GW00459097

San Marco Press/Atlanta
Copyright 2016

Other books by Susan Kiernan-Lewis:

Free Falling
Going Gone
Heading Home
Blind Sided
Rising Tides
Cold Comfort
Never Never
Dead On (February 2017)
Murder in the South of France
Murder à la Carte
Murder in Provence
Murder in Paris
Murder in Aix
Murder in Nice
Murder in the Latin Quarter
Murder in the Abbey
Murder in the Bistro
Murder in Cannes (October 2016)
Swept Away
Carried Away
Stolen Away
Reckless
Shameless
Breathless
Heartless
Witless (December 2016)

Wit's End

Book Eight
The Irish End Games

Susan Kiernan-Lewis

Susan Kiernan-Lewis

1

Mike wasn't sure what genius decided they should celebrate the harvest when they were only halfway through it. But since the idea of a market fair seemed to be a generally popular one among the people in the castle and since he'd been encouraged of late by his good wife to work on tamping down his dictatorial tendencies, he found himself driving a wagon full of cakes, pies, handmade baskets and soaps to the fairground midway between Henredon Castle and the nearest village.

In other words he was buggered.

His wife Sarah sat beside him with their two year old daughter Siobhan on her lap.

It had been a long eighteen months since they'd come to live at Henredon Castle, an occasion marked by blood and betrayal and the loss of too many loved ones.

But for the most part they'd survived, by God. And they'd survived well enough to fashion a first annual county fair in order to reach out to the surrounding communities. But mostly they did it because they had reason to celebrate.

They were still alive.

"You look like you just ate a sour pickle," Sarah said, squinting at him. She was American and while he'd heard most of her Yank idioms in the five years they'd been married, it seemed she could still surprise him.

"Not a-tall," he said, forcing a smile. "Sure it's not like there's anything for us to do back at the castle. It's glad that I am to be larking about instead of doing any of the million things calling to me in the name of our very survival."

"It's one afternoon, Mike," Sarah said. "The castle will still be there when we get back."

She was awfully sure about that, it seemed to Mike. It wasn't so long ago he'd prayed for a more confident Sarah or at least one who wasn't wracked with constant worry and anxiety. And truth be told, she wasn't totally wrong. After a dangerously shaky beginning that had nearly been their end, their lives at the castle had been nothing but peaceful.

Sure why wouldn't any sane person expect it to continue that way?

A rider on horseback galloped up to the wagon and pulled to an abrupt stop.

"Hey, Dad, hold up!" the young rider said. John Woodson was Sarah's son from her first marriage. Although true enough the lad couldn't be more different from Mike's own son Gavin Mike loved him as his own.

"Aunt Fi says she forgot the ice cream crank and she needs one of the wagons to manage it."

Siobhan reached her arms out to John. "Me ride!" she squealed.

John took the little girl and settled her on the saddle in front of him.

"Promise you'll keep it at a walk?" Sarah said.

"Don't worry. We'll be fine. Won't we, Shivvy? See you at the picnic." He goosed his mount into a trot, the trill of Siobhan's laughter following behind them as they rode away.

Mike turned to Sarah. "You okay with going the rest of the way on foot while I go back for Fiona's fecking ice cream churn?"

"Of course." She gave him a quick kiss on the cheek before hopping down. "After all, what would a fair be without fecking ice cream?"

Sarah watched her husband turn the horse back toward the castle looming in the distance. She could never look at

Henredon Castle without remembering the first time she'd laid eyes on it.

A classic example of Norman architecture, Henredon was a well maintained thirteenth century fortress perched high on a bluff over the Atlantic Ocean. Storybook crenellated towers —two of them easily visible even from this distance— anchored the broad expanse of towering limestone walls in between. In the beginning, it had looked ominous, even wicked, to Sarah.

And yet somehow it had become more like home than any place she'd ever lived.

A trickle of people trudged out from under the raised portcullis of the castle. They had left a small cadre of defenders—mostly archers on the castle walls—who would be relieved in a few hours so that everyone might enjoy the fair.

Sarah watched as Nuala O'Connell walked toward her. Nuala was tall and tan, with a smile always ready. She held her two year old daughter Darcy's hand and carried a wicker basket full of soap and knitted wash cloths that Sarah knew Nuala hoped to trade at the fair.

"Lost your ride, did you, Sarah?" Nuala said as she approached.

"It's a nice day for a walk," Sarah said as she gently pinched the baby's chubby cheek. "How's this little one today?"

"Sure she's a terrible brat," Nuala said. "I'm that sorry I didn't have another boy and that's the truth."

Nuala's two boys Damian and Dennis were already at the fair.

"Oh, you can't mean that," Sarah said as they continued on past the half harvested fields to the green square that Mike had selected for the site of the fair.

Midway between the village of Kilbaha and near enough to the main road such that the fair might benefit from any travelers or peddlers that came along, the most important feature of the location was that it was on high enough ground that anyone approaching could be seen from ten kilometers away.

The things we think about nowadays, Sarah thought, remembering the many family reunions she'd attended as a child in the American south. Needing to keep the ocean to your back, your powder dry, or posted sentries just hadn't been part of the party planning.

But of course that was then.

From what little information they'd been able to learn from passing travelers, Sarah knew that America continued to remain largely unaffected by the second electromagnetic pulse, or EMP, which had crippled Europe and re-crippled Ireland the year before. On the one hand that knowledge reassured Sarah immensely. After all her parents were still in the States. On the other hand it was difficult to understand how the US could be so limited in its response to Ireland's distress.

As in, not at all.

"Did you hear that Regan and Tommy got in last night?" Nuala asked.

The two had been traveling the southern part of Ireland to return two girls who'd been stolen away from their homes the year before. Unfortunately, the girls' homecomings also featured two babies borne of rape as a result of their time spent in a prison camp.

"Mike mentioned it," Sarah said. "He said they went right back out on the road this morning."

"So they'll miss the fair?" Nuala said in surprise.

"Regan didn't want Hannah to have to wait any longer."

"Regan's a changed lass, so she is," Nuala said. "She's been through a lot. I'm just surprised. I thought Hannah wanted to stay with us in the castle? Wasn't she one of the archers?"

"She was. She initially asked Mike for her family to be allowed to come *here*."

Post-EMP Ireland was a very dangerous place to be unless you had a community behind you—and a decent stockpile of weapons. Sarah was surprised more of the rape camp victims hadn't asked if their families could come live at the castle.

But they probably they already knew the answer.

"Well, I'm shocked Mike allowed it," Nuala said shaking her head in disbelief.

"He didn't," Sarah said. "I hate to lose her but Mike's adamant that we keep our numbers small and manageable."

"Sure your husband's a stubborn man, Sarah Donovan, so he is," Nuala said grimly. "I heard Hannah was an amazing shot with the bow."

Sarah didn't answer. It was a sore subject with her. She and Mike had argued about it for days. But he felt strongly about keeping the castle population down. And in the end, his view prevailed.

She and Nuala crested the hill to see that the villagers from Kilbaha had already set up their tables along the sides of the green square. In the center a large metal spit had been erected on which hung a hog that Davey, one of the castle men, had butchered the day before. Davey's wife Liddy and her sister Mary had been basting and seasoning the slowly rotating pork all morning. Sarah could smell the heavenly aroma as she approached, just imagining the meal later when the meat would be falling off the spit in tender, juicy slabs.

Nuala waved to one of the castle women and hurried off to join her leaving Sarah to survey the scene of the castle and village communities coming together.

Looking at all the tables of food lining the square and the people bustling about them gave Sarah a feeling of pride. It had been a long hard year in so many ways. They'd started with so little when they'd arrived at the castle. The garden had needed to be tilled and replanted. And there had been no stores except for those that they had brought with them.

One table was loaded with baked goods—pies and cakes, cookies, bannocks and scones. Another table near the rotating pork was covered with platters of roasted potatoes and crocks of fresh creamery butter and plate after plate of baked carrots, parsnips, broccoli and cauliflower. At last year's fair, the village had provided most of the fresh food and Mike and Sarah had been relieved to see that their neighbors were well advanced in farming the land around them.

Many people after the bomb hadn't been as prudent.

Beyond the food tables, Sarah could already see that some of the men had set up competition sites for horseshoes, sack races, tug-of-war, and an archery competition. The latter would likely only have castle participants but Sarah knew it was a match that the castle girls had been talking about for weeks.

A few of the villagers sat with guitars which reminded Sarah of the days when the gypsies used to live with them. The gypsies had always kept their little community humming with music. Hearing it now reminded her of Declan and her heart squeezed in pain at the memory. He had been so brave and so strong. And then taken from them way too soon.

Not for the first time Sarah found herself wondering where the gypsies had gone after the compound was raided by the Garda two years earlier.

She caught sight of John and Siobhan at one of the sweets tables and she hurried over. Siobhan's face was already covered with jam. She looked up at Sarah and grinned.

"Can you take her now, Mom?" John said, his eyes searching the crowd. Sarah didn't approve of the young woman John had chosen to spend his time with but he was nineteen and—especially these days—long past the day when she could weigh in on the matter.

"Yes, yes," Sarah said reaching for Siobhan's sticky hand. "How did you pay for the jam muffin?"

John moved off into the crowd. "Catch you later," he said.

Sarah smiled at the stout woman standing behind the jam and bannocks table. "Hi. What do I owe you?"

"Sure, not a thing, Missus," the woman said beaming down at Siobhan. "I love to see the little uns with their sweets."

"Siobhan? What do you say?"

"Fank you," Siobhan said, her eyes hungrily eyeing a tray of berry muffins on the table.

"You're the American, are ye not?" the woman said.

Sarah smiled warily. Most Irish didn't love Americans these days. They blamed them for the two EMPs that had destroyed their infrastructure and thrown the country back—for all intents and purposes—to the eighteenth century.

"I am, yes," Sarah said, keeping her smile firmly in place. The woman, although looking like she hadn't missed too many meals, was wearing rags—stitched together and laundered—but rags nonetheless. Sarah had found too many people prone to laying their current troubles at her doorstep—or who were resentful because the castle wouldn't accept new members.

"Sure I don't mean a thing by it. Not at-tall," the woman said. "I'm Gilly. I used to love your American TV, sure I did. Watched it all the time."

Sarah had to bite her tongue to keep from apologizing.

"Oh, well, I'm glad," she said.

"Sarah!"

Sarah gratefully turned away to see her daughter-in-law Sophia walking toward her, a heavy basket of relishes and jars of stewed fruit in her arms. Sarah smiled regretfully at Gilly and went to Sophia.

"You made good time," Sarah said to her. "Where's the baby?"

"I left her with the nuns," Sophia said in her lilting Italian accent. "She has a cold."

The Sisters, members of Our Lady of Perpetual Sorrow, had come to live with them at the castle when their convent burned down the winter before.

"Oh, poor dear," Sarah said. "But she's really too young to know what she's missing. Besides, now you can help me watch Siobhan. Wait until Maggie hits two. That's when you'll need all your strength. Just ask Nuala if you don't think so."

"Isn't today Siobhan's birthday?" Sophia asked as she waved to one of the castle women.

"It is," Sarah said.

Siobhan had been born the day that Archie Kelly, a beloved family member and a special friend to Sarah, had died. She was sure she'd never be able to truly celebrate Siobhan's birthday without feeling the pain of that loss.

Sophia thumped her basket down on an empty table and began pulling out jars of stuffed eggs, pickled relish and crocks of fresh goat cheese.

Sarah looked out over the gathered crowd. Including the castle residents there were about fifty people all total. Not surprisingly, the villagers interacted with the castle group guardedly. They were friendly, but they were inevitably aware that if anything truly awful should happen, everyone who lived in the castle would survive.

And everyone who lived in the village likely wouldn't.

It was the kind of distinction that didn't promote strong friendships.

Past the area where the food tables and the hog was roasting there was a stretch of weeds and gorse interspersed with rocks and dirt. Last year's fair or *lughnasa* as the Irish called it had been sparsely attended. With no real harvest to celebrate and a growing distrust on both sides, it was a wonder the two communities had gotten together at all. Since then Mike had reached out to the village to assure its people of the goodwill of all in the castle—offering everything except, of course, an invitation to join them inside.

Sarah saw Mike now on the other side of the square. He must have unloaded Fiona's churn because she was nowhere to be seen. He stood—always the tallest man in any group—his hands on his hips and his head tilted downward listening to an older gentleman who Sarah recognized as Artemus Morgan, the village leader at Kilbaha.

I wonder what that is all about?

Beyond Mike stood the brothers Frank and Robbie Murphy with Gavin—Mike's son—each holding the bridle of a horse. Frank and Robbie had been a part of the armed assault on the castle last year. Their contribution to the community since then had earned both of them a place within the castle. Frank had been a teacher before the EMP and had stepped into the role of schoolmaster in the castle. Both young men had put in double the hours of anyone else to plow and weed and harvest the crops this year.

Sarah knew a horse race typically began the *lughnasa* and for the life of her she couldn't understand why Mike allowed it. There was always roughhousing and it wasn't unusual to have a broken arm to deal with later.

One year back at the compound, they'd had to put a horse down who'd broken his leg. Nowadays having to kill a perfectly healthy horse for no good reason except the pleasure of a race didn't make sense in anybody's ledger book.

"Will John race this year?" Sophia asked as she set out her wares. While many people used the fair as an opportunity to trade for items they didn't have themselves, it was generally understood to be a picnic to be shared with their neighbors.

"I've asked him not to," Sarah said. "It's too dangerous."

"Everything's dangerous these days," Sophia said with a shrug and turned to watch her husband Gavin as he checked over his horse.

Sarah looked in the direction where Mike still stood with Mr. Morgan.

"Yeah, well there's dangerous and then there's just asking for trouble," she said.

Susan Kiernan-Lewis

2

Mike stood in the center of the grassy square. More weeds than grass, it had obviously been a state-owned verge before the bomb dropped. Good for little else now but a place for two communities to come together and try to enjoy the benefits of each other—without envy or suspicion.

If at all possible.

Two of the Kilbaha men were strumming guitars and one young girl was playing a fast and snappy reel on a fiddle that looked like it had seen better days. As Mike watched her, he wondered when she found time to practice. She looked to be about fourteen. That meant the new world order had been in effect for nearly half her life. He looked around to see if he could spot her parents. What kind of people would insist their child practice the fiddle with the world crumbling around their ears? Mike had a feeling he would probably like them very much.

"Have you tried the poteen, squire?"

Mike turned to look at Artemus Morgan. Ruddy, sunburned face, with muscular arms, Morgan was easily in his mid to late sixties.

Mike took the cup of alcohol from him. He imagined it would taste like kerosene going down but he knew he had to drink it. The last thing he'd want any of the men from the village to know was that there was a fairly decent supply of real Irish whiskey in the castle. It was one of the many useless but necessary things Sarah had brought back from her trip to the States five years earlier. And it was one of the things that

Mike had been most grateful had survived the burning of their first home, Donovan's Lot.

He nodded his thanks. "Much obliged," he said before throwing the drink back. It burned all the way down and he found himself hoping he'd still have his vocal chords afterward.

"Sure it's a fine thing you've done here, your honor," Morgan said waving a hand at the activity of the two groups clustered around the roasting hog. Mike could see twenty of his own people from the castle and another twenty or more from the village.

It had been no small feat for Morgan to have kept so many people alive and working and living together. The fact that Kilbaha had put together a working farm was unusual in itself. Without basic infrastructure, most people were at a loss to do the necessary, elemental things. Morgan was a natural leader. And from the ease with which he carried the military-issue handgun in his shoulder holster, he was no stranger to making difficult decisions when the occasion called for it either.

This afternoon however Mike knew Morgan had something specific on his mind.

"And the harvest was good at the castle this year?" Morgan asked.

"We're only half way through it but aye, it'll do."

"What did you plant then?"

Mike knew the man was perfectly aware of the castle crops but he also knew this was the accepted procedure for leading up to whatever was on Morgan's mind.

"Some corn," Mike said. "And we've begun the replanting with cabbages and potatoes. We should survive the winter."

Morgan laughed. "Was there ever a fear of that?"

"There's always a fear. And yourself?"

Morgan shrugged and indicated the line of people gathered around the hog roast. One of the castle men was slicing off thick steaming slabs of meat onto plates. "This will be the first meat most of us have had this spring. But we're healthier for it, eh?"

Mike knew he didn't mean that. Not at-tall.

A rumbling sound erupted in the distance and both men paused and turned in the direction of the sound. It was so far away that most of the other people laughing and gathered around the food tables didn't react. The musicians didn't stop playing and the children didn't stop running about. Mike caught a glimpse of two of his girl archers—not eighteen years old—sitting with two of the village girls, their heads close together in intimate conference.

"Any idea of what that sound would be?" Mike asked. "I've heard it before."

"I was going to ask you the same thing, squire," Morgan said. "Sounds like an explosion of some kind. It's always off in the distance. Let's hope it stays there."

Mike made a face and threw the dregs of his drink into the grass.

"I'm not sure any of us has the right to hope for shite these days," he said.

"You'll be going to see what it is?" Morgan asked with surprise.

"Rather than have it sneak up and bite me on the arse? Aye. I'll need to. For all our sakes."

"What if it's something ye can do feck-all about?"

Mike looked at Morgan and grinned.

"Do ye believe that, Mister Morgan? That there's anything in this world we can do feck-all about?"

Morgan turned as if to survey the crowd of people before him, forming the very picture of a marketplace in the eighteen hundreds. Horses and wagons waited patiently under trees while people sat or stood and talked and ate and drank moonshine while children raced around squealing.

"I've a few good men," Morgan said. "Trustworthy men who might be of use if you're thinking of getting together a party to find the source of yon noise."

"They would be welcome," Mike said carefully. "Would there be something I might do for you in return?"

Morgan laughed, his deep set blue eyes crinkling and nearly disappearing in his weathered face.

"I'm not subtle, am I?"

"And I appreciate it. What's the problem then?"

Morgan rubbed his hands on his pants—an ill-fitting pair of denim trousers that Mike couldn't help but think weren't originally bought for him. Morgan wouldn't be the first man to acquire his wardrobe from a dead man. After all, they weren't using them any more.

"A band of gobshites visited us last week," Morgan said. "Thugs. As bold as chalk. Led by a bastard who calls himself Thor if ye can believe it."

Mike frowned and looked at the village people, all of whom looked relaxed and happy. If they'd been recently terrorized, they'd obviously gotten over it. He saw Sarah walking through the crowd and saw that she was trying to keep up with little Siobhan who was running on chubby legs toward the roasting hog.

"What does this Thor want then?" Mike asked.

"Tribute, he calls it."

Mike looked at him in confusion.

"Food," Morgan said. "Or sex with any of our women who are willing. Basically anything of value we might have."

"For what in return?"

Morgan snorted. "In return for not burning us out."

Mike sighed. It was a sick tiresome world they lived in now. There were always those who would try to take advantage of the weaker ones rather than build something themselves.

"I take it this Thor and his gang our well armed?"

"Oh, aye, he made sure I saw that they were. They call themselves the Yanks, ye see."

"Are they American then?"

"Not at-all. What would an American be doing in this shite?" Morgan blushed. "I'll not be meaning your wife, squire. I meant no disrespect."

Mike waved away the comment. He well knew the general feeling toward Americans in Ireland wasn't a positive one. It was actually dead clever for a gang to label themselves as such. It was nearly as effective as calling themselves the Demons.

"I can't ask your lot into the castle," Mike said. "I'm sorry if that's where this is going but we're already at the limit for sustaining the people we have now."

"Sure no, I wouldn't ask that," Morgan said making Mike think that was exactly what Morgan *had* hoped. "Just help when the time comes."

Mike didn't immediately respond. He looked at the village people as they mingled with his own. He knew there were some things that the castle could use—a different kind of soap, more kinds of honey, perhaps an herb or two that their healer Sister Alphonse hadn't heard of. Certainly more manpower. But beyond that, was there any real point to associating with any of the villages that surrounded the castle?

The villagers would always be the vulnerable ones, the ones on the outside looking in. What in the world could Mike do to help? Sending castle men to Kilbaha would leave his men just as vulnerable as the villagers. It was only the castle itself that gave Mike and his people any advantage.

And he was pretty sure this wily old Irishman knew that very well.

Mike clapped a hand on Morgan's shoulder.

"Enough business for now," he said. "Let's see if there's any pork left. I'll be needing you to try my wife's cornbread. I grant you it takes some getting used to and I'll be the first to say so, but at least try it before you make up your mind."

Morgan moved with Mike to join the others.

"I would never do that, your honor," he said easily. "Sure it's not in me nature to reject any offer honestly made."

Susan Kiernan-Lewis

3

Later as the sun began to sink in the sky Sarah waited at the perimeter of the firepit for Fiona to bring the wagon around. John and his girlfriend Cassidy had taken most of the children back already and now there were only a few of the village men standing around the campfire, mostly drinking.

Mike had left hours ago and he'd made it clear to the castle men that he expected them back in short order too. Sarah was sorry Mike didn't seem to be able to enjoy a full hour of fellowship and relaxing but she understood it too. The castle and everyone in it was a massive responsibility.

And one Mike took very seriously.

Sarah saw Fiona headed her way with the wagon. Nuala was in the back which was piled full of more children and some of the other castle women.

The nuns hadn't come to the fair and the castle's archers had left when Mike did. The archers were a standoffish bunch. The girl archers usually wouldn't be caught fraternizing with anyone but themselves.

Although now that Sarah thought of it, she had seen some of them talking with a few of the village girls. When it came right down to it, she imagined girls would be girls. And in the absence of CDs and makeup and the Internet there would always be clothes and boys and gossip. Not even an EMP could obliterate the power of those for a teenage girl.

"Shall we call it a success then?"

Sarah turned to see Artemus Morgan approaching her from the campfire. She was surprised that he spoke to her. From what Mike had told her, Mr. Morgan was very definitely old school and felt that women were now finally back where they belonged—firmly ensconced in second-class status—and not really good for much beyond making babies and supper.

The fact that Morgan was approaching her with a smile told her that the man mustn't have gotten what he'd wanted from his conversation with Mike.

"I'd say so," she said, smiling politely.

"Himself back to the big house is he then?" Morgan asked, nodding in the direction of the castle.

"We left in the middle of the harvest," Sarah said shrugging.

"Aye, so he said," Morgan said. "Might I have a word with your good self in his stead?"

"I thought I saw you talking with him earlier," Sarah said mildly.

"So you did, so you did," Morgan said nodding. "I'd like to take a moment to put my case before the entire leadership of Henredon Castle."

Sarah bit back a grin. The auld leprechaun was slathering it on pretty good but she'd listen. Why not?

"And what case would that be, Mr. Morgan?"

"It's a fine thing what you've done here, so it is," Morgan said. "All of us coming together as a community."

"But?"

"Do ye remember how it was when ye first came I wonder, Mrs. Donovan?"

"I do. You helped us immensely."

"Aye, even your husband said ye'd never have made it without our help."

"He might have been exaggerating a tad to be congenial," Sarah said carefully.

"It's sure I am that he was doing exactly that," Morgan said nodding. "But still…" He looked at Sarah and narrowed his eyes. "We helped ye when we needn't have. You know that full well, aye?"

"And now you need help in return."

"That's the way of it, Missus," he said, all amusement and light gone from his face.

"And did my husband give you an answer today?"

"Sure no. He didn't."

Fiona pulled the wagon up beside Sarah and gave her a quizzical look encompassing the old man. Sarah threw her bag onto the floor of the front seat of the wagon.

"That's a handsome lad you have. Young John, is it?" Morgan said. "He must be a big help to you."

Sarah turned to him.

"I understand you have two lads of your own?"

Morgan nodded. "Me grandsons. Both their parents…me daughter and son-in-law are gone now these past three years."

"I'm sorry," Sarah said. She swung up into the wagon but put her hand on Fiona's rein hand to stop her.

"All of us appreciate the help you gave us when we came," Sarah said. "We haven't forgotten that."

Morgan raised an eyebrow as if to indicate he had serious doubts about that.

"Why don't you bring your grandsons to the castle for dinner day after tomorrow?" Sarah said. "And we'll talk more then."

Morgan's face brightened.

"The lads'll love that, so they will," he said.

Marcus Dennehy sat down heavily at the campfire, drawn to it by the allure of the aroma of the roasting goat on a makeshift spit and the exhaustion of his morning.

They'd only traveled ten miles on the highway but all of those on foot. He looked over at Emma as she stacked the metal plates on top of each other and then headed in the direction of the stream they'd discovered earlier. Marcus grunted and his man Jocko turned to look at him.

"Go with her," Marcus said.

"It's broad fecking daylight," Jocko said, but he got to his feet.

"Where's Rose?" Marcus asked, ignoring the man's comment.

"How the feck should I know?"

"Rose!" Marcus pulled himself to his feet, feeling every ache, every blister and every stretched and abused muscle in his thighs as he did.

"Da, I'm right here," a young voice called out. "Trying to have a bit of privacy in the fecking bushes!"

"Sorry, lass," Marcus said, heaving himself back down in front of the roasting meat. "Oy! Jocko!"

His man stopped in his slow slog to follow Emma and turned only his head.

"Send her back to the camp. You can wash the fecking dishes."

"Bugger that!" But the man continued toward the creek.

Marcus ran a hand over his face. Across from him sat five other men. Two of them were cleaning their weapons while the others picked greasy strips off the meat on the spit and ate it with their fingers. Behind them, he could hear the rest of his men setting up camp in a nearby clearing in the woods. Twenty men in all. Most of them his mates from the time before the bomb. The rest just men who knew how to follow orders for a full belly—and sometimes a little more.

His own tent would go up first. They'd stayed in their last village for more than a fortnight and if it hadn't been for the fact that Rose had gotten too friendly with some of the other kids, they would have stayed longer. It had been a good place to rest.

He watched Emma appear from out of the bushes, her hands free and swinging at her side. There'd been a clothing store in the last village. Like most stores it had been looted but Emma had still found something she liked. The jeans were too baggy but Marcus had to admit that the top was bonny. All sparkly like it had been made for a disco party.

Watching her wear it now as she came out of the bushes was almost fecking funny.

"Jocko said you needed me?" Emma said as she approached.

"I need ye not to work like a fecking field hand all the time," he said, patting the spot next to him by the fire.

"The dishes won't get as clean if I don't wash them," Emma said as she seated herself next to him. "We can't afford to get sick."

"I can't afford to have you working yourself to death either."

A rustling sound came from behind them and Rose appeared, adjusting her cotton shorts. Her legs were covered with red welts from bites and scratches.

"Is it time to eat yet?" she asked.

"Wash your hands, Rose," Emma said.

"Mum, no! It's too hard and too far!"

Marcus sighed. "Do what your mum says, Rose. We don't need ye keeling over from botulism or some such shite."

"Salmonella," Emma said.

"Aye, that too."

Rose turned still grumbling and headed in the direction of the stream.

Emma watched her go. "Take soap!" she called and then turned to look at Marcus as if Rose's behavior was somehow his fault.

"She's thirteen," Marcus said with a shrug. "She'd be a pain in the arse even if she wasn't living in the woods."

"I really hate camping out, Marcus. You know that."

"Aye, lass, I do. And I'm working on getting you a lovely new home."

"One where we can stay for longer than two weeks?"

"Aye. This one's grand, so it is. There's gardens everywhere with fresh vegetables and a whole string of apple trees for all the pies and cobblers ye can stand."

"And they'll let us take what we need? And live there?"

"Sure they *asked* me to come. Said they needed protection from bandits and other criminals on the road."

"Really? Oh, Marcus, that would be lovely. To finally settle down again."

"I know, lass. Soon enough. I promise ye."

"What's the name of the village? Have I ever heard of it?"

Marcus knew Emma was thinking about her life before the EMP. In those days he'd run a petrol station in Galway and Emma had worked at the local insurance office. She'd loved traveling around to the villages then. She said it gave her something interesting to talk about at tea with Marcus and Rose of an evening. Before Marcus could respond, Gil, one of Marcus's men, emerged from the direction of the clearing where they were erecting the tents.

"Oy, Thor! We got a problem. Amos is motherless again."

"Can't you deal with it?" Marcus said with a frown.

"Nah, he's polluted something rotten. Sommat's going to get fecked-up."

Marcus cursed under his breath and stood up. He could see Rose coming up the trail from the creek wiping her hands on her shorts.

"Stay here with the lass," he said quietly to Emma.

"Oh, Marcus, must you?" Emma said. "Amos is just an auld fool. Can't you let him off?"

Marcus patted her shoulder and left the campfire, striding toward the ring of men surrounding the last tent in the clearing.

All of the men were filthy. With no women to urge them to wash or give them the desire to, they'd mostly devolved into a pack of homeless miscreants. It wasn't that women weren't allowed in the group—just not the sort of women most of this lot preferred.

How could Marcus have hoors living in the same camp with his wife and daughter?

The first man Marcus saw when he pushed into the scrum of men was Amos himself who was off to the side and an obvious spectator–not the villain in the piece after all. Marcus felt a rush of relief to see Amos wasn't shite-faced at all, but at the same time he felt a wave of dread. What was so bad Gil couldn't say it in front of Emma?

One man, Neil, stood facing Marcus, his hands loose at his sides as if ready to defend or protect the person behind him.

Shite.

Marcus glanced at Gil who shrugged.

"Who is she, then?" Marcus asked.

The girl—barely older than Rose—peeked out from behind Neil and grinned. She was scantily clad with harsh eyeliner and rings in her lip and nose.

Marcus tensed at the sight of her. His rule was one of only a very few that he insisted upon. It was uncomplicated and it was inviolate. *No hoors.* Not on the road and certainly not in the camp. Whatever Neil had gotten up to with this lass back in the last village had been discreet and no matter to Marcus.

"You know the rules," Marcus said to Neil, working to keep his voice calm and his face impassive.

"It's a crap rule, Thor," Neil said, licking his lips and flexing his fingers. His eyes darted around the ring of men. He wouldn't find anyone to back him here. He'd be mad to think it.

"Be that as it may," Marcus said. "You've caused some problems for yourself now."

"I won't take 'er back," Neil said. "I promised I wouldn't."

"Ye intend to marry her then?"

The other men laughed.

Marcus saw the tension leave Neil's shoulders at the sound of the laughter. He was beat. And he knew it.

"Nah," he said, dipping his head.

Does someone want to escort this lass off the premises?" Marcus said. "Or do you think you might handle that little chore, Neil?" The message was clear and except for the poor girl there wasn't a man there who didn't understand it.

"I'll take her," Neil said quietly, still not looking at Marcus.

Marcus shrugged. "Well, then, good." He turned back to the other men. "So, are we done?"

He went over to Amos and slapped him on the shoulder.

"My good wife was asking about yourself earlier, Amos," he said. "Do ye think ye might sit with us by the fire and relieve her mind?"

Amos blinked in surprise and a smile spread across his face.

Marcus began to walk back to the campfire where his wife and daughter waited for him. Neil would bring him proof of the deed later—a finger or an ear—and of course there would be confirmation from one of the other lads who'd watch the killing from a distance.

All tidily done and quickly. They weren't animals after all.

Of course, if Neil didn't slit the hoor's throat, he'd have his own done for him in short order.

Spit spot.

It was all the very essence of simplicity and clarity. As any successfully run company should be.

4

Sarah sank into the hot bath and groaned as she felt the heat penetrate her sore muscles. The late spring day had become a chilly night. She was grateful for the two salvaged solar panels on the castle roof Mike had insisted on recovering from the old compound. The midday sun had heated the water to allow most of the children of the castle to have warm baths when they returned from the fair.

With enough water left over for a few tired mothers, too.

Mike came into the bathing room—a stone room no bigger than the average walk-in closet in any suburban neighborhood back in America—and sat on a stool in the corner.

"Siobhan finally go down?" Sarah asked as she closed her eyes and enjoyed the fragrance of the bath. She was using one of the floral-scented soaps that Sophia had made. Along with the moon, a tiny candle in a dish by the tub faucet provided a flickering light to the room.

"Aye," Mike said, clearly distracted.

There was a sheet of clear plastic over the window in the room but Sarah could hear laughter outside in the courtyard where some of the young people were sitting around a small fire pit. She knew John was down there with his girlfriend Cassidy, the Murphy brothers and some of the rape camp women who'd escaped pregnancy but hadn't wanted to return to their homes.

Everyone else—Fiona, Nuala, Mary, Liddy—either had a child to tend to or was too exhausted from the day's activities to drink cheap wine and sit around a fire pit giggling about nothing.

She knew she shouldn't begrudge the young people their fun. Life was hard nowadays.

"One of these days we'll have to celebrate her birthday proper," Mike said.

"I know. Next year. Definitely. What were you and Artemus Morgan talking about so seriously?" Sarah opened one eye and watched Mike rub his face with both hands.

"Just the usual shite," he said eventually. "Nothing to worry about."

Sarah watched him for a moment. For something that was *nothing to worry about* he certainly seemed to be giving a good impersonation of someone worried.

"How many archers are on watch?" she asked.

Henredon Castle had one hundred and forty people in it. Half were nuns, men, and small children. The other half were women and forty of them—in their late teens mostly—were trained to shoot a bow and were tasked with the security and general defense of the castle.

Even now, Sarah marveled at how during a time when women all over Ireland were reduced to second-class citizenry, here at Henredon, they had been made the first bastion of defense for the whole castle.

All day and all night, no fewer than ten archers patrolled the top parapet perimeter of the castle walls ever watchful of the woods and the long drive leading to the front gate.

"The usual," Mike said. "Ten."

Sarah held out her hand for the towel on the bench next to Mike. He stood and held it out to her as she stood. He wrapped her in the towel as she stepped out of the tub. His arms remained around her and his lips found the curve of her neck.

"You smell wonderful, lass," he murmured into her skin.

They kissed. The moon shone in through the window, distorted into waves of light by the plastic onto the stone floor. The young people's laughter was muted in the still night.

Mike broke off the kiss—a first as far as Sarah could remember. She saw in his eyes that he was thinking of something else.

"Is it Tilly?" Sarah asked.

Before the picnic one of the archers, a young woman named Tilly had been restricted to quarters until something could be decided about the fact that she'd been caught sleeping with another woman's husband.

Sarah had argued that it wasn't a case that should involve the castle council—the judicial panel that had been set up to decide guilt in cases of rule infractions—mostly because the council was made up largely of married castle women.

If it had been up to Sarah the man involved—Mary O'Malley's husband Kevin—would be tossed in the castle dungeon but Mike insisted he needed him to finish bringing in the harvest on time and that longer hours in the fields would be punishment enough.

Before now they'd had very little need for this sort of internal regulation but already Sarah had heard talk that ranged from head shaving to public whipping. Sarah knew Mike wouldn't allow the girl to be physically hurt, but that didn't mean he had decided about what to do.

In the last couple of years Mike had tended toward taking a hard line on all kinds of crimes. The memory of one Chezzie Walsh came to mind for Sarah.

Chezzie been held accountable with another man for crimes committed against the women during the time the women had been held in a prison camp. Although complicit, Chezzie hadn't done any actual raping and after three months living in a dungeon cell he had been released.

The other man, Bill, had been taken to a far orchard and hung.

"Don't you think it was punishment enough that Tilly missed the fair?" Sarah asked.

Mike snorted and released her. "You think the women of the castle will be content with that? You think *Mary* will?"

"She will if you take a stand and dictate what's appropriate punishment and what's not," Sarah said.

"You'd have me let the lass off with a hand slap?"

"I'm not sure what she did was a crime," Sarah said, shrugging. "It didn't endanger the community. It didn't impair security."

"You'll be saying morals don't matter then?" Mike narrowed his eyes at her.

"I'm saying maybe you should be careful about thinking *you're* the one to say what morals are these days."

The next morning Mike was up early and standing in the half-harvested cornfield two kilometers from the castle.

Directly south of the castle, opposite the field and nearest to the entrance of the castle, was the castle's parking lot which was nearly the size of a football field. Before the first EMP, Henredon Castle had been a popular tourist destination. Two decrepit vehicles parked there now, their interiors stripped down to the metal, their tires long since stolen, forlornly rusting in the ocean air.

Mike wasn't sure what to do with the car park. The thought of breaking up the asphalt to create more pasture or planting fields always ended the same—with the realization that it was too much work for too little return.

As it was it had taken backbreaking work to till the existing gardens and fields for that first harvest last summer. Few people in their castle were farmers. As usual, they'd had to learn the hard way every step of the way.

Mike felt a vague wave of guilt as he thought back to the help that Morgan and his group had given them during their first few months at the castle. Not just seeds and advice but physical labor too as the castle group learned to create their own tools and make their own way.

If it hadn't been for Morgan they wouldn't have had the paltry first crop they'd had last year. And paltry or not—it had helped them survive the winter.

Being American, Sarah had pushed hard for a corn crop, saying they could make everything from oil and polenta from it and the husks could be used to feed the pigs. While most people in the castle didn't much care for corn as a food, they had to admit the crop made sense for livestock and basic calories than even wheat or potatoes.

Now Mike stood in the bright sunlight and watched men and women busily planting potatoes and cabbages in a row where corn had just been harvested. Behind them on the next row people were quickly removing ears of corn from the tall stalks. He didn't know why he felt like he was in a hurry. Maybe he always felt that way these days.

Maybe he always felt like danger or disaster was right around the corner. He only knew that the corn in the field wasn't as good as the corn safely stored away in the food cellars of the castle.

He glanced up at the clear blue sky. There was no threat of rain or storm.

There was nothing to worry about.

Right.

"Oy, Mike!" He turned to see Frank Murphy walking up from the direction of the castle. Murphy had been a good addition as schoolmaster to the castle population although at the time his physical proximity to Declan's murder had made most people hesitant to accept him or his brother.

"There's a problem with one of the lasses," Murphy said as he reached Mike.

"What kind of problem?" Mike asked. "Why can't the women handle it?"

But as soon as the words were out of his mouth Mike knew the problem had to be with one of the archers. The young women who patrolled the top parapet and daily practiced their archery skills fell into a totally different category from the other people of the castle. And they knew it too.

"Seems your Missus let Tilly out of her room and now Mrs. O'Malley is crying foul."

"Bloody hell," Mike swore.

His mission discharged, Murphy moved past Mike into the field. Mike had no option but to return to the castle to sort out the stramash.

Of the forty women trained to shoot a bow and arrow, seven were so good they could shoot buttons off a jacket at a hundred yards. These seven were referred to in the castle as *Les Crème*. And without doubt they were exactly that.

Les Crème archers ate first and best. Their needs were met first, their comfort was the primary concern in the castle hierarchy. And it wasn't only because they stood between danger and the rest of the community although that was part of it. It was also because the young women trained hard to be good at what they did, to hit the eye out of a field mouse at a hundred paces, not just now and then but *every time*. And they trained not to blink when the target looked back and spoke, lived and breathed.

It wasn't an easy task by any means and not everyone was cut out to do it. But for the ones who could—it was a skill that the castle couldn't live without.

Mike was willing to endure a whole lot of drama for the benefits the archers provided—but there was a limit. He just didn't quite know yet what that limit was.

As he walked back to the castle, he began to see the silhouettes of the archers moving on the parapet behind the open gaps in the crenellation. He knew that each young woman had her bow at the ready as she scanned the surrounding landscape for enemies. Arrogant they may be and a huge pain in the arse most of the time, but they did their jobs well.

He nodded at the tallest figure and recognized her as Aibreann, the unofficial leader of *Les Crème*. Aibreann was in her mid-twenties. She was one of the ones rescued from the rape camp two years ago. Her child, little Bill, was being raised by Fiona who had lost her own baby at the rape camp. The arrangement seemed to work out well for everyone.

He watched now as Aibreann turned to talk to someone behind her, probably Briana, letting her know that Mike was returning.

From the castle gate tower, Kevin O'Malley was manning the drawbridge that could be lowered across the wide moat around the castle. It had been Mike's plan to put sharpened spikes in the moat and fill it with water, but there was so much work in the fields that they had only been able to outfit a portion of the moat with spikes—and Mike couldn't for the life of him imagine when they'd be able to spare any water to fill the damn thing.

The gate tower was nearly three stories high and jutted out from the front castle wall. From here the drawbridge operator was able to raise and lower the portcullis using a winch that controlled the heavy ropes.

Mike waited patiently as the drawbridge was manually cranked down to allow him across the moat. There had never been a time when he thought they could leave the bridge down—even for a quick jaunt outside to check on the crops or the people working them. The castle was their safety. But it was only that as long as the drawbridge was up and secured.

He entered the castle and was immediately confronted by Sister Alphonse, Mary O'Malley, Nuala with a toddler on her hip and Robbie Murphy who had his hand on the arm of the errant archer Tilly. Although whether he held her to keep her from running or to protect her from Mary was anybody's guess. Probably a little bit of both.

Mike held his hand up. "What happened?" he asked tiredly.

"Your *wife*!" Mary said, her hands in fists on her hips as she glared at Tilly. "*Sarah* said Tilly had been 'punished enough' and she let her out!"

Mike glanced up at the parapet and saw that several archers were looking down at them where they stood in the courtyard. He waved at Aibreann and made a circling motion with this finger to indicate they were to turn around and focus on their jobs.

He turned back to Mary. "Where is Sarah now?" he asked.

"How should I know? When I told her she hadn't cleared it through the council she said she didn't need to! I guess we all take our orders from Sarah Donovan now, is that right?"

Mike looked at Sister Alphonse. "Are you a part of this, Sister?"

Sister Alphonse shook her head. "The very idea. Nay, I'm needing an escort into the field to search for herbs." She jabbed a thumb in the direction of Robbie. "But me usual escort is busy playing jailer, it seems."

Nuala spoke up. "That's not fair, Sister. Robbie was just walking by minding his own business when Mary O'Malley comes shrieking through the courtyard like a banshee!" She looked at Mike. "Sure I thought we were being invaded or murdered in our beds at the very least."

Mike felt his temper edge up dangerously.

"Do none of ye have any concept of how busy we are right now trying to get the second half of the harvest in? And planting the other half of the cornfield? And the insanity of keeping a perfectly able lass locked up when she's needed? Do I have to forbid the *lughnasa* next year to get any work done?"

"Sarah had no right to release her! The strumpet hasn't been tried yet!" Mary said, her eyes raking the young archer with fury. Tilly stood beside Robbie, her stance relaxed, with her weight resting on one leg and her hand on her hip. She looked the very picture of a cocky fighter pilot.

"Right," Mike said. "Robbie, unhand her. Tilly, you've served your time so get back to your post. And stay away from other people's husbands."

Tilly grinned, glancing briefly at Mary who had to be restrained by Mike.

"Settle down!" he growled. "You've work to do, Mary O'Malley, and bairns to mind."

"But she—"!

"She *nothing*," Mike said between clenched teeth. "Talk with your *husband*. If you want me to talk with him, I'll be happy to." He turned to the nun. "I'm sorry, Sister, but I need Robbie out in the field pulling corn so we don't all starve this winter. He can take you out to look for herbs when the harvest is in."

"But that might be too late for the herbs I need," she protested. "They have a growing season too ye ken!"

Mike released Mary who stomped away shooting bitter looks at him over her shoulder. A small cheer went up from the parapet and Mike imagined Tilly had rejoined her pals. He hated that their crowing was so public. That would only cause more problems with the other women.

Sister Alphonse turned in a huff and stormed back to the side of the castle where the rest of the nuns had set up a convent and chapel area in the castle's inner bailey.

Robbie called up to Kevin to let the drawbridge down in order to let him out to join the others in the field.

Mike looked at Nuala. "Well?" he said, fully expecting an argument from her too.

"Heavy is the crown, eh, Mike?" Nuala said with a shrug as she headed for the castle nursery on the second level of the principle living quarters.

She was right about that, he thought with frustration.

Even though he'd been pushed into it by Sarah's action, once he'd finally made the decision—for the protection and wellbeing of everyone in the castle—he knew he could count on the fact that nobody was going to be happy about it.

Bugger.

Susan Kiernan-Lewis

5

Sarah stepped out of the kitchen and massaged the small of her back. Everyone in the castle had a job and some, like herself, had rotating duties. This week had been her week to cook. If she had to do it full time she'd probably go screaming into the nursery begging to rock one of the many babies in the castle.

But then if all she was doing was changing diapers and trying to get the little ones down for naps, she was sure she'd be begging to spend her time in an overly hot kitchen keeping the massive castle ovens roaring. Her sister-in-law Fiona, who was standing next to her, wiped her hands on the towel that hung from her apron.

"Sure, I'll never get used to chicken and dumplings," Fiona said. "Nor understand why you insist on making it."

"Well, now you know how I feel about haggis."

"Go on with you! You know full well that's Scottish not Irish."

"It's all the same," Sarah said with a grin. She was glad she'd pulled kitchen duty with Fiona. As busy as they were all the time, it had been too many days since she'd spent time with her and she'd missed her.

Fiona had suffered too many gut-punching losses in the last two years—her child and her dear husband Declan—and there had been a time when Sarah wasn't sure her friend was going to come out on the other side of it.

They hesitated at the entrance to the large center courtyard of the castle. There had been plans for that courtyard—mostly to plant grass for the cow that they'd managed to find last winter during a raid. In the end they'd put the cow in a nearby pasture long enough to keep it alive and producing milk. The castle would readdress the idea of turning the courtyard into a lawn in the fall.

Two of the archers, Tilly and a chubby blonde named Nola were standing in the corner of the courtyard talking with John's girlfriend Cassidy. Sarah could feel herself stiffen when she saw her.

"Steady on, Mama bear," Fiona said under her breath.

"Easy for you to say," Sarah said, her eyes still on the girl. Cassidy was wearing jeans and a baggy cardigan sweater. She wasn't unattractive but for the life of her Sarah couldn't see what John saw in her. Cassidy had tried out to be an archer but hadn't been able to get the hang of it. She hadn't worked out in the nursery either, where she tended to make the children fussier than they were before.

The sisters Mary and Liddy who were in charge of anything that had to do with feeding the castle had finally put her to work as full time dishwasher in the castle kitchen. John insisted that Cassidy wasn't stupid—not at all—but her skills didn't lend themselves to homesteading.

Sarah couldn't help but think how that was a satisfactory answer since living like pioneers was essentially the world they lived in now.

"Liddy says she's only doing the pots and pans now," Fiona said, "because she broke too much of the crockery."

"Can she ride?" Sarah asked, forcing herself to look away from Cassidy who was laughing and whooping loudly with the two archers. "Maybe she can learn how to set a trap or shoot a rabbit."

"You really want to see that eejit on the business end of a gun, Sarah?"

"You've got a point."

Tilly and Nola broke away and headed toward the section of the castle where the targets were set up and Sarah couldn't help but think that Cassidy wistfully watched them go.

One thing was certain about every one of the archers—they clearly loved what they did. They all came from different backgrounds with different paths that brought them to

Henredon but they all shared a love of competition and athleticism. If Ireland hadn't folded like a bad hand at the first EMP, any one of them would have been happy serving in the army.

Except none of them were any good at following orders.

You'd think with how much Mike loves to give orders, Sarah thought with a smile, that that wouldn't be a problem. But it was their very femaleness that confounded Mike. A natural leader, he knew how to make a man knuckle under and do his bidding in nearly any situation

But girls were a whole other kettle of herring.

"Mary came undone when you let Tilly out. You ken that, right?" Fiona said.

Sarah snorted. "Mary needs to deal with her husband and quit acting like him sleeping around is someone else's fault."

"I agree with you. Still, the lasses are out of control."

"No one's arguing that," Sarah said tiredly.

Fiona squinted up at the dropping sun.

"Summer feels like it's over before it's started," she said. "Can it really be that late?"

"You're right. It does seem to be a little darker than usual. Maybe there's a storm system coming in."

"Mike will go off his nut if it rains," Fiona said. "He didn't want us to break for the fair and wasn't the weather lovely for a picnic?"

Sarah laughed. "We needed the break."

"Aye, but we need the weather to hold until we get the crops in too."

Sarah shrugged. "It probably wasn't sensible to stop in the middle of the harvest," she admitted.

"Did you talk to many of the villagers?"

Sarah looked at her. "Not really. Did you?"

Fiona shook her head. "They don't love us."

"Of course not."

"They want inside," Fiona said.

"I know."

"But there's no room," Fiona said. "At least that what Mike insists."

"If we let more people in we'd have more hands to work the harvest," Sarah said.

"Aye, and more mouths to feed and more cat fights like Mike broke up this morning."

Sarah shrugged. "That's just living in a community. Nothing's ever perfect. You want to go watch the girls' target practice?"

"And risk Mike seeing us having a lark instead of working? No, thank you. I've got laundry to do."

Just then Nuala came out of a nearby doorway leading a small cadre of children behind her. They headed in the direction of the archery target range. Nuala was holding her own daughter Darcy on one hip and Sarah's daughter Siobhan on the other.

"Oh, there's my precious lamb!" Fiona said, waving to five year old Ciara who waved back.

"At least someone is getting to watch the show," Sarah said.

"Mike wants the little un's to all grow up to be warriors," Fiona said as they watched the children.

"Well, at least all the girls," Sarah said. "We need *everyone* skilled on the bow and arrow. Wouldn't hurt for the nuns to know how."

"Sure now I know you're taking the piss!" Fiona laughed.

While the boys were encouraged to learn how to shoot as well as train in hand-to-hand combat, Sarah knew that Mike believed their greater physical strength was better used for doing the heavy lifting around the castle. The girls—if they had a gift for it—were a more natural choice as the castle's archers.

"I'd give anything if Ciara could grow up to be something besides a dishwasher or a fecking sentry," Fiona said softly.

"It's a different world, Fi," Sarah said gently.

Dinner in the great hall that night was noisier than usual. While an exhausting day in many ways, it had also been unusually eventful. A trio of starving wolves had crept too close to the harvesters and had to be shot before work could continue.

Sarah knew Mike wasn't happy with the interruption. He'd been hoping they'd be a lot further along than they were. Sophia had been stung by a bee and had to quit for the day and Sister Alphonse had gone off on her own expedition and gotten lost, forcing two of the men to stop planting and find her.

While there were no fewer than a thousand things for Mike to attend to back at the castle, his apprehension over their production schedule had him out in the field harvesting corn with the rest of them. The result was a ferocious sunburn that would keep a normal and more sane man indoors the next day—if not in bed.

As dinner finished up, Mike sat at the head of the table with Siobhan on his lap flanked by Sarah and John. His son Gavin sat beside Sarah with Sophia and little Maggie.

In spite of what Fiona had said about the chicken and dumplings, not a plate was left uncleaned—although Sarah knew that could be as much about the uneasiness of wasting food as anything else.

"We'll have to bring the cow in full time," Mike said to John.

"The wolves?" John said.

"Aye. Probably a miracle they haven't found her already."

"I brought her in as soon as I heard they'd gotten so close," John said.

"Good lad," Mike said, smiling wanly. "Thank God for you. One less thing for me to deal with."

Sarah was glad Gavin hadn't heard Mike's words— although he'd certainly heard versions of them throughout his life. Gavin was an intelligent young man but he was often impractical and had a strong immature streak.

Sarah turned to Mike.

"Did I mention I invited Morgan and his two grandsons to come to the castle tomorrow?"

He looked at her and his mouth fell open.

"You're kidding me. Tell me you are," he said.

"We owe him, Mike."

"The last thing I want is that auld bastard getting a good look inside the castle."

"Well, he can probably guess what it's like. What does he want from us anyway?"

Mike sighed. "He's having a spot of trouble with gangs."

Gavin looked up from his plate. "I heard talk of it at the *lughnasa*," he said. "They call themselves the Yanks." He grinned at John.

Sarah looked at Mike. "But they're not—"

"Nay, lass. They're just taking the piss."

"So what does Morgan want you to do?" she asked.

Nuala came to the head of the table and held out her arms for Siobhan. "It's movie night in the nursery," she sang gaily.

"Very funny," Sarah said with a laugh.

"I'd give anything for a laptop and just one movie," John said with a sigh.

"You and me both, mate," Gavin said. "What was your favorite?"

"Well, since I was only nine when the bomb dropped, I was pretty much a *Sponge Bob Square Pants* fanatic."

Sophia laughed. "I remember that cartoon!" she said as she got up to follow behind Nuala who was leading most of the children out of the dining hall.

Sarah turned back to Mike. "What does Morgan want us to do?"

"I don't know," he said with a sigh.

"We can't give him men," she said.

"I know."

"Guns, maybe?"

"For all the good they'd do. We only have a handful of bullets left."

"I'd like to be there when you talk to him."

He cocked an eyebrow at her.

"I just want my voice heard," she said.

"You've never had any trouble getting your voice heard."

"I'm serious."

"Would ye settle for having John and Gavin there in your place?"

"You don't want me there because I'm a woman!"

"It's not that and sure you've cut me to the quick to suggest it," Mike said. "But as you've put me feet to the fire by inviting Morgan to the castle you should know that the auld scoundrel will talk more freely without a member of the more sensitive sex there."

"You mean weaker."

He leaned and kissed her on her mouth. "Could I be married to you for an hour and possibly mean that?"

Sarah grinned in spite of herself. "Nice to see the Blarney Stone wasn't effected by the EMP. Fine. John can be my proxy." She looked at her son but before he could respond the large wooden doors that led to the dining hall flew open and Terry Donaghue burst in.

"Someone's coming!" he yelled.

Mike was on his feet in an instant.

"Gavin, go find out what the sentries are seeing," he said as he headed toward the door.

Sarah jumped up as several men in the dining room, including John ran past her. Many people had gone back to their rooms for the night and she gave a silent prayer of thanks that Nuala had already taken the children away.

"I'm sure it's nothing," she said to no one in particular. "Let's all just sit tight until we find out who it is."

Briana came in and looked around for a place to sit. She'd clearly just come off patrol. Fiona went to the kitchen to fetch the girl her dinner.

"What's happening out front, Briana?" Sarah asked.

"It's only a wagon coming down the front drive," Briana said, shrugging.

"Well, then why is Terry freaking out?"

Briana threw down her gloves on the table.

"I dunno, Mrs. Donovan," she said, "maybe because he's an auld tosser afraid of his own shadow?"

Sarah bit her lip. Terry had been through hell in the last few years. If he jumped at shadows, it was because he had good reason to.

"So there's nothing suspicious about it?" Sarah pressed her.

"Except for the fact that it's coming at night," Briana said with a shrug. "That's not usual."

Fiona appeared and placed a plate of chicken and dumplings in front of Briana.

"Did you wash your hands?" Fiona's hand hovered near the plate as if to snatch it away again.

"Aye," Briana said picking up a fork. "Cor, this is me favorite!" She began to shovel the food in. Fiona pushed a plate of cornbread and a bowl of freshly whipped butter toward the girl.

She and Sarah looked at each other.

It was probably nothing. And even if it *wasn't*, they were safe inside the castle.

6

It was Regan and Tommy returning with Hannah and her family.

The four had driven all day and most of the previous night in order to try to reach the castle before nightfall. They hadn't managed that but they had definitely managed to take everyone by surprise.

Not the least of which was the fact that instead of returning with one person fewer than they'd started out, they'd returned with three more—in direct violation of Mike's orders.

Sarah stood with the other castle women in the square and watched the wagon pull fully into the courtyard. She noticed the girls on the parapet—half of them facing the interior of the castle and the other half still scouting the woods and front drive for any sight of threats.

Sarah couldn't help but wonder just how itchy those girls' trigger fingers really were. Aibreann may be their de facto leader but in many ways she was an insecure young woman. She was hardly in a position to make the kinds of decisions that would mean the life or death of the people inside the castle.

Sarah could see Mike literally vibrating with fury as he stood by the wagon. Regan dipped her head as he railed at her. She may have gone out in tandem with Tommy Donahue to deliver Hannah to her family but there was no doubt to anyone who knew Regan who it was who'd made the decision to bring Hannah's family back to the castle.

Mike knew it. The castle knew it.

Hannah hopped out of the wagon and ran up the stone stairway to the parapet. Instantly she and the other archer girls hugged and began chattering.

John walked over to Sarah. He had his arm around Cassidy's waist.

"Da's flipping out," John said with a grin, nodding toward where Mike was talking heatedly to Regan, who wisely kept her head down.

Cassidy giggled.

"Nearly as good as movie night," he said.

Sarah turned her attention back to the couple sitting in the wagon with Regan. A woman near her own age sat listening to Mike's sharp words to Regan. Next to her sat a young man about John's age. He had bright eyes and looked around the castle interior like he'd just won the lottery.

Sarah made her way over to where they sat.

"I'm not done with you, Regan," Mike said in a low threatening voice. "You'll meet me in me den first thing in the morning and we'll discuss the finer points of what you've done."

Mike turned to Sarah as she approached and jerked his head at the couple in the wagon.

"Hannah's mother, Mrs. Eliza Bartlett," he said. "My wife Sarah Donovan."

"Hello, Mrs. Donovan," Eliza said as she held out her hand. "I can't thank ye enough. Sure you've saved our lives and that's a fact."

"Pleased to meet you," Sarah said, smiling.

Mike frowned at the young man sitting next to Eliza. "What's your name, lad?"

"Jordie sir."

Mike glanced up at the girls on the parapet. Sarah knew he was watching Hannah and probably weighing the worth of her skill with the bow with the burden of two more mouths to feed.

"Do you know anything about horses?"

"No sir."

Gavin appeared on the other side of the wagon. "Oy, mate," he said. "I'm Gavin. Come with me and I'll teach you everything you need to know."

Jordie jumped down from the wagon while Mike helped Eliza down.

"How long have you been traveling?" Sarah asked as Eliza steadied herself with a hand against the side of the wagon.

"Not too long. Maybe ten hours. We're from near Tralee."

Mike grunted and turned away, clearly exhausted with the effort of being civil. He stalked back toward his den.

"That's a good ways," Sarah said. "Have you eaten?"

Eliza's eyes filled with tears. "Sure no, but I can't thank ye enough for taking us in."

Sarah took the woman's hand to lead her to the main castle living chambers which faced the back of the castle and the ocean.

"Don't worry about that now," Sarah said. "There's a hot bath waiting for you and a bed with real cotton sheets."

Eliza shook her head and Sarah felt her arm trembling at Sarah's touch.

"I'll never be able to thank ye enough. Never."

Thor stepped out of the wagon where Rose and Emma were still sleeping. He jumped to the ground and then went to a nearby bush to relieve himself. His men were up and moving about in the process of breaking down the camp.

Getting ready.

He saw Jocko standing over the cache of rocket launchers. It was his job to make sure they were kept dry and in good working order. They'd been lifted—along with a dozen warheads—from one of the army depots in Dublin. Which was very strange since the RPGs were Russian.

Thor made his way over to Jocko.

"Tell me we'll be ready tonight," he said as he touched the toe of his boot to the tarp covering the pile of missiles.

49

Finding them had been a boon, to be sure. The fact that Jocko and Digby both were fast learners when it came to any kind of gun—even better.

"The weather's shite," Jocko said, looking up into the murky air. "Might want to wait for it to clear some."

"Me wife's sick of camping out," Thor said. "We'll go in tonight."

Jocko shrugged. "What about the castle?"

Thor stopped in his half turn back to the wagon. He frowned at Jocko's words. He knew very well of the castle in the area. What he didn't know was whether it was worth the effort to capture it.

With their rocket launchers they could easily take it, but Thor was keenly aware that once the warheads were gone, they went back to doing things the hard way.

"First things first," he said.

"Just as well," Jocko replied. "Rumor has it they're all cannibals there anyway."

7

The next morning saw reduced numbers in the dining hall which didn't surprise Sarah. New people or not, Mike would have every able-bodied man and woman out in the fields tending to the harvest and planting the potato field. It was just as well there wasn't a crowd at breakfast. Eliza Bartlett seemed a sensitive sort, prone to tears and shaking.

God only knew how the poor woman had survived the past seven years.

Jordie, who had been thirteen when the first bomb dropped in the Irish Sea, was clearly made of sturdier stuff. John and Gavin had both taken him under their wings and given him a tour of the castle along with rudimentary instruction on how to stable a horse and wagon.

If Jordie was like most normal people in the twenty-first century, he'd need to have it explained to him a few more times before getting it right without getting kicked, stepped on or bitten in the process.

Sarah knew Mike was somewhat mollified by the fact that Jordie was old enough to do a full day's work. Before he and Sarah had gone to sleep last night, he'd sketched out a plan where Jordie could be in charge of the pigs. Sarah had serious doubts about that.

Eliza sat at the breakfast table and gazed down the long expanse of table as if she was seated at Buckingham Palace. Gavin had taken Jordie with him to the fields at sun up.

Liddy and Mary O'Malley—sisters who'd married brothers and so kept a common last name—served up oatmeal in heavy crockery bowls with slabs of rough toast drenched in fresh butter. It was the job of three preteen girls to collect berries and make the jam that also sat on the table at every meal—which they did when they weren't practicing their bow and arrow skills.

"I can't believe how you live," Eliza said breathlessly, tears once more filling her eyes.

How the hell did you survive? Sarah couldn't help wondering for the thousandth time.

"Well, we all work together," Sarah said. "Everyone has a skill and we all as a community benefit from that."

Eliza picked up a piece of toast. Her hand shook. "I…I don't think I have a skill."

"Don't worry. We find out what your skill is even if you don't know yourself," Sarah said.

"Sometimes it's a skill for shoveling manure," said Terry's nine year old son Darby.

"Darby Donaghue!" Fiona said sharply before thumping down a fresh plate of steaming scones on the table. "Are ye not expected in the stable about now?"

The boy grinned and stood up. "See?" he said to Eliza before snatching a hot scone and scampering off.

"Everyone seems so happy here," Eliza said as she watched Darby disappear out the main door of the dining hall. "Hot food, hot baths…"

Fiona sat down next to Eliza as Liddy appeared and silently poured all of them fresh tea before going back to the kitchen.

"How was life where you were then?" Fiona asked gently.

Sarah was glad Fi had asked. As the only American in the group Sarah tended to be too blunt and sometimes just hearing her accent got people's backs up. Eliza didn't look like that type but the question was still a hard one and better coming from another Irish woman.

"It…wasn't too bad at first," Eliza said, reaching for her tea and taking a long sip before resuming. "Me Marty moved us into one of the summer cottages that were vacant."

"Marty is your husband?" Sarah asked.

"He was."

Sarah glanced at Fiona.

"When did you lose him?" Fiona asked.

Eliza took a long breath. "Not until the second year. He...he went out to find us food and...just never came back."

Sarah let out the breath she was holding. There were worst ways to lose your husband and both she and Fiona had cause to know that.

Fiona's husband Declan was shot in front of her in their first weeks at Henredon. Sarah's own husband David had been killed in front of her too in the pasture of the remote cottage where they'd lived with John the year after the first EMP.

"After Marty never came back, me and Jordie and Hannah did whatever we had to do. We ate garbage. We hid. We ran. We stole. Hannah was a big help and always such a sensible girl." Eliza's voice trembled and Sarah knew she was coming to the part where Hannah was stolen away.

"And then she was gone. Just like her father, aye?" Eliza said. "Gone and nary a word for two years until yesterday when she shows up happy and hearty as you please. I...I couldn't believe it. There she was like nothing had happened. As cheerful and good natured as ever."

Only Sarah knew something *had* happened. Something terrible and relentless. And Fiona knew it too because Fiona had been there. Hannah was a survivor and if she was cheerful and good-natured it was because she was unnaturally resilient and had overcome something horrific and somehow come out whole on the other side—not because it hadn't happened.

It was fairly clear that Hannah had not told her mother the truth of what had happened to her. All the girls who were returned to their homes always had the option of keeping silent but most of them had opted to tell their families the truth.

If Hannah was trying to protect her mother from the pain of the ordeal Hannah had survived, she must know it wouldn't be kept secret from Eliza for long. Here in the castle everyone knew which girls had been rescued from the rape camp, which girls had borne babies of rape, and which girls were never really the same again after.

"You're safe here, Eliza," Sarah said, putting a hand on the woman's trembling hand. "No one can get you here."

Eliza looked at Sarah and nodded, her eyes full of tears. The thought came to Sarah like a cold dagger in the ribs that if demons lived in Eliza's own breast, all the iron gates or high limestone walls in the world wouldn't protect her from them.

Could it be another eclipse? Was it just a bad storm system coming in?

Mike stood at the window of his study and stared out into the darkening gloom. Although the castle stood high on a seaside bluff, it was not unusual for thick morning fog to roll in and hang about the castle well into the afternoon. Mike was trying to remember the last time the sky looked as dark as this when a knock at the door jerked him out of his thoughts.

The field workers had returned to the castle for their midday meal. With the presence of the wolves in the area, it made more sense to have them come back to the castle rather than post guards for the whole time. The main benefit of the archers was they could discourage the wolves coming too close.

And Mike was trying to save bullets.

"Come in," he said, moving back to his desk which was a massive mahogany secretary with matching hutch and bookshelves. The heavy furniture had been left in the castle from its days as a museum and had proven too heavy for the average looter to carry off.

Later in one of their own raids that Mike, Gavin and John had made of the countryside last fall, they'd come upon a mansion that had been stripped, defaced and abandoned years earlier. It also had several rooms of oriental rugs and a full untouched library of books.

They'd recreated the room in Mike's den.

Regan stepped into the room. She easily looked a decade older than her twenty-five years and nothing at all like the young woman who'd sold her body to passersby two years earlier or who'd betrayed Mike's son Gavin at nearly the cost of his life. Her once pretty face was leathery, tanned and creased with worry lines, and she clearly made no attempt at cosmetic enhancement. Her hair was tied and braided down her back with a leather thong

No, the years had not been kind to Regan, but they'd been the making of her.

Mike noticed the armband that she wore over her black t-shirt. It was the insignia that the archers had created to identify themselves.

As if anyone needed an armband to know that.

"You knew the rules," Mike said briskly. "You knew we don't accept any new members to the castle."

"I knew we needed Hannah," Regan said. "She's the best archer we have. And she wouldn't stay without her family."

"And so you just made the decision in spite of what my orders were?"

Regan swallowed but kept her gaze level. "I…I made a field decision," she said. "It was spur of the moment."

"So you didn't plan it all along?"

She looked surprised. "No. Not at-tall! Until we got to Tralee, Hannah wanted to go home. It wasn't until we got there that she begged me to bring them back with her."

"At which point you made your executive decision."

"I'm sorry, Mike."

"Are you? Because I really don't think you are."

Regan looked at her boots. "I'm sorry you're so upset," she mumbled.

Mike stared at her for several long moments, letting the silence build between them. Regan wasn't a talker—not like a lot of girls—but even she shifted uncomfortably as the tension built between them.

Regan was a special case and discipline was always a delicate matter with her. In many ways—except for her brokenness—she reminded him of Sarah. That strength, that spike of steel in her spine. Regan was a natural leader too. Which was why disobeying orders came so easily to her.

Mike sighed. What's done was done. With any luck the two new castle members would prove beneficial to the group. It was all that Mike could hope.

"I see you've passed the archery test," Mike said, nodding at the armband. "Thinking of joining the army, are ye?"

"I only barely passed," she said with a grin. "I didn't qualify for Les Crème but I'll get better. I have other things to offer the group."

Mike had to admit that if archery skill and the ability to kill without hesitation were the two prerequisites of becoming a Henredon archer, he knew Regan had at least one qualification in spades.

"Such as?" he said.

"Leadership skills," she said.

Like making field decisions when it suits you? Mike couldn't help but think.

"I thought Aibreann Kieran was the leader of the band."

Regan nodded. "For now."

"I'll not be having ye cause trouble, Regan," Mike said, giving her his best glowering look.

"Everything I do is for the good of the castle."

That's what troublemakers always say just before they wreak havoc.

"Anyroad," she said, "There are no more people to be returned to their families. That job's done."

Mike nodded. He was actually relieved that Regan thought she might want to be one of the archers. He couldn't see her settling down and he could easily imagine the devastation a bored and idle Regan could cause in the castle. She needed to be kept busy, did Regan, and darning socks by the fire wasn't going to cut it.

"I need you to help get the harvest in first. I need all hands."

He watched a muscle clench in her jaw.

"Sure," she said.

"You can train of an evening after you come in from the fields."

"Is that all?"

"Ye did a grand job, lass. Ye helped put all the pieces back together for a lot of people. I'm that proud of you. And I know your parents would be too."

Regan flushed and bit back a proud smile.

"Ta, Mike," she said, then turned and left the room.

Mike stood up and went back to the window. The clouds had darkened and there were more of them now. The storm was definitely coming and half the corn was still on the stalk.

Shite.

Susan Kiernan-Lewis

8

Sarah stood in front of the small bookcase that faced the king-size bed, her hand on the back of one of the leather-bound books she'd read many times over.

Most of the castle living chambers faced the ocean or the south side of the castle. Mike and Sarah's rooms were closer to the castle front. From the large mullioned windows in their bedroom, they could see the gardens and all the pastureland that stretched to the south in the direction of the village of Kilbaha.

Their bedroom was large and had a separate living room off it. While Mike's den held books looted from the mansion they'd found, this room held most of the books that Sarah had brought back with her from the States years earlier. They'd made several trips back to Ameriland in the past year to recover them.

Most of those books were kept in the schoolroom where Frank Murphy taught the children. Sarah had thought of the books as a balm to her guilt of bringing John back to post-apocalyptic Ireland. She'd brought them with the hope that they could help John keep up with his studies.

A brilliant boy with a love of learning, he'd gone through them all in a summer.

The book she had her hand on was a novel—something most people nowadays would consider an indulgence. She knew for a fact that Mike read only manuals and nonfiction.

"I thought I'd find you here," Mike said from the doorway.

She turned, surprised to see him. The man never stopped moving from sun up to sun down. Seeing him upstairs anywhere near their bedroom in the middle of the day was unusual.

"I can't say the same about you," she said turning to face him.

"Sure I'm just here to see if I left me glasses up here." He went to his bedside table and rifled under a stack of books. "How's Mrs. Bartlett doing then?"

"Honestly, she's pretty fragile. I put her to doing laundry and mending."

"I thought the nuns were doing that work?"

"Yes, she's helping them."

"And that's all she's good for?"

"Do you hear yourself?" Sarah laughed. "I'm sure she has other skills and as soon as we get to know her better, we'll discover them. You did a good thing allowing her to come here, Mike."

He grunted and turned away from the table, his hands empty.

"Did she say how she was managing before?" he asked as he scanned the bookshelves.

"She's not offered any specifics, no."

"That's usually telling right there."

"I know. So I haven't pressed her. What about Jordie?"

Mike snorted. "Gavin says he's useless. Afraid of the horses and the cow. Stabbed his foot with the manure fork first off."

"That explains why I saw him limping earlier, I guess."

"He spent the afternoon in the clinic and then copped an attitude when I sent him to the kitchen to wash dishes since that's all he was fit for."

"Maybe he and Cassidy will get together."

"Don't get your hopes up," he said.

"Speaking of the kitchen, I'm afraid Mary is on the warpath about our letting Tilly off the hook. You might want to think about using a food taster for the next few weeks."

Mike sighed in exasperation. "*Our* letting her off?"

"Well, it was a team effort, you know. I let her go and you backed me up. Thank you for that way by the way."

"Is it possible Mary has too much time on her hands?" Mike said. "She went mental on me when you ordered Tilly released."

"She's just frustrated," Sarah said. "In fact all the women are. They feel like the archers are considered to be more valuable than they are."

"They *are* more valuable! That's a fact!" Mike said heatedly. "Which would you rather have, Sarah? Someone who can create a scone to weep for or someone who can shoot the eye out of the blackguard scaling the wall of Siobhan's nursery?"

"I'm just telling you to be aware of what's brewing."

"Can't you talk to the women? Talk sense into them?"

"Maybe. But someone needs to control the archers. Someone needs to *lead* them and be in charge of them."

"And you're saying that's not me?"

"So far it's not," Sarah said, trying to soften her words. "They need a fellow warrior to keep them in line and tell them what to do."

"Know anybody to fit that bill, do ye, Sarah?"

"No," Sarah admitted.

"Sure it's glad I am we had this little talk," Mike said. "Always nice to have a discussion about a problem with no fecking solution to it."

Sarah put down her book and went to him.

"When do you think Mr. Morgan might arrive?" she asked.

Mike sighed and glanced out the window.

"If he tries to miss the rain probably any time now."

"Where will you meet with him? Your den?"

"Nay, absolutely not," Mike said firmly. "No sense in making this harder than it already is. I'll meet with him in the stables."

"Seriously? And will we put him up there for the night too?"

"Bloody hell, Sarah! Is it the whole night ye promised him?"

"Mike, I invited him to dinner. The village is three miles away through the woods. We can't send him out in the dark with two little boys!"

"Aye, fine, fine," Mike said impatiently.

"And we'll help him if at all possible?"

"I said we would, didn't I?"

"He did help us out when we first came here."

"I'm well aware, Sarah."

"Some might think we owe him."

"Is that what you think?"

"I do, of course. The question isn't do we owe him? The question is *what* do we owe him?"

Mike laughed and stepped over to her and pulled her into his arms.

"I love ye, Sarah Donovan," he said, kissing her. "Do ye ken that?"

"I do, Mike Donovan," Sarah said in a whisper, feeling the rush of tenderness tingling through her hands as she ran them through his hair. "Like I've never known anything else in my life." She kissed him again.

The knock at the door broke them apart.

"Good Lord," Sarah said, straightening her shirt and fanning herself. "God forbid we should have five minutes in the middle of the day to ourselves."

Mike turned to look at the open door where Gavin stood grinning on the threshold.

"What?" Mike barked in annoyance.

"Sorry, Da," Gavin said. "Hope I didn't interrupt anything."

"Don't be a smart arse, ye smirking eejit. This had better be an emergency."

"Am I right in thinking we'll not be working the fields this afternoon?" As if timed to synchronize with Gavin's words, Mike heard the unmistakable sound of rain pattering against the window.

"Aye," Mike said with a sigh. "So?"

"So Frank and Robbie and I'd like to head out for an overnight deer-hunting trip. Mary won't let us touch any of the pigs until fall and that's a long time to eat cornbread and cabbages."

Mike frowned and looked outside. It wasn't coming down that hard but working the fields was out of the question. Might as well come out ahead in another way.

"Where will you go?" he asked.

"We haven't hit the Foynes yet," Gavin said. "It might be tapped out but we know for sure it is around here."

"Horses only or a wagon too?"

"Just horses. Three to ride and an extra one to carry the meat."

"You know we only have fifty bullets to last us," Mike said, dropping his voice. He wouldn't want to cause a panic if people were to find out how few bullets they actually had left.

"So we'll make them count," Gavin said with a shrug. "We might even find more."

"No raiding," Mike said firmly. "Unless the place looks abandoned. I'll not risk the loss of any horses just so we can grab a couple of bullets that probably won't fit our guns."

"I promise, Da. No raiding unless it's just sitting there ripe for the picking."

Mike didn't like the sound of that but then he didn't like the sound of most things these days.

Susan Kiernan-Lewis

9

Artemus Morgan thought it unusual for the light to have faded so quickly even with the heavy rain that had been falling for the past hour. By the time they'd reached the castle it was nearly dark out although he knew it was only late afternoon.

The figures positioned along the parapet were obviously expecting them but there were no waves or shouts of greeting. Even in the gloom, Morgan could just make out the wicked outlines of each of the bows the lasses held.

He lifted his hand and one of the archers waved back. Minutes later the drawbridge began to descend and the portcullis in the castle entrance rose.

When the heavy wooden door pounded down across the moat in front of them he and Matt and Macaulay walked across it—the lads so excited they practically skipped. But the biggest surprise was when they stepped into the interior of the castle.

Morgan had an idea of what the inside of Henredon Castle would look like from what he remembered of it before the EMP went off. But he hadn't been prepared for what he saw when the drawbridge cranked down and he and his two lads were allowed inside.

There were electric lights illuminating the castle courtyard.

They have electricity? he thought with astonishment. *How did I not know this?*

Donovan was striding across the courtyard towards them, his good wife behind him with her son at her side. Matt and Mac— eight years old twins—had talked to John at the fair and both exclaimed when they saw him again.

Morgan shook hands with Donovan.

"Welcome, Mr. Morgan," Donovan said. "I believe you've met my wife?"

Sarah Donovan smiled at him and then turned her attention to the lads.

"Dinner won't be for an hour or so," she said. "But John said you wanted to see the castle dungeons."

"Aye, Missus!" the boys said in unison.

"Off ye go, lads," Artemus said and watched his grandsons as they scampered off with John.

A few people were standing in the courtyard talking. In the far corner Morgan could see a cow standing by a bale of hay. A few chickens were running about.

"Cor, I didn't know you lot still had the lights on," Morgan said as he followed Donovan through the nearest archway into a long interior tunnel illuminated by large candles on the walls every twenty feet. The flickering light from the candles made eerie shadows across the walkway.

"We were able to salvage a few solar panels and a battery from our old place," Donovan's wife said. "It's not enough to work the ovens or give us security lighting on the walls. But there's enough in summer to heat the water for washing and to power the lights in the courtyard."

Morgan wasn't use to a woman speaking as authoritatively as this one did. Not often before the crisis and never after.

Must be her being American and all.

"Naturally, come winter it's all bollocks since there's no sun to charge the battery," Donovan said leading them toward a stone stairwell.

"So you have hot baths in the summer when you don't need them," Morgan said, "and in the winter you're like the rest of us, chipping ice off a block in the cellar?"

"That's about the size of it."

"I'll leave you men now," Donovan's wife said. "As long as you promise not to talk about anything too important while I'm gone."

Morgan had absolutely no idea how to respond—and from a woman!—but Donovan kissed her and gave her waist a squeeze which seemed to satisfy her.

"I'll see you at dinner, Mr. Morgan," she said with a smile before turning and disappearing down the hallway.

Donovan's sister Fiona appeared in the hallway.

"Mike! Terry says he needs to see you in the workshop straight away."

Donovan looked apologetically at Morgan.

"No worries, squire," Morgan said. "Do what you need to do. I'm fine right here."

"I won't be a tick," Donovan said, turning to walk back out into the courtyard.

Donovan's sister turned to Morgan and smiled.

"Sure we're glad to have you and your lads to visit," she said. "I'll show you upstairs to Mike's den where you can wait for him. It's just this way."

Donovan's den was a pure shocker, so it was.

Morgan knew he must have stood with his mouth open for at least two full minutes before recovering because Donovan entered the room behind him and immediately began to downplay what he was seeing.

"It's a cold bloody fortress come winter," Donovan said. "The rugs and the drapes help to make it a sight less noisy and so I'm not freezing me bollocks off come January."

"Of course." Morgan went to the large leather chair opposite the massive oak desk where Donovan now sat. Every wall was lined with floor to ceiling bookcases. And the shelves were filled. It made sense they would be. Unless you used them to start a fire to keep warm, books were the last thing any sane person would think to loot.

"It looks like before the Crisis," Morgan said, gazing around the room. He coughed until his eyes watered and Donovan waited for him to recover. Morgan had been a committed smoker for most of his life. The fact that fags were hard to get a hold of now had helped him quit but clearly the damage was done.

"Trust me, everything about my life reminds me on a constant basis that nothing is like it was before the Crisis," Donovan said, still trying to explain away the luxury of the room.

Morgan had told himself he wouldn't think about it. He told himself he wouldn't *want* it—if he could help it. But sitting here now in this beautiful room with every imaginable comfort, the yearning welled up inside his chest and he couldn't make it stop.

There simply had to be a way to bring his people into this world between life and death, pain and ease. This man, this Donovan who seemed so fair and compassionate, he had to be convinced to allow it.

He just had to.

Mike knew what the man was thinking.

How else would any normal person process the relative luxury inside the castle? People were human. They wanted security and fellowship and food.

But they also longed for comfort.

He was going to kill Fiona for bringing Morgan here.

Did the lass not have any sense at all?

It's why Mike hadn't wanted Morgan to see his den. Oh, the rest of the castle would impress, he had no doubt. The big dining hall with platters of hot food and drink, the beds in all the rooms with cotton sheets and wool blankets and freshly laundered duvets and goose down pillows.

All of that would grandstand the hardest heart. But this was the room that gave the message that the rest of it only hinted at.

This is the room that said *somehow it will all be fine.*

When you sat in this room, surrounded by knowledge—both in maps and novels—a thick rug beneath your feet, a crackling fire in winter before you—there was a chance to believe that the world hadn't changed. That the world could still be civilized. *Would* be civilized once more.

It was a room of unabashed hope and Mike always made a point to tread carefully when he entered it.

Hope could get you killed these days.

And it was a room that today was going to make his conversation with Morgan about a thousand times harder.

"We met your lad on the road," Morgan said. "Said he was off hunting?"

"Oh, aye. Since the rain ended work in the fields at least for the next day or so."

"Bad luck that."

Mike shrugged. He'd hated that it had happened—just as he'd feared it would—but a delayed harvest wasn't the end of the world.

He knew bloody well what *that* looked like.

"We might lose some to mold," Mike said. "It'll just mean our women will have to work double time to can it all. Less will be available as fresh."

"Would you be needing extra hands from the village women perhaps to help out?"

"I'm not sure how we'd pay them."

Mike left it at that and was grateful that Morgan did too.

"Your women seem to do a lot to keep the castle running," Morgan said. "Everyone within a twenty mile radius knows about your archer lasses."

"We have more women than men." Mike shrugged. "So everybody does what they do best."

"Have they been tested?"

Mike was well aware that Morgan knew the answer to that. No amount of drilling or practice or lectures from Mike could prepare the girls for the first time an army or invader showed up at their gate. Would they fight? Would they shoot to kill? Would they panic? To hear them talk, it wasn't a worry.

But what happens in battle was always a worry.

"Not yet," Mike said, arching an eyebrow at the man. He didn't mean to make it sound like a threat but in his experience, it didn't hurt to underscore his strengths and de-emphasize any perception of weakness. No, the lasses weren't tried. But they would fight and Morgan shouldn't think for a minute that they wouldn't.

"How many men do you have in the castle?" Morgan asked innocently.

Mike narrowed his eyes but before he could answer there was a knock at the door. Mary O'Malley appeared carrying a heavy silver tray with teapot, two mugs and a creamer. She swept into the office and thumped the tray down on Mike's desk.

"Shall I pour, your grace?" she said sarcastically.

Mike flushed. For her to attempt to embarrass him in front of an outsider showed the extent of her fury with him. But he bit his tongue.

"Not at-tall, Mary," he said. "This will be grand, so it will."

He knew she expected him to introduce her formally and if it had been anybody but Morgan, he might have. But this was a delicate negotiation between two leaders and he wouldn't give Morgan the advantage.

At least not right out of the gate.

Mary hesitated and then turned on her heel and flounced out without another word.

Morgan's eyebrows shot up. "Are ye sure you're not married to that one?" he said.

Mike laughed in spite of himself.

"I made a recent decision related to the archers that didn't sit well with the rest of the women."

"Ah. Jealous, are they?"

Mike poured the tea and handed Morgan a mug.

"Do ye not have to deal with such bullshite in your own community, Mr. Morgan?"

"Call me Artie and aye, now that you mention it, that would be the truth of it." They drank in silence for a moment.

"So," Mike said. "This Thor bugger. How well armed is he?"

"I'm reliably informed he has rocket launchers."

Mike worked not to let the surprise and dismay show on his face. If that was true, they were all in trouble.

"But you don't know for sure?"

Morgan shook his head. "I haven't seen them with me own eyes. But we have two families with us from the last village that didn't capitulate."

"Did he destroy their village?"

"Nay. But he blew a fairly large hole in it. Enough to get people paying attention to his demands."

"You can't fight him," Mike said flatly. "And unless I bring your people into the castle, I can't protect you. Maybe not even then. These walls are limestone, not iron."

"What would you have me do? Let him have the village? Call it the price of our times?"

Mike saw the anger simmering behind Morgan's expression. He tried to tell himself it wasn't him that Morgan was angry with. He put a hand up to try to slow the progression of whatever was building in Morgan's head.

"Steady on. It's early days yet. We've a lot to discuss and we're not near ready to call it."

Morgan visibly worked to calm himself. His lips curled, showing his teeth.

"Meanwhile, are ye having trouble with wolves?" Mike asked, hoping to distract the man from the far thornier subject.

Morgan ran a hand over his face, his tea cold and forgotten on the side table by his chair.

"Aye. Nobody hurt yet but we've lost goats. They're getting bolder."

"And you have enough ammunition to protect your people from them?"

A glittering look of distrust slipped into Morgan's expression. "For now," he grunted.

A bell ringing in the distance punctured Mike with a spasm of relief. Dinnertime. Maybe the old wanker would relax a bit during the meal.

He'd been barking not to offer the bastard whisky straight off.

Susan Kiernan-Lewis

10

Sarah had been torn between wanting to put on a celebratory spread for their guest and downplaying all that they had in the castle. In the end she decided that she would receive Mr. Morgan as she would want to be received.

It would be an average meal in the castle dining hall. No more, no less.

The dining hall was roughly one hundred feet in length and forty feet wide with a thirty foot ceiling. It was anchored at one end by a massive floor to ceiling stone fireplace which in summer was not lit. At the other end were two wooden doors that opened outward onto the stone hallway.

The four dining hall tables—each seating twenty per table—were parallel to each other. Ever since they moved into the castle it had been their habit to eat together as a community as much as possible.

Given patrol, kitchen and nursery duties, it wasn't possible for everyone to sit down together, but there was usually at least eighty people at one time seated together for each of the three daily meals.

Candles flickered in hurricane lamps positioned at intervals down the long table. Kerosene sconces were outfitted on the walls. The overall feeling was one of warmth and conviviality.

Mike sat at the head of the first table with Sarah to his right. Normally John sat to his left but tonight that place was reserved for their guest Artemus Morgan.

Each family in the castle had their chosen seating places at the tables. To have an outsider dining with them was an unusual occurrence and there was a buzz of excitement and expectation as the castle residents filed in and took their seats.

Even more than the thrum of voices and laughter, the aroma of whatever the cooks had created in the castle kitchens wafted about the long room. Tonight it would be chicken—an extravagance to be sure and one that gave testimony to the status of their visitor.

Before the wolves got so bad, the chickens had been kept in movable coops in the nearest pasture beyond the car park. Mike had moved them into the interior of the castle in one corner of the courtyard. It was not an ideal situation from anyone's perspective—least of all for the chickens.

The kitchen staff had made the decision to keep a dozen chickens for laying purposes. The rest of the birds had gone into last night's and tonight's dinners.

Sarah watched Mr. Morgan's eyes widen as Liddy came to the head of the table and poured each of them a glass of red wine. She hadn't asked Mike ahead of time if they should hold back while Morgan was here but he didn't seem to react negatively. He just picked up his glass, nodded to Morgan in a toast, and drank it fully down.

Uh-oh. Perhaps their talk hadn't gone so well?

John and the two boys had yet to show up when Liddy and Mary and a few of the nuns began bringing out the plates of food. Sarah heard exclamations of astonishment when several people realized they were having chicken twice in a week.

Well, enjoy it, Sarah thought as Sister Margarita set a plate in front of her. *Because this will be the last of it for awhile.*

"Rice!" Morgan exclaimed. "Am I really seeing rice?"

"It's a popular staple from my wife's area of the US," Mike said, topping up Morgan's wine glass and then his own. "She brought back a rather large quantity of dried rice that we're having some trouble using up."

Mike raised an eyebrow at Sarah. As a Southerner, rice was integral to Sarah's diet back home. For the Irish—especially post EMP—it was practically exotic.

"I can't imagine what's keeping John and the boys," Sarah said.

Sophia was sitting with Eliza and Nuala a few seats away. Since Nuala was in charge of the nursery and often opted to eat there Sarah was surprised to see her in the dining hall. She was glad to see her enjoying adult company for a change.

Eliza ate slowly as if every morsel was a marvel to her. Her naturally taciturn nature seemed to work well with the talkativeness of the other two. Sarah gave a silent prayer that Mr. Morgan wouldn't get around to talking to Eliza and find out she'd been allowed into the castle for no good reason but that she was the mother of one of the archer girls.

Sarah was glad to see that Eliza seemed to be settling down. But even in just the two days the pair had been in the castle, Sarah had already heard less good things about Jordie.

"For those two to risk missing a meal," Morgan said. "your lad must be showing them a facsimile of the space shuttle at the very least." He turned to Mike. "Which, squire, I would not be at all surprised to hear you have here."

Mike laughed good-naturedly but Sarah could tell there was tension underneath it. Negotiations were clearly still in process.

A shrill titter of laughter broke through the hum of conversation and the clink of silverware against crockery. Sarah recognized the laugh as Cassidy's and she sought the girl out. At the far end of the table—where she would have no worry of being easily observed by Sarah—Cassidy sat between Jordie and young Tommy, Terry and Jill's son. Tommy and Regan had been an item for at least three months and had done the last two runs to deliver the rape victims to their homes.

From Cassidy's giggling and Tommy's red face it appeared he and Regan were no longer together.

Sarah sipped her wine and scanned the rest of the diners. The archers always sat apart from everyone else at the end of the head table. Sarah wasn't sure whether that was planned or it had just happened. There were always at least ten archers on duty at any given time. The archers didn't always come to breakfast or lunch but they often showed up for dinner which was always a hot meal and often with wine.

Tonight Sarah saw Regan, Aibreann, Tilly and Briana sitting hunched over their plates and talking heatedly among themselves. All four of them had long hair tied back in a low ponytail. Their buckskin-brown clothes that made them appear from a distance like young Indian warriors. The dark armbands were easily visible on each of their arms.

When Mike had mentioned that Regan had joined the archers, Sarah had agreed it made sense for Regan. But Regan wasn't a joiner and she tended to see things strictly in black and white with no gray areas.

It didn't typically make for the most cohesive of team experiences.

"Oy! Young Darby!" Mike called to Tommy and Jill's youngest. "Have you seen John about?"

Darby, his mouth full of food and a chunk of corn bread in one hand, shook his head. His father slapped him lightly on the back of the head.

"Go off and find him, ye git!" he said with a grin.

Darby swallowed, jumped up from the table, and bolted for the door.

"I really can't imagine where they are," Sarah said to Morgan.

The sound of a chair scraping back and then falling with a loud clatter on the stone floor was followed by a loud curse.

Both Regan and Aibreann jumped to their feet, their faces close to each other. The other two archers scooted away but watched intently.

"Oy!" Mike bellowed. "Sit yer arses down!"

Neither Regan nor Aibreann looked in Mike's direction. Aibreann said something under her breath and a second later Regan shot out a hand and pushed Aibreann on top of the overturned chair. Aibreann launched herself with a banshee shriek at Regan, grabbing her by the hair with both hands.

"Bugger!" Mike muttered. He reached them in four strides and grabbed Aibreann around the hips and pulled her off Regan. Before Mike could stop her, Aibreann punched

Regan in the stomach. Mike twisted Aibreann around and slammed her facedown on the dining table. Plates and drinks smashed and scattered to the floor.

Regan was on her feet. Mike roared over his shoulder, "Regan, if ye try anything I swear I'll tan yer hide myself!"

Regan turned to the other two archers and slapped Tilly across the face. Both girls lunged at Regan at once, knocking more dishes to the floor.

Before Mike could see what was happening, he heard a strangled yelp and turned around, releasing Aibreann in the process to see Morgan raising a warning eyebrow at the two archers who stood panting and glowering at Regan—who was held by Morgan with her arm twisted up behind her back.

"Look at this mess!" Mike bellowed. "The lot of ye, take it outside. Dinner's over for you. Get out!"

Regan jerked out of Morgan's hands and stalked out the door, followed by the other three.

"You'll not punish them for fighting?" Morgan asked as he watched the girls go.

"What would you suggest?" Mike said with frustration. One of the nuns began picking up the shards of crockery from the floor.

"I dunno. Clean up the mess they made?"

"They'll just break more doing it."

"It's an interesting problem," Morgan mused. "They are your army on the one hand, but on the other hand they're lasses—and young. Ye don't want to puncture their confidence, yet they need to know you're in command."

Even Sarah could hear the unspoken observation: *And they don't know that.*

As Mike and Morgan made their way back to their seats, John, Darby and one of the twins came through the door. Darby went to his seat at the table and pulled a chair over beside him for the other boy. John came to the head of the table.

"What is it, John?" Sarah asked. "Where's the other one?"

John addressed Morgan.

"I'm sorry, sir. Mac had a fall. He's okay but Sister Alphonse says his arm is broken."

"Oh, John, no!" Sarah said, her hand to her throat. "What happened?"

"We were just checking out the oriel window above the postern gate and I told them it had a great view of the ocean and the next thing I know—"

"He's a born spider monkey, is Macaulay," Morgan said with a sigh. "There's no keeping him down if there's something to climb."

"I'm really sorry," John said with a shrug. "He was having fun up until then."

Morgan sighed and stood up from his chair.

"You'll be needing to take me to him, then," he said, eyeing his wine with resignation.

11

Macaulay looked very small where he sat bundled up in blankets on a cot in the clinic. Sister Alphonse, a bulky, bullheaded woman with a gentle touch and a love of herbs, held a can of warm cola with a straw to the boy. He looked up at the nun as if he were ready to propose to her.

"Ach, lad!" Morgan clucked as he entered the clinic. "Can I not even leave ye for a quarter of an hour?"

Mac grimaced. "Sorry, Grandda," he said.

Sarah smiled at Sister Alphonse. Before the nuns came to the castle, the clinic had been a disorganized and depressing place—even though fairly well stocked from the compound's inventory. Sister had turned it into an efficient working infirmary

Morgan sat next to the boy and put his hand on his cheek.

"Drinking soda, are ye? I'll wager Matt will want to be breaking *his* arm next!"

Mac grinned wanly. His face was white and his eyes closed briefly.

Morgan turned to the nun. "Did ye drug him, then?" he asked with surprise.

"Sure, the lad won't be hurting. Not on my watch."

Morgan shook his head in wonder.

Sarah touched Sister Alphonse's shoulder. "We brought him some supper. Is he up for it?"

Sarah set the covered bowl on the table next to the bed.

"Maybe later," the nun said. "If he wakes hungry, I'll give it to him then."

Morgan looked at her in surprise. "You intend to spend the night here?"

"Of course. Where else would I be? He's me patient."

Morgan turned back to Mac who had now given up the battle to stay awake, cola or no cola.

Sarah knew what Morgan was thinking: *What do I have to do to give this life to my lads?*

"We'll leave you then, Sister," Sarah said softly. "I've brought your dinner too."

The evening had been stressful and there was still a few things yet to do. Summer or not, at least the other twin would have the benefit of the first warm bath. Sarah would need to oversee that.

Before she and Morgan had left the dining hall Sarah had noticed that John had disappeared with Cassidy. She told herself there was nothing to worry about and she wouldn't borrow trouble before its time.

Because that had always worked so well in the past.

When she and Morgan left the clinic, she watched him put out a hand to touch the stone walls of the hallway almost as though he needed to prove to himself that they were real. She didn't know what to make of him.

So many of the Irish were masters at holding their cards close to the vest and Artemus Morgan definitely fell into that category. But there was something else about him too. Something as yet undefinable.

"I'm so sorry this happened," Sarah said as they walked down the hall together.

"No worries, lass," he said. "Lads'll will be lads, will they not?"

"I'm going to get Matt settled for the night but I know Mike would like to see you. Do you remember the way to his den?"

Morgan nodded but his eyes narrowed. "You'll not be joining us then?"

Sarah knew Mike was right. If he was going to have any real dialogue with Morgan, it would have to be without the presence of a woman—especially an American one.

"Best laid plans, Mr. Morgan," she said. "I have a few other things I need to do before I'm ready to call it a night. I'm sure Mrs. O'Malley will be in with a drop of something and otherwise I hope you get what you came for tonight."

"How likely is that do ye think?"

"Probably depends on what you have to offer. Goodnight, Mr. Morgan."

As they approached the village, Thor noted that the night was darker than he'd like. While he didn't expect any trouble—his preliminary visit had found Kilbaha peopled with mostly women and old men—he still preferred every foreseeable element on his side.

Not for the first time he wished he'd been able to score night goggles.

He'd left a man with Emma and Rose although there was feck-all in the woods to worry about—except possibly the wolves. But even those they'd only ever heard.

There was something in the air tonight that made a night raid preferable to waiting until morning. Thor couldn't put his finger on exactly why, but even Jocko had mentioned it. A tingling seemed to permeate the air like a harbinger.

His men fanned out in a solid channel line. Every man was armed with rifles or handguns. Jocko and Digby were carrying one loaded rocket launcher each. Thor didn't expect the need to use them. But the weapons were too valuable to leave back at camp with Emma and Rose.

It just made practical sense. If, God forbid, something did happen to his wife and daughter while he was gone, at least they'd save the guns.

Susan Kiernan-Lewis

12

It was nearly dawn by the time Mike finally made it to his bed. While much of what he and Morgan had discussed was about what Morgan needed and what Mike was willing to give, inevitably they spent a lot of time exchanging stories and commiserating in a way that only two men responsible for the lives of large communities could do.

The question of discipline and order was one of the discussions they had long into the night—especially in the case of Mike's female archers.

How to maintain order without breaking the spirit of the young warriors you were attempting to mold? How to maintain order and stay civilized? How to be firm without being brutal? Should one just accept that these times called for stronger, harsher measures?

Mike wished that Morgan had felt comfortable with Sarah being at the meeting. But it had still felt good to have another leader—and a man—to talk these things over with. Sarah was a strong leader and didn't flinch at making the tough calls. But being a woman—and American make no mistake—often created a divide between them that at least with Morgan didn't need to be crossed first.

There had been a certain comfort in talking with Morgan. But the *discomfort* of hearing the man's requests—all reasonable—was made worse by the fact that Mike genuinely liked Morgan. Before the Crisis, they might not have been friends—they were of two different generations—but even then Mike had no doubt Morgan would always have had a wise word in a difficult situation.

In the end, he promised to help Morgan with his Thor problem—the specifics of that help to be determined once the threat actually materialized—and Morgan promised five men to help the castle get its crop in and then accompany Mike on the expedition to find out what the explosions were about.

Mike slept in late. Sarah was long gone when he awoke, but there was a cup of now cold tea on his bedside. As he sat up and ran a hand across his face, he realized that the sunlight which normally streamed in through the mullioned window in his bedroom was missing. He listened to the sound of rain bucketing against the window—which explained the lack of sunlight.

Dressing quickly, he walked down the curving stone staircase that led into the dining hall. By his estimation, it was only a little after eight in the morning—much later than he normally rose—but with the rain, many of the castle folk would probably only just be at breakfast themselves.

He thought of Morgan last night and the man's intense determination to protect the people in his village. Before the Crisis, Morgan had been a taxi driver in Limerick. A widower, he'd walked the one hundred kilometers to Kilbaha to reach the home where his daughter and husband lived with their toddler twins.

Morgan's experience during the early years after the EMP mirrored much of what Mike had endured himself. Morgan had defended the village against looters, rogue gypsies and due to his military service decades earlier even negotiated a pact with the *Garda Socha* when they came looking for new recruits.

The fact that Morgan had been a career sergeant in the Irish Army for twenty years was probably the only thing that kept the Garda from demolishing the village. As it was they took every man over the age of twenty.

But if it hadn't been for Morgan's service, they'd have taken the women too.

Eventually most of the men found their way back to the village.

Mike pushed into the dining hall and glanced around. Most mornings people just grabbed an egg and bacon sandwich on the run, which Mike encouraged. They had plenty of time to sit and enjoy a meal at lunch or dinner. He didn't advocate starting the day out in leisurely fashion and he passed that preference on to his people.

This morning he was surprised to see that almost two dining tables were full.

Sarah spotted him and hurried over from the swinging doors that led from the kitchen. Her face was flushed. Siobhan and Fiona's little lass Ciara walked beside her. The two girls were serious for a change—a purer indication than any red flag that something was wrong.

At the head of the table where Mike normally sat, Tommy and Kevin O'Malley stood bending over someone seated in a chair who was blocked from Mike's view. Mike was surprised to see Morgan seated at the table too.

Did the man not go to bed?

Sarah reached Mike, her face tense.

"I didn't want to wake you since you practically just got to bed," Sarah said.

"What's going on?"

"It's Jordie," she said. Mike could now see the young man's face. He looked afraid.

Sarah put a hand on Mike's arm before he could move forward to the group waiting for him.

"Mike," she said in a low voice. "He's new. John said he didn't know the rules."

Mike's body tensed at her words.

"Should I punish *John* then for not telling the lad the rules?"

Siobhan looked up at her father with wide eyes but her bottom lip quivered.

"Oh, Mr. Donovan!" Jordie's mother Eliza Bartlett pushed from behind Sarah. "My lad didn't know! I am so sorry! If anyone's to be punished...please don't throw us out!"

Sarah patted Eliza on the shoulder and pulled her away.

"Come on, Eliza," she said. "I'm taking the girls up to the nursery. Will you give me a hand?"

Eliza looked fearfully at Jordie, his head hanging as he listened to whatever Kevin and Tommy were telling him. She gave Mike one last pleading look and then turned away with Sarah.

He wasn't sure why but the combination of the boy's mother's tears and the looks of expectation from everyone gathered in the dining hall that ratcheted up his exasperation over the situation.

Why is it so hard to play by the damn rules? And this boyo a fecking newcomer?

He walked up to the head of the table. Kevin's wife Mary appeared from the direction of the kitchen with a tray of steaming tea mugs which she set on the table. Instead of leaving, she stepped back to watch.

"What happened?" Mike asked gruffly, nodding a greeting to Morgan who looked as if he'd slept eight hours, washed and shaved since they'd parted company four hours earlier.

"Caught stealing from the kitchen," Tommy said bluntly.

Mike put his hands on his hips and towered over the young man in the chair. He forced himself to count to ten. He forced himself to realize his antipathy toward the lad had to do with the fact that the survival of everyone in this castle depended on them having the very best people working together and that Mike had allowed one of those precious spots to be filled by this idiot plonker.

And that had been Mike's call. He was the one who'd allowed it to happen.

Which just made him all the madder.

"What do ye have to say for yourself?" he thundered to Jordie.

"I'm sorry," Jordie said, looking up into Mike's face without fear or—from what Mike could see—contrition. "I didn't know it was against the rules."

"What did he steal?"

"A plate of cold chicken," Kevin said. "Two knives. And a pie meant for tonight's tea."

"You didn't know those things weren't yours to take?" Mike asked the young man.

"How would I?"

"Ye do know that none of the lasses here are yours to rape, do ye not?"

The boy blushed. "That's different," he said. "This was communal food. Why was it okay to have it at dinnertime but not okay just a few hours later?"

Mike resisted the urge to look at Morgan. He already knew how the older man would handle this. He didn't believe in giving second changes or warnings. If you let someone off with a warning, you gave them every reason to think you were weak and they would do worse next time.

Mike understood the concept.

He wasn't there yet. But he was getting there.

"Do you know better now?" Mike asked.

Jordie nodded his head vigorously. "Aye," he said. "I'll never take another thing that's not given to me."

Mary cleared her throat but Mike refused to look at her. It didn't matter what he did as far as she was concerned. If he let the boy off, he was too soft. If he punished him, he was a brute. After the Tilly fiasco, Mary had made up her mind about Mike's way of handling things.

"No dessert for a month," Mike said. Out of the corner of his eye he saw the stances of both Terry and Kevin relax— whether from relief or disgust he didn't know. "And you'll put new hay down for the cow and drag the old out to the compost heap."

The boy nodded less vigorously now.

"After which—in addition to your usual chores—you'll bring the archers their tea up on the parapet every day from now on."

"Even in the *rain*?" Jordie looked at him with dismay.

Mike stared at him. He knew what he wanted to do. In some ways it was also probably what he should do. But he'd found a piece of himself lately going down a road that was hard and cruel. He hadn't liked what he saw. He was even afraid of it. He bit back the bile, the instinct and the urge and took a long breath.

"And when it snows, too. Now get out of me sight."

Jordie sprang from the chair and ran the length of the room and out.

Without looking at anyone, Mike turned and picked up one of the mugs of tea and sat down. Kevin and Terry walked away without a word and the rest of the people in the hall began to talk amongst themselves.

"Tough crowd, squire," Morgan murmured, his eyes unreadable as he drank his tea. Liddy came to the table and set down before them two bowls of oatmeal along with a ceramic ewer of thick cream and a dish of honey.

"Bloody hell of a way to start the day," Mike said, pushing his food away and then feeling ashamed of the gesture. Likely Morgan already thought the castle didn't appreciate all that they had.

As he listened to the hum of conversation around him, all Mike could hear was the sound of his own voice telling the little gobshite he couldn't have dessert for a month like he was a naughty toddler. The memory of it made his ears burn.

"It's a tricky dilemma, so it is," Morgan said as he poured cream on his oatmeal. "Ye can hardly reduce his rations and expect to get more work out of him."

"Aye," Mike said, relaxing a little at the man's words. "And I can't beat him either."

"Sure I don't know why not but I won't argue with you, squire. This is your kingdom, not mine."

"How would *you* have handled it?" Mike asked in frustration.

"For stealing?" Morgan drizzled honey over his bowl and took his time with his answer. He picked up his spoon and met Mike's eyes. "Exile. Immediately and no pardon or reprieve. A community that can't trust its members will soon tear itself a part. And for stealing food? He'd be lucky to leave with both hands."

"That's severe."

"So is life nowadays, Donovan. Or hadn't ye noticed?"

Sarah came to the table and put her hand on Mike's shoulder, giving it a reassuring squeeze, but she spoke to Morgan.

"I'm hoping you'll allow Matt and Mac to stay on," she said. "Mac is still quite uncomfortable this morning and the Sisters want to keep him for a while longer."

The door to the dining room burst open and Tommy hurried toward them.

"Aye," Morgan said. "The lads can stay for a day or two."

"They won't be the only ones," Tommy said as he got nearer, slapping great clouds of dust off his pants with his hat. "We have a problem outside."

Mike and Morgan both jumped to their feet and were moving toward the door at Tommy's words.

"What kind of problem?" Mike said. Visions of the archers brawling in the courtyard or throwing each other off the castle walls or Jordie garroting half the laying chickens sprang to mind. He opened the outer door that led to the courtyard and stopped, stunned.

It looked like nighttime outside with swirls of black snow churning the air. Visibility was no more than thirty yards.

"What the hell?" he said his mouth slack in astonishment. "I've never seen fog this bad before."

"That's because it's not fog," Morgan said, his voice tense. "It's volcanic ash."

Susan Kiernan-Lewis

13

"Volcanic ash?" Mike stared into the swirling powdery soot.

"From Iceland most like," Morgan said. "Seen it in 2010. Brought most of the UK to its knees so it did. Not sure it was ever this bad."

Mike stepped out into the courtyard and instantly the dust settled on his arms and shoulders. He brushed it off and looked at his hand.

"It's not like any kind of ash I ever saw," he said.

Terry's son Tommy emerged from the fog. He was covered in grey ash

"That's because it's not soft like ye'd expect," he said. "We'll need to get people to cover their faces. It won't be good to breathe this shite."

"The crops?" Mike said, looking first at Tommy and then at Morgan as if they had the answer.

Tommy shrugged helplessly. "It depends on how long it lasts. Sure it'll kill everything it covers for long."

Mike ran his hands through his hair. He felt the throbbing tension in his jaw.

The corn crop was only half in. The potato field wasn't even planted and what was planted would die if it didn't have access to light and water. He watched helplessly as the ash swirled and then drifted downward to coat the courtyard pavers. He turned to Tommy.

"If we can get enough water to the fields we can wash it away," Mike said.

"Worse thing we could do," Tommy said. "Water turns it into cement. Anything under it'll be dead for certain."

"How long will it last?" Mike said, running his hands through his hair again.

"I've heard it can last anywhere from a couple of days to six months," Morgan said. He turned to Mike. "I need to get back to the village." His voice was laced with urgency.

"How, man?" Mike said, waving to where the front gate was no longer visible. "Ye can't see ten meters ahead of you. The wolves are in the woods. You'll get lost."

Sarah came from behind them and stared out at the fog. "What is it? What's happening?"

Mike took in a long breath.

"Tommy, find your way to the parapet and see that the archers all have scarves for their noses and mouths."

Tommy slipped away into the fog.

Mike turned to Terry. "Go to the Sisters. Tell 'em to stay indoors. I'll find John and some of the other lads to see if we can protect the water reservoir on the roof and cover any other openings."

Terry pulled his neck scarf over his mouth and darted into the fog.

"Sarah, lass, gather everyone in the dining hall. They'll need to know what's going on and what's being done about it. Not the bairns, mind. Tell Nuala to stay put and I'll come talk with her directly. Mr. Morgan, will ye come with me?"

Morgan gave one last frustrated look in the direction of his village and then nodded.

Before Sarah turned toward the interior of the castle she grabbed Mike's arm. "Mike! What about Gavin and the hunters? How will they get back?"

Mike stared into the dark sky and watched the ash pour down, coating everything inside the castle courtyard. In the space of time it took to enjoy a cup of tea, he'd lost his son, half his crop, and any hope of saving the castle's water supply.

And the hell of it was he wasn't even surprised.

Thor stood at the edge of village, his gun in his hand. He was confused and he wasn't taking another step forward until his head cleared and he knew exactly what he was walking into.

The shite coming out of the sky just didn't make sense.

Snow in June? A forest fire somewhere?

It had taken a full hour to walk to the village in the dark —another bollocks Thor could lay at Jocko's feet. Why were they afraid of these berks? Why not just drive their wagons right in the center of town and go door to door ripping people out of their beds?

They'd done it plenty of times before.

Truth be told there was something about the falling flakes that unnerved all of them. Most of the men now stood looking up at the sky and then at each other with confusion written on their faces. And doubt.

And that was not what you wanted when you were in the act of taking a village.

Without looking at Thor, Jocko motioned for the two men beside him to go around to the back of the village. He gave a similar order to two other men. Thor's shoulders and hair were already coated with ash—like he'd walked too close to someone's bonfire.

Jocko looked over at Thor. Thor nodded and gripped his gun as a feeling of breathless anticipation spread through his chest.

There was nothing like action to eradicate a feeling of helplessness. If he didn't know that, he knew nothing.

Just as they began to converge on the sleeping villagers, Thor heard the unmistakable drone of an airplane overhead.

Susan Kiernan-Lewis

14

The place was officially a madhouse.

Sarah stood in the doorway between the outside and the corridor leading to the great hall and swept. She swept when anyone came in or went out and she swept when someone walked past and tracked the ash from their shoes. She swept if they walked too close to the front door, open or closed, and it didn't make a bit of difference. The ash lay in a thick layer everywhere it landed.

The swirl of silver and black snow-like dust continued to fall. Everything it touched, it stained black—hands, hair, cobblestones, the cow. While it was only a little after noon, it was dark out with visibility reduced to tattered glimpses peeking through the swirling gloom.

Sarah watched through the open door as the rain pummeled the ground and turned the ash to sludge. Already the roof of the chicken coop had collapsed from the weight of it. The cow had been moved into the stable with the horses.

It was a nightmare of the first order.

Mike had organized a small group to race outside to cover the two wells—which had proven to be useless as the ash had already contaminated both of them. And then they'd hurried to see what could be done with the mill house, only to find it effectively destroyed, clogged with ash that became concrete as soon as it had mixed with the rain.

John had climbed the back parapet to check on the roof-fed water system they'd established when they first arrived at the castle but all the collected rainwater had been polluted the instant the ash hit. And the reservoir tubs too. Mike put a young sentry by the outdoor water cisterns to make sure no one used them until they could be disposed of.

They had several reserve barrels of water in the kitchen and the stables but not enough to last the castle for longer than a week. Sarah had no idea what they'd do if the ash didn't stop coming down before then.

Fiona tapped her on the shoulder and Sarah jumped, startled.

"The bairns think it's a party," Fiona said. "Sure even little Bill was clapping and grinning."

Sarah still wasn't sure how it was all going to work out with all of them living together for the next twenty years when Bill eventually found out Aibreann, his real mother, hadn't wanted him.

Kind of hard not to take that personally when you see your biological mother every day across the lunch table.

Sarah very much hoped for Fiona's sake that Aibreann didn't change her mind down the line.

"Well, at any rate, I'm glad *somebody's* happy," Sarah said. "Is Nuala having trouble keeping the bigger ones indoors?"

"Not the babies but the older children are mostly lads. Cassidy's in charge of them and she's begging for John to be allowed to help her keep them in line."

Sarah snorted and turned away. Everyone in the castle was working double time to try to secure the place and mitigate the damage of the ash. And Cassidy was whining.

Typical.

"We'll never hear the end of it from Mike you know," Fiona said. "He didn't want us to go to the fair. He'll say if we'd stayed home and picked corn instead..."

"If we're playing the *if-only-I* game," Sarah said, "I never should have bought those vacation tickets to Ireland six years ago."

A ghost of a smile passed across Fiona's face.

"Sure you don't mean that, Sarah. And never to have known us all...and Mike?"

"I'm just saying there's no point imagining doing things differently when we didn't."

They stood silently and watched the ash fall in small, slow-motion eddies as it drifted gently to the ground.

From where they stood Sarah could just make out the outlines of the archers poised, still as statues, on top of the parapet. They were watching for wolves as the castle men worked outside picking corn, then shoveling the ash from the fields. They then carried it in wheelbarrows to the parking lot and dumped it there where it mixed with the rain and hardened.

The crop wasn't a total loss anyway. At least the husk protected the corn. For now.

"I'd still have bought the tickets," Sarah said quietly. "Even if I'd known all that would happen."

"Of course you would."

"But I would've done some things differently."

"Oh aye?"

"I'd have forced David to come live in the compound."

It was because Sarah's first husband had insisted they live in their own cottage in the country that they'd been attacked. If they'd been living with Mike and Fiona in the compound, David would still be alive.

The implication of that thought passed silently between them.

But then I wouldn't have Mike.

When it was all over two villagers lay dead at Thor's feet, and the rest of the people stood in the street cowering and weeping in the morning air.

All total the village acquisition had taken less than an hour. Thor had already sent three men back to camp to collect Emma and Rose.

He could only marvel at the perfect timing of it all. The volcanic ash—one of the villagers had informed him what it was—had blanketed every outdoor surface and crept in around open doors and windows.

Just the thought of living in the woods in this shite made Thor shiver.

Jocko stood in front of the line of quaking village men—seven in all. The women and children watched, wide-eyed and moaning—their eyes alternatively focused on the two dead bodies in the street and their unarmed men.

"Oy!" Jocko said loudly as he waved his handgun in the men's faces. "Listen up, ye bogtrotters!"

Thor approached the men.

"Your village leader was informed I was coming," Thor said. "I'm surprised he's not here to greet me personally. Where is Mr. Morgan?"

The men looked dully at him but didn't answer.

"Well, no matter. I'll deal with him when he returns. Meanwhile, I'll direct your attention to the poor unfortunates who attempted to question my men's actions this morning." Thor pointed to the corpses.

"Because I am not a murderer, I'll ask ye to leave the village of your own free will. I don't care where you go as long as you don't come back."

"But…when…I mean, we need to…" One of the men gestured to the bodies, his eyes full of anguish.

"Not to worry, lad," Thor said. "We'll bury your dead and you're welcome. Now off you go and be quick about it. Come back and you'll be killed. Simple enough, eh?"

The men looked at each other in confusion until Jocko cocked his gun and aimed at the nearest man's head. They began to walk quickly backwards.

"I'll find ye, Imogen!" one of them yelled to the crowd of women.

"Da! Don't leave us!" a child screamed.

Jocko pointed his pistol in the air and fired twice, prompting all the men to break into a run down the main road of the village. Thor watched them disappear before turning back to the women.

"I don't know how you lot have survived this long," Thor said, "but trust me on this—most people would have killed your men so that they didn't have to look over their shoulder forever."

He smiled and then turned away to explore the village. He'd need a place large and comfortable for his family.

Two dead wasn't bad. Not bad at-tall.

After all, he wasn't a murderer.

He was a loving husband and father just trying to do his best in a changed and challenging world.

Susan Kiernan-Lewis

15

The ash drifted down languidly. But the rest of the world was in a whirling turmoil of activity and chaos.

In fact the only thing in Mary's mind that seemed to match the lazy descent of the destructive volcanic ash was the picture of five girlish forms lounging high above the rest of them. Even from where Mary walked at the far end of the courtyard on her way back from the nun's quarters, she could glimpse them through the patches of ash and fog.

They were above it all, quite literally. Watching the rest of them run around like demented beasts of burden as if this latest disaster had nothing to do with them.

Every now and then Mary heard a laugh—soon joined by the others—indicating the lark it all was.

"Mary?"

Mary turned from the sight of the girls on the parapet to Eliza Bartlett who stood with a basket of just baked scones in her hands.

"Are you all right?" Eliza asked, her voice laced with concern.

Mary forced a tight smile but her voice was hard.

"Sure I won't be all right until we have real leadership in this place," she said.

Eliza glanced up at the parapet. A look of understanding swept her face.

The whole castle knows! They all know what a fool those young bitches made of her. And then they go prancing about unpunished while Mary was forced to serve them. Every day it took all her strength not to throw their food in their faces!

"Come inside, Mary," Eliza said gently. "The ash is coating your hair, so it is."

Not that Kevin would care, Mary thought bitterly. She could be dipped in tar for all he would mind. He and that oaf Mike Donovan only had eyes for the saucy lasses on the parapet.

"Mary?"

"You've seen how the men slobber all over them?" Mary said bitingly. "And meanwhile, they do what they want and sod the rest of us."

"Why not go to Sarah Donovan?" Eliza said.

"Sarah Donovan is no friend to the rest of the women in this castle," Mary spat the words out.

Eliza put an arm around Mary and begin to gently tug her back toward the great dining hall.

Mary had to admit it helped not to look at them.

But one thing her auld grandma used to say was that sticking your head in the sand was *not* the way to solve a problem that needing solving. Her stomach still tensed painfully at the receding sounds of their laughter.

That much Mary knew if she knew anything.

John wedged his knee against the frame of the windowsill as the rain pounded on his shoulders. He knew what he was trying to do was hopeless. Even if he and Jordie managed to seal the windows on this section of the castle against the invading ash, there was another hundred windows they'd never get to before winter.

Jordie held three nails in his mouth and juggled the hammer while John stretched the piece of plastic across the opening.

"Think the rain's slowing?" Jordie asked, his words muffled by the nails in his mouth.

John squinted up at the sky. This high up the swirl of ash looked more like snow than anything. When he held out his hand to collect it in his palm he was always surprised that it wasn't cold to the touch.

"Maybe a bit," John said.

"So you and bonny Cassidy, aye?"

John grinned. "Pretty much," he said.

"She's cracking, so she is. How long?"

"Not long," John said. "We're not engaged or anything."

"But she's not seeing anyone else."

John cocked his head. "You interested in Cassidy, Jordie?"

"Blimey, no! You're the only friend I have. Would I be that much of an eejit? Not-at-all. Just trying to get the lay of the land so to speak."

John held the piece of plastic taut against the window while Jordie hammered down one side of it by driving the nail into a crevice between the stonework.

"You know this is hopeless what we're doing," Jordie said.

"Just keep doing it."

"Sure I wouldn't dream of stopping. When Himself speaks, ye just fall in line, don't you?"

John had to admit he liked the guy for the most part. It was true Jordie was lazy and remarkably unskilled at just about everything which was odd for someone who'd lived this long during the Crisis. But he was good-natured and cheerful. That was a hard thing to come across these days. John realized he'd laughed more since Jordie came to live at the castle than he had in the six months before.

"You know you got off easy, right?" John said.

"So everyone tells me."

"And you've been here, what? Five minutes?"

"But he didn't even hear my side of things."

"Did you *have* a side of things? I thought you were guilty."

Jordie gave him a chagrinned look.

"Now your mum," Jordie said. "I've never met anyone like her. She's Wonder Woman, so she is."

John grinned. "I guess that's one way to describe her."

Jordie patted the finished job over the window and tossed down the hammer. It started to roll off the roof and John lunged for it to stop it just in time.

"So if your mum's married to the governor," Jordie said, "they must have had their eyes on each other while your da was still alive, eh?"

John was taken aback by the comment and sat, staring at Jordie with the rescued hammer in his hand. It wasn't the first time the thought had come to him but since it always left him feeling like shit, he tended to push the idea of it away.

"What are you saying, Jordie?" John said coldly. "That my mother and Mike—?"

"Blimey, no! Not-at all, mate! Sure anybody could see that the two strongest forces would draw toward each other. That's all I'm saying."

"My father wasn't like Mike," John admitted. "He was a man of ideas and…and intellect. I'm not saying he wasn't handy. He was. He did what he had to do in order to survive and he learned what he needed to know—as we all do," John said with a raised eyebrow at Jordie.

"Aye, I know. I'm rubbish at all the important stuff and that's a fact. But I was wizard at video games."

"Yeah, well that's real useful now," John said with a laugh.

"Well, it might be if you consider the strategies involved."

"There's a big difference between blowing a guy away on a screen with a push of a button," John said calmly.

"Have you done that, then?"

John narrowed his eyes. "You haven't?"

Jordie shook his head. "Bugger me, no. Not even close."

How is it possible that in six years of running and living scared Jordie hadn't had to defend himself—or his sister and mother—to the point of violence?

"We're not all warriors, John," Jordie said as if reading his mind. "But I'm a grand hider."

"Hell of a way to live."

"Mebbe. But then I haven't had the luxury of a gang behind me either. It's always just been me and me mum and Hannah. And for two years just me and Mum."

"I'm sorry, Jordie. I know that must have been rough."

"So us being here?" Jordie waved a hand to encompass the castle interior. "With you lot? It's the saving of us and no mistake."

"Well, that's thanks to Hannah," John said.

Hannah had endured two years in a rape camp with no hope of rescue until Fiona and the rest of the compound women had showed up. She'd risked her life for Fiona and the others and since then she'd worked hard—night and day—to prove herself worthy on the parapet.

Did Jordie think for one minute he was here for any other reason than the castle's high regard for his sister?

John spotted Matt sitting alone in the courtyard below with his arm around one of the castle dogs. He remembered how both Matt and Macaulay had been dumbstruck with awe when he gave them the castle tour.

They were eager to please and hoping beyond hope that someday this life might be theirs too. And they were good kids. John could tell. They'd make a good addition to the castle population—especially being male since they had so damn few. But there was no question of them being allowed to stay. John felt a wave of sadness.

We can't save everyone, he thought, shaking off the feeling and turning away from the sight of Matt with the dog. *As much as we may want to.*

All of a sudden John felt a tremor in the scaffolding where he sat. He looked at Jordie to see if he was causing it. The abrupt sound of thunder sounded in the distance.

"Feck me!" Jordie said. "What the hell was that?"

John turned his head to look beyond the castle walls but the falling ash and fog wouldn't allow him to see anything.

It was another one of the explosions, he was sure of it.

Only this time it was louder.

And much closer.

Susan Kiernan-Lewis

16

Mike stood at the perimeter of the cornfield and looked in the direction of the explosion. As far as he was concerned it sounded just like the usual bombing he'd been hearing on and off all spring.

Only louder.

It was Morgan who suggested that the plane itself might have crashed, compliments of the ash storm.

Either way it was past time to get a group together and investigate what they were dealing with.

It was late afternoon now and while both the ash and rain had recently stopped it almost didn't matter. The damage was done. Mike watched a few ash flakes drift lazily to the ground.

Every man from the castle and several of the older children were working to salvage what they could of the corn. Mike wouldn't allow the horses out in this muck so they were putting the corn on a wide sled that could be dragged by two or three men back to the castle.

The field they'd been trying to plant was a complete loss. There was no point even looking there. Every available hand was pulling the corn out of the field.

Mike watched the parapet. He could make out the shapes of the lasses on the castle wall—at the ready. A movement behind them caught his eye and he groaned when he saw the two figures picking their way along the roof apse of the chapel.

It had been folly to send John and Jordie up there. They couldn't make a difference and there was a real risk of them falling. What had he been thinking? That any action was better than nothing?

He turned to Tommy.

"Oy, Tommy lad. Tell John and Jordie to come down and check on the livestock. Then go see if Mrs. Donovan needs help at the castle."

Tommy nodded and jogged back toward the castle. The drawbridge had been down all morning. Mike turned to make his way into the field to help pull corn from their stalks.

He figured if anyone chose today to travel through this shite to take the castle, they deserved it.

Morgan ate silently in the grand dining hall with Mac and Matt beside him. Mac was enjoying the novelty of his cast and sling. Both lads were delighted to be eating another hot meal so soon after breakfast.

While Morgan's first instinct had been to race back to Kilbaha, he'd breathed in too much of the ash the first afternoon. Combined with his age and a lifetime of smoking unfiltered fags, he'd been fortunate to make the steps leading up to the dining hall without having to stop and rest.

He tried to imagine how Kilbaha was managing. Surely they'd cover the water reserves? And get the cows and the goats inside? He ran a hand over his face. At least he needn't worry about Thor's gang showing up. Only a fool would be out in this shite.

One of the castle men stomped into the dining room, slapping the ash from his clothes and pulling off his wet jacket. He nodded at Morgan in greeting and went off to find his lunch.

Donovan may not have wanted to divulge how many men he had in the castle but it didn't take a university degree to count heads.

There were only twenty.

For a castle this size. For all the effort and heavy lifting needed to keep it running, Donovan had only twenty able bodied men—and all the rest were women and children.

Morgan looked up to see Jordie enter the room. Instantly he ran over to one of the archers. Unlike the other girls, she didn't immediately rebuff him, which surprised Morgan. From what he'd seen, the archers didn't mix with the rest of the castle population if they could help it.

"Oy, Grandda," Matt said. "Jordie said he'd show me how to use his Game Boy if we stay long enough. Even though it's got no battery."

"Oh, aye?" Morgan said absently. "Perhaps that's the line he's using on yon bonny lass there."

Matt turned to look and frowned.

"That's his sister," he said. "Hannah."

His sister? Well, that explains why she hasn't sent him packing.

"John says Jordie came to the castle with his mum two days ago," Mac said. "How come they let him in and not us?"

Good question, Morgan thought as he watched Jordie talk to his sister who was still doing a cracker job of ignoring him, brother or not.

"And he's not the only one, Grandda," Matt said. "There's a lad named Aedan who got to come live here with his mum after his group attacked the castle people! Only they weren't living in the castle back then."

"Attacked them, did he?" Morgan said with a frown. "And lost, presumably?"

"Oh, aye. Ground them into the dirt. Druids, they were. "

"And then invited the lad and his mother to live with them?" Morgan said.

Matt shrugged. "That's what Aedan said."

"Maybe we should try invading them too," Morgan said.

The boys laughed and Mac pulled out two energy bars and handed one to his twin.

"Where in the world did you get those?" Morgan said.

"Mrs. Donovan gave 'em to me," Mac said. "Says I need to keep me strength up. Want one? She's got heaps."

Morgan shook his head and felt a flush of longing as he watched the two boys happily munching their treat. He longed to give them simple treats. And safety.

Two more archers entered the dining room. Morgan recognized them as Regan and Tillie. It appeared whatever issues the two had last night were resolved. They walked over to Jordie and his sister. There was ash on their shoulders and their boots tracked mud across the floor.

Regan growled something that Morgan couldn't hear from this distance but Jordie jumped up and then she and Tillie sat down. None of the three archers bothered to look at a single other person since coming into the room.

As soon as Jordie wandered away from the group, the girls relaxed, their expressions of aloofness gone.

They don't feel like they're a part of the community, Morgan realized. *The castle is in crisis but that has nothing to do with them. They're apart from it.*

Which was good.

He could use that.

"Grandda, why are you frowning?"

"Am I, lad? Just thinking."

"You're staring at the archers. Matt wants to marry one!"

"Does he now?" Morgan forced a chuckle. "Well, who could fault him for that? They're bonny every one of them, so they are."

"Is that why you're frowning, Grandda? Do *you* want to marry one of them?"

His brother laughed and Morgan gave him a playful cuff.

"Settle down, ye young ruffian," he said. But when his eyes went back to the girls there was nothing playful in his gaze.

17

Sarah always felt that the night seemed to make everything worse. Maybe it was because at night there was nothing more they could do to remedy anything and so a feeling of helplessness settled over the castle.

Dinner was quiet. It was as if even the children knew the very water that the soup was made with was precious—with no guarantee there would be more.

Sarah sat at her place at the table with Siobhan. Mike hadn't shown for dinner but Sarah had overheard Liddy say he'd requested a sandwich sent to him in the dungeon where he was working with a few of the men to get the chickens settled in. The birds needed light and the dungeon—situated at the back of the castle—had numerous windows. Plus, it wasn't working having the chickens in the barn with the goats, horses and the cow.

Cassidy sat across from Sarah. She and John had arrived together but John left soon after the soup was served to have a word with Tommy who was stationed outside the gate tower.

There were no archers in the dining hall tonight. Normally, if they weren't on duty, they were sleeping or getting ready to be. Sarah imagined with the reduced visibility that the patrols would be increased. More eyes would help mitigate the lack of light.

Sarah watched Morgan eat and talk with his two grandsons seated on either side of him. She noticed Morgan ate heartily—his affect unchanged with the disaster caused by the ash. While initially upset that he wouldn't be able to return to his village, he seemed to have accepted the disappointment well enough.

But like many of the castle men, he was coughing a good bit.

Two of the castle dogs lay at the feet of Nuala's boys and Sarah hoped—tonight more than ever—that the boys weren't feeding them scraps. The dogs had their food, what there was of it, and the castle couldn't spare any more.

Fiona and her daughter Ciara were seated down the table from Sarah and Cassidy.

"Oy, Cassidy," Fiona called. "You're on duty tonight aren't you? With the older children?"

Cassidy nodded. "I think so, Missus," she said.

She thinks so? Sarah forced herself to keep her focus on Siobhan's dinner plate as the child ate.

"When you're finished eating, go on and collect them," Fiona said to Cassidy. "That'll be Nuala's two, then the two village lads, Mac and Matt, and also young Darby. Am I missing anyone?"

Cassidy grimaced at her plate. "I don't think so. Only… can John help me? He says his chores are done for the day."

Sarah cleared her throat.

"I'm sure he's needed elsewhere," Sarah said. "What do you plan on doing with the kids?"

Cassidy looked at her blankly.

"Aye," Fiona said, "Mrs. Donovan wants to know if ye'll be taking the tykes bowling or just making popcorn for an all-night Disney cartoon marathon."

"I…I…" Cassidy looked at Fiona and then Sarah in confusion.

"Never mind," Sarah said, arching an eyebrow at Fiona. "Just play games with them until it's bedtime and don't let anyone break any more bones."

"I would never!"

"Me come with John and Cassie!" Siobhan said. "Me not a baby!"

Sarah looked at her child. "Didn't Mrs. O'Malley say there were cookies tonight?"

Siobhan's eyes widened and she looked in the direction of the kitchen. "She did," she said in hushed awe.

"Cassie, would you mind taking Shivvy to the kitchen for her cookie?" Sarah asked. "And then deliver her to Mrs. O'Connell? Ciara? Want to go with Cassie and Shivvy?"

Ciara jumped to her feet and she and Siobhan ran to Cassidy's chair. Each of the little girls grabbed one of Cassidy's hands and they trooped off to the kitchen together.

"Sure you're a master at delegation and distraction, Sarah Donovan," Fiona said, laughing.

Sarah smiled as she watched Cassidy and the little girls leave. Her gaze fell on Sophia who was standing with her baby in her arms talking to Eliza Bartlett. Sophia was trying so hard to be brave but Sarah knew she was worried about Gavin. Eliza's hand was on Sophia's arm and Sarah could see she was talking encouragingly to the girl.

Maybe that was her special gift? You could do worse than being able to offer succor in a world where there was little else but terror and pain.

"Have you had much time to talk with Eliza yet, Sarah?" Fiona asked as she moved closer down the long dining table.

"I haven't," Sarah said. "I'm glad to see how well she seems to be integrating though."

"Oh, aye, people love her, so they do." The way Fiona said it made Sarah look over at her. The Irish had a special way of saying a thing that was the opposite of the words they used. Sarah had become better at recognizing it over the years.

But she was still pretty hopeless at understanding it.

Tonight she thought she might have gotten it right.

"Jordie again?" Sarah asked, dropping her voice.

"Just rumors mind," Fiona said, shaking her head as if to say they were still as true as a legal deposition as far as she was concerned.

"What rumors?"

Fiona warmed to her topic, leaning toward Sarah conspiratorially. "It seems that before he was dragged up before his honor for nicking the pie in the kitchen, he'd been missing for a good four hours where no one could find him— and of course none of his chores done."

"Missing?" Sarah glanced around the room to try to spot Jordie but she couldn't see him. "Where did he say he was?"

"He said he'd had a violent stomach ache and didn't want anyone to worry about him so he'd gone into the corner of the stable to be sick."

"Did he."

"And that's testimony to how sick he was, what with him so afraid of anything with hooves."

"All of which live in the stable."

"Don't they just."

Sarah had half a mind to go to the stable to see if there was any evidence to back up Jordie's story. But a wave of exhaustion gripped her shoulders. Didn't she have enough on her plate? Mike was discouraged—more than she'd ever seen him. John was falling in love with a shallow little piece. And they had a five-day supply of drinking water at best.

Maybe she should just let it go?

She looked over at Jordie's mother Eliza again.

Even if he was a lying lazy little weasel, what harm was he doing, really?

"Well, Eliza and Hannah are a good addition to our group anyway," Sarah said finally.

"That's what I like about you, Sarah," Fiona said sipping her wine. "Always taking the bitter with the sweet."

An hour later Sarah and Fiona had helped clear the tables and stack the dishes for Jordie to wash. Sarah went upstairs to the nursery. Nuala met her at the door with a finger to her lips.

"Sure they were all tuckered out," she said in a whisper. "No goodnight kisses tonight, luv. Sorry."

Sarah smiled faintly. Siobhan didn't often sleep in the nursery but when she did it was because she'd worn herself out playing during the day. Sarah saw there were at least four other toddlers and babies also sleeping in cots next to Siobhan—Ciara and Nuala's girl Darcy included.

"That's all right," Sarah said. "I'll collect her tomorrow before breakfast."

As soon as Sister Mary arrived, Nuala would go back to her rooms to be with her boys Dennis and Damian. Sister Mary took turns with another nun watching the children in the night nursery.

After Sarah left the nursery she ran into John in the hall.

"Everything else all right outside?" she asked. "How goes it with the corn?"

"So far so good. We saved most of it. Now we just have to hope it doesn't mold with all this wet weather. Is Cassidy in the upstairs play room with the bigger kids?"

Sarah nodded. "She's waiting for you."

He hesitated. "I know you don't like her, Mom."

"It's not that I don't like her. I just think she's a little... wild for you."

"You would've said the same thing about Regan at one time."

"Probably. I love Regan but I still wouldn't want to see you with her."

"Because I'm so much better than her? I've done some things too, you know, Mom. Bad things."

"We've all done what we had to do to survive," Sarah said, trying to keep her voice down. Their words seemed to ring out against the unforgiving stone walls.

"But the fact is Regan is damaged," Sarah said. "I'm not sure she can even give love and she definitely can't love herself."

"Cassie is nothing like Regan, Mom."

That's true. She doesn't have Regan's bravery or her loyalty. But instead Sarah said,

"I just want you to be happy."

After John left, Sarah felt depleted. She'd really been hoping she wouldn't have to tell John how she felt about Cassidy. She'd prayed it would all just come to a natural end before then. As she approached Mike's den on the second level at the front of the castle, she could see a flicker of candle lights under the crack of the door.

It had been a long day. All she wanted now was the strong reassuring arms of her husband and to lead him back to their room—to their little cozy oasis against the storm.

She opened the door to see Artemus Morgan seated in one of the tufted leather club chairs in front of the bookcase, a large book in his lap, and a glass of sherry on the side table.

"Oh!" Sarah said, looking around the otherwise empty room.

"Himself's not here, Mrs. Donovan," Morgan said, coughing noisily into his hands.

"You should have Sister check on that cough, Mr. Morgan."

He shrugged. "I breathed in too much of the ash. It'll pass." He coughed again as if for emphasis.

Sarah hesitated in the doorway, her hand still on the doorknob.

"What a nightmare this must be for you," she said.

"No more than yourselves."

"But you must be eaten up with worry about the village. Not knowing how they are."

There was something about Artemus Morgan that bothered Sarah. Something she couldn't put her finger on.

He shrugged. "While I've no doubt they're uncomfortable, I'm confident I'll find them all alive upon my return."

He flipped a page in his book.

Your mind is at ease because your boys are safe and sound, Sarah thought. That's the important thing.

That's always the important thing.

And she of all people couldn't fault him for it.

She bid him goodnight and went to find her husband.

Fifteen minutes later she found Mike alone in the back stall of the stable. There was a main entrance to the barn—a massive double door that swung outward and where they brought the animals and wagons through—and a single door in the far back that allowed access to the stable from inside the castle.

The stable was dimly illuminated by a burning lantern hanging from a wall hook. Mike stood with his back to her grooming his favorite gelding Buck—something he tended to do when he needed a moment without the constant demands and noise of his responsibilities.

"I thought I might find you here," Sarah said as she stood at one of the stall gates. Because Gavin and his hunting party had taken four horses, there was plenty of room for the cow and the three goats that normally stayed outdoors in summer.

Mike smiled at her. She tried to remember if she'd ever seen him look more discouraged. She slipped through the slats of the stall and into his arms. She felt him hold her tightly, one hand still gripping the dandy brush.

"The potatoes are lost," he said into her hair.

"I know," she whispered back. "It doesn't matter. We didn't have potatoes last year and we survived."

"I feel like we work so hard and then we take so many steps backward."

"I know. But we'll get through this too."

Mike was trying hard to present a show of confidence and strength to their people in the castle. They needed to see it. But only a machine could show strength twenty-four seven.

And then there was Gavin. Sarah knew very well the agony that accompanied a son somewhere out on the road—the dangerous, treacherous road. She had to believe he would have found a safe place to hole up to wait out the ash.

But believing and knowing were two different things. The relentless worry for Gavin's safety was just one more thing pressing in on Mike.

"We'll clean up and start over," she said. "Nobody died. That's what matters."

"Aye." Mike patted the horse's neck and tossed the dandy brush in a bucket in the corner. "It's just I have a bad feeling about all this."

"You're not allowed any Irish premonitions," she said, rising up on tiptoe to kiss his mouth. "We have enough trouble."

He held her close and deepened the kiss. "What would I do without ye, lass?" he murmured.

"You'll never have to worry about that."

"Well, then how did I get so lucky to have ye love me?"

Sarah put a hand to his cheek and her eyes glittered with emotion.

"I was thinking the same thing about you."

She was sure she loved him more each day. Oh, he drove her slowly mad on a daily basis over the little things. But when he entered a room or she saw him when she wasn't expecting to or when he appeared in a crowd among other men, her stomach always gave that delightful lurch. To know he was hers was a gift she never tired of relishing—over and over again.

"Siobhan's in the nursery tonight," she whispered.

He gave her a crooked grin. "Oh aye? What are we doing standing in the fecking barn then?"

18

Kylie stamped her feet and let her hips rest against the front of the parapet while she leaned with her elbows. It was a warm night. But she was impatient. She was ready.

She was bloody tired of waiting.

Unlike the other girls, Kylie wasn't somebody's daughter or a rape victim trying to feel good about herself. She'd been plucked out of the woods three months ago where she'd been living with a group of gypsies. The governor had been out hunting and happened to see her bring down a hare with her slingshot.

If she'd known he'd been watching, she would have aimed at something smaller.

She'd gone with him that very day and never looked back. Never even said *see youse* to the lads she'd lived with for two years either. She was older than the other girls here at the castle. Not by much but enough. They all thought they'd lived through so much. Especially Aibreann who'd never dream of crawling down from her cross, she'd *endured* so much.

And her with a sweet little lad she hardly ever saw.

The governor had assigned Kylie to learning the bow and arrow before she'd even had her first hot meal in the castle. It hadn't taken long to prove her skill. She'd played around with archery in school—and she was always good.

Once she realized the only thing that would ever be required of her at Henredon Castle was to walk the castle parapet or barbican and keep a sharp eye out, she'd begun to explore other opportunities within the castle.

The first time she followed Tommy Donaghue into the back tower that faced the sea and housed the castle workshop, she felt like she had stepped into a wonderland of possibilities.

Tommy, who knew feck-all about carpentry, had only gone in search of his da, Terry. His da was fecking brilliant at it, same as Kylie's own da. Kylie felt a flinch of revulsion at the thought of her father and she pushed the memory aside quickly. Sure the auld bastard wasn't totally useless and although he'd not taught her near what he could've if she'd been a son, she'd at least discovered she had a knack for working with wood.

Mr. Donaghue on the other hand seemed disappointed that neither of his sons were interested in woodworking. Tommy was a right git, no matter what Regan said. He was only keen on electronics and computers. *Hello! We've none of any of that rubbish any more!*

She'd learned that Mr. Donaghue had fashioned and hung the massive double door of the stable. The workshop itself was a long rectangular room with floor to ceiling loophole windows that faced the sea and gave light to the work area. There was a potbellied stove in one corner.

Two narrow wooden workbenches stood against the long back wall. Over one Mr. Donaghue hung his tools: hand saws, shavers, sanders, wrenches, hammers, carpenter's braces, bits, screwdrivers, push drills, and various sized hatchets. A jug of oil sat on the table along with a large wooden bowl of fletches prepared to be attached to the arrows always in production. The workshop floor was covered with a thick carpet of wood shavings.

The workshop was where the castle's every day needs were met, problems were solved and ideas created to make life if not easier then at least manageable.

But most important as far as Kylie was concerned was the fact that the workshop was the command center for the castle's defenses.

It was where all the bows and arrows were made, repaired and modified.

The governor had set Mr. Donaghue to making lightweight long bows for all the girls—which was grand. The old antique bows they'd found in the castle broke easily and were too heavy to swing about easily. To look at his work, you'd think Mr. Donaghue had been making bows his whole life. Someone told Kylie that he'd been a postal clerk before the bomb but Kylie would no more believe that than she believed she'd have her own cell phone again some day.

"Oy! Kylie!" Aibreann spoke sharply to her. "Tits up!"

Kylie flushed and raised the arrow already notched in her bow an inch higher.

Bugger her. No one could convince Kylie that they needed to have the arrows fit in the strings. Hell, Kylie could have her bow on the ground with her foot on it and a steaming cuppa in her hand and she'd still get it up and launched before anything could get near the castle.

But she wasn't in charge of that. She couldn't rightly remember who died and made Princess Aibreann the boss of them. Her eyes sought out Regan's form fifty meters away, her shoulders tense and pushed forward, her head slowly moving as she scanned the dark bushes and the line of trees before them.

The guard would be changing soon, that was clear for anyone with eyes to see. As far as Kylie was concerned it couldn't happen too soon.

Her stomach rumbled. She'd eaten a sandwich three hours ago but it hadn't been enough. She was heavier than the other girls—but she wasn't fat. She was solid. She needed the extra fuel was all.

Where was that useless gobshite with their tea? The governor said Hannah's brother was to come once a watch and the lazy sod hadn't come a single time since Kylie was on duty.

She felt the tension in her arms as she scanned the bushes, her bow held up.

She allowed her mind to detach from the bushes and the hunger in her belly and the lack of tea. She allowed herself to think of the secret she shared with Mr. Donaghue. He hadn't mentioned it in awhile and the last time Kylie had indicated to him that she was free to meet with him, he'd put her off.

No worries. It was just this fecking ash shite throwing everything out of kilter.

As soon as it was cleaned up they'd go back to their normal schedules. Kylie felt the excitement thrum in her chest as she thought of meeting with Mr. Donaghue. He'd told her not to tell a soul what they were doing but he needn't have bothered. Sure her own group would look at her as if she were barking if they knew what she and Mr. D were getting up to.

A smile touched her lips at the image of him standing in the workshop, his back straight, his expression sure, his hands skilled and knowing...

...and the crossbow on the bench before him.

She nearly moaned with pleasure at the thought of it.

Her own crossbow. Fitted to her, weighted to her hand. Just like the Normans used.

It was nearly ready. Just a few more finishing touches. It would be more powerful than anything they had now. Once Kylie mastered it, she'd teach the others.

And then let the bastards come.

Let any of them come.

A crossbow could pierce an armored tank.

Suddenly she saw a movement on the ground. Every muscle in both her arms stretched taut and tingled. She didn't look to see if Regan or anybody else was seeing what she saw. She didn't take her eyes off the motion until she was sure it wasn't just a whirl of windblown ash in the dark gloom.

Was it a wolf? Was it her imagination? Whatever it was, it seemed to take amorphous shape and then recede back into the darkness as the wind blew the ash above the ground. She strained forward, the bow string biting into her fingers.

The fog broke and drifted into a patch of perfect clarity. Yes! There were three of them. Large shaggy beasts. More shadow than form. They were hanging back, hesitant to approach.

And they had something. Something that was trying to get away.

"Oy!" Kylie shouted. "Four o'clock!"

The first arrow flew from her bow before she even knew she'd pulled back the string. She saw it disappear in a soft whistle through the fog. She heard the scream of pain as it hit its mark.

She pulled another arrow from the quiver on her back but before she fitted it to her bow she watched two other arrows fly from the other archers—both followed by startled yelps.

"Stop! Stop!" Aibreann called. "Hold fire!"

Kylie's finger vibrated in agony, her longing to let go the poised arrow in her bow nearly overpowered her discipline.

The wolves slunk off into the mist. Kylie strained her neck to see better. She moved closer to where Regan stood, both with their bows raised and ready above the crenel of the wall.

There...she saw the body of one wolf. And next to it...

A man.

A man on his hands and knees.

Susan Kiernan-Lewis

19

The dungeons were the only place in the castle that stayed cool in the summer—and were nearly arctic in the winter. Mike and Morgan walked past a series of rooms that had in centuries past served as the castle garderobes. Now they stored meat and vegetables.

Down the narrow stone hall they came to the anteroom outside the holding cells. Mike pointed to the two barrels of fresh water, kept cold in the dungeon.

"That's it," he said. The barrels looked smaller than he'd remembered.

"How long should they last you?" Morgan asked.

"If we're careful," Mike said, "a week." He eyed Morgan. "How are you set up for drinking water in the village?"

Suddenly Tommy burst through the archway. He caught himself from falling and struggled to catch his breath.

"What is it?" Mike asked, his heart pounding.

"Someone is trying to get in!" Tommy gasped. "At the front gate. Wolves are after him!"

Mike pushed past the boy and took the narrow and slippery stone steps up to the courtyard two at a time.

Although no longer falling, the ash was still swirling in the air from the winds off the ocean.

Who the hell could be out in this mess?

Mike squinted across the courtyard at the gate tower and went in that direction.

Morgan was right behind him. He didn't need anyone to tell him it could well be someone from village.

Kevin leaned out of the window of the gate tower, not quite level with the girls on the parapet. One hand was on the windlass ready to lower the drawbridge.

Aibreann stood at the railing of the wallwalk that overlooked the courtyard.

"How many?" Mike called up to her.

"Looks like just the one," she shouted. "And he's hurt."

"Open the gate."

"What if his friends are waiting in the woods?" Aibreann called back. "What if they—"

"Open the damn gate!" Mike yelled to Kevin before turning to Morgan. "Are ye armed?"

Morgan nodded and pulled a semi-automatic from his shoulder holster. Mike turned as Terry, John, and Davey ran up to join them. Davey held a gun in his hand.

Tommy ran to the gate.

"If you have to shoot," Mike said in a low voice, "try not to shoot Tommy in the process."

The portcullis cranked up slowly and the massive drawbridge began to lower. Tommy went through the archway and perched on the descending gate, ready to drag the wounded man into the castle.

Once the bridge was down, Tommy disappeared across it and out of sight.

"Come on, lad," Mike said under his breath. "Get him in."

Tommy reappeared, walking backwards and dragging the body of a man over the stone threshold of the gate entrance and immediately the steel tines of the portcullis began descending behind them.

Mike heard the archers yelling "All clear! All clear!"

Mike's arms sagged to his side and he let out the breath he was holding.

Mike turned to Davey. "Tell Sister Alphonse to get the clinic ready. Then bring back a stretcher."

Mike realized a part of him had feared it might be Gavin or one of his hunting party—either situation would have been bad. But Tommy had given no indication that he knew the man who now lay silent and unmoving.

John and Terry had joined them now. Mike looked up at the archers and called to Aibreann.

"When was the last change of the guard?" he called.

She shrugged. "Three hours ago. We usually do every six."

"Go to four hours. Send someone to tell the next shift they're up in one hour."

Aibreann motioned to Nola who put her bow down and ran down the stairs to the ground. She jogged past Mike and headed across the courtyard to the great hall.

Satisfied, Mike turned to the group now huddled around the man on the ground. John stood with his hands on his hips murmuring to Tommy. Morgan was kneeling by the man, shaking his head.

"Is he hurt bad?" Mike asked, pushing past Terry and Tommy.

"He's not one of ours," Morgan said.

Mike knelt by the body. The man's clothes had been torn by the wolves and Mike could see great patches of gore striping down the man's legs and arms.

Where had he come from?

He touched the man's shoulder gingerly to pull him over from his side to his back and to get a better look at his face. When he did, the man groaned loudly.

Mike was startled to feel John push past him and drop to his knees by the man whose face was covered with blood and ash.

John's voice came out in a strangled croak.

"Dad?"

Susan Kiernan-Lewis

20

Mike stood for a moment in the darkened room. He could see Sarah's form in the bed. He ran a hand across his face, the exhaustion seeping into his shoulders like an anvil pressing down from above.

How was this possible?

They'd piled the wounded man onto a stretcher and carried him up to the clinic where he lay unconscious, the blood sponged from his face and identified without a shadow of a doubt as David Woodson.

John's missing father. Sarah's missing...husband.

How was this possible?

Woodson's wounds were deep and the ones in his neck, dangerous. Sister Alphonse had whirled around the bed like a maniacal dervish, muttering to herself, wiping away the blood. And all the time John was at his father's side, his hand clutching David's, his face shining with hope, euphoria and fear.

How was this possible?

They'd buried David Woodson six years ago in a deserted pasture three miles south of the compound at Ameriland.

How was it possible he was alive and lying in a bed at Henredon Castle?

Mike moved into the bedroom and sat down on the bed. Sarah, still asleep, shifted away. He put his hand lightly on her hip and she made a noise, half awake.

"Sarah? Lass?" he said softly.

Her eyes fluttered open immediately.

"What's wrong?" she said, instantly awake. "Siobhan? John?"

"No, lass. They're fine."

She sat up in bed. "What is it? What's happened?"

"Sure it's a miracle," he said, searching her eyes and seeing only confusion and worry in them. "I'm not exactly sure how to tell you."

"You're scaring me, Mike. What's happened?"

Mike held both hands out helplessly. "It's…David," he said.

She frowned. "David?" Her eyes widened and she shook her head. "What are you talking about?"

"It's David," he repeated, more firmly. "He's come back, lass, so he has."

She stared at him. "I don't understand what you're saying," she whispered. "That can't be."

"I don't understand it either," Mike said. "But sure he's alive and upstairs in the clinic with John. Right this minute."

Sarah sat frozen in the bed, her hand over her mouth, her eyes wide and uncomprehending.

"That's impossible," she said.

❉ ❉ ❉ ❉ ❉

Fifteen minutes later Sarah stood ramrod straight in the cold clinic. She had a faint buzzing in her brain.

John stood beside her, his hand in hers, his eyes riveted to the back of the two nuns and Fiona who were bent over the man on the bed.

This is what shock feels like, Sarah thought. When the backs of the nuns parted, she saw David's face clearly.

"Oh, my God," she whispered.

It was him. Dear Lord it was really him.

There was conversation behind her, low and urgent like a conference of angry bees with their cadence rising and lowering.

It was so cold in this room. Or maybe that was just her.

"Sarah? Lass?" Mike came up behind her and put his hand on her waist.

She jumped at his touch. But she felt the spell break.

David was alive. David was in that bed fighting for his life—a second time.

She watched the face of the man in the bed. It was a face she knew so well. The strong English nose, the lantern jaw. The tiny scar on his chin where he'd fallen out of a shopping cart as a child.

Dear God, it was him. It was really him.

She felt a rush of heat and a heavy feeling thickened in her stomach.

David had not died that day in Seamus and Deirdre's pasture…the day Sarah was taken bound and gagged in a wagon across the sea to London.

How? How could it be?

"I don't know, lass," Mike said quietly.

She must have spoken out loud. She turned to him and saw the worry and guarded questions in his eyes. She saw the questions he had. Not just for David, but for her too.

What did this mean? What did any of this mean?

"Mom?"

She looked at John. Astonished that she hadn't really done so before now. His face showed only joy. Unbridled, intense joy.

His father was back.

She squeezed his hand. Before she could find any words for him, Fiona turned and joined them.

"Sure he's terrible wounded," Fiona said. "I still can't believe it. Where's he been all this time?" She looked over at Mike. "And who did we bury in Seamus's pasture?"

Mike shook his head. "I have no idea," he said, his gaze once more going to Sarah.

"Sister Alphonse has given him something so he'll sleep," Fiona said.

"How…how badly is he…" Sarah said. David's eyes were closed, his face chalk white. But it was him. There was no mistake.

It was her husband David.

"Some of the bites are fairly deep," Fiona said in a low voice. "But they're cleaned and stitched now. It's the bite to the…to his throat." She looked at John.

"It's okay, Aunt Fi," John said. "I know he's going to be okay."

He's thinking it's not believable to lose a father twice in one lifetime, Sarah thought. She squeezed his hand again and then turned abruptly toward the door.

"Need air," she gasped and stumbled out into the hall.

Mike was right behind her, his hand on her back, supporting her. She couldn't help but wish he wasn't. She didn't know what she was feeling. She knew he was too close. She couldn't breathe.

"Sarah…" he began.

"What happened?" she croaked, one hand on the cold stone wall. She leaned her head on it. "What happened that day? What did I *see*?" She turned to look at Mike. His face a twisted mask of worry and apprehension. "How can this be?"

And then guilt slammed her like a physical assault. Her eyes widened at the realization. Of all the things she was feeling now—shock, confusion, uncertainty—the one thing she *hadn't* felt was the unquestioning joy of a resurrected loved one.

21

Rose Dennehy stood at the pasture gate and watched the ash drift lazily to the ground. It had mostly stopped now but it still fascinated her. She'd never seen anything like it. How could it look like snow but not be cold? And drift and float like snow, but not be fluffy and soft to the touch?

Her mind drifted like the falling ash for a moment and before she could stop herself she found herself thinking about the boy she'd met in the woods. She had gone out alone—just for a moment!—while her father and his men were gone. She pushed the thought of the boy out of her head. No sense thinking about it, she scolded herself as tears of anger filled her eyes.

There was nothing to be done about any of it now.

She held her hand out and let several flakes of the ash collect before slapping her hands together. When she did, she heard a loud gasp from the other side of the fence.

Her first thought was to run away. As it was, her father would skin her to be this far from the house. But there was something about the noise that made her move toward it instead.

That's when she saw the girl.

She was one of the village girls. Rose remembered her from when she and her mum had ridden into town that morning. She was about Rose's age.

The girl stood up slowly from where she'd been sitting on the ground. She would be pretty if she lost a few stone.

Rose smiled, hoping she wouldn't run away.

"I'm Rose," she said. "You're Betsy, right? I heard your mum talking to my mum."

Betsy seemed to examine her suspiciously and then sat back down. Rose felt a gush of relief that the girl still hadn't run off.

"Got a fag?" Rose asked and then blushed. She was sure this girl had nothing. She was only trying to sound cool. And now she felt like an idiot.

"I *wish*," Betsy said. "The girls in the castle?" Betsy motioned in the direction across the fence line. "I met a few at the fair last week. They always have fags."

"Really?" Rose said, her eyes wide with delight at Betsy's seeming acceptance of her.

"You know they have telly there?" Betsy said.

"Go on with you," Rose said. She slid to a seated position next to her new friend.

"It's true!" Betsy said. "You should see them. They dress like Indian princesses. One of 'em told me they're the archers for the castle."

"I'd love to meet one."

"Oh, they're nice too. Not stuck into themselves. Not a bit. Not like you'd expect anyway."

"Indian princesses…" Rose said dreamily as she glanced in the direction Betsy had indicated.

"The one I met…her name's Briana," Betsy said. "She said they have Coca-Cola and electricity at the castle. She said she and the other lasses are in charge there. Can you believe it?"

"Sure it sounds like a magical castle," Rose said.

"Oh, aye," Betsy said, "that's just what it is." And both girls looked across the fields and pastures as if they might somehow be able to see the magical castle ruled by the beautiful Indian princesses with bows an arrows.

Mike didn't know whether to give Sarah space or support her. He didn't know whether to hold her or give her a whisky and put her to bed.

The way she was staring into space—stunned and mute—it didn't look like she knew either.

Mike's own shock had dissipated with the effort of getting Woodson up to the clinic and calming John who'd practically tried to climb onto the stretcher with his father. If it hadn't been for John's instant recognition of his father's voice, Mike was sure he wouldn't have recognized David Woodson.

It wasn't because the man had changed so much. Bizarrely, he seemed to have changed not at all. It had only been the camouflaging blood and dirt that had prevented Mike from seeing who he was.

And who he was…was absolutely unbelievable. Even now, a full hour after breaking the news to Sarah and watching the Sisters tend to him, Mike still couldn't wrap his head around what had happened.

"We'll get all our answers when he wakes," he said.

Sarah looked at him and then back at the door to the clinic.

"You mean like how is it he's not dead?" she asked bluntly. "And where he's been for the last six years? And how he came to be here? Unarmed and crawling up to our drawbridge?"

He could tell she was a half step from full-blown hysteria. He knew her well enough to know a calming tactic on his part would only push her over the edge. He bit his tongue and waited.

"Or maybe how it is that he appears well fed with a recent haircut and clothes that look like he just bought them in the Men's department at Macy's?"

Mike had wondered if he'd been the only one to notice David's condition. Except for his injuries from the wolves, he didn't look like he'd spent any time in the Ireland of the last six years.

Leave it to Sarah to leap past the whole *my-dead-husband-is-alive* issue and get right to the part that didn't smell right.

"How is it he is alive?" she asked in a whisper.

They could do this all night and until David woke up it would just leave them exhausted and more wrought up than when they started.

Mike put his hand on Sarah's elbow and pulled her away from the wall.

"Come on," he said gruffly.

"Where are we going?"

"We're going to get the first round of answers before he wakes up."

He led her to the end of the hall where a group of women was huddled. Mike spotted Mary in the pack.

"Mary, Sarah's had a bit of a shock. Will ye send a few sandwiches and a bottle up to me den?"

Mary nodded, her eyes on Sarah as Mike pushed past her to the stairwell that led to the second level of suites and rooms.

Sarah came along quietly but Mike could tell her mind was miles away. He pushed open the door to his den and settled her in the nearest chair. Her eyes darted everywhere around the room, seeing nothing.

Mike pulled a chair up in front of her and sat down. He took her hands—frozen and cold even on a warm June day—in his own.

"Sarah, lass," he said gently.

She looked over his shoulder, oblivious to where she was. Not seeing Mike. Not seeing the room she sat in.

There was a knock at the door and it opened, revealing Liddy with a basket in one hand and a bottle of Irish whiskey in the other.

"Mary said the sandwiches were already made," she said in a quiet voice, watching Sarah. "How is she?"

"Ta, Liddy," Mike said as Liddy put the basket of sandwiches down next to him. She went to the hutch and brought out two cut crystal whisky glasses.

"Shocked, as we all are," Mike said.

Liddy poured the glasses and set them on the table by Mike. She squeezed Sarah's shoulder. "It's wonderful news, love," she said and then left.

Sarah shook her head and tears streamed down her face.

"It *is* wonderful news," she said. "It's a miracle. Did you see John's face?"

"Aye." Mike handed her the whiskey. "Drink this."

Sarah took the glass in her hand and looked into the depths of the liquid.

"Because I look like I've seen a ghost?" she said, shaking her head in anguish.

"Because you look like ye need it."

She looked up and met his eyes.

"I don't know how to feel, Mike. I'm...I'm happy, of course. I mean I'm ecstatic but..."

"Drink it, Sarah."

She did. He took the glass and held her hands in his.

"Now," he said firmly. "Tell me exactly what you remember of that day."

Susan Kiernan-Lewis

22

"I was baking bread. John had gone off to the compound. David was working in the south pasture. I don't even remember what he was doing. Fixing the fence maybe. I remember it was a pretty day. Warm. I remember because I wondered if John would be swimming with Gavin or going fishing."

Sarah remembered the feel of the air and the smell of the yeast as she molded the dough into Deirdre's bread pan and slid it into the hot oven.

She swore to herself she'd never forget a minute of that day.

"I got this weird feeling. Like something crawling over my grave. I can't describe it. Something felt wrong. I stepped outside to listen. I should have heard the sound of David working. Hammering, whistling. Something. Instead I heard voices."

Sarah swallowed hard as she remembered that afternoon, that moment when she turned and saw three men standing with David in the pasture.

David had his hands in the air.

"I ran back inside and grabbed the Glock. We hadn't used it in months and I remember I had to look for it and then make sure it had a clip in it."

She wiped her hands on her pants and forced herself to remember the rest of it.

"I ran to the pasture...the whole way with the gun in my hand. They all saw me coming. One of them...lifted the butt of his rifle and...and smashed it in David's face. He fell."

"He knocked him out?" Mike asked gently.

"He...no, I think David was stunned. He groaned but he was on the ground. I told them to leave and they laughed. One guy held the barrel of his rifle to David's head."

"Was he one of the men who kidnapped you?"

Sarah looked at Mike and for a moment she didn't see him. For six years she'd been remembering this terrible day a certain way. And now...now that she knew David had survived it...she was trying to see if her mind had filled in the gaps in her memory without her realizing it.

"He was," she said, her eyes wide with revelation. "But one of the other men there...I never saw him again. I don't know why I didn't remember that. There were three men. The leader shot and killed David...*I thought*. And then he and the other two put me in the wagon."

"But not the same two?"

"No! I remember now! One of them I never saw again."

Mike nodded. "That would be the poor bastard who got buried in the field wearing David's plaid shirt."

Sarah put a hand to her mouth.

"They never shot David," she said with awe and comprehension.

"But you thought you saw them shoot him?"

"I...I heard the shot. They said they were going to...to blow his head off and I heard the shot."

"But you didn't see it?"

She looked at him helplessly. "I thought I did but everything happened so fast. They said they were going to kill him and when I heard the shot I...I thought they did. I was sure they did!"

"Do you remember getting in the wagon?"

Sarah shook her head numbly.

"I don't know how I got in there. One minute I was losing my mind in the field where they were threatening to kill my husband and the next I was in the back of the wagon. But I saw him, Mike! I saw him—blood everywhere—dead on the ground!"

"You saw someone, lass. But it wasn't David. David's upstairs recovering from a wolf attack. Trust me his head is in one piece."

"I don't understand! Why would they want to fool me? Why would they care? And what did they do with David? And who did you bury?"

Mike poured both of them more whiskey. "When we heard the gun shot, I sent Gavin to investigate. He saw a man's body—dressed in David's shirt—with his head blown away. He reported back that John's father was dead. I went racing over there to see for myself."

"You assumed the body you found was David."

"Who else would be wearing his clothes?"

"Did he have a wedding band on? The body?"

"Lass, I didn't notice."

"He's not wearing one now."

Mike looked at Sarah in surprise. "You looked to see if David was wearing a wedding band?"

Sarah drained her glass. "I guess I was looking for proof that it was really him. I don't know what any of it means."

Mike took her hands in his. "John has his father back and your David is alive and well. It's a miracle, sure it is."

"You're right. It is a miracle," Sarah said. "A wonderful, extraordinary miracle—no matter what the explanation for it is." She stood and walked to Mike's desk and gazed out the floor to ceiling window into the darkness outside.

"But he's not *my* David."

Susan Kiernan-Lewis

23

Fiona brought her plate over to Mike at the head of the table. The chairs beside him were empty. Siobhan was in the nursery with the other children, and John and Sarah were both in the clinic with David.

The rest of the castle was still eating breakfast or just finishing. Each man and woman knew their tasks for the day especially those related to the ash clean up.

It was true the ash had finally stopped falling.

But now the fog had rolled in.

Fiona noticed that bugger Morgan had finished his breakfast in two gulps and gone out to watch the lasses on the parapet. *The old perv*, Fiona thought with disgust. More than one person had remarked on the auld bastard's unusual interest in the archers going about their rounds.

The sooner he was gone, the better. It was a shame about his twin grandsons. Sweeter lads Fiona had never met. Good manners and eager to help too. She glanced over at Jordie seated with Tommy. *Not like some.*

"Is it today you'll be talking to me, Fi?" Mike said gruffly, "Or were you waiting for an invitation from the Prince of Wales?"

Fiona turned her attention back to her brother. His plate of eggs and fried ham and toast sat untouched before him.

"How's Herself, then?" Fi asked, reaching for her mug of tea.

"As you'd expect," he said. "Shocked like the rest of us."

"I should say so. John must be beside himself."

"You saw him."

"Aye. Joy in its purest form, so it was. And Sarah?"

"You already asked that, Fiona." Mike drank his tea and stood up. "A lot to do today," he said.

"Can I ask you, brother dear, what David's showing up means for the rest of us?"

"It means feck-all," he said.

"Sure then what does it mean for you and Sarah?"

"I'm not understanding you."

"Don't play games with me, Mike! Is Siobhan a wee bastard now?"

Mike sat back down and grabbed his sister's wrist. "Whisht!" he hissed. "That her own auntie could say the words! Sarah and I are legally wed, Fiona. As you well know since you danced at our wedding."

"Oh, are ye now? And what do you call the strapping Yank upstairs in the clinic bed?"

"That has nothing to do with…me."

"Are ye daft? She's married to him!"

"She *was*," Mike said standing up again, his eyes looking over Fiona's shoulder. He didn't look happy or at all sure he believed his own words.

"Is he staying?"

"Sure you know what I know," Mike said abruptly and walked out of the dining hall.

Several people turned in their seats to watch him go and then looked at Fiona.

Everyone had questions. It was all very well to say that David's coming didn't affect the castle but when it came to Mike and Sarah—everything affected the castle.

Mary stirred the heavy cauldron of rabbit stew and wiped the perspiration from her face. It was always boiling hot in the castle kitchen—especially in summer.

Sophia Donovan poked her head in the kitchen and looked around.

"Yes, Sophia," Mary said briskly. "What is it?"

"There's been a request for more of the berry compote, if there's any left."

Gone were the days when Mary took praise for her cooking as anything but a demand of more work from her. She tried to feel even a glimmer of what she once had—before the EMP—when Kev used to tell her what a grand cook she was.

She grimaced at the memory.

"Liddy!" Mary called over her shoulder.

Her sister, a smaller, less hardy version of herself, stepped out of the walk-in pantry and frowned.

"Do we have any more of the compote left?" Mary said. She turned to Sophia. "Is it for Himself?"

Mike loved Mary's compote, so he did. And as much as she'd like to see him choke on it just now, it didn't hurt to remind him that she had worth too.

Sophia flushed and glanced back into the grand hall.

Before Mary could react that eejit girl Cassidy dropped a dish on the stone floor, shattering it and what was left of Mary's control. Cassidy turned away from the giant stone sink, her arms red to the elbows, tear tracks down both cheeks as she looked at the broken shards on the floor.

"Well, don't just stand there!" Mary said sharply.

"Nay," Liddy said, looking at Sophia and shaking her head. "Sure there's none left to be found."

Mary turned back to Sophia. But she'd gotten her answer and was gone.

On impulse, Mary ripped off her apron and pushed open the door from the kitchen into the great dining hall.

It was past lunchtime but there were about twenty people still eating. It infuriated Mary that Mike wouldn't enforce set eating times. He allowed the archers to eat whenever they were off duty which meant that Mary or Liddy had to be there to serve them and clean up afterward. And so of course, the others felt they didn't have to pay attention to the rules either.

She looked around the room but Mike was nowhere to be seen. Frowning, she looked for Sophia and caught a glimpse of her long dress as she scooted out the far door and up the staircase.

"Oy! So is there any of that fruit shite left or isn't there then?" a female voice called out.

Mary turned to see three archers at their usual table. They'd finished eating and their plates were shoved away. A fork had fallen to the floor where it lay unnoticed by anyone but Mary.

As she watched the ease and nonchalance of the lasses, the fury began to build inside her. Not a care. These ungrateful girls had not a care in the world. Their rooms were cleaned for them, their beds made, their food set before them...everyone else ran around like fiends frantically sweeping up the ash, sealing all open windows, cleaning up after the livestock which now lived indoors.

But these girls just laughed.

"Nay," Mary said evenly. "There's not. The rats got it, more's the pity."

"You're an odd one, so ye are," one of the girls said, smirking. "No wonder your Kev prefers his sauce on the side."

The other girls guffawed and Mary felt her cheeks flame.

Was it true? Was Kevin still shagging that lass?

She turned and fled back to the kitchen, the sound of the girls' laughter pushing her from behind like a battering ram.

If he was sleeping with her there was no one in the whole castle to stop him. Certainly not Mike Donovan.

She shut their raucous laughter out with the slamming of the kitchen door and stood against it, her breath heaving in her chest, the sound of their jeers thrumming in her ears.

There's no one who'll stop this, she thought, blinking back tears. *No one but myself.*

Thor knew that this was without question the best situation they'd ever found for themselves. Partly that was because the village had plenty of water and food put by—and for that he would thank that old geezer if he ever came back.

His very brief conversation with Morgan had assured Thor he would no doubt have to kill the auld tosser. One look

in those eyes and you could see he wasn't one to be conned—
or at least not easily.

Thor was in the large sitting room of the best house in the
village. It was still a relatively poor village and the Crisis
hadn't improved anyone's situation but it beat living on the
road. And the village women could be prevailed to wait on
them—something Thor had been promising his Emma nearly
from the day he married her.

As he reflected on his good circumstances, one of the
women came into the room with a tray with tea, milk, sugar
and biscuits. She set it down on the table in front of the
fireplace—which had a nice little fire going even though it was
summer.

"Do I see sugar?" Thor asked jovially, pouring his tea.
When the woman didn't answer, he looked at her. She
appeared terrified.

"Aye," she said in a whisper. "From the castle."

"I see. The castle seems to be well stocked then, so it
does."

When the woman still didn't speak, Thor sighed and sent
her away. Immediately the door opened and Emma and Rose
came in, accompanied by Red, the young man who was
usually assigned to guarding them.

"Marcus," Emma said, "we need to talk."

Thor looked at Rose who was gripping her jumper with
her hands, and looking down at the ground.

Jaysus, Thor thought. *Now what?*

"Is it something you've done, then, lass?" Thor said
sternly to Rose. "Look at me, Rose."

"It weren't my fault," Rose said breathlessly, still
studying the dirty and worn rug in front of the fireplace.

"What weren't your fault?"

"She was out...picking flowers in the woods—" Emma
began.

"When?" Thor asked, his eyes on Red now. "Were you
with her?"

Rose spoke up. "Da, it's not Red's fault! I slipped away so
I could be alone!"

"What happened?" Thor said, standing up, his teacup knocking to the floor.

"She was attacked," Emma said, pressing her lips together tightly. "Sexually."

"What?!" Thor flexed the fingers on his hand and felt his face flush.

Rose burst into tears. "I was just picking flowers," she sobbed.

Thor turned to Red in a rage. "Where were you when you were supposed to be watching me daughter?"

Red glanced at Rose, his eyes wide with fear. "I never saw her leave," he said, licking his lips. "I swear I had me eyes on her every—"

In one movement, Thor grabbed his gun from the tea table and shot the man.

Red grabbed his chest as an abrupt fountain of blood gushed out between his fingers. Rose screamed and buried her face in her mother's shoulder.

Red tumbled face-first to the rug.

"I'll kill them all!" Thor raged. "Every one of the fecking villagers, one by one! By God, I will! Jocko!" Thor stormed to the door but Emma ran after him.

"Marcus, no!" Emma cried as she grabbed his arm.

Jocko was waiting in the hallway. He pulled his gun and entered the room, his eyes flicking briefly to the body on the floor.

"Get ten men together," Thor said. "The village men can't have gone far. Comb the woods until you find the bastards!"

"Marcus, stop! Please, listen," Emma said.

"What?" Thor said whirling around on her. "What could ye possibly tell me that would stay my hand against the blackguard who soiled me only daughter?"

"It wasn't any of the village men," Emma said. She stepped back to allow Rose to stumble forward, her face ashen and her chin trembling.

"Who was it did this to you?" Thor shouted at her, spittle flying and catching her across the face.

Rose blinked back tears and bit her lip.

"He said he lived in the castle on the hill," she said.

24

John and Sarah sat next to David's bed. Sarah watched John as he gazed at his father's face. He had spent the night in the clinic but he didn't look exhausted. He looked expectant and jubilant.

"I just can't believe it," John said softly.

"It is pretty unbelievable," Sarah said.

"Everyone keeps saying it's a miracle. I think that's a perfect word for it."

How Sarah wished she could share John's feelings. She hated herself because she couldn't. To look at David's sleeping face—just as she'd seen it so many times in her marriage to him—made her feel like she was in a dream sequence of her own life.

Except Sarah didn't trust dreams any more.

As she gazed at his face—so relaxed and free from pain or care—she remembered the agony she'd felt— unending months of it as she thought back to the day she thought she'd seen him murdered. She remembered the horror that had come back to her at unexpected moments throughout the long days until time had faded her memories.

And then the guilt. The towering, monumental guilt over finding happiness again with Mike.

And all of it—the loss, the mourning, the nightmares— were because of an event...a terrible event...that had never happened.

Where's he been these last six years? Did he know where we were? Could he not have found his way back to Donovan's Lot?

149

She looked at John and wondered—as much as he loved Mike—if he was assuming Sarah would now be back with his father again.

"I can't wait to hear him speak, you know?" John said. "Sometimes I think it was his voice I missed the most."

"He had a wonderful voice."

"I can't even imagine what he has to tell us. I've tried to piece together scenarios and I just can't even begin to imagine where he's been. He looks good, doesn't he, Mom?"

"He does," Sarah said. *Too good.* The thought came to her before she could stop it. And when it did she realized that a part of her was angry with David. That surprised her but it explained why she wasn't feeling the same delight that John was.

Had David left of his own free will? Is that possible?

She shook the feelings away and gave John's arm a squeeze. "I'm going to go check on Siobhan," she said.

"I want to be here when he opens his eyes."

Sarah kissed her son on the forehead. "I love you, John," she said. "This is just the best thing that could have happened."

"It washes everything else away," John said, his eyes wet with tears. "You know?"

Sarah smiled and nodded. "It does," she said.

Sarah left the clinic, her mind roiling with confusion, her emotions bubbling uncomfortably inside her.

Nuala was standing outside the nursery door talking with one of the other mothers. She held her arms out and hugged Sarah.

"Cor, most of us have never met your David," she said, "but we're all chuffed for you, Sarah!"

"Thanks," Sarah said. "John is over the moon."

"Is it Siobhan you're looking for? She's happy playing but I can fetch her."

"No, let her play. I'm supposed to be helping in the kitchen this week."

"Sure, Fiona said you're to do no such thing!" Nuala said. "Sit by your man's bedside and there's no worries for the rest of it."

Is that how everyone thinks? That David is my man?
Is that what David thinks?

"You wouldn't know where Mike is, would you?" Sarah asked.

She should have known she'd find him in the stable. The fog in the courtyard was thick and wet, wrapping around everything like a heavy blanket.

At least it's better than the ash, Sarah thought zipping her jacket up and slipping through the double gated barn door. She could hear men's voices in the back.

"Mike?" she called.

"Aye, back here, lass," he called from the woodshop behind the stables.

It had never made sense to Sarah that they would set up a workshop so close to the horses. All that hammering and clanging was bound to upset the beasts on a daily basis. But Mike, who knew more about horses than anyone in their group, insisted that horses could handle the noise of farriers and that it would desensitize them. Sarah thought that sounded like he was trying to get them used to the sounds of battle.

She went and stood in the doorway of the workshop. Terry Donaghue was bent over a bench where row upon row of metal arrowheads glittered in the dim light.

"Is he awake?" Mike asked.

She was surprised to see he looked tired. He'd been such a rock to her last night, so soothing and even-keeled that she hadn't noticed the stress in his face.

"Not yet. John's with him."

"Sure it's a miracle, Sarah," Terry said, nodding at her from his workbench. "An answer to prayer, so it is."

Mike laid down the arrow he'd been holding and he and Sarah walked outside to the stall area.

She wasn't sure why she'd needed to see him, why she'd felt the need to connect with him after her morning sitting by David's bedside.

"How's the ash clean up coming?" she said.

"Tommy thinks the ground will be ruined for future planting if we don't remove it quickly so I've got everyone outside trying to brush the shite off the best they can. The corn is fine for this year. But the potatoes and cauliflower are both buggered."

"How's the water supply?"

He ran a hand across his face. "We've cleaned out the reservoirs and disposed of what was in there. I don't know how long it'll take us to clean out the wells or honestly even if we can."

"So we just pray for rain to fill our drinking water back up?"

"That's about the size of it."

"I thought I'd do an inventory of what food we've got," she said. She realized she was standing well away from Mike —as if she was afraid he might reach out and touch her.

"Good idea."

"I'll work with Mary and Liddy on that."

He narrowed his eyes. "Are ye all right, Sarah?"

"Of course."

"Nay now don't say that when you've every reason be banjaxed something desperate."

"Well, I'm not."

"No?" He reached out with one hand and pulled her to him.

She gasped and pushed him away with both hands. "Don't!"

He cocked his head and watched her.

"I ...I just don't want to be hemmed in right now."

"Is that what I'm doing? *Hemming you in?*"

"Don't put words in my mouth. That's not what I meant."

"Those are your very words, so they are."

"Just give me some space, for God's sakes."

"I'm your husband," he said in gruff voice. "Or are ye not too sure of that?"

"Don't be ridiculous." She moved away and rubbed her arms as if she'd gone cold. "I just came in here to tell you what I'm doing today. That's all."

"So I shouldn't get any other ideas, is that it? Will ye be moving out of our bedroom?"

"I don't know! Can't you just give me some space?"

Mike didn't answer. A muscle twitched in his jaw as if he were holding himself back at great effort. She could hear the musical tapping of Terry's hammer as he worked on the archers' arrows.

"I've...I've had a shock," Sarah said. That sounded weak even to her.

"Oh, aye?" he said, his eyes narrowed and clouded with hurt. "And space is what will mend that?"

"Look, Mike. Don't make a big deal out of this."

"Out of what? Out of the fact that me own wife doesn't want me to touch her? Or that she's thinking she's really married to someone else?"

"I never said that!"

"Well, why don't you say it now? Do ye ken whose bed you'll be crawling into tonight?"

Both of them were shouting now, all pretense at calm gone.

"Well, it won't be *yours*! That's for sure!" She stood facing him, her hands on her hips, her heart pounding in her chest.

As for Mike, he stood and clenched and unclenched his fists by his side.

"Take all the time ye need," he said, grinding out the words. "Sure I can see how confusing this must be for you. Two husbands and you not knowing which one is real. Or is it you don't know which one you want?"

"You're putting words in my mouth again," Sarah said taking a step toward him, her fists clenched at her side. "Or maybe it's just thoughts in my head!"

Neither of them noticed Fiona's arrival until she was nearly standing between them.

"Oy! I could hear you two from the upstairs nursery," she said breathlessly. "I'll wager you woke up bairns trying to nap in *Dublin*."

"What is it, Fiona?" Mike said angrily, his eyes snapping and never leaving Sarah's.

"Oh, not all that much," Fiona said, patting Sarah on the shoulder as she turned to go. "Just that your first husband appears to be waking up."

25

Thor watched the center road that dissected the town from the double window in the house he'd commandeered. There wasn't a soul visible but that didn't mean there wasn't plenty of activity going on behind every door. He had instructed his men to shepherd all the women and children into their houses where they were to remain.

He couldn't imagine the village women were plotting or scheming. In his experience, women—especially if they had children to bother with—spent the majority of their time during a crisis crying or praying. In his four years of kicking in doors and taking villages—and taking everything they had of value in them—he had never once confronted a woman who did more than beg or cry.

Some just did it louder.

"What are you looking for, Marcus?" Emma asked from behind him. He turned to smile at her.

"I'm expecting Jocko back with a report on the distance to the castle," he said tersely, his tone belying the smile on his lips.

"Is that really necessary?" She stood up from her chair with a cup of tea in her hand.

He thought she looked every inch a queen.

His queen.

Emma had been his true love since they were children. Sometimes he honestly couldn't imagine how it was he'd gotten her to love him back. It was always the first thing he thought of when he found himself wondering if there really were miracles in this life.

"You know the answer to that," he said and turned back to watch.

In the hours since Rose's attack was revealed Emma had made it clear that she felt forgiveness—both for the bastard who'd done the deed as well as for Rose who'd managed to allow it—was the answer.

Thor loved Emma all the more for this.

You want a soft woman, so ye do, he thought. *That's what makes them a woman, the softness.*

"Digby told me this morning that some of the men are coughing up blood," Emma said. "This ash has sickened all of us one way or the other. And now with the fog..."

Thor turned and walked to his wife. He took the teacup from her and placed it carefully on a nearby table. Then he kissed her lips.

"Let me handle it, Em. You do trust me, don't you?"

She put a hand to his cheek and smiled sadly. "Of course, Marcus."

"What was Rose doing out by herself?"

"Collecting flowers, as she said."

"Is she such a fan of flowers then?" Thor raised an eyebrow to his wife.

"Marcus, she's just a young lass. She was picking wildflowers." She put her hand on her husband's arm. "Did you have to kill Red? It was so upsetting for...for all of us."

He looked at her with surprise and sputtered, "How am I to keep order with the men if they see Red get away with allowing me daughter to be raped?"

"It was just so shocking. And right in front of Rose! She's been in tears ever since."

Thor grunted and turned back to the window. It was true he hated to upset Rose. She took after her mother in that way.

Sensitive, moody, softhearted.

Suddenly he spotted Jocko and five men striding down the street. They were back from the scouting mission to the castle. Thor went to the door and stepped out into the street.

"Well?" he asked abruptly.

Jocko waved off the men behind him and they dispersed, disappearing into doorways along the main street.

"Castle's right up against the ocean, but it's socked in something brutal," Jocko said. "We barely found our way there and Liam tripped on the way back and busted his wrist."

Thor cursed and shoved his hands into his pockets.

The man who'd attacked his daughter was in that castle—drinking tea and warming his feet in front of a fire no doubt—and all Thor could do was stand here, helplessly?

He knew Jocko was waiting for his answer—and it took all his power of self-control to be able to deliver it.

"They're not going anywhere. We wait until the fog lifts."

Jocko nodded and turned on his heel. Already he seemed to have found a lass in the village who'd tolerate his attentions.

Thor closed the door and returned to the sitting room where Emma waited for him. The only sounds were the muffled sobs of their daughter in one of the upstairs bedrooms.

"Well?" Emma said. "What did they find out?"

Thor went to the tea service and poured himself a cup of tea. It was tepid by now but he knew one of the village women would be in soon to refresh it. He sat on the couch opposite his wife with his teacup and smiled.

"They found out what I already knew," he said. "That life is long and if you're lucky—as me auld grandmother used to say—all good things will come to those who wait."

Emma nodded. "I'm glad," she said. "It will give us time to temper our reactions. Honestly, isn't forgiveness the only thing that stands between any of us and our just deserts?"

"Well said, my love," Thor said, his smile broadening as the door opened and the village woman scurried in with a kettle of hot water for the tea.

He would wait. After all, didn't all the proverbs down through time say that waiting was always the wisest course of action?

And he would use the time to steep his hate and nurture his fury.

Susan Kiernan-Lewis

26

Sarah walked into the room and went straight to his bed. John was sitting on the bed embracing his father. Sniffing and wiping the tears from his face with his sleeve, John quickly pulled away to make room for his mother.

Hesitating only briefly, Sarah leaned down and put her arms around David. Instantly she felt the familiarity of his touch as he held her. She felt the firmness in his grip, the way his hand glided across her back.

The way he used to do.

Only the sounds of shuffling feet and throat clearing behind her prompted her to finally pull back. She gazed into his eyes. David's eyes.

"I can't believe it's really you," Sarah said softly. "*How*? How are you here? How did you survive...that day?"

"Mom! Give him five seconds to adjust, would you?" John said with exasperation, his face still streaked with tears. "Dad, are you hungry?"

David looked at John and smiled. "Water would be great," he said.

John turned but Sister Alphonse had the cup ready for him.

"I can't believe I'm really seeing you again." David said as he gazed from John to Sarah's face. He drank deeply from the cup and then held each of their hands. "I've waited so long for this."

Sarah saw David look over John's shoulder at Fiona, Sister Alphonse and at Mike, who was standing near the door. Something passed across David's face. Something unpleasant.

"Can you tell us what happened?" Sarah asked again. "Where have you been all this time?"

David struggled to sit up and John and Sister Alphonse adjusted his pillows for him. He let go of John's hand so he could hold Sarah's with both of his.

"I thought they killed you," Sarah said. She was surprised to hear the emotion in her voice. She was very near tears.

"I know. I agonized when I knew that's what you thought." He turned to John. "What you both thought."

"So you weren't kidnapped?" John asked stiffly.

"No, I *was*. I most certainly was."

"But you didn't try to escape?" John said.

"At first I did." His eyes went again to Mike and something flinched in his jaw as if he were steeling himself for what he needed to say. Sarah didn't dare look at Mike.

"That's all I thought about. But let me go back to the beginning."

David drank more from the cup of water. It looked like the act of drinking and the few words he'd said had exhausted him.

A thick white bandage covered his neck where the worst of the wolf bites had been. Sister Alphonse was confident the wound would leave a scar but heal well going forward. David's bottom lip had been stitched where the wolves had ripped it too. His face looked bone white and he closed his eyes frequently as if fighting to stay awake.

"There is a…group that has been in existence for several decades."

"What group?" Mike asked. "What's the name of it?"

David's eyes narrowed at the sound of Mike's voice.

"You wouldn't know it." He turned to John. "It is a group of scientists and scholars and military experts—all dedicated to protecting the world's knowledge."

John frowned. "You mean like a think tank?"

"Well, it's more than that," David said. "And I've come to tell you all about it."

"You mean you came here *deliberately?*" Mike asked with surprise.

David ignored him.

"Until last month I didn't know you and your mother were still in Ireland," David said. "I would have come sooner if I'd known."

"Why did you not think we were in Ireland?" Sarah asked. "Isn't Ireland where you last saw us?"

He turned to her. "Yes but I also saw a video of both of you climbing on board a USAF helicopter where I was told you were flown to an interim airbase in Ireland and then later shown documentation that proved you'd landed safely in the US."

His voice grew firm and accusatory.

"It was beyond my wildest imagination that once safely back in America you might actually bring my brilliant son back to a third-world country that had been thrown into medieval survivalist mode."

Sarah blanched. She had agonized over the decision to return to Ireland. And she had wrestled with the guilt of having done it every time she saw her genius son digging a ditch or repairing a thatched roof. She couldn't meet David's eyes.

He still held her hand. Now he tapped the ring on her finger.

"You've remarried," he said softly.

Sarah stared at the wedding ring on her hand with David's fingers wrapped around it.

"And I suppose that would be Donovan?" David said. "No real surprise there."

"Now steady on, mate—" Mike began.

"I'm not your *mate*, Donovan," David said tightly, "and I wasn't speaking to you." He turned to Sarah.

"Look, Sarah, I know I have a lot of explaining to do and I want to tell you and John everything." He turned and smiled at John before turning back to Sarah. "But if you ever cared for me…if you ever loved me—"

"John, will you give us a minute?" Sarah asked breathlessly. She felt the room getting very small and she was finding it difficult to breathe.

"Mom, no! I want to stay," John said.

"If you ever loved me," David continued, squeezing her hand, "then I'm asking you to please give me the benefit of the doubt and hear me out."

"Of course," Sarah said breathlessly, surprised she was able to get the words out.

"Until all this gets sorted out between us," David said, "I'm asking you not to make it harder on any of us by going back to the room you share with him."

Mike surged forward, knocking over a chair. Sarah turned and laid a hand against his chest as if she would stop him. It was the first time she'd touched him since David arrived in the castle.

"Mike, stop it," she said fiercely. "Don't make this harder than it is."

"Harder on whom?" he asked, his eyes blazing. "You're not really thinking of agreeing to this bullshite?"

"Mike, *please.*"

"I don't believe this." He turned and walked out of the room, slamming the door behind him.

Sarah stared after him, her mouth open in astonishment. She had never seen Mike lose control like that.

Ever since David's arrival he'd been so balanced and even-keeled. She looked at Fiona who shrugged and looked back at David.

"I'm sorry about that, Sarah," David said. "I hope you can see it from my point of view."

"Of course," Sarah said woodenly. "Perfectly understandable until we get this all sorted out. Now please continue with your story."

"The men who came to our cottage that day were hired thugs from the UK."

Sarah stiffened. She knew very well who they were. She'd traveled a thousand miles with them in the back of a horse-drawn wagon. She glanced over at John.

He had been twelve years old when he set the bomb that blew up one of those men not three months later—the man whom Sarah believed to have murdered his father.

It was the first time John had killed a man.

And that, in a way, was courtesy of David Woodson.

"The people who hired them—my group—you have to understand, are intensely secretive and in the days to come I hope to explain why." He looked at John when he said this. "They were aware of my whereabouts in Ireland and set out to procure my...talents to the cause."

"Are you serious?" Sarah asked.

"They couldn't take the chance that I might be accidentally killed. You know yourself how easily that can happen these days."

"I was dragged screaming and kicking to a whore house outside of London," Sarah said, fighting to keep her voice low. "I fought to survive every day. So yes. I know."

"Look, Sarah," David said. "It was a horrible day. I'm not trying to say it wasn't. My group is...can be...ruthless and I'm sorry. But I've come to understand that it's sometimes necessary."

"Continue with your story, Dad." John reached over to briefly squeeze Sarah's hand and she made an effort to stay calm.

"Because of...what we're trying to do, it was necessary that my family believe I was killed that day. You have to believe me when I say I had no idea that was going to happen —or who they were. Once they had me, they put everything in motion for you and John to be flown back to the States. The thinking was that if you thought I was alive somewhere in Ireland you wouldn't leave. You wouldn't have applied for my death benefits with the US government—all things necessary to make the US believe I was unrecoverable."

"What body was it that we buried?" Sarah asked coldly. "What body is in the grave that John and I visited and wept over for four years? Was it anybody special or just a member of your group taking a big one for the team?"

"I see you're angry and I don't blame you."

"Yeah, David. I'm angry. I was lied to. Tricked." Sarah said hotly, flinging off his hand.

"Mom!"

But Sarah could tell John was disconcerted too about what he was hearing.

"I had nothing to do with how I was procured!" David said.

"And the fact that I was thrown in the back of a wagon and taken across the Irish Sea to work in a prostitute ring?"

"They told me you were left unharmed at the cottage!"

"Well, I wasn't, David."

"Sarah, I'm sorry. I know some of my group's methods are—"

"What is the name of this mysterious group of yours? Do you have your own bible and your own megachurch?"

"It's not a religion. It's...for your purposes, you can call it The Island of Secret Knowledge."

Fiona snorted with laughter and Sarah shook her head.

"Dear God, are you kidding me? You think you're the effing Hardy Boys? Do you hear yourself?"

"I can't tell you the real name," David said. "We are an intensely secret group. A hidden government, if you want to know, and the work we are doing is second to none in importance anywhere in the world."

"Dad..."

"I know that sounds crazy, but it's true! Look at all of you now! Living like you're in the eighteen hundreds! Hell, most of Europe is the same way. The second EMP took out most cars, electronics and communications pretty much everywhere, not just here. And it won't be long before the Middle East implodes and then the US won't be far behind."

"So your club is dedicated to bringing peace to the world?" Sarah said sarcastically.

"No. We are dedicated to preserving the world's knowledge for that time when all societies' infrastructures are destroyed. When all of it—the Internet, cars, jets, anything that made us civilized—is gone. And if we're not careful, our knowledge will be gone too. That's why we exist. To make sure that doesn't happen."

"Wow," Sarah said. "You must really be in your element."

"Don't, Mom," John said in a low voice. "Don't be mean."

"It's all right, John," David said. "I know how it sounds. I do."

"Where are your people now?" Fiona asked.

David smiled at her. "I can't tell you," he said.

"But you all live on an island?"

"It's not really an island. I'm sorry I can't tell you more."

"Well, can you tell us why you've come back now," Sarah said. "And why, if you're all so smart, you nearly ended up as a wolf's chew toy?"

David grinned. "That was a slight miscalculation, I admit. They dropped me near enough to the castle not to cause suspicion. But we didn't take into account the wolf problem. It's worse than our Intel had shown."

"*Your Intel*?" John asked. "So you still have computers and satellites and all?"

David turned to him. "We do. We have everything they have back in the States. And we're using it all to collect the information—the knowledge we need—and keeping it safe in repositories that will withstand…well, whatever happens next."

John frowned and looked out the castle window by his father's bed. Sarah could not imagine what he must be thinking…or feeling. She appreciated that David paused to let John attempt to process it.

Finally, John said, "And all this time you thought we were in the States?"

David nodded. "I did, son. I would have come years ago if I'd known you were here."

"Your pals opted not to tell you?" Sarah asked.

"They thought it was for the best. If you knew the magnitude of what we're trying to do, you'd cut them some slack on the logistics."

"Logistics."

"So what happened a month ago?" John asked.

"What do you mean?"

"You said something happened a month ago that made you realize we were still in Ireland."

"Yes. I met someone who told me you'd returned to Ireland."

"Who?"

"Dr. Sandra Lynch from Oxford."

27

Mike could feel his muscles quivering as he stormed down the stone hall and out into the courtyard. The air was hot and thick with the fog, the sight of which just served to make him madder.

The blighter comes back after six years and thinks he can throw me out of me own bed?

He couldn't believe he'd heard what he had.

Or that he'd watched Sarah nod her head when Woodson had said it like it was a completely reasonable thing to say.

As he strode across the courtyard, the sounds of arrows thumping into their dense straw targets carried to him from the far side of the courtyard.

Enough.

The whole world felt like it was squatting on his shoulders. First the fecking ash ruining half the year's harvest —and possibly all future harvests—and then Mary going after him night and day about the Tilly situation—*and don't get me started on the fecking archers.*

Heat seemed to vibrate through his body as he reached the barn door and jerked it open with both hands.

A part of him was imagining Woodson's neck in his hands as he flung the doors back. A startled whinny greeted him. He went straight to Buck's stall and his hand reached for the bridle hanging by a hook before Mike even knew that's what he wanted.

Yes, by God. I need to get out.

"Hey, governor," Terry called to him from the door of the workshop.

Mike drew Buck out into the center aisle and tied him to the hitching post. Within seconds he had a saddle pad and saddle on the horse's back.

Terry drew nearer, a perplexed look on his face.

"Everything all right, Mike?"

"As rain," Mike said tersely as he snaked Buck's bridle over the horse's nose and slid the bit between its teeth. "Just a little errand I need to run."

"Not outside the castle, I trust."

But Mike wasn't listening. He felt like he couldn't breathe in the barn. He led the horse through the double doors into the dense fog of the courtyard. It wasn't much better out there.

He couldn't *breathe*.

Terry ran alongside him into the courtyard.

"Mike, mate, what's wrong? Sure you can't be thinking of going out of the castle? The fog is as thick as two planks!"

"I need to find the explosion site and see if there's anything to be learned."

"That can wait, Mike!"

"No! It can't!" Mike snarled. He glimpsed Terry's startled face and a part of him felt a splinter of guilt for snapping at the man.

But the other part of him just needed *out* at any cost.

"It's too dangerous to go alone. Visibility is shite out there. At least wait until I can tack up and go with you," Terry said.

"I can't stay here another minute," Mike said as he swung up into the saddle. "Oy! Regan!"

A form morphed out of the fog and stood at the back of the fence high up on the parapet at the front of the castle.

"Here," she called.

"I'm going out," he said. "Mind you lot don't accidentally shoot me in all this fog."

Without waiting for her reply, he trotted to the gate tower where Kevin O'Malley stood watching him come.

"Are ye sure, governor?" Kevin said, his hand resting on the windlass that operated the pulley system to raise the portcullis and lower the drawbridge.

"Open the fecking door," Mike growled, using all his willpower to wait for his escape.

Morgan sat shrouded in fog on the stone bench in the courtyard. He watched as Donovan barreled past, his horse's hooves thundering against the massive wooden drawbridge. Then he stood and walked over to where Dongaghue, the castle farrier, stood watching in obvious frustration as the drawbridge was slowly hauled back up into place.

"Just be glad he didn't order anyone to go with him," Morgan said with disgust.

"I wish I *had* gone with him!" Terry said heatedly. "I should never have let him go alone. He's not in his right mind."

"Your responsibility is to the people in the castle," Morgan said coolly. "Not one hot head having a bad day. No matter how good a mate he is."

Terry turned to look at Morgan as if seeing him for the first time. He held an arrow in one hand. It looked to Morgan as if he'd been stopped in the act of attaching its flinthead.

"Mike has saved this community a hundred times over," Terry said. "He's sacrificed everything for the good of the whole. Many times."

Morgan shrugged and glanced up at the archers. The girls had spent part of their morning wasting arrows shooting at a few wolves sniffing around the castle perimeter—even though Morgan had heard Donovan tell them not to.

Their voices—and their laughter—seemed to carry further in the fog. Or maybe that was just the other senses kicking in when one was diminished, he thought.

He noticed that aside from Mike and Terry he hadn't seen a male over the age of ten all morning. Most of the men were busy cleaning ash off the windows and from any machinery it had found its way into.

A loud squeal of mirth made him turn to look toward the parapet again. One girl shoved another and more giggling ensued. The girl who was shoved dropped her quiver and a dozen razor-sharp arrows rained down onto the courtyard. *Lucky nobody had been walking under there at the time.* Morgan had already noted the fact that besides the archers there were no other lines of defense at the castle. No boiling pitch or even a working moat. He'd heard whispers that the castle was low on ammunition too.

So that meant whatever guns they had in the castle were likely useless.

It seemed—at least from what Morgan could see—that it was only the girl archers who stood between the castle and anyone wanting in.

Another squeal of laughter erupted from above. Morgan sat back down on the bench and fingered the handgun in his shoulder holster.

Henredon Castle's defense was a fake.

Take out the little girls playing soldier and the whole place falls down like a house of cards.

28

Sarah bolted from the clinic room as soon as she could. David had fallen back to sleep and John was staring out the window immersed in his own thoughts. When Sarah tried to talk to him, he'd made it clear he wanted to be alone.

She knew exactly how he felt.

Her mind was swirling with all that David had said as well as with the hints of what he would say in the days to come when the whole puzzle was finally pieced together. As it was, enough had been said.

There wasn't anything so mysterious about it all now. David wasn't Lazarus raised from the dead. There was a perfectly logical if slightly ugly explanation. And it made Sarah want to throw up just thinking of it.

Nuala had tapped on the clinic door and asked Fiona for help in the nursery. That left Sarah on her own.

She hurried upstairs to the bedroom she shared with Mike. She knew he wouldn't be here—had prayed in fact that he wouldn't be. She had never seen him lose his cool like that.

It occurred to her that as long as they'd been together she had never seen him jealous before.

It wasn't pretty.

She paused for a moment in the doorway of the small living room connecting to the bedroom. Rank definitely had its privileges and nowhere was that more evident than in this room. While they'd worked hard to make each of the rooms in the cold, drafty castle comfortable, this room was downright sumptuous.

She stepped onto the thick Oriental rug and sank into her reading chair. Without thinking what she was doing, she drew her favorite wool afghan rug across her knees.

From this chair she could look out the window and see fair weather clouds skate across the blue Irish sky. She had a small bookcase facing her and sometimes when she sat and looked at the spines of all those books—most of which she'd brought back from the States—she found herself thinking life couldn't really be so bad.

No matter how hard she worked, or how hard she worried about things, being able to relax in this chair and in this room made it all bearable. Here she still could curl up with a cup of tea and lose herself in a book. The room truly was her sanctuary.

Her eye strayed to the bed in the other room.

It was true she'd never seen him so angry but it was worse than that. She had never seen him look so…betrayed.

She rubbed her face with her hands and tried to blot out the look on Mike's face when she'd asked him to be reasonable about moving out.

It had been her involuntary reaction to a request from a man she'd trusted and loved.

David.

The familiar way he crinkled his eyes when he smiled, the way he looked off to the left when he was thinking. The cowlick in his hair that gave him a perennially tousled look.

Hearing David's voice again—especially his wry laugh—had sent Sarah time-tripping in spite of her best intentions back to that afternoon in Dierdre and Seamus's pasture.

That horrible autumn afternoon when the men and their wagon had come…

She shook the image from her mind and tried to focus instead on what David had said.

Could it be true? Could any of it be true?

Had he really been kidnapped by a secret society trying to save the world's knowledge in advance of a world apocalypse?

It sounded so…crazy.

It wasn't until David told them that Oxford's foremost chemist and immunologist Sandra Lynch had joined them that Sarah began to believe David might be telling the truth. While she'd never met Dr. Lynch, the woman had taken good care of John during his time in Oxford—even flinging herself in front of him to protect him against a rain of bullets on a London street.

If Dr. Lynch was a part of the plan, it instantly elevated David's crackpot da Vinci Code group into a real possibility. But it didn't just help make David's group make a little more sense, unfortunately it also did something way more ominous.

It made it clear that David was here to bring John back with him.

How could it be anything else?

Sarah's stomach churned with anxiety at the thought. She remembered John's expression as he looked at his father—the joy and the conviction there. David was just like him. It had always been that way. Both scholars, both brilliant, both intellectuals. In a way it was a relief to see John with someone who understood him and how his mind worked.

Then why am I so terrified at the thought?

She heard a tap at the door and looked up to see Sophia enter the room. Sarah felt a prick of guilt. She knew Sophia was worried about Gavin. He'd been gone two full nights and nearly three days now.

"Fi thought you might like a cup of tea," Sophia said in her lilting Italian accent. She carried a tray into the room and set it on the table by Sarah's chair.

"Oh, darling Fi. Always thinking of me. How are you doing, Sophia?"

"I am well. I cannot stay. I told Nuala I would help with the older children."

"Where's Cassidy? I thought that was her job."

"I do not know. Fiona told me to tell you not to worry about Da."

Sarah poured her tea and stirred in a teaspoon of sugar.

"You mean him storming out of the clinic like he did?" Sarah shook her head. "Sometimes I don't think I know him at all."

"No. I mean because he left the castle. At full gallop on his horse."

Sarah's mouth dropped open. "Mike left the castle?"

"In a rare rage, Fi said. We are all a little worried."

Sarah put her teacup down and went to the window. The fog was too thick to see anything.

Mike went out in this?

"Why?" Sarah said, her heart beating quickly. She felt her cheeks flush. "Where was he going?"

"Mr. Donaghue said Da went to find the source of the explosion we all heard yesterday."

"In this *fog*?" Sarah heard her voice crack and her breath begin to quicken. Her fingers tingled unpleasantly.

But Sophia had already left the room. There were children to mind and chores to do.

Sarah stood at the window and let her tea go cold. She didn't know whether she was angry or terrified. Or both.

Even with the patchy fog flitting between the trees the view from the parapet was better than Artemus Morgan had expected. He stepped from the top of the stairs and dropped the quiver of arrows he'd picked up from below onto the wall walk. There were ten archers on duty. All ten stood facing him.

They were not happy to see him.

"You're not allowed up here, auld man," one of the girls said. Morgan thought he remembered her name was Hannah.

"Am I not? My mistake then. Thought I'd return something you dropped."

"Don't be touching me arrows, Granddad," the girl Tilly said as she knelt to inspect the arrows he'd placed on the walkway, looking at him as if she wasn't sure he hadn't damaged them in some way.

"It's a wonder ye can see anything in all this fog. Am I right in hearing you've killed a wolf this morning?"

The girls hooted.

"*One?*" Tilly said. "We killed *four*."

"And how many arrows did you waste to do that?"

Regan stepped closer to Morgan and looked him up and down.

"If it's any of your business, ye auld tosser, we 'wasted' four. One for each beastie."

"That's good shooting. Each one a kill shot?"

"Naturally."

"And will ye then retrieve your arrows or do they grow on trees here in Cinderella's castle?"

"Sure the others will do that," Hannah said. "Since they're useless for anything else."

Another wave of laughter passed through the girls. One by one they turned away from him to focus on the ground outside the castle.

"Oy, Regan," Hannah said. "Aibreann said to tell ye she's not fit for patrol tonight. You'll have to take her watch."

This is exactly what Morgan would have expected. No doubt it was the lass's time of the month or perhaps she was peeved at one of the other girls. Lasses were notorious for not getting along for more time than it took to sneeze.

One thing Morgan knew was that the natural order of things would always win out. And women were meant to be wives and mothers—not warriors.

Sooner or later, who they really were would bob to the surface.

And then where would the castle be?

"So do each of you have a post? Is that it?" Morgan asked easily. "I see you're spread out. Is that by design?"

"Thinking of starting your own all-girl army, Granddad?" Regan asked.

The other archers tittered.

"Oh, you never know."

Regan watched him and seemed to make up her mind about something. She lowered her bow and approached him.

"We're set up at intervals," she said. "With four on the front spread out like we are there's no section of the approach we can't see."

"So you each have your area that you're responsible for?"

"That's right."

"Do you ever switch up? Stand some place different the next time?"

Regan narrowed her eyes but she frowned as if she was thinking about it.

"No," she said. "Why would we?"

"Well, no reason. Except have you ever noticed how you see a certain thing and maybe it's the most beautiful thing you've ever seen—like a waterfall on your way to work or something?"

The girls laughed. "Or maybe a unicorn!"

"Only about the tenth time you drive by it—in the days when we used to drive—you stop seeing it. It's still there, but your mind expects to see it and so you don't. Like your nose that's always in your field of vision. The same principle applies to a standing sentry. If you mix it up, you might find you see more clearly."

"Are ye saying ye've been a sentry before, Granddad?"

"Back before the Norman invasion, aye," he said with a grin.

Two of the girls turned to look at him. "Where? In the Garda?"

"The Irish Army," Morgan said. "So, where would you say your blind spots are up here?"

"Don't have any, Granddad."

"Really? No spots at all that are harder to see than others?"

Tilly shrugged. "Maybe by the north corner of the car park. It'd be a bugger to try to hit anything there."

One of the girls tensed and brought her bow up, her arrow poised to fly. Instantly the other three struck the same pose. Their eyes and bows were pointed in the direction by the front of the woods.

"What is it?" Morgan whispered. "What did ye see, lass?"

The silence held for a long moment before the girls relaxed one by one. Morgan had to admit that when it was time to get serious, all play and laughter vanished.

That surprised him.

"Ye remind me of someone I used to know," Regan said as she relaxed her bow by her side. She still stood at her post but she was watching him quizzically.

"Oh? Your auld Grandda, I suppose?"

"Nah. I never knew me Grandda. No, you remind me of someone...who lived with us once. He was old like you. Name even sounded a little like yours. *Archie.*"

That was an unexpected boon. Morgan had pegged Regan early on as the hardest nut of them all. She had a tough demeanor that didn't indulge fools—and she was wary. If he resembled this Archie bloke in her eyes that meant she'd be open to trusting him.

He would find that useful as things came to pass.

Mike couldn't see shite in this muck.

Pure adrenalin had taken him a full mile down the front drive of the castle approach. The fact that he couldn't see twenty feet in front of him didn't bother him. All he could see in his mind was Sarah's eager yet tearful face nodding in agreement with her first husband that they should probably be reasonable and pretend that the whole Mike Donovan portion of her life had never happened.

He ground his teeth and felt his horse accelerate out of the trot into a loping canter. He pulled him back into a trot. Something about the canter was too languorous and easy-going to be endured at the moment. He'd rather have his teeth rattled out of his skull with the roughest trot known to man than feel like he was on a fecking rocking horse.

And just hours before she wasn't even sure how she felt about the bastard's return.

Guess she made her mind up about it.

The air was thick and warm. Mike felt like he was wearing too many layers although he'd only come out in a t-shirt and jeans. The fog bunched up in front of him and then whipped away as he penetrated it—only to reveal more fog.

A thought occurred to him. A thought far off and barely perceptible in the distance.

Maybe this was a mad stupid idea coming out here in fog so thick half the time you can't see your hand in front of you.

His body tensed in frustration and Buck again took it as a signal to speed up. This time, before Mike could correct him he felt Buck stumble.

Mike leaned back into the saddle and reined in hard, trying to help the horse recover by giving him something to push against. The horse hesitated—almost as if thinking about it—and then dipped his head.

And fell all the way down.

29

Mike stood at the side of the road, his reins in one hand.

Buck was back on his feet but the field trip was officially cancelled. Whether it was a twist in an unforeseen pothole—*hell, everything was unforeseen in this fog!*—or a bruised frog, he'd find out back at the castle.

He glanced in the direction of the castle.

He'd been mad. A nutter. Not the full shilling.

He shook his head and began to lead Buck back home.

The anger had faded with the scare. What if Buck was permanently damaged? Did they have enough horses to risk losing one to Mike's temper tantrum? He tried to imagine how he would've reacted if somebody from the castle had done something so stupid.

A sound broke through the soft clip clop of Buck's unshod hooves against the asphalt drive. Mike paused. He wasn't sure exactly what he'd heard. Voices? He turned and peered into the thick mist around him.

He could only see glimpses of trees in the woods that lined the drive.

Was someone out there? Watching him?

He reached for his holster before realizing he'd left in such a rush that he hadn't grabbed it.

He turned and began to walk again, a little quicker now, his ears straining to hear any sound, his heart pounding in his throat.

Sarah folded the laundered diaper and placed it in the stack by the cupboard in the nursery. Her mind was a million miles away. Or perhaps only one or two miles...

Mike still wasn't back.

Sarah had asked Fiona to ask Hannah—whom she knew from the rape camp—to please notify her as soon as she saw Mike returning.

The fact that Mike would put her through this kind of worry—on top of everything else she had to stress about with David—made Sarah grind her teeth with fury as she paced the nursery and looked out the window for a glimpse of movement in the twilight gloom.

"Oy, Sarah," Nuala said as Sarah went to the window for the hundredth time. "Sure as much help as ye are to me, would ye mind pissing off and fetching me a cuppa?"

Sarah turned to look at Nuala who stood with a baby in each arm and a look of frustration on her face.

"I'm sorry, Nuala," Sarah said. "I meant to be a help."

Two of the smaller children were seated on the floor wailing. Their little faces were wet with tears. Sarah couldn't believe she hadn't heard them. She bent to pick one of them up, little Bill.

"Well, ye can help by bringing me a cuppa, sure ye can. And asking if Sophia is free."

"But Sophia's been on duty all day long," Sarah said. "She needs tonight off."

"Then somebody else!" Nuala said, her voice strident.

Sarah had never seen Nuala so frustrated. She was reminded that Nuala was sweet on Robbie—who'd gone off with Gavin three days ago. She hid it well, but of course Nuala must be worried sick. Sarah jiggled Bill in her arms but the baby only screamed louder.

"Sure he can tell you're tense and you're doing none of us any good!" Nuala said. "No offense, Sarah, but please go!"

Sarah put Bill back down on the floor where he crawled over to Siobhan and instantly started gnawing on her foot.

"I'll send someone up. I'm sorry, Nuala," Sarah said.

"No worries," Nuala said, depositing one of her babies in his crib and reaching for Bill before Siobhan started howling. "Just go. And don't forget that cuppa!"

Sarah waggled her fingers at Siobhan but the child was too absorbed in a game she was playing with Ciara. Sarah slipped out of the room.

It surprised her how warm it had been in the nursery. She realized that when she stepped into the cool hall, lined with limestone blocks.

Liddy O'Malley was coming down the hall with a tray in her hands.

"Is that for Nuala?" Sarah asked. "You're an angel and a mind reader if it is."

"Sure I bring it to her every evening at this time," Liddy said. Sarah couldn't help but notice that Liddy was cooler to her than usual.

"Is everything okay?" Sarah asked.

"And why wouldn't it be?" Liddy asked curtly, nodding at the nursery door to indicate that Sarah should open it for her.

"No reason I guess." Sarah opened the door and the din of the wailing children spilled out into the hallway. She bit her tongue to keep from asking Liddy if she could stay and help Nuala. Sarah was pretty sure that Nuala would mention she was all on her own now that Sarah had proved to be worse than useless. Liddy would no doubt volunteer to help.

Sarah hated herself for allowing that to happen. She closed the door on the noise and warmth and felt the relief invade her bones when she did.

Damn Mike! Why would he leave like that? How dare he leave the castle with the fog and the wolves out there?

Was this his way of getting back at her?

She'd never seen him behave so immaturely. To deliberately make her worry like this—and now of all times! It was almost like he was someone she didn't know.

As she walked down the hall, she neared the door of the clinic.

Speaking of someone I don't know...

She hesitated outside the door and then opened it. There was a lantern on the table by the window and Sister Alphonse was napping in the large tub chair. John wasn't in the room and Sarah found herself relieved about that.

As soon as we all go back to normal, the better.

David was sitting up in bed. He was awake.

"Come in," he said in a loud whisper. His voice woke up the nun and she pulled herself to her feet and looked around as if unsure of where she was.

"Sorry, Sister," David said.

"If you want to go get dinner," Sarah said coming into the room, "I'll take over."

Sister Alphonse nodded and went to David's bed. She put her hand on his forehead and then picked up his wrist to check his pulse before turning to Sarah. "Thank ye, lass. I think I will."

Sarah sat in the chair next to David's bed and waited for the nun to leave. David seemed to be waiting too.

"So," Sarah said. "You're back."

"So it would appear."

Sarah narrowed her eyes.

"Sarah. I'm sorry. I know how you must feel."

"We thought you were dead. You let us think that."

"It was a terrible thing. I absolutely cop to that."

"I suppose that's an apology in somebody's world."

"I've said I'm sorry. I don't know how to say it in a way that makes what happened—*not* have happened. I can't reverse time. I'm sorry, Sarah. It killed me knowing you and John were going through that."

"You missed his childhood, you know. You missed who he was at thirteen. And fifteen. You missed all the things he discovered about himself and life. You missed it all."

David's eyes filled with tears. She knew it was just about the worst thing she could have said to him. If he was still even a little bit the David she used to know, she was sure he'd tortured himself with that loss for the last six years.

"I know," he whispered, as a tear streaked down his cheek.

"And you never got to weigh in. You never got to advise him or teach him. All he had were memories of what you said to him when he was eleven."

"Sarah, please. I know what I lost. I know."

"Do you?"

"Of course I do. You don't think I didn't mourn the loss of us as a family? Or the fact that I'd never see you again?"

"I have no idea what you thought. The man I knew couldn't have walked away from his family."

"I didn't walk away! I was drugged and carried away! Why won't you believe that?"

"Because you never came back! Because once you found out who had taken you and why, you didn't say *screw this, I'm going back to my wife and child!*"

"I...I did at first. I really did."

"And then what? You forgot how much you loved us? Or did you meet someone you loved more?"

"It wasn't like that."

"It *wasn't* like that," Sarah repeated, her eyes widening. "Past tense. So it *is* like that now." She jammed her fists against her hips and spoke through her teeth with forced restraint. "Did you really have the balls to ask me to stay away from Mike when you yourself have remarried?"

"I haven't remarried!"

"Oh, excuse me. Shacking up, then."

"Give me a break, Sarah! It's been over six years. Was I supposed to be celibate that whole time? At least I didn't cheat on you while we were still together."

"What are you talking about? I never cheated on you!"

"Didn't you, Sarah? Every time you looked at Donovan? Every time you waited for him to visit us at the cottage and made sure your hair was just so or you'd bake something special just for him?"

"You're crazy."

"If you say so. But it doesn't matter. We are where we are."

"You never did say why you've come now."

"I told you. I didn't know you were in Ireland until last month."

"And now that you know…"

"I wanted to see John. And you."

"That's bullshit, David."

"Sarah, I…"

"You've come to take John."

David licked his lips and looked away. Even though Sarah had been fairly sure that's why he'd come back, the confirmation of it felt like a kick in the stomach.

"You can't have him."

"He's my son, too."

"And you walked away from him!"

"I told you! I didn't walk away! Besides, don't you have another child?"

Sarah gaped at him in astonishment. "You think children are interchangeable? Is that what you brainiacs believe on your Island of Magical Thinking? That it's okay for you to swoop in here and take my son because I have a backup kid?"

"No. I'm sorry. I shouldn't have said that."

Sarah stood up. "You can't have him."

"I didn't want it to be like this, Sarah." He reached for her hand and she let him take it. Her shoulders vibrated with anger.

"But it *is* like this," she said in a low voice. "Because of what you set in motion six years ago, it is like this."

She started to pull her hand from his grip just as the door opened. Sarah turned to see John step into the room, his face flushed with pleasure at the sight of both his parents together and holding hands.

30

That night Mike ate in the dining hall alone. It was long past dinnertime and except for the sounds of pots being washed in the kitchen, there was no indication of life in the room. Most people were either putting the livestock to bed—or their children.

Mike's dinner of fish soup and turnip greens sat before him and—after everything that was going on in his head—he surprised himself to discover he was hungry.

After he'd handed a limping Buck over to Davey at the stable, Mike had asked Liddy to prepare one of the empty bedrooms for him. He hated to alert the whole damn castle that David's coming had driven a wedge between him and Sarah. But short of sleeping in the barn, there was nothing for it.

He looked up to see his sister enter the hall. She held her little lad Bill in her arms.

Mike smiled at her as she approached. It had been a long hard year since losing Declan but Fiona seemed to have come out on the other side with her optimism and good humor intact.

God knows they needed both these days.

"So you're back, are you?" she said as she sat down. The baby moaned in his sleep but quickly settled.

"As you see. How's this little one then?"

"Sure how can I be surprised that boys are more trouble than lasses?"

"That is a totally skewed perspective, I'll have ye know," Mike said. "As far as I'm concerned, every lass in this fecking castle is the biggest pain in my arse. Present company excepted." He readdressed his meal for a moment until it became clear that Fiona didn't intend to tell him what had happened without prompting.

"So what did the wanker have to say for himself?" he asked.

Fiona rearranged the blankets around Bill before she quietly filled him in on the details of what Mike had missed. He listened solemnly, his appetite and food forgotten. When Fiona finished, he sat there and shook his head in disbelief.

"So basically the same thugs who took Sarah were hired to take David Woodson to some secret laboratory where, as the smartest people in the world, they're all trying to figure out how to save the world before the rest of us mucks destroy it?"

"Aye. You've got it in one."

"And Sarah believed this?"

"You'll have to ask her."

"How did Woodson get to the castle?"

"He said his group knew where we were."

"Oh, right. Because they're the smartest people in the world."

"Something like that."

"If he's so smart how is it he ended up on his hands and knees with teeth marks in his neck?"

"Slight miscalculation he said."

"So now what? He's here to collect his missing family?"

"I don't know, Mike. He didn't say beyond that. If you'd have stayed, you'd likely know for yourself."

"The bastard asked Sarah to leave our bedroom!"

"Sure *that's* not what turned you arseways, now is it?"

Fiona was right of course. It wasn't the bugger saying it. It was the ready agreeing to it from Sarah that had done him in.

"She's banjaxed at the moment, Mike. As anyone would be. Her first husband's come back from the dead! Sure you can see she's just placating him until she can—"

"That's *not* what I see."

"Of course it's not. Because honestly you're *not* the smartest person in the world."

"You didn't see how she was with him? All gentle and nearly about to cry? *Sarah*?"

"What I saw was someone who'd had a traumatic experience trying to make sense of it. Nothing more."

Mike snorted in disbelief.

Fiona shrugged. "But you know your wife better than I do. Oops, I meant to say another man's wife."

"Sure you're pissing me off something fierce, Fiona."

"Well, good. Because I need you to focus on what's happening in the castle and leave the soap opera dramatics for another time. The very idea of you bolting out of here like a pissed off teenager! I couldn't believe it when they told me! What got into you?"

"Never mind." The thought of how close he'd come to nearly crippling his horse made Mike flush.

"There's things boiling beneath the surface here in the castle and I don't like the sounds of it," Fiona said.

"Like what?"

"Mary is talking to everyone who'll listen about how the archers are running the show and think they can do no wrong. You can't let it come to a head or you'll have worse problems. And you can't throw this on Sarah because she's got her hands full at the moment."

"How's the ash clean up coming?"

"Changing the subject isn't the answer either."

"What do you expect me to do, Fi? Is dealing with one disgruntled housewife more important than finding the wreckage of an airplane that's been bombing all around us for two months and finding answers that might affect our very existence here at Henredon?"

"You really think they were dropping bombs?"

"I don't know what to think. That's the point. We need to find out."

"So you're going back out?"

"Aye, but I'll bring one of the men with me."

"Just one?"

"I hate to bring more. There's still so much work to be done on the ash clean up."

"Why don't you bring Mr. Morgan with you? We won't miss him and I'm sure he'd appreciate having something to do besides ogling the archers and eating three squares a day."

"Something on your mind, Fi?"

"Don't you think it's strange that he hasn't gone back to his village yet?"

"The man's coughing up a lung for Jaysus sake! He can barely walk from one room to another. And the fog's still fair bad."

"It was good enough for you to go tearing out of here at a dead gallop over hill and coop."

"Is his boy fine to travel, then?"

"Even if he wasn't, Morgan knows he can leave both lads here a few days longer. But he doesn't seemed worried about all those people he left in Kilbaha."

"You think he doesn't want to return?"

"I don't know. It's just bloody odd."

The next morning Mike visited Siobhan briefly in the nursery with the other children and then skipped breakfast to avoid running into Sarah in the dining hall. He went straight to Morgan to ask him to accompany him to the plane crash site—if indeed that's what it was.

"Sure you were in the army, were ye not, Mr. Morgan? You might be able to say whether the plane is friend or foe. Do ye mind?"

Morgan shrugged. "Me breathing's better today. I was thinking of heading back to Kilbaha," he said.

"Delay it a few hours," Mike said. "Then after we're done, take the horse the rest of the way to the village. Return it when you come back for your lads."

Mike caught a glimpse of Sarah crossing the courtyard. She didn't look in his direction.

"Sounds a plan, governor," Morgan said.

"That's grand," Mike said brusquely. "Go on and tell your lads and I'll saddle up two horses."

Thirty minutes later, Kevin cranked up the portcullis and lowered the drawbridge for them.

David didn't think he'd ever get tired of looking at his boy. At first he caught himself looking for signs of the little boy he'd left over six years ago. He realized that he had half expected to see the silly grin, the open naiveté in John's eyes, the eagerness to greet each day and embrace each new fact as it came to him.

But of course Sarah was right. He'd missed all that.

He eased his legs off the bed. Sister Alphonse slept noisily in the large chair in the corner of the room. It was early. John would be by soon.

Sarah, who knows?

David pushed thoughts of his wife away. He didn't have to make any decisions about her right this minute. He had a simple mission. How she reacted to it would determine where she fit in and how he dealt with her.

He needn't get ahead of himself.

No, it was all about John now. And the man the boy had become.

David looked out the narrow window. The fog made it impossible to see much but the ever-present roar of the ocean told him what he'd see if it were clear.

One thing was certain. The young man John had become no longer looked at David as if he had all the answers to the world's questions.

He didn't look like he greeted the world with any particular eagerness either.

The things that had happened—things that David hadn't been there for—those things had rerouted the natural bent of John Woodson. Whoever John had been intended to be, that person never got a chance to exist.

Clearly, John had seen things, done things. Even the joy with which he embraced his long lost father—even that was somehow tempered.

The father who John remembered—that man was still lost to him.

David felt a chill crawl up on his arms.

He'd seen that realization in John's face the instant he'd looked into David's eyes for the first time in six years.

The surprise. The joy.

And the disappointment.

David gingerly touched the bandage at his throat and carefully peeled it away. It stung but there was no foul odor or seepage. It was healing.

When David thought of John he saw an image in his brain of a twelve-year old boy. He shook his head. He wasn't sure what he'd been expecting.

No. He knew what he'd been expecting. He'd been expecting to see the boy who listened to his every word, copied his inflection, and loved him without condition or thought.

And that expectation had been misguided.

Sandra had told him as much. But he'd wanted to come so badly. He'd wanted to see John…and Sarah…so desperately, that he hadn't listened. Hadn't believed.

That was probably a mistake.

The fog was still dense but not as bad as the day before. As they rode, Mike kept an eye on the bushes that lined the verge of the woods for anything that moved. He didn't expect a wolf attack—they preferred to hunt at night—but they weren't the only threat.

Creatures did all kinds of things they didn't normally do when they were desperate.

The air was warm and the light seemed to be struggling to break through the mist.

He was grateful that Morgan didn't seem in a mood to talk. Likely he'd already heard all there was to know about David Woodson and who he really was.

Mike led the way down the long drive away from the castle. One side was hemmed by thick woods and the other by pastureland. Normally he wouldn't cross the pasture to where the planting fields were but with the damage done by the ash, what disturbance the two horses did would be negligible. If they could get the field cleaned up—even just a portion of it —they might be able to plant at least once more before the season was totally gone.

The thought buoyed him even as he picked his way through the field and saw how thick the ash was on the ground and how little his men had been able to clear.

Yesterday when Mike had come through here he'd been too upset to look for signs of Gavin—something he intended to do today. He knew the lad would have traveled this way although he was probably long gone by the time the ash started to fall. Gavin had said he wanted to try the woods around Foynes, thirty kilometers north.

It had been nearly four days since Gavin had headed out with Frank and Robbie. And in that time the ash had effectively covered all tracks and all signs of their passing.

An hour into their ride, Mike stopped to orient himself. He'd decided that the sound of the explosion had come from the southwest. Up to now they'd travelled through pastureland. Visibility increased as tattered wisps of fog parted the further they got from the castle.

Morgan should easily be able to make it back to the village once they finished their mission today.

If he had a mind to go.

Did the auld bastard think Mike wouldn't eventually throw him out?

"Are ye thinking it's past yon stand of beech trees?" Morgan pointed to the forest edge that loomed on the other side of the pasture.

"Aye. What do you think?"

Morgan shrugged. "Hard to tell. Sound carries and then pops up in places you'd never think. I reckon it's as good a place as any to start looking."

They turned their horses toward the forest. As soon as they entered the woods, the fog dissipated. The sound of their horses picking their way through the woods over roots and rotting logs competed with the sounds of startled shrews and voles bolting for their cozy burrows.

They rode alongside a bramble-choked gully bordered by a narrow path. The path quickly became too treacherous for riding as the open ground gave way to many large flat stones that were slick from the moss covering them. Mike held up his hand and they stopped.

They dismounted and led their horses through the woods until they found a new path. The way was boggy from the recent rain and the water squelched beneath their boots as they walked.

Irregularly shaped tree branches jutted out against the sky creating a disconcerting and haphazard pattern. A brisk breeze seemed to push them along, giving a chill to the summer day absent before they'd entered the woods.

They walked in single file. Mike scanned the darkest recesses of the woods for any sign of wolves—or human predators—but saw no movement.

Except for the field mice, there seemed to be no life in the woods to tempt a hungry hunter. At one point, Mike turned in the direction of where he imagined the castle to be. They'd been gone a little more than two hours. The explosion they'd heard had been loud enough to startle everyone in the castle but it was difficult to gauge how far the sound might have traveled. Especially muffled by the trees.

"Are we lost, squire?"

"No. Just listening."

Mike forced himself to look through the tree branches, squinting into the gloom for anything that looked like it didn't belong in the woods. He focused his mind and worked to keep the other thoughts away.

Thoughts of Sarah bent over David's hospital bed, her arms around him, her face near his.

Thoughts of David's arms wrapped around her waist. Holding her like he knew every inch of her. Holding her like it hadn't been six years since he'd last—

"Oy! Squire! Hold up!" Morgan called out. "Look! Through there! Do ye see it?"

Mike turned to where Morgan pointed. He wasn't sure what he was seeing. He shoved his reins into Morgan's hands and slid down the muddy embankment, grabbing saplings as he went to stay on his feet.

He hadn't taken three steps up the other side of the ravine before he knew they'd found it.

His heart pounded. It had been totally hidden except for the splash of red on the side which jumped out of the dense underbrush.

"Squire? Is it the plane?" Morgan called.

Mike stared at the wreckage and chills crawled up his arms in spite of the heat. It was broken in half—the tail nowhere to be seen—and the cockpit gone too.

Just a ragged chunk of metal torn into pieces. Its impact had created an elongated crater where it skid to its final resting place.

A fuselage.

With the words *USAF* visible on the side.

Susan Kiernan-Lewis

31

Mike sat on a log in a small clearing with a flask of Irish whisky in his hand while the horses grazed. After making a second complete circuit around the wreckage Morgan approached and Mike handed him the flask without speaking.

Five minutes after joining him with the horses, Morgan had spotted the dead pilot hanging in a tree thirty yards away. No parachute. He'd been ejected on impact.

"American," Morgan said shaking his head. "What do ye make of that?"

"It makes no sense," Mike said. "Are you sure it carried a bomb?"

"This one probably didn't," Morgan said. "Or there'd have been nothing left for us to find. I don't know what it was doing out here—maybe reconnaissance? But the equipment is definitely *capable* of carrying a bomb."

"So does this mean the Yanks are bombing the countryside?" Mike said in bewilderment. "What the hell sense does that make?"

"None, squire," Morgan said, handing the flask back to him. "None what so fecking ever."

Sarah hated that John wanted to do this.

She stood outside the clinic with him and Cassie while John spoke in a low voice to Cassie telling her how his father was going to love her. Cassie looked how Sarah felt: totally unconvinced.

When John first mentioned he wanted to introduce Cassie to David, Sarah had tried to talk him out of it.

Bad tactic.

John had immediately closed down discussion on the topic—and anything else between them.

In the old days, John and David had often aligned themselves on one side of the fence with Sarah on the other. They were both male and they both lived in a world of the mind that Sarah wasn't privy to. It wasn't uncommon for that bond to overstep into other areas leaving Sarah feeling left out and outvoted.

For the moment, because of the years he'd been gone, David was on the outside but with just the few conversations Sarah and John had had with David she could tell that wouldn't last long.

John was eager to regain the old connection. Set up the old alliances.

And for David's purposes of course that would suit him only too well. Sarah had no doubt that David would welcome Cassie into the family with open arms.

It reminded her of those times when she was forced into playing the bad cop while David spoiled John's appetite with ice cream in order to retain the title of the preferred parent.

"Ready?" John said to Cassie with a smile.

The girl dipped her head, but nodded.

John glanced over at Sarah and his face hardened. His message was unavoidable.

Don't spoil this.

Sister Alphonse got up and left the room when they came in.

John's eyes went first to his father sitting on the side of the bed. His bandage was off and the harsh red stripes on his throat were easily visible from the doorway. Cassie gasped and held back at the sight of him.

"It's all right, Cass," John said. "Come on."

Sarah brought up the rear. She watched as David's eyes went first to John, then her, and finally to the girl John was tugging by the arm. She saw a cloud pass across his face.

"Dad," John said, "I'd like you to meet my girlfriend, Cassidy Reardon. Cassie, this is my dad."

David's face cleared and he broke out into a wide smile.

"So this is Cassidy," he said. "Come closer. I won't bite. Promise."

John laughed and Cassidy edged closer.

She can't even look him in the eye, Sarah thought.

Sarah glanced at John so see if he was registering how abnormally his girlfriend was behaving, but he was beaming as Cassie stuck her hand out to shake hands with David.

"Pleased, I'm sure," she mumbled.

"Wow, you are certainly very pretty," David said. "I can see why my son is so crazy about you." He grinned at John who was smiling and watching Cassie. David's eyes flitted to Sarah and his face was pinched and cold.

In that moment, the years rolled away and disappeared. Their visual shorthand came roaring back as clearly as if they'd just used it yesterday. As if they'd never been parted.

David's eyes connected with Sarah and his silent message was as clear as if he'd shouted it.

Who the hell is this girl and what is she doing with our son?

Sarah felt a wave of relief that she hadn't been expecting. What a fool she'd been to think David would try to use Cassie to cater to John. When it came down to the things that really mattered—riding his bike without a helmet, or crossing the street unattended—David had always been an equal parenting partner with her.

What was best for John always came first.

And one thing was for sure.

That was not Cassidy Reardon.

Sarah was so startled to realize that she and David were on the same page, that she missed several seconds of attempted conversation among the three of them.

She'd been hit with a lightning bolt of a realization and she needed a minute to recover. Because the truth was as real as a slap in the face but she hadn't realized it until this moment.

And that truth was that no matter how much Mike loved John—and she had no doubt that he did—only John's real parent—only David—cared about him the way Sarah did.

It was hot in the late afternoon as Mike pulled the pilot's body down from the tree and searched him for identification. There was none. After going through the pilot's pockets, he cut the patch off of the man's uniform—a red and gold badge with the letters *MPC* stitched on it. He handed the patch to Morgan.

Mike went to his saddlebag and pulled out a retracted shovel.

He'd gone looking for a plane crash. He'd come prepared.

He was drenched in sweat by the time he and Morgan dragged the body to the shallow grave. After they'd filled it in, Mike rested long enough to drain the flask while Morgan explored the inside of the broken fuselage for anything useful that might be salvaged.

"It can't be a one off," Mike said as he stared at the red, white and blue letters of the US insignia on the side of the plane. "But who's the pilot?"

"He's not American," Morgan said. "Or at least his uniform isn't. Nor Irish either or British. But the fact that he's wearing a uniform at all means he belongs to a larger force." He examined the patch. It showed a mongoose and a snake. The letters *MPC* were wedged in the snake's mouth.

"One thing is certain, he wasn't some bloke out joyriding on his own bombing the shite out of Ireland for his health."

"So," Mike said carefully, "what we know now is that there's a force out there with connections to the US intent on bombing the Irish countryside. For some reason."

"That looks to be the size of it."

Mike stood and stared at the wreck. "And the plane was brought down by the ash, do ye imagine?"

"I'm no airplane mechanic but that would be my guess."

"Why the feck would they bomb the countryside?"

"We don't know for sure that that's all they were bombing," Morgan said ominously.

Suddenly Morgan snapped his head around as if he'd heard something behind him.

"Morgan?" Mike said, reaching for his handgun.

Morgan held up a hand for silence and reached for his own gun, his eyes squinting into the woods.

"We're not alone," he said in a low whisper.

Susan Kiernan-Lewis

32

They came at them with a roar that curdled Mike's blood. Half naked, their eyes crazed, they materialized out of the bushes. Three charged from his side flank, screaming, waving branches and knives.

Mike took aim on the biggest—and closest—but his arm was batted down, the gun wrenched from his hand. He felt the impact as two hit him at once. He fought to stay on his feet, grabbing the hair of the biggest bastard. The man screamed and Mike jerked his head back to snap his neck.

Morgan swung the butt of his gun into the side of Mike's face.

Mike spun around and fell heavily to the ground. All sound and motion stopped as he lay there, his face numb and yet on fire.

He saw their shoes as they stood around him. One man put a toe to Mike's head and pushed. Mike rolled over on his back and stared up at the canopy of trees overhead.

His head reverberated like a jackhammer on steroids.

Noises, voices came to him as the trees shimmied and spun.

He closed his eyes.

A man cheered. More men cheered.

"Hurt him bad?" a voice said.

"Still breathing," someone else said.

Mike opened his eyes and saw Morgan squatting beside him.

"How do ye feel, squire?" he said.

Mike blinked but his vision swam and darkened.

"See if he can sit up," another voice said.

Mike felt hands grab him and pull him up. His head pounded and he felt wetness dripping off his chin.

"Look out. He's going to heave," one of the men said, laughing.

Morgan's face swam in front of Mike.

"Nah, he's grand. Aren't ye, squire? Sure I didn't hit ye that hard, now did I?"

Mike licked his lips. He didn't dare look around or turn his head. He tried to focus on Morgan's face.

"Bastard," Mike said in a rasp.

"Nay, now don't be that way," Morgan said. "I could hardly let ye kill me own men, could I?"

More laughter floated up into Mike's consciousness as he fought to stay awake.

And then lost the fight.

"So he won't listen to you?" David said. "Well, there's your mistake. You should have let the relationship run its course. Now he'll hang on to the bitter end just to spite you."

After Cassie and John left the room, Sarah lingered in David's room. She needed an ally with the Cassidy problem. And whatever David was otherwise, she knew when it came to John's welfare, he would always be that.

"What was I supposed to do, David? Lie to him? He asked me why I didn't like her."

"Yes, Sarah. Lie to him. Is that a new concept for you? Can you see where your precious honesty has gotten us now?"

"It's not serious."

"Bullshit it's not serious! It's serious to him! Are you totally blind?"

"I just can't believe he'd choose someone like her. He's so grounded and astute in every other way."

"Oh, you can't believe he couldn't find a nice girl living in a commune in post-apocalyptic Ireland?"

"Look, David. I won't argue with you. I'll grant you it wasn't the best thing for John bringing him back. But neither was being separated from him. He'd already lost one parent."

"Oh, very good. Bulls eye, Sarah. You got me."

"Do you mind if we stop bickering for five minutes and talk about what to do?"

David let out a frustrated sigh.

"I'm not sure there's anything we can do. God! What does he see in her?"

Sarah narrowed her eyes. "You're afraid he won't want to leave her to come with you."

David didn't answer.

"And taking her with you isn't an option, am I right? Not to your magic island of superior intellect."

"Were you always this contemptuous of me? And I just missed it?"

"No, David," Sarah said heatedly. "I *loved* you. And then you left. And when you had the chance to come back to us— you didn't."

"And what if I had? At what point did I still have a window to come back? Three months? Six months? Or did Donovan start to *comfort* you right after I was taken?"

"No, David," Sarah said between her teeth, "because as I keep reminding you, I was busy fighting for my life in a human trafficking ring in London right after you were taken."

David looked uncomfortable.

"You know my people had nothing to do with that," he said.

"I don't know that at all, actually. The same people who took *you* took me."

"That's not true as I've said at least twice now. The people who took you were *hired*."

"What difference does it make? It was your people who set the whole catastrophe in motion. If they'd never come to our farm, I'd never have ended up in the back of a wagon on my way to England."

"Can we please stop? It was a disaster and badly done. I admit that. I was not told the truth about what happened to you and I can tell you there will be hell to pay when I get back."

Sarah turned away. Why was she arguing with him? What possible difference could it make now?

She stood at the open window and hugged her arms, her back to him.

Except she'd lost something with his coming back. Something precious and irretrievable.

She'd lost the memory of who he had been up until then. The memory she'd kept safe and pristine in her heart.

The David she remembered. The David she mourned. The David she'd loved.

That David was gone.

Because the real David wasn't a hero who died tragically.

The real David was a victim who'd survived—and then made the decision not to return to her.

Tears welled up in her eyes and Sarah wondered if John felt like this—cheated out of the memory of the man they had loved.

Or was he just so happy to have his father again it didn't matter to him?

David watched Sarah go to the window for the fourth time in twenty minutes.

She looked older of course. If wasn't just the extra years that had passed. It was the hardships she'd endured. The creases around her mouth, the sunbaked effects on her face of seven years spent out in the elements—cementing and hardening the lines that had only been hinted at before.

He turned to glance out the window. The fog wasn't nearly as bad as it had been yesterday. In fact, it showed definite signs of lifting. Even so, he was pretty sure Sarah couldn't see much of anything out there.

He watched her face as she stared out the window. She chewed her lip as if in thought but he'd known her long enough to know what that really meant.

She was worried.

She was looking for Donovan in the mist below. Even though any fool knew—and Sarah was no fool—that that was impossible.

And for a moment, for one intensely painful moment, David felt the full brunt of the dagger-sharp jealousy he'd hoped never to feel again. As he watched his wife looking out the window in hopes of catching a glimpse of the man she loved, it occurred to David in a roiling spasm of nausea that she'd never loved him like that.

The moment he realized it, all the pretense and the contention fell away.

Sarah was Donovan's now.

And David flat hated him for it.

The next time Mike opened his eyes, he could see Morgan squatting in a circle with several other men.

He knew immediately who they were. They were the men from the village of Kilbaha. He recognized one of the men from the fair.

And the fact that they were all out here in the woods also told Mike what had happened.

The village had been attacked.

He groaned and shifted in his position against the sycamore tree. He put a hand to his head and felt the soft folds of a t-shirt that had been tied around his face.

"He's awake, Artie," one of the men said, standing up.

Morgan came over to Mike. All laughter was gone now. Morgan's eyes were clouded with worry.

"Thor attacked the village two days ago," Morgan said without preamble. "Just as the ash was coming down."

Without waiting for Mike to answer, Morgan signaled for one of his men to bring the water canteen from Mike's horse. Morgan held it out to him.

"We need to go straight to the village from here," Morgan said.

Mike took the canteen and drank deeply. Afterward, he dropped it in the dirt beside him.

"Ye do know well ye bashed me in the head with a fecking tree branch, don't ye, ye fecking lunatic?"

"I'm sorry about that, squire," Morgan said patiently. "And it was just the butt of me gun. But I couldn't let ye kill me own men over a case of mistaken identity, now could I?"

Mike looked at the men standing behind Morgan. As terrifying as they'd been during the attack, now that he got a good look at them, they looked like accountants and mail carriers who'd had the bejesus scared out of them—who were starving and living in the woods—with no idea of how to survive or where to go from here.

Bugger me.

"They've managed to keep an eye on the village from a distance and while they can report it hasn't been torched neither have the buggers left," Morgan said.

"At the risk of being bashed in the head again for telling you something you don't want to hear—"

"Aw, now, Donovan," Morgan said. "I explained that and apologized too so we'll need to move past it, so we will, if we're to come up with a plan to help Kilbaha."

"Wasn't it yourself who told me these bastards are well-armed?" Mike said, unwinding the bloody t-shirt from his head.

"So they are," Morgan said. "Denny here said the blighters came into the place guns blazing. Killed two men—to show they meant business—and ran the rest of this lot out."

Mike struggled to stand and two of Morgan's men hurried to assist him up. Mike shrugged them off once he was on his feet.

"What did you have in mind?" Mike asked, his head pounding and the light leaching from the sky with every minute. "Is it ten bullets we have between us or eight? As I don't know what you have in your clip, you'll excuse me for asking."

Morgan glanced at his men who stood waiting for the two men to decide what they should do. His shoulders slumped at Mike's words.

"The bastard's taken me village, squire," he said in a low voice. "Ye can't expect me to do nothing."

"I expect ye not to be a damn eejit and walk in and get your head blown off—or ask me to do the same." Mike looked at one of the men. "You've been watching the place?"

The man called Denny nodded. "Aye."

"And?"

Denny shrugged. "It's been quiet."

"No screams?"

Denny's face flushed and he looked at the other men. "That doesn't mean they're having a fecking tea party in there," Denny said.

"I know, mate," Mike said. "But it sounds like we at least have time to come up with a plan." He turned to Morgan. "That okay with you, Mr. Morgan? If we come up with a plan instead of going off half-cocked and all of us going down in a blaze of bullets before nightfall?"

Morgan's jaw flinched with frustration and he looked in the direction of where his village lay. But he said nothing.

Mike looked at the men. His head throbbed but he raised his voice.

"Someone bring me my horse. We're going back to the castle. There we'll come up with something. Although God knows what." He turned to Morgan. "We'll think of something."

"Aye," Morgan said dejectedly.

Mary paused and slipped quietly into the arcading that led from the courtyard to the front of the castle. She held a basket of meat pies—likely the last of the season unless Gavin came back with game—and watched the gate tower where her husband spent nearly twelve hours of every day.

If it hadn't been for the fact that physical strength was needed to raise and lower the portcullis, and her Kev was one of the strongest in the castle, it would be a better job for anyone else. Mary knew for a fact that the real problem was having to endure hours of boredom on the off chance that they needed to get the door up in a hurry.

As usual, it was Mike who'd decided that Kevin should spend his days in the gate tower.

The gate tower, whose operator needed to be in constant close communication with the archers in case the worst happened.

The gate tower. Where Kevin and one of the archers had had sex—protected by the united confederation of the other archers.

And Mike Donovan too since nothing was done about the offense once it became publicly known.

Oh, Kev had been contrite. He'd said *sorry* a million times in that laughing, half-sincere way of his.

Eliza had encouraged Mary to forgive him and to forget about what happened. Forget Tilly who still openly flirted with Kev—and with just about every other male in the castle. Forget the humiliation and the broken trust.

It was Eliza who begged Mary to bring her man a surprise lunch in the middle of his day. *Try and make a little bit more of an effort*, Eliza had said.

Mary stood now in the arcading, hidden from view, her fingers tightening on the wicker handle of the picnic basket and watched her husband locked in a passionate embrace with the same little bitch he'd been caught with before.

Angry tears filled Mary's eyes and she watched her husband and Tilly. She was close enough to hear the girl's giggle and the thick burr of Kevin's voice—warm and inviting.

If she'd had less self-control, she would have approached the two and thrown every meat pie in her basket into their lying, laughing faces.

If she'd had less self-respect, she would go back to the room she shared with him and burn every piece of clothing he owned.

But she couldn't do any of that.

People counted on her. They expected her to do what was right.

She turned back toward the kitchen and took in a long, cleansing breath, erasing the image of Kevin and the archer from her mind.

She would rise above this. She would handle it with grace and bearing. Eliza would approve. Especially after Mary told her about what she'd seen today, Eliza would understand completely.

Mary entered through the archway that led to the grand dining hall and to the kitchen beyond. She straightened her shoulders and felt the burn of self-righteousness surge through her.

Tonight was the night everyone got a little justice.

And oh to be sure that would include Mike and Sarah Donovan too.

Susan Kiernan-Lewis

33

The fog had lifted.

Thor turned in bed and put a hand on Emma's hip beneath the duvet. He could see for himself out his window.

Today was the day.

He'd already planned out his moment of triumph in detail with Jocko. They'd line up in front of the castle, while keeping Emma and Rose safely back at the village with two good men. With the rocket launchers, Thor wouldn't need more than twenty men including himself. Just enough to provide the required show of force.

He swung his legs out of bed and rubbed the sleep from his face.

He could only imagine how the castle would respond. Either they'd be cocky enough to think they were safe inside —which would bring a different kind of amusement when Thor created his own personal entrance right through the middle of their drawbridge.

Or they'd be cowering in fear, wetting themselves at the sight of Thor and his gang.

Either way worked.

Emma groaned and turned away, still half asleep. He would let her have a lie-in. God knows she'd earned it. He knew this whole disaster with Rose was emotionally wearing on her. It would be best to get his part done with as soon as possible for Emma's sake.

He stood and pulled on his trousers, his mood rising with every moment that took him to the door. Soon, he'd be out of the village and on the way to the castle on the bluff by the sea.

There he would say the words he'd rehearsed for three long torturous days.

There he would demand they give up the bastard who'd befouled his precious Rose.

And no matter how they responded, there he would systematically destroy the castle and every single person in it.

By the time Mike, Morgan and the tattered, ragged band of village men made it back to the castle, Mike was exhausted, confused and discouraged.

Plus he had a terrible headache.

The expedition had focused his thoughts sufficiently such that he'd had little time to obsess about what was going on with Sarah and David. But even so it was always there at the fringes of his mind.

When Davey and Terry met them in the courtyard, Mike quickly introduced the village men and had them escorted to the bathhouse across from the nuns' quarters. He instructed Davey to tell his wife Liddy that there would be seven more for dinner and to ask Fiona to prepare bedrooms for the men.

He was relieved when Morgan opted to go with his men. Mike wanted to wash off the dust from the road himself and have at least a moment to try to put together what he'd learned from the day and what might possibly be a solution to the problem at Morgan's village.

As he trudged up the stairs to his bedroom, it occurred to him that he'd neglected to ask the village men not to mention the crashed American airplane. The people in the castle had enough on their plates without thinking the fecking Yanks were trying to bomb them too.

Upstairs he saw evidence that Sarah had not moved out of their rooms but whether that was because she expected *him* to, he didn't know. It was nearly dinnertime so he quickly washed and changed clothes.

On his way to the great hall he stopped at the clinic to pick up a couple of pain killers for the thundering in his skull. Stepping inside, he saw the clinic was empty except for Sister

Alphonse and Terry's youngest Darby who sat on the table with a trembling bottom lip and a skinned knee.

"Hello, boyo," Mike said cheerfully to the boy, his eyes scanning the room as if he expected Woodson to be hiding under one of the beds. "All on your own then?"

"My other patient felt well enough to go down to dinner," the Sister said. "Your good wife and John collected him not ten minutes ago."

Mike grunted as he dug out two aspirin from the medicine closet and waited for the nun to put a bandage on Darby's knee.

"Come on, lad," he said. "I hear there's corn on the menu tonight."

Darby jumped down and tapped his foot on the floor, testing the feel of the bandage on his leg. He looked up at Mike and grinned.

"Sure there's always corn," he said.

Mike walked into the great hall and immediately saw that Morgan had settled his men at the end of the archers' table. Three archers were at dinner tonight—all *Les Crème* archers —Briana, Nola and Tilly. As usual, they were only talking amongst themselves.

Darby ran to join his family and Mike walked to the head of the table. His seat was empty and Sophia, John and Cassidy were seated on each side.

Mike's glance went first to Sarah who sat next to Woodson—a good five seats away from where she normally sat. She sat with a straight back, her long hair pulled back in a single braid down her back. Her body was turned away from him and she was talking quietly to Woodson who was nodding and looking around the grand hall at the same time.

Mike could see Siobhan was seated with the other children as she often preferred. Tonight, he couldn't help but feel disappointed that she was not at his table.

Unless Sarah had insisted on it so as not to upset Woodson?

Mike forced the thought away.

"Up and about I see," Mike said gruffly to Woodson.

Woodson nodded and seemed to lean toward Sarah almost proprietarily.

"Healing nicely," Woodson said.

Mike tried to catch Sarah's eye but she was clearly working hard to make sure that didn't happen. Her cheeks were flushed pink.

Right. So that's how it is.

He turned to survey the long table of diners. It was a full house tonight, easily eighty in attendance.

"Oy!" he said loudly. Everyone stopped talking and looked in his direction. He saw Mary and Liddy, their hands full of trays of food, continue to hand out the meals.

"We have guests tonight as you'll have noticed," Mike said. He nodded his head in the direction of the men seated at the end of his table. "They're from Kilbaha and will be with us one night. I expect you to make them welcome. They've had some misfortune in the village that we are hoping to help them with. After dinner I need Mr. Morgan, Terry, Davey and John to meet with me in my den. If ye would be so kind."

"And my dad," John said. "He should be there too." John looked between his father and Mike.

Mike opened his mouth to speak when Sarah spoke up.

"I would like to be there, too," she said, looking at him for the first time, her eyes direct and challenging.

Bugger it. Whatever.

"Fine," Mike said and then sat down. No wine was in his glass and Mary had lately taken to serving his plate last so he stared at an empty setting.

"Does this misfortune in the village have anything to do with the explosion?" Kevin called out. "That *is* why you went out this morning, isn't it, governor?"

Mike stood back up.

"Right. The explosion—if that's what it was—was just one of the old villages burning. Probably a lightning strike. Nothing at-tall to do with us here at Henredon."

"That is a lie!" a shrill voice called out as Mike started to sit back down. He recognized the voice and faced it now, his expression one of annoyance and long-suffering.

Mary stood with both hands on her hips and faced the people seated in the dining hall.

"He's lying to us! It wasn't a burning village at-tall. It was an American bomber!"

A gasp erupted from the audience.

"He won't tell us the truth because he's protecting his Yank wife!" Mary said, approaching the head table.

"That's enough, Mary," Mike said firmly.

"Is that true?" one of the men asked. "Was it an American bomber you found?"

"The men from Kilbaha told Davey that it was!" Mary said. "So ask yourself why your so-called leader is lying to you about it."

Mike's face reddened as he held his hands up to the people, now talking loudly, their faces turned to him in building anger.

"Aye, she's right," Mike said. "There was no sense in worrying everybody until we—"

"No sense in telling us the truth, you mean!" Mary said. "Is that the kind of leader we want?"

"Sit down, Mary," Mike said gruffly. As soon as the words were out of his mouth, he was sorry for them.

"Cor, he's trying to shut her up! And her with the only truth that's been said tonight!" a woman called out.

"If we'll accept lies from the people who lead us, what else will we accept?" Mary said.

"He was only trying to protect us, Mary," Fiona said. Even Mike heard how lame the argument sounded. He wished she hadn't tried to help.

"*Protect us*?" Mary said, her voice strident and shrill. "By letting the archers get away with murder? By lying to us so we don't know what's going on? Is there anybody here who believes that rubbish about the village having a *misfortune*? Why are all their men here? And look at them! Their clothes are ripped, they haven't shaved. Davey said they'd been living in the woods! Why won't anyone tell us the truth?"

Mike looked helplessly around the room, his eyes landing on Morgan who just shook his head.

"Fine. You're right," Mike said. "Kilbaha was attacked by a group of thugs who are holding their women and children hostage."

Another louder gasp erupted from the group and some of the children started to cry.

Are ye happy now, Mary, Mike thought in mounting irritation.

"What can we do?" Liddy called out, her voice bordering on hysteria. "I don't want my Davey going out there to fight their battles! Is that why you're talking to them tonight?" She looked in horror at her husband, Davey, who just looked bewildered.

Mary strode to the front of the dining hall.

"I didn't want to have to do this," she said to everyone. "If Mike Donovan hadn't lied to us, I swore to myself that I wouldn't."

"What the feck are ye going on about, Mary?" Mike said, a vein pulsating in his temple.

She turned to him and glanced at Sarah before a look of triumph came over her.

"Sure I'm talking about the fact that our leader has been sleeping with the newest member of the castle."

An exclamation erupted from the crowd and Mary turned to Sarah.

"While it's true ye may not be Mrs. Donovan any more or Queen of the Castle, Sarah, I'll wager ye didn't know your man was bedding someone else."

"That's a lie," Sarah said, her face flushed pink.

"Is it now?" Mary turned to the audience. "Mrs. Bartlett? Would ye stand up, if ye please?"

Mike watched with astonishment as meek and shy Eliza Bartlett stood up, her head hanging in shame, her shoulders shaking.

"No way," Mike said under his breath. He looked around the room as if this must be a joke. Any moment now people would start laughing.

Nobody laughed.

"Go on, Eliza," Mary said. "you might as well tell the world. Is it the truth that you and Mike Donovan have been doing the dirty?"

A titter of nervous laughter rippled through the crowd and then was quiet.

Eliza lifted her head and looked directly at Mike, her expression apologetic.

"He knows it's true, sure he does."

"You have got to be shitting me," Mike said, his mouth hanging open. "Does anybody believe this shite?"

He resisted the urge to look at Sarah to see if by some horrible twist of the way his luck was going, she might think it could be true.

"I would like to nominate Terry Donaghue as our new leader!" Mary said. "A show of hands to all those who're with me."

No one raised a hand.

"You're barking, Mary," Mike said angrily. "And everyone here knows it. I don't know how you talked Mrs. Bartlett into telling such a lie but—"

"Oy! I slept with Himself, too," a young voice called out.

Mike started in disbelief as one of the archers, Kylie, stood up at the table and put her hands on her hips.

The crowd exclaimed loudly, the roar of their reaction swelling and falling. Mike felt lightheaded as he looked out at the crowd as individuals looked back at him with horror and disgust.

"Me too!" Another voice said, as Nola jumped to her feet to stand by Briana.

"And me," Tilly said, standing up too.

217

Susan Kiernan-Lewis

34

Sarah watched Mike toss down his napkin and go to face off with Mary who ran into the kitchen.

Everyone was speaking at once and the sheer noise of it caused the babies to respond in full throat. Nuala was already putting the little ones in carriers and pushcarts to remove them.

"Go help Nuala!" Sarah hissed at Cassidy who was watching all the activity as if it had nothing to do with her.

"Mom!" John said angrily. "Could you cut her some slack?"

Sarah jumped up to go herself but David grabbed her hand. She shook him off and went to where Nuala was trying to get two screaming toddlers in a single buggy. Sarah scooped up Siobhan in one arm and Ciara—although she was really too big to be carried—in the other.

"This is the last time I bring them to the hall," Nuala said between gritted teeth. The din of the outraged mostly female castle residents was nearly overwhelming. Sarah looked over her shoulder to see the three accusing archers, seated once more and laughing amongst themselves.

How in the world had Mary recruited them into her plan? Mary hates the archers and vice versa.

A needle of unease pierced Sarah's between the shoulder blades.

If Mary didn't put them up to it...?

"Oy, Sarah," Fiona said pulling Ciara out of her arms. "I'll take this monkey. Nuala, can you manage Bill?"

Bill was sitting in a carrier and was literally the only baby not crying or looking in anyway upset.

Boys, Sarah thought with chagrin. *They thrive on the chaos.*

Her eyes swept the dining hall as many people left their seats. Some had already gotten their dinners and were eating. The person Sarah was looking for sat cowering in her chair, her face down.

Still holding Siobhan, Sarah walked over to Eliza Bartlett and kicked her chair, causing the woman to jump and look up in alarm. When she saw Sarah, she bit her lip and looked away.

"So," Sarah said. "Sleeping with my husband, huh? Look at me when I'm talking to you, Eliza."

"I'm sorry, Sarah," Eliza whispered.

"Don't call me by my first name," Sarah said. "I'm Mrs. Donovan to you."

"Mommy mad?" Siobhan said, a worried expression on her face as she looked from Sarah to Eliza Bartlett.

"You might say that, Siobhan," Sarah said. "This bad woman says she stole something from me. You remember what I said about taking things that don't belong to you?"

Siobhan nodded, her wide gaze glued to the top of Eliza's bent head.

Sarah put Siobhan down and squatted next to Eliza's chair.

"What the hell did you think you were doing, Eliza?"

The woman closed her eyes and shook her head as if by doing so it might make Sarah go away.

"Oy! Sarah Donovan!" Mary said, charging toward her from the kitchen. "You leave her be!"

Sarah stood up and caught John's eye. She pointed to Siobhan and he headed toward her. She turned back to Mary.

"Payback, Mary?" Sarah said. "Are you feeling better now?"

"It's your own fault, so it is," Mary said breathlessly as she stood protectively by Eliza's chair. "This castle has had it with you and your husband kowtowing to those brazen young things."

John picked up Siobhan and walked away without a word. Sarah waited until he'd gone and then turned and slapped Mary soundly across the face.

Mary rocked back on her heels. A hand flew to her face where a red mark was forming. Eliza screamed and the surrounding diners went instantly quiet.

Mary straightened her apron, her eyes flashing with fury.

"Sure there'll be no punishment for you now, will there? Ye can slap and pummel anyone ye like with no consequence and we're all tired of it."

"Then why don't you leave?" Sarah said.

"That's your answer to everything!" Mary said, her fists bunched at her side. "'My way or the highway!' That's what every despot has said since Ivan the Terrible!"

"Glad you understand the concept," Sarah said heatedly. "If you don't like how things are here, you should definitely piss off."

"*Nobody* likes it and we're sick of taking it! Your husband favors his pets and it's bollocks for the rest of us!"

"It's true he weren't fair to my Jordie," Eliza said meekly.

Sarah turned on her. "Your Jordie was found stealing from the kitchen!"

"Even so," Eliza said, sniffling now, "he didn't treat him fair. Forcing Jordie to climb up there in all weather to serve those hussies."

"I can see you're unhappy about that, Eliza," Sarah said tartly. "So I'll be happy to make arrangements to have you and your son escorted back to the village you were rescued from."

"This is what we're talking about!" Mary said, looking around and speaking to everyone who could hear her. "She thinks she's God! Her and Himself!" She turned back to Sarah.

"You can't throw Eliza out! No more than you can throw me or anyone else here."

Sarah put her face near hers. "I wouldn't be so sure about that," she said menacingly.

What a bollocks.

Mike stood behind his desk in his den and waited for the men gathered there to settle down. He'd had a brief word with Morgan who understood and agreed with not having his own men present for the meeting. They'd need to get the castle men on board first. No sense adding more drama to the mix than was necessary.

Drama.

Dear God, he'd wanted to throttle Mary at dinner. What in the hell had gotten into her? And her husband Kevin sitting there—sure the total cause of all the aggro—not opening his mouth to say a word.

Mind you, Mike could well imagine that saying any word to Mary in her state could get more than a bloke's nose bit off. But if Kevin hadn't shagged one of the archer girls, they'd all have had their dinners in peace tonight without the background music of a dozen screaming infants.

He turned toward the door as Fiona came in with a tray of sandwiches and a bottle of Irish whiskey.

John sat next to his father across from Mike's desk, with Morgan to one side and Terry and Davey on the other. Kevin wasn't at the meeting. He wouldn't be going to the village with the rest of them. Mike needed him on the gate, not gallivanting across the countryside throwing rocks at a gang of thugs with automatic weapons.

Mike sighed. *How is it anyone still had any ammunition after all these years?*

Sarah hadn't joined them. At least not yet. As Mike had been leaving the dining hall, he saw her talking with Eliza Bartlett but the tenor of that conversation had been difficult to determine from where he stood.

Surely she doesn't believe it? How could she?

He ran a hand over his face. Anything was possible at this point. Sarah believing he could betray her like that—and with the lasses? She just might.

"Mike?" John said, looking at him questioningly.

Normally the lad called him 'Dad.' Not 'Da' as an Irish son would, but *Dad*. Stood to reason Mike would be demoted as soon as the lad's real father showed up. But reason didn't ease the blow. Reason didn't salve the punch to the gut after six years of loving the lad as his own.

"Right," he said briskly. "Thank ye, Fiona. The food is much appreciated."

"And the whiskey," Davey said with a grin as he poured six glasses and began handing them out.

"So I'll get to it," Mike said as Fiona slipped out the door. "I need volunteers to come with me in the morning to see the state of the village."

There was a brief silence. Then, John spoke.

"What do you think the state is?" he asked.

"The men you saw at dinner were thrown out of the village two days ago," Mike said. "Two of their number were killed in the process so we're not dealing with idle threats."

"A gang attacked the village?" Terry said, frowning.

"Aye," Morgan said. "He calls himself Thor. He goes from village to village—taking what he needs and then moving on."

"I hate to ask," Woodson said, the evidence of his healing wound stark against his white shirt. "But why couldn't you just wait for him to move on? Is he…interfering with the women?"

Morgan looked at Woodson as if he were a laboratory specimen.

"Sure I don't know how ye do things in America," he said, "but we don't roll over so easily in Ireland."

"My dad didn't mean it like that," John said, flushing. "I think it's a fair question."

"You're right," Morgan said to Woodson. "We've no reason to believe he's hurting our women and children. But no confidence he isn't. If it were your wife and young laddie there, could you just stand back and wait?"

Woodson blushed and looked down at his hands. "No," he said. "I guess not."

The sound of the door creaked open and Mike looked up to see Sarah enter the room. Again, she didn't look at him, just took a seat behind Terry.

"In any case," Mike said, "I've promised our help and I'm hoping you'll see your way to doing just that."

Morgan snorted but Mike didn't look at him. He well knew the old duffer thought he was weak. That was plain. In Morgan's world, he'd just order the men to go. And that would be the end of it.

Would Mike have done that if Mary hadn't given her fine performance tonight? Would he have just ordered them out there—armed with only bows and arrows that none of the men were any good at—and hope for the best?

Maybe. But tonight he wasn't up for it.

Or was he looking for a way out of his promise to Morgan?

That's probably exactly what Morgan thought.

"It will be dangerous, won't it?" Davie asked, smacking his lips on his glass of whiskey.

"Oh, aye," Mike said.

"It is what it is," Terry said. "There's women and children there." He looked at Morgan. "If we can't retake the village, we'll at least rescue your people."

"And bring them where? Here?" Davey asked.

"Why don't we deal with that after we've saved their lives?" Mike said bitingly. "If we're all in agreement, we'll head out in the morning at first light. The fog's lifted enough. Terry, do ye have enough extra bows to hand out tomorrow?"

Terry nodded. "Aye, and I've made a hundred more arrows. If any of us can pull a bow, we shouldn't be too bad."

Mike nodded. When no one spoke, Sarah cleared her throat.

"Yes, Sarah," Mike said. It was the first time he'd addressed her since he stormed out of Woodson's clinic room two days ago.

"The plane wreck you discovered," she said. "Was it an American pilot too?"

Mike sat on the edge of the desk and picked up his whiskey. He could feel the exhaustion of the day mingle with the throb in his head from where Morgan had hit him earlier.

"It didn't appear to be," he said. "He was wearing a different kind of uniform. None that any of us recognized."

"But even so, an American airplane doesn't make sense!" John said. "Why was it in the area? Was it the one responsible for the bombing we've been hearing?"

"That's all we can assume," Mike said.

"But what does it mean that it's American?" Terry said. "Does it mean the Yanks are bombing us? What in the world for?"

"Again. Great question," Mike said wearily. "And I haven't a baldy notion."

David turned to see Sarah in the back of the room. He smiled at her but she was intent on listening to what Donovan was saying about the American plane.

The evening had been very interesting all in all—especially the vote of no confidence at dinner that half the women in the castle seem ready to make against Donovan.

David bit back a grin and chided himself for enjoying Donovan's misery so much.

After all, this was a very serious meeting with a bunch of well-meaning and very serious citizens who all believed that they were somehow making decisions that would control their future. Perhaps even affect whether they all lived or died.

Smiling was not an appropriate response in such a meeting. Smiling might even look to them like he knew something.

It might look like he knew exactly what that American airplane was and precisely what its mission was.

Susan Kiernan-Lewis

35

After everyone left, Mike lingered in his den.

Sarah had been the first to bolt from the room. It was true she'd been sitting closest to the door but Mike had watched her wait in the hallway for David and John. She never looked in Mike's direction.

Not once.

He sat behind his desk and tried to push the events of the day out of his head.

His still slightly aching head.

An image of Mary storming over to him at dinnertime, her hands on her hips and fire in her eyes came to him and he rubbed his eyes as if he might physically be able to expunge the memory.

As big a pain in his arse as Mary had become to him—and especially tonight what with revealing the American bomber to everyone—it was the archer girls' accusations that bothered him the most. That didn't make any sense at all. Why would they back up Mary? Why would they come forward like that against him? In a lie? For what possible purpose?

Just to show the castle how little they respected him?

Maybe Mary was right.

Tender young egos be damned.

Maybe he should have come down on them like a ton of bricks at the first infraction. Would that have mattered?

You only needed to glance at Mr. Artemus Morgan to see his thoughts on the subject, Mike thought bitterly. It was pretty clear Morgan thought it was a damn miracle the castle was still standing under Mike's leadership.

He turned in his chair to glance at the bookcase behind him. He kept his fishing tackle box there. Inside were the handmade lures he'd made last winter when there were more days to sit and reflect than spring or summer allowed.

The ocean behind the castle didn't give up much in the way of fishing although they fished there anyway and were glad for whatever they caught. It was nothing like his days in Killmilloch. Endless days of dropping a line from his dinghy and bringing in bass and turbot by the boatful.

He tore his eyes away from the bookcase and memories of Killmilloch. He glanced back at the door where Sarah had slipped away.

Not a word, not a look. His *wife.*

Wasn't she?

He wondered if she was already in bed. He wondered what she had made of the evening. He wondered...

A light tap on the door broke his reverie and when he refocused, Sarah stood in the doorway as if she'd just materialized there. His heart soared at the sight of her. Her hair was pulled back away from her face and her eyes were determined and sharp.

"We need to talk," she said.

His heart sank.

"You can't have made up your mind so soon, lass," he said fiercely standing up.

She walked to where he stood at the desk.

"Don't be ridiculous," she said. "I was never struggling to make up my mind." She slipped into his arms and laid her cheek against his chest. "I'm sorry I made you think so."

"Oh, Sarah, lass..."

The relief was paramount. He felt a weightlessness in his whole body. He struggled to speak. Sarah pulled back to look into his eyes.

"It was the guilt," she said. "I didn't want to admit it. Not even to myself but David was right. I did want you before I lost him. I wanted you from the first moment I pulled a gun on you at Devon O'Shay's cottage."

Mike laughed in spite of himself.

"And David knew it," Sarah said with a sad smile. "Hell, *you* knew it. So when David was out of the picture—as much as losing him devastated me at the time—the truth was I got what I wanted." She cupped her hand to his cheek.

"And now he's back to expose the horrid, shallow truth of who I really am," she said.

"And yet you're here with me now anyway," Mike said softly, letting out a long breath.

"That's because I decided not to hate myself for feeling the most natural thing I've ever felt. Loving you. And I guess I've decided I don't care how it looks to the world."

"So...you're not thinking of going back to David?"

"I love you, Mike. But you're an idiot. No. *That* thought never crossed my mind."

The sensation of relief and joy radiated through him as he swung her around and held her tight.

"And will ye be sleeping in your own bed tonight, Sarah?"

"Only if you're in it, too."

The next day Mike woke to Sarah asleep in their bed and the sound of a hard rain pounding against the plastic on the window in their room. He got up to peer out.

"What is it?" Sarah mumbled sleepily. "What's happening?"

Mike came back to bed.

"Looks like our drinking water is being replenished," he said. "But it's lashing something brutal. We'll have to put off the trip to the village."

"Win-win," Sarah said with a yawn.

A tremendous crack of thunder made them both bolt into upright positions.

"Holy crap," Sarah whispered, her eyes wide as she looked in the direction of the window. "What kind of storm is this?"

Mike was already pulling on clothes.

It wasn't your typical summer rainstorm.

Of course not, Mike thought as he sloshed across the courtyard from the stable to the main dining hall.

No mere rainstorm would include hail, mixed with fog and bring down trees and damage rooftops.

He'd spent the morning putting the castle men to work trying to secure anything loose around the courtyard—but it was too late for the convent roof. Portions of that had already flung about the bailey like shrapnel terrifying the horses and forcing everyone inside.

A quick glance at the parapet revealed a reduced number of archers watching the front. Whoever had made the decision to cut ranks hadn't asked him first—a dangerous precedent—even though it made sense. What lunatic would think of attacking them in a cyclone?

Mike entered the dining hall to see Morgan already in intense conference with his men. Each of them had a mug of tea in front of them. Even as deep into the castle as they were, the sound of the wind battering the castle ramparts was pronounced and undeniable.

Mike walked over to the group and held up his hands before Morgan could speak.

"It won't be today, Mr. Morgan," Mike said. He fully expected an argument and he was ready for it.

"We understand, Donovan," Morgan said. "I was just talking to the lads. Likely the bastard will be holed up today himself."

Mike was surprised to see Morgan cave so easily.

Morgan continued. "My men were just telling me that Thor—for being a bastard—almost seemed like a reasonable sort in that he gave his word that none of our women would be hurt as long as the men left."

"What a prince," Mike said.

"Aye, well," Morgan said, "we still intend to cut his tongue out and hang his carcass for the buzzards before the end of the week but it does give us a bit of comfort even so."

"I'm glad we're all on the same page," Mike said.

"Aye. But as my lot aren't used to drinking tea with their boots on the table, may I offer their services today in helping to secure the castle against the storm?"

Mike looked at the village men with surprise. With his own manpower in the castle so severely limited, an extra set of strong backs and hands was an unexpected gift.

"I would be grateful," he said.

As he watched Morgan direct his men to the nunnery, Mike's attention was distracted by loud clanging sounds from the kitchen—almost as if someone were having a particularly nasty tantrum with the pots and pans.

Sarah had filled Mike in on her conversation with Mary and Eliza. He hadn't been surprised that Eliza was put up to it by Mary.

The archers were another matter.

He smiled at the thought of his wife—who showed him during their reunion last night that she was completely his in every sense there was. He promised her not to doubt her again —no matter what came or what it looked like. After last night, he couldn't imagine having any trouble honoring that promise.

As Morgan's men began to file out, Mike saw Kevin O'Malley dash into the dining hall to grab a stack of old towels by the door. He toweled off his hair and then draped the towel on his head ready to dash back outside when Mike hailed him—and put a hand on Morgan's arm to detain him.

"Oy, Kev!" Mike said.

Kevin looked up in surprised but when he saw Mike, he immediately stared down at his feet, his hands stuffed into his pocket, the very picture of guilt.

As well you might, you wanker, Mike thought, keeping his face impassive. *All of this mess is because of you not being able to keep your willy in your jeans.*

"I'll have a word with you, mate," Mike said. "And your good wife too."

Kevin nodded dejectedly.

"One hour. Right here," Mike said. "Have Mary here if you have to drag her."

"So I will," Kevin said and then turned and hurried out the door.

Mike turned to Morgan.

"I didn't have the opportunity to ask what you thought of our little dinner entertainment last night."

Morgan snorted.

"Sure you can't just let it go, squire. They're serious charges, so they are."

"I don't intend to."

"You know why Mrs. Bartlett said what she did," Morgan continued. "But what about the lasses?"

"Just what I was getting to," Mike said. "Did I see you talking with Regan this morning?"

Morgan shrugged. "I remind the lass of someone she used to know."

"That would be Archie. My ex father-in-law. I've marked the similarities myself."

"Us both being old and decrepit, ye mean?" Morgan said with a wry smile.

"Not at-all. But you've connected with Regan and that's not something most people ever manage."

"Regan wasn't one of the lasses last night."

"I know. But if she'll listen to you—even for a minute— it means the other lasses will too."

"You want me to question the lasses then?"

"That would be grand."

With the storm continuing to cause more damage by the minute, the hour passed quickly. The reserve water barrels were soon full and overflowing.

Morgan's men worked with the castle men to secure the livestock and make sure the more vulnerable members of the castle—the nuns and the women taking care of the children— had what they needed.

Twice Mike saw one of the village men on the stairway going up to the parapet to hand out food and protective gear to the archers.

He tried to remember the last time any of the castle population had climbed up there. He reflected that he'd accepted the shortage of manpower in the castle for so long that he'd stopped being aware of those things he'd given up.

There were seven men from the village. They'd been divided into four rooms.

Mike knew what he was sure Morgan had already noted: there was plenty of room for the men in the castle as well as their families.

The only possible concern now was Morgan.

Mike watched the man direct the men and he watched how they followed him without hesitation. Morgan was a natural leader.

Except Henredon already had a leader.

An hour later Mike dropped his dripping and soaked denim jacket in a pile on the stone pavers of the dining room entryway and grabbed a towel before entering. He dried his hair and left the towel draped around his shoulders.

Kevin and Mary sat at the table furthest from the door and closest to the kitchen.

A relatively meek Kevin was watching the door as if waiting for reinforcements. Mary had her arms crossed in front of her and her chin tilted stubbornly downward.

"Oy, governor!"

Mike turned to see Morgan entering the hallway but hesitate to enter the dining room. Mike was pretty sure the *governor* reference was at the very least meant ironically.

He nodded at Morgan. "What did you learn?"

Morgan shrugged. "It was a lark."

"Mary never spoke to them?" Mike asked.

"Nay. Briana stood up as a joke once she saw Eliza do it and the other two followed suit."

Mike snorted in frustration. "Just making mischief?"

"That's the size of it. They're nearly out of control, squire. You do know that, aye?"

Maybe I should let Mary take over after all.

Except if she tried to lead the archers they'd end up using her for target practice.

Mike thanked Morgan and walked over to where the O'Malleys waited.

"Sure you took your sweet time," Mary said sourly. "Is it today we were to meet or were you waiting for nicer weather?"

"Mary," Kevin said in a low voice.

"I'm glad you wanted to talk," Mary said. "Although I can see why you didn't want the rest of the castle involved. Your personal shenanigans—"

"You know that is rubbish," Mike said, toweling off his hair and not bothering to sit down.

"I must insist that you hand over the reins of leadership of Henredon to Terry Donaghue," Mary said stiffly.

Kevin groaned.

"Have you talked to Terry about this, Mary?" Mike asked. "Because he made it clear to me this morning that he's not interested in the job."

"Fine," she said. "Then Kevin."

"Mary, for Jaysus sakes," Kevin said. "What is the matter with you?"

"Then I'll do it!" Mary said, raising her voice. "I can't do a worse job!"

"I've listened to your nonsense and here's an end to it," Mike said. "It's all bollocks, as ye well know. I don't know how ye got poor Mrs. Bartlett to lie for you but ye did her no favors."

Mary sputtered and jumped to her feet but before she could speak, Mike turned to Kevin.

"Fix this between you and your Missus or I'll separate you. And if that doesn't work, you'll have to leave, Kev. As sure as I'm standing here I'll throw your arse out. So however you need to do it, *fix it*."

As Mike turned and walked away, Mary shrieked after him.

"You haven't heard the last of this, Mike Donovan! Not by a long chalk! You'll be sorry with your threats! I promise ye that! Do ye hear me? I'm not done yet!"

Susan Kiernan-Lewis

36

The rain was coming down in fecking buckets.

Thor sat at one of the pub tables, his men gathered around him. They'd gone through what poteen or plunk there was to drink in the first few hours of arriving at the village. But even with only tea it was still a decent place to spend an afternoon.

Especially one where it was pissing down so hard, that one step outside filled your shoes with mud and your shirt collar with a torrent.

If Thor had been a religious man, he might be tempted to see all these natural delays as a sign of some kind.

But God involving himself in what happened in Thor's life—or anyone else's for that matter—was bollocks.

Bad luck didn't know any religion. It just was.

The door to the pub opened tentatively and all heads turned toward it. The village women knew to stay hidden—until they were needed. Thor saw Rose stick her head in and look around until she saw him. Her eyes grew wide with alarm.

Now what was the little scamp up to?

She turned her head as if conferring with someone behind her and Thor was immediately on his feet. Unless it was her mother—whom he knew for a fact was taking a nap for a migraine—there was no one his daughter should be conferring with.

He opened the pub door wide to see one of the village girls standing next to Rose. She was plump and her hair was plastered down against her skull from the onslaught of the rain. She blushed furiously and her eyes darted around the interior of the room in fear.

"Hello, luv," Thor said to her. "Who do we have here then?"

"This is Betsy, Da," Rose said. "We just came in for a jug of water if there was any."

Thor yelled over his shoulder. "Jamie! Fetch me one of those water bottles, lad." He smiled at Betsy until Jamie appeared with the water.

"What are you two lasses up to today?" he asked easily.

"Nothing," Rose said. "We're just reading some books we found."

"Are ye now? That's grand." He handed the water to Betsy. "Go on and run along now, lass," he said to her. "I need to borrow me daughter just for the now."

Betsy took the water and fled out the door and down the street, running through puddles as she went.

"Why did you do that?" Rose said in a plaintive voice. "Betsy is my friend."

"She seems a nice lass, so she does," Thor said, nodding at Jamie. "Escort me daughter home, lad."

Thor patted Rose on the shoulder. "Don't see her again. Off ye go now."

He watched from the doorway as Jamie and Rose ran through the rain until they reached the front steps of the house where Thor was staying with Emma. He watched Jamie open the door and Rose quickly disappeared inside.

Thor sighed and went back to his table by the window where he could watch the rain streak down the broken glass in angry rivulets.

It was nice that Rose was able to make friends. She deserved to have a normal childhood..

He sighed and fought the resentment that was building in his chest at yet another fecking delay. If it wasn't so agonizing, it would be fecking hilarious.

Jamie came back in the pub and stamped the water from his shoes and whipped his hair around like a dog trying to wring itself dry.

The fact was, the burden of fatherhood was onerous and never ending. Keeping them fed and clothed, keeping them safe, punishing the guilty on their behalf. It was a full time job, so it was.

Betsy did seem like a nice lass, he mused as he watched the rain come down. But if the two of them got any closer Rose would only be all the more hurt were she to lose the lass.

There were more things to protect a child from than just wolves and hunger.

No sense getting attached.

The rain beat against the sheet of plastic covering the big window in Donovan's den. David had chosen the room to meet John because it was the only one that reminded him of life before the bomb dropped.

It also reminded him of his own office back in MPC. The first time he'd seen this room, he'd been surprised. Not because it was so luxuriously furnished when the rest of the castle was largely barebones, but because it was Donovan's.

From the few times David had interacted with him the man seemed barely literate. In fact, while John mentioned he frequently availed himself to most of the books in Donovan's room, he admitted he'd never seen his stepfather open a single tome that wasn't a how-to.

Stepfather.

David moved to sit behind the desk.

Everyone was so determined to treat his and Sarah's situation as something normal and sane.

Even though there'd been no divorce and no agreement between the two sides.

Maybe that's what it took nowadays to make things work: a dedicated commitment to ignoring the facts.

"You okay, Dad?"

David looked at John who had been browsing the bookshelves.

"Now that I've found you, I'm always okay," David said with a smile. "Are you sure they can spare you from whatever they're doing out there?" David gestured to the hallway.

"Oh, yeah. Nothing much to do until the rain lets up," John said with a shrug. "And the women will handle the kids and the food prep."

"You've turned into a sexist society," David stated. *That will have been Donovan's doing.*

John frowned. "You think so? I never thought about it like that. You know, because Mom's so tough."

"Yes, she is, isn't she?" *But she wasn't always like that.* In fact, the Sarah that David knew—and had known through ten years of marriage—that woman was nothing like the Sarah who lived at Henredon Castle.

"I don't think it's deliberate," John said, pulling a book off the shelf. "Plus you can hardly call it sexist when our whole defense mechanism is forty girls armed with bows and arrows."

"That is indeed interesting," David mused.

John shrugged. "Mike says we need the men for the heavy lifting."

"You have what, twenty men here? Shouldn't you all know how to defend the castle?"

"Is that how it is where you live?"

David had waited for John to make the first move before telling him about MPC. It had been hard but he needed his son's natural curiosity to help fuel his acceptance of what David would tell him.

Some of it was hard to hear—let alone accept.

"Everyone on the....island has a specific job to do," David said. "It's whatever they do best."

"I thought you said they were all geniuses."

"Well, I'm not sure I put it like that, but yes, the island comprises the finest minds we could gather—so far."

"So membership is still open?"

"Membership is definitely still open." David paused. "It's why I'm here, John."

John nodded and put the book down on the desk.

"I guessed as much," he said.

"Can I tell you about the work we're doing there?"

"Sure."

David went to sit on the edge of Donovan's desk. If John was going to be open to coming with him, it was vital that he understand the importance of their mission. There was plenty of time later to fill in the details. David needed to get him on board first.

"I told you that our goal is to save civilization," David said. "Everything we do is to that end. Everything. We believe that civilization is found and maintained in the art of the world and the great writings. To a certain extent it's found in the science and new technologies, too."

"I thought you liked science," John said, frowning.

"I do. I'm not talking about biology, physics and chemistry—those things are essential. We need to retain the understanding of them."

"I can't imagine how we could unlearn it," John said, shaking his head.

"Well, we can, John. And easily," David said urgently. "If someone—if *we*—don't preserve that information and it's lost—which it well could be with the coming world wars—then we'll have to start all over again. And sure, we'll probably have another Darwin or Isaac Newton or Stephen Hawking sometime in the future but it likely won't be in time for your grandchildren's grandchildren to benefit. Or at least, why take the chance?"

"So your group is saving all the knowledge we've already amassed," John said carefully, "so we don't have to re-do everything when the world blows up."

"It's not funny, John," David said earnestly. "And it's not just preserving the knowledge—it's gathering the right people together to help keep it that way for future generations."

"You mean like genetic cleansing?"

"I do not mean that at all. More like genetic selection."

"Explain the difference to me."

"The smartest people, the most able people, the strongest people—those are the ones who will rebuild this world when the time comes."

"What about blind people? Or dwarves? What about people who only want to have sex with their own gender? Do they not have a place on your island?"

David ran a hand through his hair.

"Look, John, I understand how seductive it is to say that we're all equal and that race doesn't matter, and education doesn't matter and handicap or sexual preference doesn't matter. But we're not living in a Disney movie. All those things do matter because they make a difference in forming the result of the people we become—and I'm talking about the human race now. Look, I know it's not socially acceptable to say it but it will always be the strong and the smartest who survive—who *should* survive. That's the painful truth and most people—if they're honest—already know it in their hearts."

"I guess I don't have to point out to you that that's not what you taught me when I was seven."

"The world has changed since then," David said. "I'd give anything if we still lived in that world."

"And you want me to come with you."

"I do, yes. You can offer so much. We need people like you."

"What about Mom? Is she not smart enough to make the cut?"

"Don't be flip, John. Your mother isn't interested in coming with us."

"Would I ever see her again?"

David caught himself. He didn't want to answer too quickly. He didn't want everything he said to the boy to be a lie.

"I'm not sure," he said finally.

The door to the den swung open and three little boys peered in.

"Oy, John!" one of them with his arm in a sling said. "You said you'd show us the castle's murder hole."

"It's still pissing down rain!" John said with a grin but he stood up. He looked at his father and his smile faded. "It's a lot to think about, Dad."

"I know, son. There's no hurry. Take your time. We'll talk again later."

David watched John as he joined the three youngsters in the hallway. They all clamored for John's attention as they disappeared noisily down the hall.

David went and picked up the book that John had pulled off the shelf. It was JRR Tolkien's *The Hobbit*. He sighed and sat down in the chair that John had vacated, his words still ringing in his head: *There's no hurry.*

David stood and rubbed his arms while looking around the room. He blew out an impatient breath.

The harsh fact was he had to get John out of the castle and soon.

David's injuries had been unplanned and had seriously affected his timeline. He was running late. Dangerously late.

The next MPC bomber was scheduled to make its final run in the area in two days time.

A final run that would include the destruction of Henredon Castle and everyone in it.

Susan Kiernan-Lewis

37

Jordie sat on the bench outside the barn and watched the rain come down, his wounded hand in his lap. He'd tried to help Mr. Donaghue sharpen some tools earlier that morning but after slicing off the top part of his thumb, Donaghue had sent him packing. Even Sister Alphonse was getting less sympathetic by the day. Today she rolled her eyes when she saw Jordie step into the clinic.

Wasn't there a rule about nuns being sarcastic to penitents? If there wasn't there bloody should be.

He watched as John stood talking with Cassidy. They stood under the overhang, protected from the rain which had slowed, and were surrounded by half a dozen small boys—each jumping at John's knees like he was David effing Beckham.

Twice Jordie had caught Cassie's glance over John's shoulder.

Jordie liked her. She was nice to him—a hell of a lot nicer than most people in the castle. Maybe that's because the castle people treated her the same way—like they barely tolerated her.

He felt a needle of guilt at the memory of the kiss he'd stolen from Cassidy in the barn yesterday. But why should he feel guilty? Jordie was only a mate of John's. If anyone should fee guilty, it was Cassie! Besides, he and Cassie were two of a kind. It might take John a while to see that but sooner or later he would.

You don't walk the ground like a rock star—which even seven year olds could see—and end up with the chorus girl.

Any mog knew that.

"Oy! Bartlett!"

Jordie jumped and hugged his bandaged hand to his chest as if the noise might somehow come with a jarring motion that would cause him pain.

Terry Donaghue approached holding the leads to four horses. They each pawed the cobblestones and shook their massive heads. Jordie scooted away from them on the bench.

"Yes sir?" Jordie said, his eyes warily watching the horses.

"Mind the horses as you're just sitting there doing nothing," Donaghue said, holding the lead ropes out for Jordie to take.

Jordie pulled away. "But they bite!" he said.

"They don't bite, ye daft bugger."

"Mr. O'Malley said the big one—Chompers—is named that for good reason."

Donahue laughed but kept his arm outstretched with the leads in them.

"Mr. O'Malley is just taking the piss," he said good-naturedly. "Chompers is called that because he's a big eater."

When Jordie still didn't move to take the lead ropes, Donaghue took a step closer to him.

"Now look, lad. I'll tell you straight out that there's been some talk already that you're not pulling your weight. If ye think ye can't be expelled from Henredon you'll need to think again. Do ye ken?"

Jordie's face whitened and he looked from Dongahue's very serious but kind face to the four beasts in front of him. He nodded and slowly stood up.

"Now the only way to stop being fearful of horses is to be around them," Donaghue said reasonably. "Spend some time every day with them—feeding them, grooming them, walking them." He held the leads back out to Jordie and this time Jordie took them.

Being bitten or trampled to death by horses was only a little better than the prospect of wandering the countryside throwing rocks at wolves and eating grass to survive.

Only a little better.

But better.

Besides, if the horses did manage to hurt him, he might end up in the clinic for days in a nice clean bed being hand fed by Sister and surely no one would look at him as if he were worthless then. Jordie stiffened his back and took two leads in each hand.

Donaghue clapped him on the back and walked back to the barn and his workshop.

One of the horses jerked his head up and eyed Jordie as if he just realized somebody he didn't know—or like—had taken his rein.

"Good horse," Jordie said, his voice shaking. "Good horse."

Over the backs of the beasts, he could see Cassie watching him. That gave him the confidence to stand a little taller. *Look at me*, he thought, *with four horses on a leash*! He glanced up at the parapet and wondered if Hannah was on duty and if she was, maybe she was looking at him too.

The horse nearest to him turned his rump sideways, raised his tail and made a steaming deposit on the cobblestones by the bench. Jordie held his arm out full length to remove himself from the pile.

"Hey, wanker!" a voice yelled out.

Jordie turned to see one of the men walking by with a ladder on his shoulder.

"Clean up that mess before someone steps in it!"

Jordie looked back at the mound of droppings. The horse had already walked through it and was tracking it on the cobblestones. The gentle rain was quickly turning it to a spreading liquid mud.

How was he supposed to hold onto the horses and clean that up? Did he use a shovel? Where would he even get one? He looked around the courtyard. It was enclosed. Couldn't he just drop the ropes and go find a shovel?

He tried to think what he should do when he spotted Mary O'Malley coming out of the castle with a large basket on her hip. She looked to be heading toward the nuns' quarters across the courtyard. Mum was always going on

about what a wonderful woman Mrs. O'Malley was but Jordie
thought she was angrier than Margaret Thatcher on Hormone
Replacement Therapy.

"Oy! Jordie!" Mrs. O'Malley stopped and frowned at
him.

"Yes?" he called back, attempting to look relaxed and in
control.

"Sure it's glad I am to see you helping out with the
horses. Your mother will be proud, so she will."

Jordie felt a flush of pride that trumped his fear of the
horses—which he had to admit had been fairly docile since
he'd taken control of them.

"Just doing my part," Jordie said casually.

"Would ye be so kind as to do your part out of the
courtyard?" Mrs. O'Malley said. "So the rest of us aren't
stepping in shite?"

Jordie's pleasure crumbled in embarrassment and he
hoped Cassie hadn't heard the old bag. He looked around the
courtyard again as if to try to figure where he might move
them that wouldn't be a problem to anyone. As if she could
see him doing it, Mrs. O'Malley spoke up again.

"Sure they've scraped off enough ash on the near pasture
outside the gate," she said as she turned away. "Take 'em out
there. They could use the grass and we can save the hay for
winter."

Jordie's heart hammered in his throat.

Did she really tell him to take the horses outside the
castle? Where the wolves were?

He looked up at the parapet again. Of course the archers
would be watching. It would be safe. *Wouldn't it?*

He moved the horses slowly toward the gate and was
surprised to see that the beasts came without argument. He
hesitated at the gate though. Surely this was far enough? He
was well away from the courtyard where people gathered and
walked.

As soon as the thought came to him, another of the
horses raised its tail. Jordie watched in defeat as it too made a
large pile on the walkway by the gate tower.

"You little wanker!" Mr. O'Malley shouted out as he leaned out of the gate tower window. "Are ye really leaving that for me to enjoy the whole rest of me shift? I'll tie yer guts in knots when I'm through here!"

"I'm...I'm sorry, Mr. O'Malley!" Jordie called. "I'll clean it up."

"Sure you'll *lick* it up, when I get a hold of you, so you will!" Mr. O'Malley said.

"I'm sorry," Jordie said, staring at the pile on the ground. "I was trying to get them out of the castle to—"

"Oy! You were leaving with them? Well, why didn't you say so? I'll be happy to ease ye on your way, so I will."

O'Malley disappeared inside the gate tower and Jordie watched the portcullis as it raised. A surge of relief ran through him.

There was something about the castle—and everyone in it who were all pretty sure he was the biggest loser ever—that made Jordie glad to be free of it if just for a few minutes.

And Mr. O'Malley didn't seem to be mad at him any more. In fact, he was laughing the whole time the drawbridge was coming down.

"Have a lovely time, boyo!" Mr. O'Malley said as the drawbridge thumped down heavily across the moat.

Jordie walked quickly across the drawbridge, pulling the four horses behind him. Something about doing it filled him with a feeling of strength and confidence. Wait until he told Hannah at dinner tonight that he'd taken four horses outside the castle to graze. But then, with any luck, she'll have seen him with her own eyes from the parapet.

Sarah wasn't surprised to see the small crowd of people in the dining hall. While the rain had eased considerably, it was still more pleasant inside and it was teatime. That meant different things to different people and while it meant virtually nothing to an American, Sarah knew it had a magical aspect to most Irish—even nowadays.

Mary and Liddy worked hard to create small moments of comfort in the castle dining and they often went beyond what was necessary for providing three meals a day. Today, they had several pots of hot tea on the tables and a tray of fresh-baked scones. Because it was summer they had plenty of jam and because they had a cow, they had fresh butter and clotted cream too.

Let the world blow up on itself, Sarah thought wryly, *but post-apocalyptic Ireland will still have its Devonshire tea, thank you very much.*

John and Cassidy sat at the end of one of the tables with a swarm of small boys. Sarah saw Nuala's two sons, Dennis and Damian, as well as Morgan's grandsons Matt and Mac. There was also Aedan—a bigger boy who'd come to live with them with his mother after the druids tried to kill them all but who was very sweet and a hard worker—and there was also Terry and Jill's boy Darby.

Cassie poured tea for the boys and handed out the scones while John spoke to them. From the way he was gesticulating and waving his hands, Sarah imagined he was telling a story. Each of the boys' faces was rapt in attention.

It was a warm scene and for a moment Sarah allowed her heart to soften toward Cassie. The girl seemed intent on making sure each of the boys had a scone and a cup of tea while John told his story.

Sarah begrudgingly had to admit they seemed to make a good team—at least at the moment.

Sophia came through the door with her baby Maggie in her arms and stood next to Sarah. Sophia looked tired but Sarah recognized the look. Sophia was worried, stripped of almost any other emotion except the need to take care of her baby and pray that Gavin was safe somewhere—and would return.

How well Sarah knew that feeling.

"You could use a cup of tea," Sarah said to her.

Sophia shook her head. "Gavin loves tea," she said. "But I can't get used to it."

"If you get in the habit, it can be very comforting."

"Getting my husband back is the only comfort I want."

"He'll be back."

"The ash has stopped. The fog is gone. Even the rain is stopping."

"He'll be back, Sophia. Have faith."

"That's all I can do," Sophia said wearily as she moved into the dining hall. Sarah spotted Fiona at one of the far tables. She had Bill with her and Sophia made her way toward them.

Mike was probably in the barn or in his den. When it rained like it had today there wasn't much point in being outside. She felt a flush of pleasure when she thought of their night together. Whatever doubts or guilt she'd allowed herself to feel up to that point with David's coming to the castle had been chased away. The strength and fortitude that she always found in Mike's arms was there for her last night.

She'd been a fool to wait so long before turning to him.

The sound of a dish breaking startled Sarah and she turned her focus to the group of little boys. Suddenly, Cassie jumped up and shrieked. The boy nearest her—Damian—shrank away from her as she beat at the front of her shirt with her hands.

"You fecking sod!" she screamed.

"Come on, Cass," John said cajolingly. "It was an accident."

"Little beast!" Cassie said and turned on Damian. In a flash, she'd slapped him across the face, knocking him off his chair.

Sarah was at the table in a flash but John was faster. He stood between Cassie and Damian who was now on the floor with tears running down his little boy cheeks.

"Get a hold of yourself!" John shouted at Cassie, his eyes blazing with fury.

"That little shite spilled his tea on me!" Cassie said, but Sarah could see Cassie was realizing what she'd done.

John turned and knelt by Damian.

"Hey, sport, you okay?" John said. He glanced up at Sarah as if to say, *It's handled. Back off.*

Damian nodded and John helped him to his feet as Cassie turned and fled the hall, bumping into Kevin O'Malley as he entered.

"Whoa, lass!" Kevin said with a laugh. "Did I miss the drama?" he said as he came to the table. The little boys stared at Damian who wiped away his tears.

"Nothing to see here," John said brusquely. "Just doing some storytelling. Aren't we, guys?"

The little boys nodded, their eyes wide with what had just happened.

Yes, it's handled, Sarah thought with satisfaction. *You've seen firsthand what she's made of. Thank you, Cassie.*

Kevin tousled the heads of Matt and Mac and sat at their table.

"Stories, is it?" he said. "Any I've heard of?"

Sarah glanced around the room to see if there was anyone Kevin might be showing off for. Mike had briefed her on his meeting with Kevin and Mary earlier that day and for someone who'd been warned he might be flung out of the castle, Kevin seemed pretty pleased with himself.

"I'm paraphrasing one of the Indiana Jones movies," John said, sitting back down. "Since those are about the only movies I remember."

"Cor! I loved that bloke!" Kevin said. "Too right. Did you get to the part about the snakes?"

The little boys looked at John with even bigger eyes.

"Not yet," John said. "Hey, have you seen Jordie today? I heard he hurt his hand in the workshop and was wondering what he was up to."

Kevin threw his head back and laughed. "Speaking of great stories," he said. "That one's a good one."

John frowned. "Meaning?"

"The daft bugger decided to take four horses out to the front pasture to let 'em stretch their legs."

John stood up and looked at the doorway.

"Four?" he said. "But there's no fence around that pasture. And he doesn't know how to hobble them." He turned and looked at Kevin. "How was he leading them?"

"*Very* carefully!" Kevin laughed.

The rain had started to fall steadily again as Jordie led the horses to the first patch of green he saw in the pasture where the ash had been scraped off. It had been reasonable to assume the animals would focus their attention on the grass.

But they didn't.

As soon as they were in the pasture, each of the horses began to move in opposite directions. It was all Jordie could do to run after one, tug it back in another direction before he was pulled along by another.

And all the while the rain came down. It came down his shirt collar like cold needles. It flattened his hair and filled his eyes and ears.

A sudden sound—heard only by all four horses—made them react as one. Jordie felt the tension in both arms as the leads he held were jerked taut. It was as if he could feel the horses' fear race right through his arm and up into his pounding heart.

He turned to look up at the parapet. The girls were there —he could see their forms outlined against the grey sky—but at this distance he couldn't see who.

One of the horses bolted first, snatching his head and swiveling his hind legs into the dirt, creating small divots as the animal pivoted away from the others. He wrenched his lead rope from Jordie's hand.

Jordie turned to see what had startled the beast when the others whinnied loudly and yanked their leads away too. The sound of the first arrow whizzed past his ear and thumped into the earth by him just as one of the horses—the big one that belonged to Donovan—barreled past Jordie, knocking him to the ground.

Are the crazy bitches shooting at the fecking horses?

Jordie frantically scrambled to his feet before they shot him too.

"Oy! It's me! Can't you see me? It's Jordie! Hannah!"

253

Another arrow. Even in the rain, he could hear it singing through the air. Close.

The scream that followed turned Jordie's bowels to water. A yelp like a dog who'd had its tail stepped on.

But worse. So much worse.

Jordie turned to run back to the drawbridge, his breath robbed from him, his heart ricocheting in his chest. He tripped over something wide and large. Coming down hard into the dirt, the ground rushing up to slam into his face.

The smell of the wolf—still alive and writhing—was in Jordie's face as the sounds of the horses' hooves thundered away in the distance.

38

The whole castle was in an uproar.

Naturally, there couldn't be a single afternoon without something going majorly arsewise, Mike thought as he stormed up the stone steps from the dungeon.

Artemus Morgan and his men lined up in the outer courtyard. The rain had stopped but it was evening now. *Surely the auld bugger didn't expect them to go tonight?*

"In the morning, Mr. Morgan," Mike said as he passed the older man. "Have your men ready at first light again."

"Might I make a suggestion, squire?" Morgan said as he turned to trot alongside Mike, wheezing as he struggled to keep pace with him.

Mike slowed and then stopped, his hands on his hips. The rest of the castle was waiting for him in the dining hall. He could take a breath before facing them.

"Let's hear it," Mike said.

"Public flogging for the both of them," Morgan said, jerking his head in the direction of the dungeon where Mike had flung both Jordie and Kevin.

Mike sighed and was about to turn away when Morgan grabbed his sleeve.

"That way ye don't have a goodly percentage of the castle's manpower loitering in a cell instead of working. I understand you were leaving O'Malley behind tomorrow in any event but at least he could be doing his job."

"Thank you for your input," Mike said tersely.

He nodded at the village men who watched him with calculating eyes as he pushed past them and into the dining hall. Once inside he was gratified to see that there was only a small knot of people waiting for him. His eyes went to Sarah and she nodded. *That would be her doing*, he thought. She'd made sure everyone else had their dinner and went back to their quarters.

Thank you, lass, he thought as he walked into the hall, Morgan and his men close behind.

Eliza Bartlett leapt up from one of the near tables and clutched his arm.

"Mr. Donovan," she wept, "I'm begging you! Please! He was just trying to help!"

Mike shook her off but she'd unnerved him, even so. Crying women always did.

"Take a seat, Mrs. Bartlett," he said gruffly.

Sarah moved to touch the woman's elbow to lead her away but Eliza jerked her arm from Sarah.

"Mary's right!" Eliza snarled. "This is payback for what happened yesterday. My Jordie is being punished to get back at me for what I did."

"Ye'll calm yourself or I'll have ye removed," Mike said to her. "I'll not countenance screaming so make up your mind." Without waiting to hear her answer, he turned to the rest of the gathered group.

Mary sat at the table beside her sister Liddy who had one arm around her. Kevin's brother Davey sat at the same table but his eyes were hooded and unreadable. Terry, John, Tommy, David Woodson and at least half of the castle men were also in attendance.

"We're here first to discuss the loss of the horses," Mike said evenly. "And what's to be done about it."

"I'll go out first thing in the morning," John said, "to track them down."

Mike nodded but his eye caught Sarah's. She wouldn't love the idea of John out there on his own but Mike would give him the gun at least. And it beat trying to rescue the village armed only with rocks.

"The wolves will get them, that's sure," Davey said.

"Not necessarily," David Woodson said. "Horses are flight animals. They're used to running from predators."

"What about our men?" Mary said loudly. "The ones you have locked up in the dungeon!"

"They're not going anywhere tonight," Mike said firmly. "The loss of the horses is a significant one and both Jordie and Kevin share equally in that crime."

"My Kevin only opened the gate like he was told to do!" Mary said.

"If it's true what you say, Mary," Mike said evenly, "and Kevin is that big of an idiot not to know that opening the gate to someone as green as Jordie—leading every horse we have in the castle—if that is true, he'll be expelled in the morning as we can't survive long depending on people that stupid."

Mary flushed. "But Jordie is the one who sashayed outside with them! If you want to point fingers for stupidity."

"You bitch!" Eliza screamed at Mary.

"Shut up," Mike said to her. He looked at Mary. "Jordie isn't stupid or mean-spirited. He's green, that's all. Your husband took advantage of that greenness. If anyone's to be punished for this it'll be Kevin O'Malley—who knew exactly what he was doing—not Jordie who didn't."

Mike glanced at Eliza who flushed and dabbed the tears from her face. She looked at Mike gratefully.

"So they stay put for tonight. John goes out in the morning—with Tommy—to see if they can find the horses— whatever's left of them. Davey, I'll ask you to take your brother's post on the gate in the meantime."

Davey nodded solemnly.

"That's all there is to discuss," Mike said. "The men who've volunteered to come with me to Kilbaha tomorrow, we'll leave at first light tomorrow. On foot."

Morgan stood up and faced the group as they were about to break up.

"I just want to thank everyone for their hospitality," he said. "To me and me grandsons and on behalf of the men of Kilbaha. The people of Henredon are true friends to Kilbaha and we won't forget it." He turned and shook hands with Mike and then led his men out of the room and to their quarters for the night.

Sarah came over to stand next to Mike as the others in the room filed out.

Woodson was the last one to leave and he hesitated. John turned and saw him but Woodson motioned for him to go on and he'd catch up. John glanced briefly at his mother and then left.

"I'd like a word, Donovan," Woodson said.

Mike noticed Woodson deliberately didn't look at Sarah. Without thinking about it beforehand or knowing he was about to do it, Mike turned to Sarah and patted her on the bottom.

"All right, lass," he said. "Off you go then. I'll see you upstairs."

Sarah froze when he did it but smiled graciously, if somewhat woodenly, at him.

"Of course, darling," she said, her voice light. But her eyes said something else. She turned and walked out of the room without saying another word.

Mike had done it for Woodson's benefit of course. Because sometimes words just weren't enough to communicate a man's meaning.

Of course, later when they were alone he was pretty sure Sarah was going to kill him.

He faced Woodson. At six foot four, Mike towered over most men. He had the advantage of height tonight.

And a little bit more.

"I should have spoken to you first," Woodson said dryly, almost sarcastically, as if to say that Mike was playacting as leader and he, Woodson, knew it.

"We've nothing to say to each other," Mike said.

"You heard how it is I came to be here?"

"I did."

"And what happened that day in Seamus and Deirdre's pasture?"

"Aye," Mike said impatiently.

"Don't you believe me, Donovan?"

"Does it matter? You're not staying."

"What makes you say that? Am I not welcome to stay?"

But Mike didn't answer. Whatever message the bastard wanted to deliver, he clearly wouldn't be hurried.

Woodson licked his lips and looked in the direction of the door where Sarah had just exited.

"I thought we had an understanding," Woodson said. "I guess it's possible that Sarah is just helpless against your charms. In that case, I'll appeal to you."

Although he smiled as he did it, Woodson tapped Mike on the chest with his forefinger.

"Until we get this all straightened out," he said. "I'd appreciate it if you didn't sleep. With. My. Wife. Is that too much to ask?"

"She's not your wife anymore."

"I don't remember getting a divorce."

"It was more like a death certificate but just as effective."

"Look, I'm trying to be nice here but trust me I have other ways of convincing you to behave like a civilized adult and not the rutting Irish you seem determined to devolve into."

"Well put, Woodson," Mike said, smiling for the first time since they started talking. "But I'll satisfy me own wife to the tune of a headboard banging that can be heard throughout the castle if I've a mind to and if ye don't like it, well, feel free to crawl back into the nearest bush—preferably on the outside of the castle."

"What's going on?" John stood in the doorway of the dining hall. "Dad? Everything okay?"

"Not really, son," David said, his eyes on Mike and blazing with hatred. "And it won't be okay until your mother stops punishing me for a crime I had no control over."

John looked at Mike, his eyes unreadable. Then without a word he turned and left the room.

"When did ye say you were leaving?" Mike asked.

"Why would I leave? I am just getting started."

Sarah was coming down the stone staircase to ask Sophia for another block of perfumed soap when she saw John leave the dining room. His face was flushed and contorted in an angry grimace.

"John?" she called. "What's wrong?"

He turned on her in the hallway, his eyes snapping with fury.

"What is the matter with *you*?" he exploded. "You can see how hard this is on Dad! What is your problem?"

Sarah swallowed and fingered the wedding ring on her hand. John had never raised his voice to her. He'd never given her anything close to the look he was giving her now—defiant and full of reckless anger.

Sarah wasn't sure what had happened in the dining hall or what John had heard or witnessed. Everything about her relationship with her son these days was a virtual powder keg.

Ever since David had shown back up.

With David lobbying hard to seduce John to his side of things, she knew that emotion held no real merit. She reached out to touch John's arm but he jerked it out of reach.

But when a loved one comes back from the dead, emotion is about the only thing to work with.

She hugged her arms and chose her words carefully.

"Sweetheart, I know this must be confusing for you," she said.

"No, Mom," John said, shaking his head, the fury evident in the pulsating vein in his temple. "I'm not confused. It's really simple. You thought Dad was dead. He's not. You're married to *Dad*."

Sarah took in a breath and wiped her now damp palms against her pants.

"No, John. I'm not," she said gently. "Not any more. And I can see without a paper showing that I legally divorced your father or separated from him—"

"But you didn't do any of those things!"

"But I did in my heart, John! Your dad was gone and I moved on. I'm not going back. I am where I want to be. If that terrible day in the pasture hadn't happened I would have stayed married and probably even happily if—"

"You mean you wouldn't have lusted after Mike the whole time?"

"Again, I can see you're upset. But the bottom line is I'm married to Mike now. That's the start and the end of it. Your Dad…I'm so glad we met because we made you and—"

"Oh, *please*," John said in disgust.

"And whether it was death or divorce or misadventure or abduction by aliens, your father ended up being my first husband. If I could legally divorce him and remarry Mike, I would."

"This is exactly what Dad said was the biggest worry about everything that's happening," John said fiercely. "We start to throw away the trappings of civilization—like bothering to get a divorce or honoring our vows—because it's too much trouble nowadays and the next thing you know we don't have a civilization any more."

"The world we live in now doesn't allow the possibility to obtain a divorce, John. You know that. It's just not possible."

"Hey, I get it, Mom," John said turning from her to walk away.

"You don't," Sarah said, calling after him. "And that breaks my heart but maybe there was no good way for all this to unravel."

"You mean Dad not being conveniently dead?" John said over his shoulder.

"That's not what I meant and I'm pretty sure you know it."

"Well, you going back to Dad and honoring the commitment you made to him would be a good way for 'all this' to unravel." John disappeared into the night and was gone.

Sarah stood in the cold hallway, listening to the sounds of Mike and David talking in the dining room and she felt the cool breeze of a summer night after a long rain. She shivered.

"I'm sorry, sweetie," she whispered. "It's too late for that."

Susan Kiernan-Lewis

39

That night after sufficiently yanking Donovan's chain, David returned to his bedroom. It was true the rain had stopped but the dampness remained in the air, in the fabric of the drapes that hung at his window overlooking the western pastures and in the very clothes he wore.

It had been so long since David had lived with this kind of primitive infrastructure. It amazed him how quickly he'd re-adapted to it after six years of fresh perked coffee, Internet access and hot showers.

Kind of like camping out, he thought ruefully. *Especially when you know you don't have to stay here and slog it out on a permanent basis.*

He pulled the heavy brocade drape back from his window but it was too dark to see anything in the moonless night. He felt the tension slowly ratchet up into his gut.

He'd have to get John out of the castle tomorrow.

At the latest.

He found himself grateful that Sarah didn't seem to be trying to influence the boy's decision. No doubt that was the result of her guilt over bringing him back to Ireland for her own selfish reasons.

He'd done his best to hammer home that point every chance he got. It seemed to be working.

One thing he could never fault Sarah for was her love for John. Whatever else was going on with her, she was a mother first and foremost.

He licked his lips at the thought of leaving her here tomorrow. But he couldn't bring her. Not after everything that had happened with her and Donovan. And then there was the kid. There was no way Sarah leave her daughter.

No, it had to be this way. It was just one more devastatingly painful, sad compromise in a lifetime of painful and sad compromises.

Sarah had been a good mother to John. And a good wife, too.

David shook the thoughts away. No point in going there. No damn point at all. The job ahead of him was to get John away safely. That was enough of a mission without getting sidetracked with sentimental history.

He was pretty sure one more heart-to-heart with the boy would have John seeing things his way. He was almost there. David could see that. Just a little bit more and he'd have him.

No, the only real impasse David could see to John leaving with him tomorrow was a seventeen year old blonde.

Cassie.

A tap at the door brought David out of his thoughts. "It's open," he called.

John poked his head in. "You still awake?"

David turned toward him and motioned toward the free chair in the room.

"I was hoping you'd stop by," David said.

"Yeah, well, I didn't want you to think I was mad at you earlier when I came into the dining room." John sat in the chair and brushed his long hair back with an impatient hand. David remembered that gesture from when he was a small boy and a knife twisted in his heart at the sight.

"It's a difficult situation," David said. "Especially if you do decide to leave and come back with me."

John nodded and then stood up as if he had too much energy to remain seated.

"That's one of the things I wanted to ask you, Dad," he said. "This Island or whatever it is…you say Mom doesn't want to come but you didn't say whether she'd be allowed to if she wanted to."

David looked at John helplessly. "I…I don't really…"

"Because if Mom's not smart enough to go there, how are they going to feel about Cassie coming?"

David wasn't sure why he was surprised that John got right to the heart of things. Naturally he would. The thought of leaving his mother was bad enough but the boy was in love. Right now, settling the question of Cassie was easily more important to John than figuring out how to provide uncontaminated water for a post-apocalyptic world.

"I'm pretty sure Cassie wouldn't like it where we're going," David said carefully.

"She will if she's with me," John said.

"Look, John. Cassie can't come with us. I'm sorry. It's best for everyone this way."

"Why? Because she's not smart enough?" John said hotly. "People don't give her enough credit."

"No, it's because she's not the one for you, John."

John looked at him and spoke in a soft, halting voice. "You sound like Mom."

"Well, when it comes to you and what's best for you, that's not surprising, is it? Or did you think my mission to save civilization was exclusive from my responsibilities as a father?"

"You haven't given Cassie a chance. You don't even know her."

"I know all I need to know. She's not right for you."

"Well, I won't go unless she comes too," John said, crossing his arms. "Is that a deal breaker for you? Cassie coming?"

David stared at him and felt a heaviness sift through his chest and limbs.

"No," he said finally. "It's not a deal breaker. If you insist on her coming, then of course she'll have to come."

The tension in John's shoulders seemed to unkink right before David's eyes.

That's all that mattered. That John was willing to return with him. Everything else could be dealt with in due time.

"I'll have to talk to Mike," John said. "And Mom too. I'd need to be able to come back from time to time. That's a given. Plus if I were to leave, it would make a difference in the castle. We don't have many men and it'll be a hardship for them. I have to take that into consideration."

"I imagine you call him 'Dad,' don't you? I suppose you would. I left when you were very young."

"He's been good to me, Dad. He's cared for me and loved me like a son."

"Except you're not his son."

"I know, but with you gone, I was glad to have him."

David tried to force his feelings of jealousy away. John was coming with him. That was all that mattered. He needed not to spoil it with hopeless longing for what he could never have—all the lost years.

"Forgive me, John," he said. "I must sound like the ultimate ingrate. I'm glad you had someone to lean on in my absence."

David stood and went to the dresser where one of the castle women had left a couple of glasses and a small half bottle of brandy. He poured two glasses and handed one to John.

"You're all grown up now," David said wistfully as he watched John drink the brandy. "Can you tell me what I missed? After I…left?"

"Well, let's see, I killed my first man when I was thirteen," John said baldly. "He didn't know I was armed. I never gave him a chance. Just shot him in the face and then went back inside the house and went to sleep."

David sat down on the bed and gripped his glass tightly. The image of the young boy he'd left, wide eyed and sweet-faced—holding a gun and firing it into a man—pierced his gut with bitterness.

"You did what you had to," he said softly.

"I was *thirteen*, Dad. And I was on my own. Alone. In Wales."

"Wales? What were you doing there?"

"I'm surprised Dr. Lynch didn't tell you. I'd gone looking for Gavin."

"Donovan's son?"

John gave him a strange look. "My *brother*," he said.

"Of course. Go on."

"I had reason to think he'd gone to Wales so that's where I went."

"When was this?"

"The plague had just shut down Ireland's borders."

David nodded as he put the timeline together.

"How did you get across the Irish Sea?" he asked.

John shrugged. "I did what I had to do. Pretty much standard operating procedure since that first night in the holiday rental cottage all those years ago when the lights went out. Remember?"

David's eyes filled with tears and he set his drink down, overcome with emotion. He couldn't look at his son. After a moment, David said in a hoarse voice, "I thought I'd never see you again."

John stiffened. "At least you knew I was alive. I *mourned* you, Dad."

David looked into John's eyes. "I know you did. And it killed me to know it."

"You couldn't try to get word to me? To us? I don't know what you think happened with Mom and Mike but she was *devastated* when you died."

"She recovered well."

John put his empty brandy glass down on the bedside table and stood up.

"The last thing you should do is fault anyone for trying to find happiness in this world, Dad. Mom *loved* you. And you...you abandoned us. You didn't just turn her into a single mother somewhere in a big city in America. You left us in a post-apocalyptic world where death and danger was everywhere."

"I saw you get on the helicopter! I thought you were both safe back in the States."

"Okay, Dad. I don't want to argue with you about that since I can see you're clinging to the idea of it with both hands but we both know there was nearly a year between the time you left and when Mom and I went back to the States.

And in that time Mom was taken away by force and had to walk across the Brecon Beacons to find her way back to me."

David put his hands up in an attempt to slow John down but the boy was wound up and ready to talk—especially about what he'd been holding back up until now.

"She walked through five hundred miles of wilderness," John said heatedly, "with an army of psychopaths tracking her every step. Mind if I ask how far away *you* were at the time?"

"They wouldn't let me leave, John. Not for the longest time."

"And you're saying that when they finally did..."

"You and your mother were back in the US."

"Pretty convenient."

"That's not fair, John."

"One more question and then I promised Mike I'd check the south perimeter wall."

"Of course, John. Anything at all you—"

"Did you re-marry on this Island of Secret Knowledge? Do you have a new wife?"

"John, listen to me—"

"Yeah, okay. I think I've heard about all I can handle for now, Dad. We'll pick this up again later when I ask you how many half brothers and sisters I have."

John turned on his heel and exited the room, not bothering to shut the door behind him.

David looked at the empty doorway with John's words ringing in the air around him.

In many ways, it occurred to Thor that having to put off his revenge—Rose's justice—had actually served to intensify the pleasure he now expected to feel as a result of finally delivering it.

He wondered if that was something to have learned from all this.

First, the waiting had been a project of its own in many ways. While his men secured the village and directed the women into service, he himself had no real occupation—beyond drinking tea and talking with his wife.

He loved his wife. Loved her dearly and with more intensity than most men could only dream of.

But tea and talking was exhausting. And in the end, he discovered that he was almost always exactly where he was when he started. No problem was ever really solved—it had merely gotten discussed endlessly.

But the act of waiting, the act of pleasure and satisfaction deferred—that had been a new sensation and one that—now that it was over, Thor found actually and inexplicably beneficial.

Bottom line, the deprivation had made him a better man.

He turned to look at his wife and daughter as they sat across from him at dinner. Emma had worked with the village women today to produce the meal and it was a fine one. Pork chops that had been hanging in the curing shed—untouched by the polluting ash—as well as corn on the cob and sliced tomatoes.

Rose picked at her food listlessly although that could very well be in retaliation for Thor forbidding her to play with her little friend, Betsy.

Ah, the role of a parent is not an easy one, he thought, *and almost always a thankless one.*

Even in her black mood, Rose looked like the flower she was named for. Her complexion was clear and pink, her big eyes a clear blue—like his own. The thought that some animal had taken her and held her down and...

"Marcus?" Emma said with concern. "Are you all right, dear?"

Thor let out a long breath and forced himself to relax.

All was well.

One more night and then they would go.

Come hell or high water—literally.

They would attack the castle at dawn.

Susan Kiernan-Lewis

40

Sarah rolled over in bed and put her hand on the spot where she should have felt her husband. The space next to her was cold and empty.

"Mike?"

"Go back to sleep, lass," Mike said from another part of the room. "It's not even sun up yet."

Sarah swung her legs out of bed, her bare toes touching the thick carpet on the floor.

"You're not leaving yet?" she asked as she reached for her jeans.

Mike was fully dressed, and just pulling on his boots.

"Aye. Soon as they're all gathered in the courtyard."

Sarah lit the kerosene lamp on the bedside table and dressed quickly.

"I can't believe you'd try to leave without waking me," she said with annoyance. "This is not a pig roast you're going to. It's dangerous, Mike."

"I don't intend to engage the blighters, Sarah," Mike said holding the door open for her as they moved into the hallway. "It's reconnaissance more than anything."

"Does Morgan know that? What are you going to do if he goes charging out of the bushes screaming bloody murder?"

"I'll encourage him not to," Mike said.

"Please don't make light of this," Sarah said, turning and putting a hand on Mike's chest to stop his forward movement.

"You are going out there with nine men—most of them office workers before the EMP went off—and all of them armed with shovels and pick handles. How many guns do you have?"

"One for every man," he said.

"And how many bullets do you have?"

"Six," he admitted.

"I rest my case. You can't engage the men holding the village. Morgan has to know that."

"I have made it as clear as I can," Mike said wrapping an arm around Sarah's waist to continue walking down the hall. "We'll be fine, Sarah. There won't be a battle today, I promise you."

"Good. Because if there is, you'll all be killed and then I'll have to go track down Mr. Morgan and kill him myself. Again."

Mike kissed her and patted her hip to urge her down the hall. She stopped abruptly and wagged a finger at him.

"That reminds me!" she said indignantly.

"Later, aye?" Mike said moving past her. "After me breakfast and the Battle of Kilbaha?" He turned and winked at her and she let him go, glad for his good humor. Hoping it meant he really didn't have any intention of storming the village with a handful of unarmed men.

Before she followed him downstairs, she paused outside David's bedroom door. She could see his light was on but it was way too early for anyone's light to be on unless they were going to storm a village.

What was he up to?

Oh, she knew very well his intention to try to talk John into going back with him to wherever he'd come from. She'd worked hard to let things develop naturally, hoping that by not pushing John he'd come to the right conclusion on his own.

The memory of her conversation with him last night came to her as swiftly and painfully as a snakebite.

What if he did go? Was he really thinking of it?

She moved away from David's door and the light that indicated he was awake. Something was definitely up with him—something beyond the story he was telling.

It may have been six years since Sarah had seen him last, but some things didn't change. She could tell there was something off about him.

Something wrong.

He never was a good liar.

Regan climbed to the walkway on the castle wall. The sky was beginning to lighten and as it did she could see the shapes and shadows on the ground in front of the castle begin to move and shift.

This was her favorite time to be up here. Not just for the feeling she always got of beginnings but also because it was the time that most of the archers hated being here. This early they were bleary-eyed and dull-witted. It would take them long minutes to sort out their gear, wake up and begin to focus on their tactical environments.

Regan quickly counted ten archers at the front of the castle lounging against the parapet wall obviously already thinking of the hot breakfast and soft beds that awaited them.

Aibreann had taken the night shift last night and she stood now, her back to the front of the castle, looking down into the courtyard. Regan had caught her yesterday watching Fiona feeding Aibreann's baby Bill. The look on Aibreann's face did not match up with a woman who didn't care. Aibreann had been downright tearful the rest of the morning and ended by going to bed early.

Regan would have to keep an eye on her.

Meanwhile, she'd taken the advice of the old tosser and switched up the posts of the sentries on duty. The archers didn't mind where they stood but Aibreann had used it as an excuse to bust Regan's chops. That was something that was happening more and more.

We probably should just throw down and get it over with.

Although Aibreann was bigger than Reagan and easily outweighed her, Regan had no doubt she could take her. Aibreann was a wounded soul and would fight from that reservoir of sadness.

That might work when she stood on top of a castle night after night and searched the bushes for invaders—but it was bollocks when it came to a face to face fight.

For that you needed fury. And you needed it in your very bones. For Regan it was a feeling she didn't have to call up when the occasion demanded.

Because it was basically always there.

"Oy, Regan!" Tilly approached her on the walkway. "Did you talk to Donaghue?"

Regan frowned and went to where her quiver was hanging on the hook by the low wall.

"Tommy or Terry?" Regan asked.

"The old one. Terry, I guess," Tilly said. "He took our surplus arrows."

Regan's hand went to her quiver where two arrows stuck out instead of the twenty it usually held.

"No, he didn't," Hannah said climbing up the stone steps. "Me mum took 'em for Terry."

Regan looked at Tilly and then down the line as the archers started to change shifts. This was a tricky time and the way they did it was flat bollocks since for at least ten minutes while the night shift moved down the steps and the morning shift moved up exactly feck-all was watching the castle front.

"So you lot only had two arrows a piece all night?" Regan asked incredulously. Her eyes went to Aibreann.

Aibreann pushed past Regan roughly.

"Not my fault," Aibreann said. "Bloody bogger took our bloody arrows. What was I supposed to do?"

Regan turned to Hannah. "Did your mum tell you *why* Terry wanted our arrows?"

Hannah yawned and stretched before answering.

"She said he needed to sharpen the arrowheads," she said.

Tilly began to climb down the steps. "Nay, I heard it was to repair the broken flits on 'em," she said.

Aibreann was already half way down the steps when she spoke.

"What difference does it make? They needed fixing and now they'll be fixed." She jumped to the ground with a soft thud and disappeared across the courtyard.

Some leader, Regan thought as she watched the girl recede from view. "Any idea when we'll get them back?" she asked.

"She said Mr. Donaghue will deliver 'em back to us midday today," Hannah said, hoisting her quiver on her back and moving to her post.

Well, that's just grand, Regan thought as her eyes went to the woods and the drive in front of the castle.

Let's just hope we don't need more than two arrows apiece in the meantime.

Sarah emerged from the kitchen. It had been her shift to help make breakfast and she'd been glad of the distraction—even if it meant working in close confines with Mary. Mary's sister Liddy had been tight-lipped and atypically unsocial but Sarah had to respect the bond of sisterhood. Of course Liddy would support Mary.

No matter how crackpot the woman was behaving.

As Sarah stepped out into the quickly emptying dining hall, she saw David seated at the table closest to the kitchens.

He was waiting for her.

In some ways it seemed so strange to see him now—so familiar—and fighting the impulse to go to him in the way she used to was so unnatural. He watched her approach and a part of her resented the familiarity with which he gazed at her.

"What's up?" she said briskly as she reached him.

"I have an idea," he said, standing. "About our Cassie problem."

Sarah glanced around the room but if John had been in it, she would have noticed him straightaway. Her motherly radar almost always picked him out first in any room she entered.

"He's not here," David said. "I think he already left to go find the lost horses."

"Right. So what's your plan?"

David touched her elbow to direct her out of the dining hall. Once in the long hallway, he pointed to the stone staircase that spiraled upward to the first level of bedrooms. She followed him up the stairs. She wanted to see Mike before he took off for the village but she estimated she had a few minutes before she needed to go looking for him.

"I don't know about you," David said as they climbed, "but Cassie does a remarkably good job of making herself scarce when she doesn't want to be found."

"That's because she has a gift for sneakiness," Sarah said.

David grinned. "Spoken like a mother. Anyway, I thought catching her before she's had a chance to find a hiding place—and doing it in tandem—we might be able to gently convince her to hunt in someone else's field."

"You've gotten poetic since you've been gone," Sarah said dryly. "Is there a second Mrs. Woodson to thank for that?"

"No," David said. "Because as you know, divorce isn't possible in post-apocalyptic Ireland." He looked at her pointedly. "And so neither is remarriage."

They reached the landing without speaking and walked down the hall.

"Do you know what we'll say to her?" Sarah asked, dropping her voice. "And more importantly, are you willing to keep this little pow-wow secret from John?"

"As I recall there were many things we kept from John," David said, "when we knew it was for his own good."

"This is her door," Sarah stopped and looked at him. "I want you to know…that it helps doing this with you."

"I know. Me, too." He raised his hand to knock on the door.

"Stop!" Sarah whispered harshly, grabbing his hand before he could knock. Her heart caught in her throat as the sounds of crying—male crying—came to her from the other side of the door.

Sarah hadn't heard her son cry in over ten years but she'd recognize the sound anywhere. She grabbed the door handle and swung open the door.

John sat on the floor, his head bent.

In his arms was Cassie's lifeless body.

Susan Kiernan-Lewis

41

Sarah was the first one in the room. She rushed in and knelt beside John. Quickly, she put her fingers to Cassie's neck but one look told her it was useless. The girl's eyes were open and her neck bent at an unnatural angle.

Sarah turned to look at David. But David didn't look surprised. Not at all. A terrible premonition flitted through Sarah's body and she felt a sudden coldness in the core of her stomach.

Did you know about this? Did you do this?

David crouched by John and put a hand on his son's shoulder.

"John, what happened?" he asked calmly.

John shook his head. The tears streamed down his face as he stared into Cassie's blank dead face.

"I…I wanted to see her before I left to find the horses," he said, sniffling. "The door was half open but she wasn't in bed. I saw her nightstand tipped over and I thought maybe she was in there." He shook his head. "I just couldn't imagine where she might be. Cassie isn't an early riser."

And then he dropped his head and he wept despondently.

Because Cassie wasn't an early anything any more.

Sarah looked at David over their son's bent head. She searched his eyes for any indication that David had known about this.

Was it possible he killed Cassie?

But David gazed back at her without flinching, his eyes direct and emotionless.

Sarah shook off her suspicions.

Just because he sees this as the answer to our problem, Sarah thought, *doesn't mean he made it happen.*

David touched the back of Cassie's head and his fingers came back with blood on them.

"Was it an accident?" David asked John gently. "Could she have fallen?"

"And stuffed herself in the armoire?" John asked angrily. "I found her in her closet with the door closed."

"David," Sarah said. "Let's move her to the bed. If this is murder, we need to—"

John jerked his head up.

"This is just another item on your to do list, isn't it, Mom?"

Sarah looked at him in astonishment. His stark pain was almost more than she could bear.

"John, I—"

"You hated her!" John said heatedly. "You're glad she's dead!"

Sarah shook her head. "John, no! I never—" She reached out to touch him but he pulled away from her.

"Makes it easy for you, doesn't it? Everyone falling in line to dance to your tune?"

"John, it's a terrible thing and we will find out whoever did this—"

"I don't care! Just leave me alone! Stay away from me!"

"John, sweetheart, listen to me. I never—"

John turned to David. "I changed my mind, Dad. I'm going with you."

David glanced nervously at Sarah and then patted John's shoulder.

"Come on, son," he said. "Let's get Cassie on the bed. Your mother's right. We need to find out what happened here."

"Will that bring her back?" John said hysterically. "You think I haven't seen death? You think I don't know how it goes? You lose someone and they're gone forever! I *know*, Dad! They don't all come back like you did!"

David gently disengaged John from the body and arranged Cassie's limbs on the carpeted floor.

"I'm so sorry, son," David said sadly. "I don't even know what to say."

"I loved her, Dad."

"I know…" David brought John into his arms and held him tightly.

Sarah watched in agony as her boy sobbed and then wiped his eyes and pulled away from his father.

"I meant what I said," John said. "I'm going with you."

He looked one last time at the dead girl on the floor and then turned and ran from the room.

"John!" Sarah said and took a step after him. But David stepped in front of her.

"You know he's just lashing out," David said. "He doesn't mean what he's saying right now. I'll go after him. Let me talk to him."

Sarah nodded and felt a sudden and pervasive exhaustion as David hurried out of the room after John.

Sarah turned back to the body. The poor girl. She'd been an orphan they'd found wandering the woods six months earlier whose entire family had either left her or been killed—the story was never clear. Cassie was a tragic case from the beginning.

All of us are struggling in this terrible new world to make a life.

I didn't want you for my son but it breaks my heart to see this is all you got.

Sarah sagged onto the bed, sick and bewildered.

Who could have done this?

Matt and Mac were still sitting at breakfast when Morgan came into the hall. They both looked like they weren't quite awake. Two large dogs sat on either side of them as the boys ate muffins and drank their sweet tea.

The sight of them gave Morgan a stab of longing—for their mother, gone these last four years—for a life where they could count on a hot breakfast and the warmth and security of the castle.

Just seeing them sitting there stiffened Morgan's resolve.

Whatever happens today, they're not leaving. If we get the village back—an absurd impossibility—or if we die trying —a much more likely possibility—these lads will stay here and be raised in safety and love.

He glanced around the dining hall as it began to slowly fill up. Many of the children here had either lost their parents or been matched up with parents who had lost their children.

If there was one single thing Morgan had noticed in his three and a half days in the castle it was that the children here were loved and cared for as if they were the fecking beacons of the future.

He would have that for Matt and Mac. For dear Lisabeth's lads.

She'd been a timid creature, his Lisabeth, and weak-willed but Morgan had loved her with his whole heart. There wasn't a day that passed that he didn't think of her. He sternly closed his heart to the memory of the day she and her husband had died, and went to join the boys at their table.

"Up early are ye?" he said jovially. "I thought we said goodbye last night."

"Me and Mac want to come too, Grandda," Matt said, his face smeared with jam from his muffin.

"Do ye now?"

"Aye, we can help!" Mac said.

"And you with a broken wing?" Morgan said, shaking his head gravely. "Nay, not a bit of it. I've already spoken to Miss Sophia and you're to help her around the castle today. Do ye hear me?"

Both boys nodded their heads in unison.

"I count on you to do what's right," Morgan said seriously. "Not just today when I'm gone but always. Do ye hear me?"

Again the boys nodded.

"So then, what are the names of these two hounds you're feeding your breakfast to?"

Matt and Mac looked at each other and grinned before turning back to their grandfather.

Minutes later, after he'd hugged them and kissed them goodbye again, Morgan made his way out to the courtyard where he saw his men waiting with Donovan and six of the castle men.

His own men were armed with pitchforks and shovels. The castle men had knives and rifles that Morgan knew for a fact were unloaded.

This was either going to be a bloodbath leaving everyone in the village dead and the entire castle without a single male over the age of fifteen to defend it, or they were going to be on the receiving end of a miracle.

And a miracle could only come if the buggers had already left the village. As Morgan approached the gathered group of men in the half light of the dawning day, he realized that that's what he would have done by now if it had been him in that village.

But then Morgan didn't often find himself thinking along the same lines as murdering thugs.

No, they'd be there waiting for them because life wasn't that easy for them to sneak up on the village only to find it abandoned by the murdering scum who'd taken it.

Still and all—if there was another way around it...maybe a way they could rescue the women and children—perhaps silently at night while the bastards slept? And then—as abhorrent as the idea was to him—perhaps then a way to overpower Donovan and his men in the woods—well, then perhaps Morgan might just get the miracle he needed.

As he walked to the waiting group, Morgan's mind raced to encompass the possibility of all of his people safely inside the castle at the end of this day and Mike Donovan lying dead in a ditch somewhere.

And at that very moment, the shrill call of one of the archers broke into the silence of the half morning and his dark thoughts.

"Oy! We have company!"

Susan Kiernan-Lewis

42

The buggers didn't even bother hiding.

Mike stood in a loophole window in the tower at the end of the parapet. No one on the ground had spoken yet. They hadn't asked to come in or in any other way made clear their intentions.

More than twenty men, still amorphous in the dim morning light but distinct enough to count. They were on foot but they had a wagon.

What was in the wagon?

But they weren't here as friendlies. That was evident although Mike couldn't say specifically how he knew that.

What was in the wagon?

Morgan gasped and wheezed as he hurried down the walkway to where Mike stood. Mike edged aside to let him see the group below.

"It's him," Morgan said. "It's Thor."

Mike grunted. "Well, that makes it easy," he said. "Doesn't make sense that he'd come to the castle though. What does he want?"

"I imagine he wants whatever you've got, squire," Morgan said.

Mike leaned out the loophole and yelled down to the gathered group.

"Oy!" he shouted. "State your business and then move along!"

No one answered for a moment and then the men that had been milling about the wagon disappeared behind it. After a few moments, a movement to the east—in a gap at the nearest stand of trees that led to the woods—caught Mike's eye.

A small child stumbled out of the woods into the clearing. She looked around and then fell to the ground and began crying.

"What the hell—?" Mike said.

Within seconds, a young woman darted out of the woods and scooped up the crying child. Behind her came more women with children—some in their arms, some walking on their own. They kept looking over their shoulders toward the woods as if someone was pushing them from behind.

"It's our women and children!" Morgan said. "Bloody hell! Why did he bring them?"

Mike turned to the archers on the parapet.

"Regan! Tell your archers to stand down!"

Regan nodded but never took her eyes off the movement below as the women and children emerged from the woods.

One man came from behind the wagon and went to intercept a woman walking alone. He grabbed her and pulled her in front of him and walked her to the castle.

"There's your answer," Mike said grimly.

Human shields.

"Good morning, Mr. Donovan," Thor called up to him. "Your lasses make me nervous, so they do." He laughed, the expulsion of air when he did making the woman's hair in front of him move with his breath. "Are they any good then?"

"Come a little closer and let's see," Mike said.

"It is Donovan, isn't it? You can call me Thor."

"What the feck do ye want?"

"Let me ask you, Mr. Donovan. You believe in justice, do you not?"

"What the feck is he on about?" Morgan said.

"I'm here today to address a crime that's been committed," Thor said.

"Would that crime be the invasion of a village and the murder of two of its own?" Mike called down.

Thor hesitated for a moment. Behind him Mike saw several of the other men break from their hiding places to attach themselves to women—and children. They stood out in the open with the innocents held closely in front of them.

"I reckon that means you have the men inside who ran squealing like little lasses when we came to Kilbaha," Thor said. "We have no quarrel with them—or yourself either, Mr. Donovan, as long as you hand over the man who has committed the crime against me and mine."

Mike turned to Morgan. "Any idea what the lunatic is talking about?"

"It's a ruse to get into the castle."

"A man attacked my daughter in the woods surrounding Kilbaha," Thor said, jutting his chin out and his voice rising.

Morgan shook his head vehemently. "He's lost the plot. My men would never hurt a lass. They're family men, every one of them."

"This bastard took advantage of me daughter," Thor continued, shaking the woman in front of him in his agitation. "She's not yet fourteen years old! I'll be needing you to hand him over to me and then we'll be on our way."

"If you're so sure none of your men could do this," Mike said to Morgan, "why is the bastard here?"

"It's a trick. He just wants in."

"Ye needn't even lower yon drawbridge, Mr. Donovan," Thor yelled. "Just lower the bastard over the front wall."

So much for Morgan's theory that the blighter is only trying to get in, Mike thought.

"Are ye a father, Mr. Donovan?" Thor shouted.

"Aye, I am."

"With a daughter, if I may be so bold?"

Mike took in a long breath. "Aye."

"I'll ask ye to imagine if it were your own wee lass at the hands of the brute who'd have his way with her? And tell me ye'd do any different than to have justice on the blighter? And then I'll ask ye to give me what's mine. Vengeance for an innocent girl who is the love of my life and the light of my heart. As I'm sure yours is to you."

"I'm truly sorry for your trouble," Mike said, "but what makes you think we have this man in the castle?"

"The blackguard told my lass that he lived in the castle."

Mike stiffened. That wasn't possible. He knew all of the men in the castle. They were his men. Hand picked. It couldn't be one of them.

"Your daughter was misinformed," Mike said, his eye watching Thor's men as they stood behind the weeping, cringing women. If the bastard didn't get what he came for, what would he do? Mike glanced again at the covered wagon.

"I have a name, Mr. Donovan. And I expect ye to do the right thing."

"What name?" Mike asked.

"The bastard told me daughter his name was *Jordie*."

43

Mike stood in front of the two cells in the dungeon. Kevin O'Malley leaned against the bars and listened intently as Mike stood facing Jordie. The temperatures in these rooms were a good thirty degrees cooler than outside. In winter they were unendurable.

They weren't pleasant now.

"Did you leave the castle?" Mike asked Jordie. "Just before the ash fell? Don't lie to me."

Jordie licked his lips and looked from Mike to Morgan who stood beside him.

"I did. Yes. Just for a few hours. Why? What's happened?"

"And did ye encounter a young lass whom ye then raped?"

Jordie reeled from the bars as if he could physically distance himself from Mike's words.

"What?! No! She said I raped her?"

"Did you have relations with her consensually?"

"No! Not even! She's lying."

"Well, her father is outside the gate with half an army and he says she named you."

"It's a lie! We just talked! I swear it!"

Eliza Bartlett pushed from behind Mike and put her hands on the bars. She looked pleadingly at Mike.

"You have to believe him!" she implored.

"Oh, aye? Because honesty is so important in your family?" Mike said before turning to go upstairs.

"Oy! Governor!" Kevin called. "What about me? I didn't rape anyone and it's colder than my granny's tit down here."

Mike ignored him. He was very much afraid that if he responded he might end up throwing *him* over the castle wall too.

Eliza stayed behind to talk with her son and Mike and Morgan hurried up the stairs to the courtyard where it looked like half the castle was waiting. Mike briefly scanned the crowd for Sarah but didn't see her.

"Do you believe him?" Morgan asked, wheezing noisily as he struggled to keep up with Mike's long strides.

"I don't know. He hasn't been a convincing liar up to now."

"That's our women out there, Donovan," Morgan said. "They don't have guns to their heads yet but that's the next step unless you give Thor the boy."

"I can't hand him over. The bastard will kill him."

"He'll kill our women and children if you don't!"

Aibreann stepped out of the crowd and stopped Mike.

"Do ye want us up top?" she asked. "I just came off duty."

"Aye, all archers at the front of the castle," Mike said.

"We don't have arrows," Aibreann said. "Mr. Donaghue was repairing them."

"What? All of them?" Mike looked around as if he could spot Terry. "Gather the rest of the girls and tell them to report up top." She nodded and darted into the crowd. Mike pointed at young Darby Donaghue standing with Matt and Mac.

"Oy! Darby! You three go to your father's workshop and gather up all the arrows you can carry and bring them to the base of the stairs at the front wall. Hurry now!"

"Donovan, you've got to give him the lad," Morgan said. "I told you the bastard has missile launchers. He can blast a hole in the middle of your front gate."

"I don't know what he has," Mike said. "So far all I've seen is threats."

"Will ye wait until he's murdered one of our women?" Morgan said, stopping.

Mike became suddenly aware that the crowd had thinned and that the men lining the way were all village men. He turned to face Morgan.

"Tell your men to stand back, Morgan," Mike said.

"Not until you give the order to drag the bastard out and give him to Thor. He wants him and it's all our women standing between us!"

"It's not that simple!" Mike said as Morgan's men stepped closer.

"It's not that simple because it's not *your* people out there with a gun to their heads!" Morgan said as he pulled his gun from his shoulder holster and aimed it at Mike's face.

"Hand the lad over or I'll be needing to take him over your dead body."

Susan Kiernan-Lewis

44

Mike stared down the barrel of Morgan's gun and didn't blink. He could hear the sounds of Thor's voice faint and braying as Thor called up to the castle. He heard the murmurs of the crowd in the courtyard.

"You shoot me and you won't get out of the castle in one piece," Mike said tensely. "Nor any of your men either."

"Denny!" Morgan said, not taking his eyes off Mike.

"Aye, Artie!"

"Get the keys off of Mr. Donovan here and go fetch the bugger from the dungeon. The skinny young one mind who looks like he's about to piss himself."

Denny pulled at Mike's jacket just as Terry came out of the crowd and directed his gun at Denny.

"Back off," Terry said.

"Don't listen to him!" Morgan said. "They have no bullets! Do as I tell ye!"

Denny hesitated, with one eye on Terry, he pulled the keys to the dungeon out of Mike's pocket. He moved away toward the dungeon.

"Giving him the boy won't stop him, Morgan," Mike said. "You throw that lad down to him and he'll still end up killing your women. You're mad if you don't think so."

"Oh, I do think so, squire," Morgan said with a shrug. "It's what I'd do if I were a heartless low-down bastard scum. So I know what he's thinking."

Mike looked at him with exasperation. "Then why—?"

"The minute I toss the boy over the wall, we have a window," Morgan said. "It's not a big one but it's the only one we'll get and it's better than standing here while he executes the women one by one. I won't lose those good women out there because you're too soft-hearted to do what's necessary to a boy whose been nothing but trouble since he came."

"So he's a diversion? You're sacrificing him to distract the bastard? Is that your reasoning, ye daft bastard?"

"That's it in one," Morgan said with satisfaction. "I'm throwing away a weaker member of the herd to save the rest of us…if it can be done. And I'll sleep fine after it's done."

"I won't let you do it."

"You are in no position to stop me," Morgan said as he pulled back the hammer on his gun.

A sudden rap on the doorjamb made Sarah jump and she looked up to see Sophia standing in the door, with her baby Maggie in her arms, and staring with her mouth open at the body on the rug.

"*Oh Dio mio!*" Sophia said. "Is she…?"

"Yes, she's dead," Sarah said. She stood up and walked wearily to the doorway. "We'll need to lock the door until we can examine the room better for any clues as to who might have done this." Sarah frowned at Sophia. "Is something wrong, Sophia?"

Sophia dragged her eyes away from Cassie's body and bobbed her head up and down.

"*Si.* I've been looking everywhere for you," she said. "There is a man outside the gate threatening to shoot the village women and children."

"What?" Sarah realized with a start that she'd lost track of the time. "Have Mike and the men left for the village yet?"

"No. The village has come to us. This is what I am trying to tell you."

Sarah didn't have a key to lock Cassie's bedroom but she couldn't deal with any of that right now anyway.

"The village people are outside, you say?" Sarah said as she and Sophia hurried down the stairs to the main hallway of the castle.

"Yes. I don't know what's happening. Nobody does."

As the two stepped out of the castle into the light the air exploded with the sound of a single gunshot.

Susan Kiernan-Lewis

45

Mike saw Morgan eyes widen as he turned his head in the direction the gunshot came from.

From the front of the castle.

It was the moment Fiona sidled up behind Morgan and placed the tip of her boot knife to his throat.

"Don't make me sorry I put extra sugar in your tea, Mr. Morgan," she said. "Lower your gun, please. I only have one brother and I don't intend to lose him today."

Morgan closed his eyes and his arm sagged to his hip. Mike quickly stepped forward and relieved him of his gun after a giving Fiona a grateful smile. He handed the gun to Terry and turned to face the village men.

"I'd just as soon not shoot any of you, but I will," Mike said drawing his own weapon. "Mr. Morgan is correct that I only have a limited number of bullets. I'd hate to use them on people within the castle before I get a chance to deal with the bastard outside of it."

"They've shot someone!" one of the village men said, his voice strident with dread.

"You see what happens when we don't give him what he wants?" Morgan said angrily.

"I've already heard from you, Mr. Morgan," Mike said tightly. "And I'll not be needing any more of your advice."

The body of an older woman lay crumpled on the ground in front of the castle, the blood pouring out of the hole in her forehead. The children were screaming, the village women were sobbing wildly as Thor's men held them firmly.

"I didn't tell you to take all day!" Thor screamed, shaking the weeping woman he held in front of him. One arm snaked around her midriff and the other now held a gun to her head.

Mike gaped in horror at the scene in front of him. Morgan stumbled against the wall and pushed past Mike to look out. He gave a sickened groan when he saw the body.

"Stop!" Mike called down to Thor. "Give us a minute to bring Jordie out!"

"So you'll give him to me?"

Mike pushed away from the window without answering and faced the line of archers. All forty of them were on the wall.

"Aibreann!" Mike bellowed.

Aibreann hurried over, a distraught look on her face.

"Where the feck are your arrows?"

"The boys said there was nothing in the workshop. They said they looked everywhere."

"Terry!" Mike called.

Terry appeared on the top step of the stone staircase.

"I'm not sure how they could have missed them," Terry said. "I have a new stockpile at the workshop!"

"Fetch them, Terry! And be quick about it."

Mike turned back to Aibreann. "Who told you the arrows would be brought to you?"

"I don't know her name."

Mike cursed. *How is it the archers don't know every single person in the castle by name?*

"I heard it from Hannah's mum," Tilly said. "She told me the arrows would be brought to us with our tea and crumpets. Sarcastic like, if you ask me."

Hannah's mother. That would be Eliza.

Could the crazy bitch really be that crazy?

"Terry will bring your arrows to you," Mike said. He turned to Morgan. "Who was it killed?"

Morgan shook his head. "Barry's old grandmum."

"Can you put aside the nightmare that's happening down there long enough to try to save the rest of them? Can you do that?"

Before Morgan could answer, Denny returned with both Kevin and Jordie. Eliza was weeping and clinging to her son from behind.

"I'm begging you, Mr. Donovan," Eliza said. "Please don't do this terrible thing. My boy is innocent."

Another gunshot from outside the castle made Mike race back to the window. Thor stood with a thin curdle of smoke from his gun, pointed straight up where he'd shot it into the air.

"I'm waiting, Mr. Donovan," Thor yelled. "Sixty seconds and I shoot another one."

In the courtyard, the sound of the second gunshot made Sophia grab Sarah's arm in fear.

"They are shooting at us!" she gasped.

Sarah squeezed Sophia's arm reassuringly and scanned the courtyard for any sign of John or David. *Were they safe? Did they know what was going on out front?*

"Oy! Sarah!"

Sarah turned to see Nuala entering the courtyard with her arms full of two squirming babies and a line of toddlers behind her.

"Can I have a hand?" Nuala called.

Sarah's daughter Siobhan ran to her mother and Sarah scooped her up and kissed her cheek.

"His Lordship's given the order that the nursery is to be moved to the dungeon for the day," Nuala said sourly. "I don't think he has a clue what a pain in the arse that is."

"We have some kind of incident going down at the front of the castle," Sarah said. She looked up at the front parapet of the castle. She saw the archers—and there definitely seemed to be a lot of them—but from here she couldn't see Mike.

The three women herded the children through the archway that led to the dungeons. The older children were playing in one of the upstairs rooms of the castle.

Thinking of them gave Sarah a twinge of sadness. Cassie was normally in charge of the older ones.

Who was watching them now?

The dungeon was exactly as it was meant to be—an uninviting, inhospitable place where no one spent any time at —or at least no one who wasn't being punished. Sarah was surprised to see both cells were empty. She was sure Jordie and Kevin O'Malley were supposed to be here.

"This is bollocks!" Nuala said in frustration as she looked around the space. "I can't stay down here with bairns! I need cots and blankets!"

"Mommy, I want my dolly," Siobhan said, pulling on Sarah's shirt.

"How long are we supposed to be here?" Nuala said looking at the debris and dirt in the cold stone corners.

Before Sarah could answer a large group of archers came into room and quickly settled on the floor, laughing and talking amongst themselves.

"Why are you down here?" Sarah said to one of the archers. "Don't we need all hands on deck for what's going on up front?"

The archer shrugged. "That blighter Donoghue lost all our arrows. Can't do much with bows but no arrows."

"Right," Sarah said picking up the nearest two year old child and depositing him in one of the archer's laps.

The girl squawked. "Oy! What'dye do that for?"

"The babies need a soft place to sleep," Sarah said. "Until you hear otherwise, that's your lap." She pointed to the other archers. "You and you and you make yourself useful. Nuala, tell them what you need them to do."

The archers grinned and began to pick up babies.

Sarah looked at Nuala over their heads and Nuala shrugged. It would do.

Sarah hurried up the stairs and stepped out into the courtyard. The first person she saw was Fiona walking quickly toward her.

"Oy, Sarah!" Fiona said. "Everyone safely below?"

"Well, not everyone," Sarah said frowning. "But the littlest ones are."

"Mike's sent me to get the rest of the castle below."

"Are things getting bad? What's happening?"

Before Fiona could answer Sarah saw Sister Alphonse approaching from across the courtyard where she worked in the clinic.

"Sister," Sarah said, nodding as she passed. "We need to move all of you to the dungeons. If you could tell the other nuns?"

As Sarah turned to join Fiona who was heading to check the kitchens and the upstairs bedrooms, Sister Alphonse called to Sarah.

"Sure I want it on the record that I was against him up and about so soon after his injury. Ye'll not be laying the blame at my door if his stitches break."

"He's just sitting at meals," Sarah called back to her. "That shouldn't hurt anything."

"Sure he's not at-tall, at-tall!" Sister Alphonse said, her voice shrill. "Didn't I just see him leave the castle this very minute?"

Susan Kiernan-Lewis

46

Sarah ran back to the nun. "What are you talking about?"

"My patient of course. One of your many husbands, I'm told?" Sister Alphonse said with a smirk. "He's well enough I'm sure but not so well to be running around outside. His stitches will—"

"Are you...are you saying David left the castle?" Sarah asked, her voice rising in pitch

"Isn't that what I just said? He and your lad both."

Sarah felt the ground move beneath her feet. "He had *John* with him?"

"Sure I know who your son is, Mrs. Donovan," Sister said impatiently. "Aye, both of them left through the secret passageway in the clinic."

That can't be. John wouldn't leave. Not without talking to her. *He wouldn't.*

"When?" Fiona asked as she joined them.

"Not ten minutes ago," Sister Alphonse said. "I asked if they would be back soon but they didn't answer. Rude, I say!"

Fiona turned to Sarah. "It doesn't mean they left for good, Sarah," she said.

Sister snorted. "Not at-tall," she said. "Sure they went for a day hike. As plain as the nose on your face."

Sarah looked at her and barely croaked out the question, "Why do you say that?"

"Because they had backpacks on, didn't they?"

303

Jordie was crying, Eliza was crying, Morgan was hammering away at him…and Mike had less than sixty seconds before another innocent hostage was murdered before his eyes. He willed himself to block out the noise, the fear, the image of the crying women below…and try to think.

If I refuse him, I sign the death warrants of eleven women and children.

If I refuse him Morgan and all his men will kill me and then they'll be killed by my men.

Mike held his hands to his head.

If I give the bastard what he wants I buy us more time. But for what?

Even with more time, can we withstand them? Or do I think for one mad moment that the bastard really will take the lad and leave us in peace?

Is it worth the risk? Is the sacrifice worth it?

One man for the good of the whole?

He glanced at the archers. *And is that all I'm sacrificing?*

More of the archers were looking around. Always before they kept their eyes glued to their tactical environment—their potential targets. Now they were looking at him and each other.

And the stairs.

Briana tried to focus on the man who was her target. He was tall and had red hair. He held Betsy loosely but the girl stood stiffly, her face expressionless. The minute Briana recognized Betsy, whom she'd met at the fair, she began to feel a queasiness that she was not used to feeling.

She was sure it was because she'd bolted her breakfast—although that normally didn't bother her most mornings.

Betsy had reminded Briana so much of her younger sister, Zita whom Briana hadn't seen in years now. Betsy had laughed easily and it had felt just like talking to Zita again.

Maybe that's because Briana had responded to Betsy as she would have with Zita.

A week ago today she'd sat and shared a ciggie with Betsy and made fun of the village men together and giggled over how cute the younger men were. And today Betsy's face was chalk white with fear, her eyes wide and frantic.

Today Briana was going to point her arrow at Betsy. She was going to aim at her, right where the redheaded man held her with his arm across her throat.

Briana bit her lip and felt a sheen of perspiration pop up on her forehead. Betsy wasn't skinny. She was covering too much of the man. And he kept moving, shifting around. The wee patch of skin that was him kept moving too. The target was mostly Betsy. The man was hunched over.

A shot to the head would have to go through Zita's… Betsy's head first.

A bead of sweat trailed down Briana's cheek. The sound of someone running up the stone stairway made her stomach tighten. But she didn't take her eyes off Betsy's face.

"Oy!" Mr. Donaghue shouted across the walkway to where Mr. Donovan stood waiting.

"The arrows. They're gone! Burned up! Every last one of them. There's nothing left but a pile of ash!"

Briana felt the sweat form on her fingers where she held her bow. She licked her lips again, her focus still on Betsy's face, on the small patch of visible skin that belonged to the man behind her.

Arrows or no arrows, she was pretty sure she wasn't going to be able to do this.

Susan Kiernan-Lewis

47

How had this happened? No bullets? No arrows except the handful each girl already had in their quivers? And that wasn't enough. Not near enough.

Mike blinked rapidly and turned to look down the line of archers. Seven women. Two arrows each. Fourteen shots. He looked at his gun. Plus eight rounds.

And at least twenty men down below.

There was no margin for failure. Every single shot needed to hit its mark. Every arrow and every bullet must be a killing one. Mike shuddered at the impossibility of what was needed.

"Squire?" Morgan said quietly. "He's going to shoot another one in fifteen seconds."

"Bring Jordie to me," Mike said.

"No! Mr. Donovan, no! I'm begging you!" Eliza threw herself at Mike, clawing and clutching at him, burying her sobbing face in his jacket. Mike shook her off and looked around as Kevin walked up holding Jordie tightly by his shoulder.

Mike grabbed Jordie and pushed him into the front of the loophole window. He was pretty sure Thor wouldn't try to shoot the lad here and now. That would be cutting short the pleasure of his justice. But in any case it was a gamble he needed to take. Jordie covered his face and his shoulders heaved as if he were about to cry.

"Put your hands down," Mike growled as he shoved Jordie as far out as he dared without toppling him over the side. He could feel the boy trembling through his denim jacket.

"Oy! Thor!" Mike bellowed. "I'll not do another thing until I have positive ID. Do ye hear me? What if someone else gave young Jordie's name here? He's not a lad known for getting in trouble. So bring your girl out and let's make sure."

Mike waited. Only the sound of Eliza's weeping could be heard for several seconds.

"Lower him down the walls," Thor said finally. "I'll not take the chance of bringing me lass out here." He waved a hand to encompass the line the archers above him.

"Not until we know for sure he's the one you're looking for," Mike said. This was the tricky part. Mike was in no position to bargain and Thor could just as easily respond to his attempt by shooting another hostage.

"Are ye saying there's someone else it could be?" Thor asked.

"Aye. That's what I'm saying."

Thor nodded. "I'm a reasonable man. I only want the blighter who hurt me daughter. That's fair."

"So?"

"And I can trust ye won't shoot down on us while I bring her and her mother to the front?"

"Ye have my word," Mike said.

Thor seemed to think for a moment and then said, "Ten minutes." He walked backwards with the woman in front of him toward the woods.

Mike pulled Jordie back from the sill.

Morgan shook his head. "That bought you ten minutes," he said.

"More than we had before," Mike said. "More than the next dead hostage had."

"Liddy? Has anyone seen Liddy?" Mary's shrill voice rose up from the courtyard. "Eliza, are you up there? Have you seen my sister?"

Kevin leaned over the inner railing of the parapet walkway and roared down at her, "She's down below in the dungeon where it's safe, ye daft bitch—where you should be! Get your arse below *now*!"

Mary hesitated, her mouth open as she looked up at everyone on the parapet and then turned and broke into a run in the direction of the dungeons.

Mike turned to Kevin. "Go help your brother in the gate tower. We may need to lower the drawbridge in a hurry."

Kevin nodded and jogged down the steps.

"Seven minutes, squire," Morgan said.

Mike nodded grimly. He'd sent Fiona to find Sarah but she'd yet to return. He needed to know Sarah and Siobhan were safe. He spotted Tommy standing next to Jordie.

"Tommy, lad, find Sarah. Make sure she's down below with the others."

Tommy nodded and hurried away.

"Gather the men, Mr. Morgan," Mike said.

Morgan nodded and went to collect the village men who were standing on the parapet walkway in helpless horror as their women and children trembled below. The castle men came too.

"Aibreann!" Mike shouted.

Aibreann walked toward him hesitantly.

"I need your fourteen best archers," Mike said tensely. "If they're not here on the parapet, go down to the dungeon and get them. Go!"

She turned and ran down the steps to the courtyard.

Mike turned toward the men.

"All right, listen up," he said to the men, "We have feck-all in the way of weapons. If it weren't for those women and children down there we'd just sit this one out until the bugger finally pissed off. But we don't have that option."

"What the hell can we do?" one of the castle men said.

"The archers will do what they can with the resources they have. After that it's up to you lot. Everyone needs to spread out in the courtyard as our second line of defense. If they breach the walls you'll need to do what you can to save the ones in the dungeons."

Mike turned to Terry. "Get the swords and Clayborns from the workshop—the ones we put there from the castle museum displays. Hand them out to anyone who's got the strength to lift one. It's not much against bullets but it's better than sticks and rocks."

Terry nodded grimly and he and the castle men broke away in a group.

Mike turned to the village men.

"Your women are down there with a madman's gun to their heads," Mike said. "If we have a hope in hell of saving them, we need to work together. Ye have to trust that I'm doing everything I can to save everyone. Castle or village members alike. If you follow my man Donaghue, he'll arm you with swords, pitchforks, shovels—whatever you can handle."

He turned to address Morgan.

"I'm going to give you your gun. You can shoot me and throw the lad over the wall and I guarantee you before he hits the ground my men will have shot and killed you and half your men. Whoever's left will be blown to shite by yon maniac out there. There's no way out of this but together, Mr. Morgan. Can you stand with me?"

Morgan hesitated and then held his hand out for his gun.

"I'll give it a shot," he said grimly.

As the only other gun, Mike would need Morgan on the wall with him to try to keep the bastards out as long as possible.

"Three minutes," Morgan said softly. "If the bastard even has a watch and is bothering to keep count."

"Has he come out of the woods with his lass yet?" he asked Morgan.

"Not a sausage since he went in," Morgan replied, checking the rounds in his revolver.

Mike walked over to where the archers stood.

"In a very few minutes," Mike said, "I'll give the order and when I do you'll fire down on the people below."

Morgan grabbed his arm. "What are you saying? They can't do that! You're telling them to murder the village women!"

"I'm not saying anything of the kind, Morgan," Mike said tensely. "I'm trying to save as many of them as I can."

"But we only have two arrows each!" Regan said.

"No," Mike said gruffly. "You have *one*. When Aibreann comes back with the other archers, I'll need each of you to hand over your extra arrow to them." He focused on Regan. "Lass, you'll need to step down. I need only the best shots today."

Regan nodded, her face grim and determined. "I'll give up me arrows, but I'm not leaving," she said.

The other girls shifted uncomfortably. One broke concentration to steal a glance at Mike.

"What if we hit one of the hostages?" she asked plaintively.

Mike turned away without responding. He didn't bother looking at Morgan. The thought occurred to him that Morgan might decide to use one of their bullets on him. But if Morgan thought about it even for a moment Mike was pretty sure he'd come to the same conclusion that he had.

Whether the archers shot the hostages or not, they were all likely to be dead by night fall anyway.

The minute John stepped out of the secret passageway outside the castle something felt wrong.

Not just the fact that Cassie was dead, or that he was leaving without saying goodbye to his mother, or that they were outside the castle without a single weapon.

He looked at his father. David was scanning the bushes as if he was looking for something.

Or someone.

A tremor of unease passed over John's skin. Something felt wrong.

It was still raining. He knew his father was counting on the ash and storm clean up to take everyone's attention to the point where their absence wouldn't be noticed immediately. It was true that they'd run into Sister Alphonse in the clinic but for someone who was so good with medicine, she was amazingly dim about most everything else.

John was pretty sure she didn't even notice them slipping out through the secret passageway.

They walked in silence for a moment. His father wanted to retrieve something he felt sure he'd lost when he first came to the castle.

"I think I dropped it just outside the gate," David said. "Not too far from the tunnel opening."

John was fairly sure what he was doing was right. His father was literally the only person in John's entire world who'd ever understood him and the things that mattered to him.

Half the time the people at the castle just applauded when John said something or managed to solve some serious problem.

Frankly it was a little annoying.

What would it be like to be surrounded by people just like him? People he didn't have to explain things to? Or who got him the first time? Better yet, what would it be like to be surrounded by people smarter than him?

Just the thought of seeing Sandra Lynch again made him speed up his steps as he and his father hurried toward the front of the castle.

The rain was coming down just hard enough to thoroughly drench them but his father had said there were provisions in the tunnels—towels, water, and even a few weapons.

"How do you know about these tunnels?" John asked. "We've lived here two years and I never found any."

"You wouldn't. They're old IRA tunnels used in the last century when the Fenians wanted to hide or ambush some English governor or whatnot."

"Wow. That is seriously cool."

"Oh, you'll have to walk bent over in them but they're constructed with cement sides to withstand the inevitable bombing the zealots all felt was coming their way from Britain."

They neared the front of the castle and John slowed. He thought he heard voices although the patter of the rain against the dead leaves tended to distort the sound.

"Speaking of bombing," John said. "The US planes that were bombing the countryside—is that your group?"

"No. I mean, yes. They are American planes contracted to MPC and flown by MPC pilots."

"MPC. So that's the real name of your organization?"

His father hesitated.

"What the hell, Dad? I'm coming with you but you won't even tell me the name?"

"We go by the initials MPC."

"Which stand for?"

"It's just a name, son."

"Which I'd like to know."

"*Meliores Priores* Consortium."

"Help me out, Dad. My Latin's a little rusty these days."

"It means...*The Better Ones First*."

"Oh, wow."

"It's just a name, John. Don't read too much into it, please."

"Okay. Then can I ask why...MPC is bombing the countryside?"

David wiped the rain from his face and shifted his backpack from his back to one hand.

"Well, because an essential part of MPC's mission is to create a safe... repository for all that we collect."

"Repository?"

"I'm sure I don't need to tell you that most of the knowledge that we need to preserve got a major leg up when Google made copies of everything and put the data online?"

"Okay," John said, frowning.

"And that's all good but it still leaves most of the world's treasures in the form of art and antiquities."

"So you're bombing Ireland to save the world's international treasure?" John shook his head in confusion.

"I'm not stating this very well. You know I work from a base that I refer to as the Island of Secret Knowledge, right?"

John nodded.

"Well, basically our bombers' mission is to transform all of Ireland into our Island base. You see? Ireland—just like back in the Middle Ages when its monks helped save the world's civilization by safeguarding all its written words—Ireland will continue to serve as the one place on earth where all knowledge and artistic achievement resides. Safe for all the generations to come."

"But why do you need to bomb the countryside to do that?" John asked patiently.

"I was really hoping to get you back to the Island itself before we got into the details of our mission."

John slowed his steps.

"Look, John. There are certain areas of Ireland—certain standing artifacts that are ruins more than anything but as long as they're standing, they serve as magnets for gypsies, refugees, and the homeless."

"I guess these people don't have a role in your mission."

"We are not against these people! We just need to temporarily remove them so that we can get the broad strokes done."

"By *remove* you mean *murder*."

"I said *temporarily*. So, no, I don't mean murder. I wish I could make you understand that!"

"Because to me it sounds an awful lot like what the Nazis did."

"I understand most people would think that. But it's much more complex than that. And here's something to keep in mind, John. Your grandchildren will be grateful for the fact that you and I did the hard work before they were born so they could live in a civilized society."

John stopped walking. He held up a hand and turned slowly to look at his father.

"Wait a minute," he said, his eyes narrowing. "Are you saying *Henredon Castle* is one of those artifacts that attract the wrong sort of people that you need to get rid of?"

The sound of a foot stepping on a sharp stick made John snap his head around. A man stood fifty feet away, his gun pointed at them.

"Hello, lads," the man said pleasantly. "Put your hands in the air or I'll shoot ye both dead where you stand."

48

Sarah thought she just might possibly lose her mind.

She stood in the courtyard, her hands to her head, and stared in the direction of the clinic and the secret passageway.

Fiona tugged at her sleeve.

"Sarah," Fiona said urgently, "you know John and David are not still at the clinic so unless you're thinking of leaving the castle, you need to come with me now and help get the rest of our people to the dungeons."

A swarm of men gathered in the courtyard around them and then surged past toward the stables. Fiona began tugging Sarah in the direction of the dungeon.

"Oy! Mrs. D!" Tommy Donaghue said as he rushed up, his face flushed with excitement. "His honor sent me to tell ye he needs you below as soon as possible. You too, Mrs. Cooper." He turned to join the other men running to the stables.

Within moments, Aibreann and a group of grim-faced archers from the dungeons. Sarah recognized one of the girls who had held Bill earlier. The girls jogged past and headed toward the stairs leading to the parapet.

"What is going on?" Sarah said in a whisper.

"Nothing we can do anything about at the moment," Fiona said fiercely, pulling again on Sarah's arm. "Now come on, Sarah. There's no point in thinking of going after your lad. Ye see that, aye?"

Sarah felt her stomach churning with anxiety. She watched as the group of men entered the stables. Terry was leading the way.

"You're right," Sarah said as she watched them disappear. "There's no point in going to the clinic now."

"Good. Glad you finally see reason."

Sarah shook off Fiona's grip and walked quickly to the stone stairs that led to the parapet.

Mike turned his head to see the fourteen archers evenly spaced across the front of the castle standing ready. Les Crème. The best they had.

Initially Mike had wanted to send all but their three best shots to the safety of the dungeons but he needed a rain of arrows when the time came and he couldn't get that with three archers shooting four arrows at a time..

It was true that more archers at the front were that many more people vulnerable to whatever firepower the bastard was hiding in his wagon. Mike could choose to possibly save eleven lives by sending all but their three best shots to safety.

Maybe it was the sight of the weeping women and children out front. But the possibility of saving eleven lives was weighed against the slightly greater odds that fourteen archers could create more havoc.

And Mike knew he needed every advantage he could create.

Jaysus, if we survive this, will I be as ruthless as this auld bastard?

Is that what's needed to survive in this new world of ours?

And what do I do if Thor comes back with the girl? Tell the lasses to open fire? Is that what we've come to? My only hope of keeping my group alive is to shoot at innocent women and children? To break my word?

If it is, by God, then so be it, he thought grimly, an image of little Siobhan coming unbidden to mind.

"Mike!" Sarah called out, breaking Mike's focus on the spot where Thor would emerge from the wood. She was running toward him on the parapet walkway.

His heart surged at the sight of her at the same time it sank because she was not below and safe.

She reached him and grabbed his arm, her face flushed with exertion.

"Mike! John and David have left the castle!"

Mike shook his head. He couldn't think about that now.

"Sarah, I need you below. Where's Siobhan?"

"In the dungeon. All the little ones are."

"I need ye to get the nuns down there too. And everyone else who can't fight. Take Mrs. Bartlett too."

Sarah glanced at Eliza clinging to Jordie by the parapet back rail. Jordie was staring straight ahead into the sky as if he'd already resigned himself to the afterlife.

"I need ye both safe and out of the way, lass," Mike said. He turned to see Fiona coming up the steps from the courtyard. "Bloody hell. And take my crazy sister with you. Sarah, please. You and Fi have children who need you."

"So does Eliza, Mike," Sarah said heatedly. "And she's not leaving."

"Then talk to her!"

"No amount of talking is going to get her to leave while her son is in danger of being tossed over a castle wall to a crazed psychopath!" Sarah said.

"Dammit, Sarah. You know I won't give him up. Make her believe it and get her below."

"Squire," Morgan said calmly. Mike looked at Morgan and saw he was staring at the woods. Mike followed his gaze. Thor was emerging from the woods.

He didn't have his daughter with him.

Sarah watched as Mike and Morgan turned their backs to her to concentrate on what was happening out front. She found herself scanning the woods for any sign of John or David.

"Come on, Sarah," Fiona said. "We need to get the rest of the castle below."

I didn't even have time to tell Mike about Cassie, Sarah thought as she turned to walk away.

Is there a murderer in our midst? Maybe sitting in the dungeon right now?

Or did he escape through the clinic passageway with my son?

Before reaching the steps, Sarah saw Jordie tucked into a recess in the back wall of the walkway. One of the village men held him there firmly, his hand wrapped around the boy's arm. Jordie's eyes were red but his face dull as if he'd shed all the tears he had left to cry.

His mother was at his side, clutching his shirt. Her face was a mask of despair. Her eyes never left her son's face.

Sarah turned to Fiona. "You go on. I'll be right behind you."

"Leave her, Sarah," Fi said. "She won't come." Then Fiona hurried to the steps and quickly descended.

Sarah went to where Jordie and Eliza stood. She put her hand on Jordie's shoulder.

"Be strong, Jordie," Sarah said. "We won't give you up. Do you hear me?"

Jordie looked at the village man who rolled his eyes as if to deny Sarah's words but the boy nodded nonetheless.

Sarah reached for Eliza's hand.

"You are not helping him," Sarah said. "I know you think you are but you are weakening him when he needs to be tough."

Eliza batted Sarah's hand away.

"I am the only thing that stands between my son and your husband throwing him to the wolves!" Eliza said heatedly.

Jordie flinched at his mother's words.

Sarah put her face close to Eliza's. "Listen to me, Eliza. You are doing the opposite of supporting him. You are weakening him. And you are doing it because it helps *you*— because it makes *you* feel better."

Eliza hesitated. She looked at Jordie.

"You are making this harder on him," Sarah said.

"No," Eliza whimpered.

"Jordie," Sarah said to the boy. "I'd like to take your mother down to the dungeons where it's safe."

"Yes, please," Jordie whimpered, a single tear tracing down his cheek.

"Jordie, no!" Eliza said.

"Let your boy be brave for you, Eliza," Sarah said, pulling her away from him. "Let him stand up and do this without having to worry about you."

"I…" Eliza looked at her son and then unclenched her grip on his shirt.

"I'm going to be okay, Mum," Jordie said, his voice trembling, his eyes still not looking at her as if he couldn't bear to lie to her face.

"Yes, you are," Sarah said, patting Jordie's shoulder. "I'm taking your mother below now."

Jordie nodded but didn't look at Sarah or his mother.

Sarah pulled Eliza away and down the walkway. Before they reached the steps, Eliza stopped. She shook her head and began to turn back but Sarah stepped in front of her.

"I know you think Jordie's weak," Eliza said. "I know he isn't clever like your boy…"

The mention of John made Sarah's insides freeze but she pushed past it.

"Eliza, listen to me. Jordie has value like everyone else in this castle. Mike won't give him up. I promise you."

Eliza looked into Sarah's eyes, her own filled with anguish.

"I pray that's true," she whispered. "Because I can't do anything about it. Can I?"

Is there anything worse than the helplessness of our worry for our children? Sarah thought. But before she could nudge Eliza toward the stairs, she heard Mike shouting down the castle front. The man out front was yelling back.

Sarah turned to see Mike standing in a crenel just enough to be seen and parlay without risking being shot.

"Sarah," Eliza said grabbing Sarah's arm. "Please find out what they're saying. Please, I have to know."

Sarah took in a long breath. "Wait for me right here," she said before sprinting back to where Mike and Morgan stood. She stopped short of reaching them. One look at Mike's face—tense and grim—as he conferred with Morgan told her that the man out front was presenting an ultimatum.

Something told her not to go any further, not to interfere with what Mike was trying to do to save the castle. Instead, she stepped to a nearby crenel and instantly saw what she hadn't seen before.

Twenty men stood facing the castle in a long line. Each of them held a woman or child in front of them. Each of them held a handgun to their hostage's head. Sarah bit back a gasp. Behind the men was a wagon with a cover thrown over the back.

The head man, Thor, stood holding a woman who looked nearly dead on her feet. He kept shaking her to force her to find her legs again. He was shouting up to the castle.

"...decided in the end—as much as I'd like to be fair—that endangering me own lass in pursuit of that fairness was bollocks," the man said.

"You are not really in a position to make demands, Donovan. So if you think it's another and not this Jordie, then I'll have them both and we'll decide in due time."

Thor gave his hostage another shake.

Sarah felt perspiration form on her top lip.

All of those poor people down there were going to die. That was as clear to her as anything. This man was not going to let them live—not any of them.

"Since you obviously don't give a shite whether we murder every single one of the women and children of Kilbaha—such is the bloodthirsty blackguard that ye are," Thor screamed, spittle flying from his mouth, "we'll go about it a different way. As luck would have it, me men have captured someone from your own castle who might make a more agreeable trade for ye."

Sarah felt the blood rush away from her head.

No. They haven't captured anyone. Please God no.

"Two blokes trying to escape the castle..."

Sarah turned and screamed. "Mike! It's John! They have John!"

She looked at Mike—only ten feet away—but he didn't turn to look at her. His whole focus was on the man below and what he was saying.

"We killed one," Thor shouted up to the castle. "But that still leaves the younger one and in good enough shape to trade. Oh, he's shot up. Be needing a doctor pretty quick. Sure it's on your head if he dies."

Sarah moaned in anguish before the words came tumbling out of the monster's mouth.

"Give me Jordie or we kill the lad."

Susan Kiernan-Lewis

49

At Thor's words all the air seemed to whoosh out of Sarah's chest. She stood, wheezing for breath, her eyes searching the grounds and the woods for any glimpse of John.

Her legs gave out on her and she fell to her knees. Before she could get back to her feet and hurtle down the walkway toward the stairs that lead to the courtyard, Mike was there, blocking her way.

"Sarah," he said, grabbing her by the shoulders.

"Get out of my way, Mike," Sarah said. "I've got to... just let me pass!"

Mike held her firmly. She could smell the sweat and fear on him. His eyes looked wild and slightly unfocused.

He knows they're going to kill John, she thought.

"They don't have him, lass!" Mike said, giving her a small shake. "It's a *ruse*. Otherwise they'd parade him front and center."

"Unless he's already dead!" she said, her voice rising hysterically.

"Then they'd parade the body! They don't have him, Sarah!" Mike said. "Do ye trust me, lass? Because I can't fight everyone inside the fecking castle, outside the castle, and you, too!"

She shook her head, her stomach clenching and her breaths hitched in her chest. But she allowed him to take her into his arms.

"Promise me, they don't really have him," she whispered into his chest. "Lie to me. But promise me."

"I promise ye, lass," he said. "Now I need ye to take Eliza and the rest of our people—the nuns, the children and the other women—and wait with them down below until this is over."

Sarah's eyes filled with tears and she shook her head but not in refusal, only in denial.

Mike kissed her and squeezed her hand before turning away. Morgan came up behind Sarah and put a hand on her shoulder.

"Go on, lass. Get your people to safety. Let yer man handle this," he said.

*****

Mike watched as Eliza and Sarah went wordlessly down the stone steps and disappeared from sight.

He was fairly certain the bastard didn't have John. Not completely sure. But fairly.

But in the end it didn't matter. It didn't matter who the bastard had or what the bastard did…there was some comfort in that.

Not much. But some.

The fact that Mike didn't immediately begin to lower Jordie to the ground was his answer as clear as he could make it without triggering a bloodbath of the innocents below: *I don't care who you have down there, we won't hand over the boy.*

Easily the most useless member of the castle, Mike thought as he glanced at Jordie shivering by the back wall. *And we're going to lose everything on account of him.*

"You were right," Morgan said as he positioned himself beside Mike again. "It's only a trick. But I'll wager it means the next thing up his sleeve will be the real deal."

"Aye," Mike said. "I fear you're right."

"I hate that we just stand and wait for whatever the bastard concocts next," Morgan said.

Mike grunted.

"We have fourteen arrows and eleven bullets between us," Mike said. "I'm not sure how good your math skills are —"

"Good enough to know there are more of them than we have killing shots," Morgan admitted.

"So we wait to see what he does next."

Thor glared up at the wall of the castle. He could see the lasses—fourteen of them. They were tucked into the windows that let them point their arrows but any bullet directed their way would likely only hit limestone and cement.

He dragged the woman backwards toward the wagon. He held her tight around the waist, lifting her feet off the ground. He found it interesting that no one had even fired a single shot at them.

Is it possible they have no guns? Or no ammunition?

Was he being more careful than was necessary? He'd promised Emma he would do everything possible before pulling out the RPGs. She asked for so little. And she was soft-hearted, so she was. It was little enough to give her.

As he edged his way backward, he could see a few of the archers retraining their sights on him.

"Jocko! Digby! Grab the tarp!" he called over his shoulder.

He was fairly confident the archers couldn't hit him at this distance but he kept the woman in front of him nonetheless. He found it more comfortable to hold onto her by her hair. It kept her neck exposed—which looked more vulnerable to the archers—and it was easier to hang onto. Tufts of it had come out in his hand because as he tensed up he had a tendency to yank on it.

Jocko threw the tarp on the ground and pulled out the first RPG.

"Should have done this straightaway," Jocko grumbled.

Thor knew he was right. But it didn't matter. It didn't matter that they'd wasted time.

What mattered was that Emma didn't want anyone hurt —unless there was nothing for it, of course. And Thor cared that Rose saw that her father was trying to be civilized about this. Those things mattered. These lugs wouldn't know that but then they didn't have families.

One thing he knew was that he was a different breed altogether from them.

The sound of Jocko and Digby loading the launch tubes with the warheads came to him from where he stood. He didn't need to watch them. They knew what they were doing. Thor kept his eyes on the castle. From here he could just see the shadow of the bastard who had ensured that this was the way it all had to end.

No one can say I didn't give him every opportunity.

Why should I feel bad? Because the bastard in the castle is willing to let all of these brave women and their bairn die rather than give up one lying, low-down rapist?

It had been painful to lose the two men they'd spotted running from the castle. Jocko reported that the slippery bastards had disappeared right in front of them—like they were swallowed up into the very earth.

But in the end it didn't matter. Even if they'd caught them, clearly this bastard in charge of the castle didn't value human life. It would have made absolutely no difference at all.

"You'll need extra women in front to hide what you're holding," he told his men. "If they see the RPGs they'll likely start shooting right through the hostages."

"We can't fire these and hold the women at the same time," Jocko complained.

"Oy! Jamie!" Thor called. "Bring one of the kids over here and two more women from the woods."

Instantly the women standing in front of Jocko and Digby began to whimper.

"That's grand," Thor said. "I prefer it when you get the picture without me having to explain it."

When the other women joined them, Thor pointed to Jocko and Digby.

"So all you women will stand in front of my men—even without hands holding ye because if ye run, the man holding his gun to little…what's your name, lass?"

The little girl that Jamie had walked over to him stared at Thor with saucer-sized eyes. "Mmm-Mary," she said softly.

"Aye, little Mary here, well…don't make me say the rest. I'm a family man with a lass of me own. Everyone know what they're about? That's grand."

"Jocko, go to the edge of the front drive there. As soon as you're in position, I'll give the word and I want ye to hit the front gate tower in a coordinated effort like. Questions?"

"You mean like why didn't we do this straight away?" Jocko said.

"Well, I was hoping to keep the castle intact, ye see," Thor said testily. "No sense taking possession of a rubble, but here we are anyway."

Story of me life: people are always forcing me to do bad things.

"Gentlemen, take your positions," he said.

He watched the two men, the Russian-made missile launchers held to their chests but hidden behind the line of women stumbling in front of them as they all scuttled toward the castle wall.

Thor waited until they were in position one each side of the gate tower. He winked at Mary who stood with Jamie's gun held to her forehead.

"Ready, lads?" he shouted.

"Aye!"

"Then what are you waiting for? Fire!"

Susan Kiernan-Lewis

50

Sarah was leading the group of little boys across the courtyard when the double thunder clap roared out over their heads.

She snapped her head around to see an orange ball of fire engulf the top of the gate tower. The sound detonated shock waves that pulsated in the air.

The boys screamed, broke ranks and ran.

Massive slaps of concrete and masonry tumbled to the courtyard as the very castle walls seemed to rumble and shudder around them. The smoke trails of twin missiles diffused overhead.

The stones and pieces of castle wall fell around them and pieces of mortar and wood littered the ground. A black smoke engulfed the courtyard, stinging Sarah's eyes as she tried to find the children.

"To the dungeons! To the dungeons!" Sarah shrieked, dashing past pockets of burning wood and smoking debris.

A man's body lay facedown directly in front of Sarah. There was a thick beam across his back and a dark pool of blood forming beneath him. A large chunk of cobblestone had ripped through the stable door which now hung by one hinge.

She leaned down and picked up one of the smaller boys. He was crying and gripped her neck tightly, burying his face in her hair. Ahead of her she saw Fiona in the mist and the smoke, rounding up more of the boys whose faces, hair and clothes were covered with dust and small debris from the explosion.

One of the castle dogs leaned in tight against Sarah's legs. It was then she realized she couldn't hear anything.

None of what she was seeing had a soundtrack. Not the crying boys, not the whimpering dog, not the sounds of loose bits of masonry still falling to earth.

Then her right ear popped and she felt blood trickle down her neck and the world came roaring back at high volume.

"Sarah!"

She looked to see Fiona motioning for her to hurry.

They needed to get the boys to the dungeon. As the smoke drifted in patches she saw all the children were between her and Fiona toward the dungeons.

She squeezed the hand of the boy that she held and saw that he had his other hand on the collar of the dog. She moved them quickly forward, the smell of burning wood and gunpowder sharp in the air around them.

Just before they reached the archway that led to the dungeons Sarah jumped over what looked like a long brick. She hesitated and then kicked it aside so the children wouldn't see it.

It was a foot. And it was wearing one of Kevin's prized trainers.

Briana had been watching the two men get in position. She couldn't make sense of the fact that the women were no longer being held but seemed to be moving willingly with them.

She watched the men stop and nod to each other—their hands hidden behind the women.

Shouldn't we shoot them? she wondered. She fingered her single arrow. But no order came.

Suddenly the men pulled out rocket launchers. They rested the launch tubes on the shoulders of the women in front of them and aimed at the castle.

Her fingers tightened on her bow, so slick with her own sweat that she nearly dropped it.

And then in tandem with a crack of unholy thunder, a blazing ball shot out of each of the launch tubes. The front tower exploded in a giant fireball gushing enormous plumes of black smoke.

Briana stared at the black cloud of smoke where the tower was. She was mesmerized as chunks of stone, wood and other debris fell through the air and into the courtyard below.

The gate tower—where both the O'Malley brothers had been standing just minutes ago.

The black cloud obscured the top of the tower as if to hide the fact that it had crumbled over onto itself.

No way anyone was still alive in there.

Briana swallowed and looked around. For the first time her stomach was flopping. She was sure she was going to throw up.

She lowered her bow and caught Tilly's eye. Tilly also had her bow lowered.

This wasn't going to work. None of this was going to work.

Donovan was screaming. She could see his face, all red. His eyes were angry and wild. He was yelling at her. At all the archers.

"Get ready!" Donovan screamed. "Archers, ready! On your mark!"

"I'll hit her," Tilly said in a loud rasp to Briana. "I can't help hitting her."

Briana looked back down at the men and saw the two with the rocket launchers were cheering. Their human shields still stayed close to them, moving when they moved. One even turned all the way around as if to better mirror her captive's movements.

And there was Betsy. She wasn't turned around. She was looking right up at Briana.

Betsy was covering too much of her captor. There was no way Briana could shoot *him* and not shoot her too. That's all there was to it.

Betsy wasn't a target. She was a girl. A flesh and blood girl who cried and bled, who laughed and…

All of a sudden Briana's arms hurt. They felt heavy. And she felt an odd tingling sensation. She was getting her period. She needed to be excused. And she wasn't the only one. She turned to look at Aibreann.

Aibreann was already heading toward the stairs.

The babies were screaming.

It looked like bedlam in the dungeons. Sarah ushered the little boys to Sophia in the corner of one of the cells that overlooked the ocean below. She felt a spasm of guilt. She should have gotten everyone to safety long before now. Was everyone here?

Mary sat huddled in the corner with her sister Liddy who kept a grip on both their young children. The nuns were doing what they could to make the cold stone floors more comfortable by bunching up a few of the museum tapestries that had been stored in adjacent rooms. But even from across the room, Sarah could feel the bite of the cold ocean breeze.

Siobhan ran to Sarah who held her in her arms until the toddler squirmed to be free again.

Fiona had her hands full with the baby Bill and Ciara—and Eliza who had renewed her weeping.

Nuala was talking heatedly to the mother superior, Mother Angelina, and the little boys were climbing over Sophia. Both castle dogs curled up in the corner as if trying not to draw attention to the fact that they were there.

"Is there any food?" Sarah asked as she approached Nuala.

Nuala shook her head, "Sure there's nothing," she said. "I have some bottles for the bairns, but that's it."

Sarah watched Liddy pull snack bars out of her pocket and hand them to her and Mary's children. Although she didn't know it yet, Mary had lost her husband today. Sarah decided they could spare a snack bar or two for the child who'd just lost her father.

"Hungry, Mommy," Siobhan said plaintively.

"I know," Sarah said. "Dinner won't be long."

A few heads turned to look at her when she said that but she took Siobhan's hand and went to Fiona who was trying to keep Bill from squalling.

The others had felt the walls shake and the dust and plaster sprinkle down from the ceiling, but only Fiona and Sarah—and the little boys—had seen the destruction of the gate tower. Sarah thought Fiona was holding little Ciara particularly tightly.

"Could you see the damage it did?" Fiona whispered as Sarah sat down next to her. "Was it the gate tower?" Fiona's lips and chin trembled as she waited to hear.

"It was."

"Are we trapped in here then? The gate tower was what made the draw bridge work."

"I don't know, Fi."

"Will there be more, do ye think? Why didn't they shoot at the front wall? Did Mike know they had that kind of firepower? Did Morgan?"

"I don't know, Fi," Sarah said tiredly, pulling a tendril of hair out of Siobhan's eyes. She kept her hand on the child's cheek for a moment. "I imagine Thor would avoid shooting anywhere where Jordie is."

"Doesn't want to damage the goods," Fiona said bitterly.

"For now."

"Mike won't give him up," Fiona said, but it was more of a question.

"You know he won't."

Fiona jostled Bill whose cries had faded into whimpers. "I can't believe this is happening," she said more to herself than anyone. "How safe do you think we are down here?"

"Safe," Sarah said. She leaned over and kissed Siobhan. "Fiona, can I ask you to watch Siobhan for me?"

"What are you talking about? Where are you going?"

"I just need to check on something up top. "

"What the feck are ye on about? You can't leave! In case you weren't aware, Sarah, they have rocket launchers up there!"

"I know," Sarah said. She reached for Fiona's hand and squeezed it. "But my husband is up there so that's where I'm going." She stood up, gave Fiona's astonished expression a brief, reassuring smile and then turned for the door, a wave of guilt spreading throughout her chest.

It was true. Her husband was up there—and directly in the line of fire.

But that was not where she was going.

51

David lay on top of John, the smell of the black earth thick in his nostrils. His hands clutched his son.

"John!" he whispered hoarsely. "Are you hit?"

John squirmed out from under him. His face was white in the dark tunnel, with streaks of mud across his cheeks to show where he'd landed.

As soon as David had swung his backpack at the man, he'd screamed *Run!* and they'd darted into the woods. The entrance to the tunnel had been only yards away under a large blackthorn bush. They'd slid into it with mere seconds to spare.

David squeezed John's arm to impress upon him not to speak. The man hunting them had been joined by others and they were running over the top of the tunnel, their voices clear and strident.

David knew from experience how difficult the tunnel openings were to see. If he hadn't been with John, the boy would never have found it.

Of course, if David hadn't been with John, the boy wouldn't be out here in the first place.

They lay in silence until they could no longer hear voices.

"Who are they?" John whispered.

"Just thugs," David said. "Remember the gypsies when we first came to Ireland?"

John nodded.

"There's nothing like a lawless world to bring out the worst of the world," David said. He shifted and sat up. "As long as we're quiet, they won't find us here."

John sat up and rubbed his shoulder. He looked around. There was a glimmer of light coming from outside the tunnel.

"Let's move a little further into the tunnel," David said softly. "And then I'll light one of the lanterns." He slid past John and felt his son's hand on his back before he moved quietly, stealthily down the tunnel. Within minutes they were in pitch darkness and total silence.

David turned on a battery-operated lantern. His hands were shaking. That had been close.

A part of David wanted to rush John right down the tunnel toward their rendezvous point. As it was it was going to take the rest of the afternoon and most of the night to get there.

And traveling subterranean was not David's favorite mode of transportation.

But he sensed John needed a moment to adjust to what had happened.

To what was happening.

"Dad, the castle must be under attack," John said. "I have to go back!"

"You're unarmed, John. What do you think you could do? There's no way anyone can get into the castle, you know that. Everyone in there is perfectly safe."

John was silent for a moment.

"I didn't say goodbye to Mom," he said softly.

"I know, son. But as I told you before, we can get word to her."

"That's not really the same. She'll flip out when she knows I'm gone."

David held his tongue. John needed to work this out in his own way and there was no fast-tracking it. As much as he wanted John on board, they weren't there yet.

"I can't believe I said all that to her about Cassie," John said.

"She knows you didn't mean it."

John rubbed a hand across his face.

John shook his head and a moment passed between them. Finally John spoke again.

"If I come with you," he said, "and I don't believe in what you're doing, will I be killed?"

David reached for John's arm. "Don't be ridiculous! John, no! But I will work to try to change your mind—"

"And will you be open to me changing yours?"

"About the mission? About working to create a safe and civilized world where we can all live without fear?" David shook his head. "Don't let softness or concern for the individual hamper your ability to help the whole."

John turned to look back the way they'd come.

"I just don't know," he said.

"You're smart for a reason, John. You have a God-given gift and that's a responsibility—not just to yourself or even your community. But to the world."

David knew he needed to get John moving and moving *now*.

"Come on, son," David said. "We can talk as we walk."

John nodded and got up to follow his father.

Once in the lead, David was keenly aware of every step that took him away from Sarah. Would John ever be able to forgive him once he knew the truth? He pushed the thought away.

One thing at a time.

David forged ahead down the tunnel and said his silent goodbyes to Sarah and steeled himself for the flood of sadness that couldn't help but follow.

Dammit, Sarah. I'm sorry but it's for the good of the whole world!

As he walked, he couldn't help but think few men had had to sacrifice as much as he had for that good.

Susan Kiernan-Lewis

52

Sarah stood in the archway that led to the courtyard. Debris from the gate tower littered the pavers everywhere. The smoke had cleared but small fires burned in spots near where the tower had been. From where she was standing, she could see through the broken wall to outside the castle.

Castle men and village men were standing in the courtyard now. They were armed with pick axes, ancient swords and battleaxes. Their faces were etched with fear.

She glanced up at the archers on the parapet. The girls still held their position. It had been only ten minutes since the assault with the rocket launchers. Sarah could hear the voices of the men as they talked amongst themselves. The fear was like a living beast. You could smell it.

Sarah moved quickly across the courtyard to the other side of the castle.

If there were to be more attacks—hand grenades or more missile launchers or whatever they had to throw at them— Thor would probably go for the side of the castle where he might guess most of the population was. But one thing was certain: he wouldn't blast the parapet as long as Jordie was on it.

That means Mike and the archers are safe at least. Doesn't it?

She slipped into the first archway and ran down the stone hall, hearing the slap of her leather shoes against the stones. She was struck by how quiet everything was. The dining hall, of course, was empty. She ran up the stairs taking them two at a time, her heart hammering in her chest.

She couldn't think about having just left Siobhan back there. She promised herself she would see her again. She couldn't think of the fact that the next bomb would surely be against the part of the castle she was in now.

All she could think of was that if there was even a slight chance that the man outside held her boy—who might be shot or hurt in someway...Sarah bit back the image and ran to the clinic door.

If John was out there, she had to find him. If they had him, she had to stop them.

Sometimes it's really that simple. You do what you have to because you can't not do it.

Sarah burst into the clinic and saw that the door to the secret passageway was open. A year ago they'd tried to block entry from the outside. The wood they'd used for the barricade was scattered on the floor.

Just the thought of John deliberately coming this way to leave the castle—to leave her—made Sarah want to break down and weep.

I trusted David. How could he have betrayed me like this? To take John—not just without discussing it with me— but when he knew John was so angry and upset with me!

What if David was dead? If what Thor said was true then David had been killed. All her anger dissipated like air escaping from a balloon. Had David been killed? And dear God, had John seen that?

Enough! She forced herself not to think about what she couldn't know. She needed to focus on one thing: John was out there and possibly hurt.

She needed to go to him.

She grabbed a small kerosene lantern on a clinic table and lit it with shaking hands. There wasn't much fuel in it but it was all she had. She knew the passageway was a steep incline. Steps had been cut into the stone but they were still slippery and dangerous.

Keeping her free hand on the wall for support, she began down the tunnel.

It should have been as cold as the dungeon but sweat quickly coated her hands and neck as she painstakingly worked her way down the tunnel. She saw the lantern flickering as the fire hungrily fed on the small amount of kerosene. It would go out soon. She needed to hurry.

Suddenly her foot hit a patch of sand and flew out from under her. She dropped the lantern and grabbed at the walls with both hands to try to stop her fall.

She fell anyway and skidded on her chin before slamming into the tunnel wall. She allowed herself a moment to get her bearings as she lay in the blackened space, and then forced herself to her feet.

Everything had gone instantly dark when she dropped the lantern. It must have run out of fuel about the time she dropped it.

She moved cautiously in the pitch darkness, steadying herself with a hand on each side of the tunnel. When she loosened her grip, she felt her feet slide and she allowed the natural momentum until she started sliding too fast.

In this way she worked her way inch by inch down the full length of the darkened passageway. After several minutes she began to see a glimmer of light ahead. The dank smell of the stone passageway was slowly transforming to one of vegetation which told her the outdoors was near.

She knew the passageway came out on the west side of the castle near the ocean and the woods.

It occurred to Sarah that with the gate tower destroyed, this passageway was now the only way in or out of the castle.

There was definitely daylight ahead and in her excitement, Sarah allowed herself to slide faster down the slippery steps, doing her best to keep upright and her hands connected to the tunnel walls to guide her and check her speed.

Her eyes were on the light—not fifteen feet away.

She stepped off into empty space, her arms flailing at the walls and trying to grab anything. But the rock face was smooth here and her fingers scratched impotently at the walls. The ground below slammed into her, smashing her knee in an explosion of pain.

A moment passed. Sarah lay at the entrance of the tunnel but didn't dare move. Her knee was on fire. She lifted her head and looked around. The steps had ended in a five-foot drop-off to the ground beside the entrance.

She could see handholds and divots on the face of the small cliff for ease of climbing up.

She turned and slowly moved to a sitting position, her knee screaming in agony. There was enough light now to see her pant leg was already dark with blood. She groaned. How bad was it? Was it broken?

Only one way to find out.

There wasn't enough head room in the space to stand up, but the mouth of the tunnel wasn't ten feet away. She could see trees swaying slightly in the breeze off the ocean. She turned onto her stomach and crawled to the entrance, her knee blazing in pain the whole way.

She pulled herself out onto the grass and as far from the castle wall as she could. In case anyone should find her, she didn't want to lead them to the passageway. She was drenched in sweat, her stomach roiling in nausea from the pain in her leg.

Once she was sure she was far enough away, she took in a bracing breath and reached for the nearest sapling to try to hoist herself to her feet.

As she tried to pull on it the small tree snapped off in her hands. Cursing, she crawled to the next one and tried again, all the while listening for any sounds of Thor's gang. If they had caught David and John, they might be near.

This time the sapling held her weight and she managed to pull herself to her feet. The blood from her knee was sticking to the inside of her jeans but the bleeding seemed to have stopped. If she had split open the knee, she could only pray the tough denim fabric would help to hold the wound together until she could get it treated.

She gingerly put weight on the leg. The pain ricocheted up into her hip and straight into her brain, making her eyes water. She bit her lip to prevent herself from crying out.

Afraid she'd snap the tree in half because she was gripping it so tightly, she forced herself to loosen her grip.

But agony or not, she was standing on the leg.

It wasn't broken.

Her relief was cut short as swiftly as a knife in the chest.

A sound came to her from the woods. A sound out of her worst nightmare.

The low-grade growl of an approaching wolf.

Susan Kiernan-Lewis

53

The wolf stood growling with his head lowered and his eyes locked onto Sarah. She was astounded at how large he was.

His stance was tense and telegraphed that he would attack at any second. She didn't dare look away to see if he was alone.

Anything could trigger the attack. Breaking eye contact would do.

The animal's fur was missing in spots with clumps growing between bare patches that looked diseased. Even five feet away, the smell of the beast was overwhelming. The odor of rotted blood and decayed meat blasted from its open mouth. Its lips curled back to reveal enormous gray teeth.

Sarah forced herself not to scream. Her hands were shaking. She couldn't remember whether she was supposed to avoid eye contact with the beast or engage him. It didn't matter. She couldn't drag her eyes from his yellow penetrating focus on her.

She inched her hand down toward her leg. Everyone in the castle was required to keep a utility knife in their boot at all times. Sarah had loathed the feel of the knife in its hard leather sheath next to her ankle. Eventually she got to where she hardly noticed it.

Now she prayed she could reach it in time.

She crept her fingers slowly down her leg. The sounds around her seemed to stop. The noise of the woods, even her own heart thundering in her ears—all of it was gone as she focused on the animal slowly moving toward her.

She couldn't wait.

She tucked her head and yanked at the knife.

Before her fingers could wrap around the handle the animal hit her full force, his teeth ramming against the top of her head. Her ears rang with the impact and Sarah tried to push him away. He twisted his face in fury, his snarls hot in her ear. His teeth flashed in her face and then clamped down hard on her exposed shoulder.

The agony jetted up her arm to her brain igniting hot convulsions of electric shocks.

Both her hands were sunk deep into his mangy coat, trying to keep his snapping, gnashing teeth from her throat. But he was too strong. She kept her face tucked and felt a section of her hair rip out as the beast bit again—but got no soft tissue.

If she tried for the knife again, he'd have enough time to rip her throat out.

Dear God, she couldn't fight a ravenous wolf with her bare hands!

The minute the thought slithered into her terrified brain, she felt her arms weaken.

Suddenly a gunshot shattered the air near her face and the wolf froze, his breath panting against her cheek. A long piercing whine emitted from his mouth. He went limp in her arms.

Over the wolf's back she saw two men running toward her.

Two men with guns.

Sarah tried to push the wolf off but the men reached her before she could and grabbed her by the hair, jerking her to her feet. The pain shot through her scalp and the first steps mushroomed the pain from her leg. She cried out and staggered and fell, taking the full force of her weight on her scalp.

The other man came beside her and grabbed her arm.

"Bugger bit her a good one," he said as he dragged her in the direction of the woods.

Sarah tried to walk but the pain was too great. She allowed herself to be half dragged and half carried into the woods. Up ahead she heard voices. Women's voices.

Sarah felt a coppery taste in her mouth. The world swirled around her, a vortex of seething pain.

She saw four women and several children sitting on a log. All of the women stood up as the men dragged Sarah and dumped her on the ground in front of them.

Sarah recognized the woman who had given Siobhan the jam muffin last week at the fair. Gilly. The woman's face was etched in fear now. She held a small baby in her arms.

"Oy!" one of the men said, nudging Sarah hard in the ribs with the toe of his boot. "Anyone know this bitch?"

No one spoke.

The man walked over to Gilly. He placed the barrel of his gun to the temple of the baby she was holding.

"I didn't hear you," he said.

Gilly looked down into the sleeping baby's face and spoke firmly but sadly.

"She's the American," she said. "She's Donovan's wife."

The cloud of black smoke had been pushed by the ocean breezes away from the castle and now hovered ominously over Thor's group.

All Mike could see of the damage to the gate tower was the top—completely gone. Rubble was strewn over the courtyard, where a few charred boards still smoked and smoldered.

He turned to Morgan. "Have Terry report on the status of the two men in the tower."

"Jaysus, Donovan," Morgan said, shaking his head. "I don't need to ask anyone about their status. It's clear to anyone with eyes."

"Just ask him!" Mike shouted.

As Morgan moved down the parapet, Mike turned his attention back to the bastard below. His gunmen didn't appear to be reloading. They were waiting to see what Mike would do.

Terry's men were in place now although what good they would do—seventeen antique swords against rocket launchers —Mike couldn't imagine. He turned to look at the archers. Every one of them was looking right back at him instead of at their marks.

Right. Desperate times, Mike thought. He turned and beckoned to Jordie who stood nearby. Jordie shook his head and closed his eyes.

Cursing, Mike took the four steps to lay hands on him. He dragged him weeping and hysterical to the loophole window and pulled out his gun.

"Oy, Thor!" Mike called. "Can ye see me well enough?"

"Aye," Thor yelled back. "I see ye."

Mike shoved Jordie to the front of the window and stepped in beside him. He held the gun to Jordie's head.

"How's this for justice, Thor?" Mike bellowed. "I shoot the bugger right in front of you and you get exactly feck-all. How does that work for you?"

Sacrifice. For the good of the whole.

Thor screamed, "No! Don't you do it! Do you hear me? I want him in one piece not a crumpled scrap of garbage insensible to the justice I'll deal out to him."

Out of the corner of his eye Mike saw that Morgan had moved among the archers. His gun was in his hand.

Mike's stomach roiled in nausea.

Is it possible the auld bastard is in league with Thor?

"I care exactly feck-all for what you want!" Mike yelled. "Leave the women and children behind and clear the feck off or I'll shoot the bastard right now!"

Suddenly a man ran out of the woods and over to where Thor stood. He wore a helmet and held a garbage can lid in front of him as a shield. He spoke to Thor and then ran back to the woods.

When Thor turned to look up at the castle, his face was nothing short of jubilant.

"Sure you're a stubborn man, Donovan, ye bastard," Thor shouted, "and I can see it wouldn't matter to you if I shot every woman and bairn in the village. Am I right?"

"Leave *now*," Donovan said, "or I kill the lad as sure as you're standing there."

But the fear that Thor had shown just a few seconds ago was gone.

What had just happened? Was the bastard really going to call Mike's bluff?

"Nay, I don't think ye will, sure I do not," Thor said as he raised his hand in a signal.

One of Thor's men emerged from the woods. In front of him he held Sarah, stumbling and limping.

Mike's arm sagged to his side and he felt his fingers grow cold.

"So, Mr. Donovan," Thor said gleefully, "you'll be sending the bastard down to me nice and gentle like or I'll kill Mrs. Donovan before your very eyes. So I will."

Susan Kiernan-Lewis

54

Mike watched in horror as Thor exchanged the woman in front of him for Sarah and put his gun to her head.

"I'll make it easy on ye," Thor said. "Lower the drawbridge and we'll come in and take possession of the bastard ourselves."

Mike licked his lips. The feel of an anvil weighed on the center of his chest.

"You blew up the gate tower," Mike said. "I can't get the drawbridge up or down now."

Even from this distance Mike could see Sarah was not standing on her own. Her right knee was stained red from ankle to knee.

What had they done to her?

"Sure I might be able to help you with that," Thor said, "but I'll be none too pleased if you force me to use any more munitions to gain entrance to the castle. So figure it out!" The maniac shook Sarah like a rag doll as he screamed his last three words.

Sacrifice. For the good of the whole.

The time was now. There was nothing more to lose.

Except there was of course everything to lose.

Fourteen arrows against rocket launchers and God knows what else.

They were all going to die. Every last one of them.

Mike's eyes filled as he watched Sarah struggle in Thor's grip.

He cleared his throat to give the order. The one that would consign them all to a bloody and immediate death.

I love ye, Sarah. From now until eternity. I'll always love ye...

Morgan reached the first girl he came to—Kyla. He put his hands on her arms from behind and she jumped at his touch. He spoke in a controlled voice clear enough to be heard by all fourteen girls,

"Anyone who makes a move for those stairs," he said calmly, "I'll throw your arse over the castle wall meself."

"But we only have one arrow," Tilly whimpered.

"So make it count," Morgan said firmly. "You know what to do. No misses now or you'll answer to me."

He watched them visibly stiffen one by one, their backs straightened, their eyes back on the targets.

"Archers," Morgan said loudly. "Are ye ready to end this bollocks?"

"Archers at the ready!" Regan shouted, her fists clenched at her side, her face a mask of determination.

Morgan had been right about that one. She was the one they would follow. If any of them survived this day, she'd be their new leader.

"You heard her!" Morgan said. "At my word, ye'll fire and by God ye'll not touch a hair of a single hostage. Archers pick your target! Draw!"

All Mike could see was Sarah's head pulled back tight against Thor's chest. Her throat was exposed and the gun was jammed to her neck.

Mike trained his gun on Thor's head. Sarah was moving too much to get a clear shot. It was impossible. No way was anyone going to be able to hit Thor without killing Sarah.

Mike's gun hand felt coated with sweat. Suddenly, Sarah convulsed in Thor's grip and shrieked, "John! Are you here? John!"

From behind her, one of the village women screamed out, "He got away! He's not here!"

Thor swiveled on one foot and jerked the gun from Sarah's head long enough to point it at the woman.

He shot her in the face.

The woman crumpled to the ground at the same time Sarah grabbed Thor's forearm and sank her teeth into it.

Mike opened his mouth to shout *fire!* or *stop!* He would never know which. His voice came out a hoarse whisper that was grabbed by the wind and flung away unheard to the four corners.

Thor howled in rage and smashed his gun against Sarah's face to loosen her bite.

Morgan's voice boomed out, vibrating through the air, each word louder than the last.

"Fire! Fire! Fire!"

Mike watched in horror as the archers let loose their arrows on everyone below.

Susan Kiernan-Lewis

55

Sarah felt the arrow as it hit her body like a small dense punch as she fell, the smell of blood and fear and urine in her nose.

Her head spun or the world did. She didn't know when Thor released her but she was free and untethered. Even the pain had let loose its grip of her as she flew, whirling and twirling.

She watched the sky spin about her as she was flung outward toward the edge of the moat. Her legs gave way immediately and she fell as if in slow motion.

The falling took forever until she was finally sliding… into the mud and the grit and the thick hardening ooze of ash and rainwater.

She felt the mud from the storm thick against the sides as her fingers opened and shut impotently to slow her descent. She knew it was impossible. She could do nothing about whatever happened now.

There was some peace in that.

Slowly she stopped sliding and felt the base of one of the large sharpened stakes that lined the moat which had halted her descent to the bottom.

Jocko stared in shock at the arrow shaft jutting out from his chest just below his heart. He groaned and released the girl in front of him. She dropped away or fled, he couldn't tell which. His legs crumpled under him and he fell to the ground in an awkward sitting position. The impact knocked the air out of him.

The arrow was all he could see in his peripheral vision. Straight out from his chest. The little feather on the end fluttered in the gentle breeze.

How had they done that? How had they possibly hit him?

He looked up and saw the girls were gone. They'd done their damage.

I'm dying. Holy shite, I'm really dying, he thought in disbelief, his handgun heavy in his hand.

Suddenly he saw movement behind one of the crenels of the parapet. A man had jumped up and was leaning over the front edge to assess the damage. And laughing. Jocko was sure the bastard was laughing in triumph.

It was the cocky bastard who'd held the gun to the rapist's head…the gobshite responsible for all this… Jocko raised his gun, the dying sun stabbing into his eyes but the bastard in his sights. His hand shook with the effort to keep the bastard's head in his cross hairs.

With his final breath, Jocko squeezed the trigger. He watched the bugger lurch as the bullet hit him. The man seemed to hesitate at first like he wasn't sure what was happening, then he turned slowly and fell over the castle wall.

With a grunt of satisfaction, Jocko dropped his gun in the dirt beside him.

And collapsed on top of it.

56

Mike gaped at the scene below—the crumpled bodies, the screaming, running women and children. Thor's limp body with an arrow protruding from his face and the sight of Sarah tumbling into the moat.

The sound of a single gunshot made him jerk his head to see Morgan clutching his throat and then slowly falling over the front wall.

Mike pushed past Jordie cowering in the alcove of the loophole window.

Regan reached the spot where Morgan fell before Mike. She stood with her hands on the edge of the crenel and stared over the side at Morgan's body on the ground, a stricken look on her face.

Mike needed to find Sarah. He turned toward the stairs when he heard a loud buzzing sound overhead. He froze.

It was the sound of an approaching plane.

He looked skyward, an ache erupting in the back of his throat. He'd never heard the plane's engine before—only the bombs it dropped. There could be only one reason why he was hearing the engine now.

He shouted down to the women outside the castle, "Go to the drawbridge! Get inside as fast as you can! Hurry! Run!"

He turned to Regan. "Get everyone to the dungeons," he shouted. As he ran down the stairs to the courtyard, he yelled to the men below.

"Lower the drawbridge! Cut the cables! Bring it down! Hurry!"

Terry was already in the smoking remains of the gate tower using a giant axe to hack at the heavy ropes holding the drawbridge vertical. Two of the village men grappled with the cables that held the portcullis in place, hauling down on them until the steel gate began to slowly lift.

Seconds felt like hours as the plane circled overhead.

Picking its spot.

"Hurry!" Mike shouted as the men worked in tandem to lift the portcullis and lower the damaged drawbridge. He sent a prayer of thanks that the castle's museum renovators had opted for the more authentic ropes instead of steel cables to raise and lower the drawbridge.

He and his people would have had no chance at all if they hadn't.

"It's free!" one of the men yelled and Mike saw the sky through the castle entrance as the drawbridge smashed down hard across the moat sending pieces of it flying as it did.

The people from outside poured over the drawbridge and under the portcullis—jammed halfway down—pushing past Mike in their panic as he tried to get out. Women holding babies, clutching the hands of screaming, crying children. Their men met them and snatched up children and ran with them while the bomber's engines droned loudly overhead.

Mike ran across the broken drawbridge.

He heard the bomb whistle as it fell and spent his last moment praying that his people would make it to the dungeons in time.

57

The impact of the blast sent Mike flying from the drawbridge as the bomb hit the corner of the parking lot in a fiery ball of red and yellow, billowing like a miniature mushroom cloud. Tossing him ten feet in the air, he landed in a splay of gorse near where Thor had held Sarah in front of the castle.

Not bothering to check his injuries he scrambled to his feet. The sound of the explosion was still reverberating in his head as he fought to keep his balance.

The blast had rattled the tops of the parapet knocking several of the top stones onto the gate tower and the moat.

The moat.

He turned and glimpsed a scrap of blue denim fabric over the edge of the ditch.

With dread and mounting panic, he ran to the moat.

She was pressed up against the sloping muddy side of the moat. Her eyes were closed. She wasn't moving.

Mike slid into the steep ditch and gently lifted her under the arms. She had an arrow in her shoulder and a bloody gash across her nose. She felt cold in his arms. Mike tried to get purchase up the steep side of the moat with her in his arms.

That was when he heard the sound of the plane returning.

He slid back into the moat.

There was no way.

Even if he managed to get them both up the sides of the steep moat, he'd never make it into the castle or to the dungeons in time.

As the sound of the plane grew louder, he bent his head and kissed her lips. He thanked God that he would be allowed to spend his last moments on earth with the woman he loved.

The woman for whom he would gladly do it all over again even if it were to end like this a thousand times.

John broke through the thick stand of horse chestnut trees on the east side of the woods, the sound of the bomb's explosion still ringing in his ears. He stared in horror at the scene before him. Bodies were scattered everywhere.

The entrance to the castle was gone.

He didn't know what had made him turn back. He and his father were a quarter of a mile down the tunnel when John simply turned and ran back to the entrance. He didn't know why. All he knew was that he had to go back. He had to see for himself that the worst hadn't happened.

When John stepped out of the woods and ran to the front of the castle, he saw Mike run to the moat, and his heart hammered in his throat.

David grabbed John's arm from behind.

"John! Listen to me!" David gasped, fighting for breath. "The bomber will make a return run. We've got to hurry! It's coming back!"

John shook off his father's arm and ran, dodging the chunks of cement blocks from the castle's western wall that were now scattered along the moat line like a set of children's blocks.

Why was Mike out here? Why wasn't he inside the castle with everyone else?

John ran to the edge of the moat. There at the bottom, Mike looked up at him from where he cradled John's unconscious mother in his arms.

"Mike!" John yelled. "Hurry! There's a tunnel in the woods!"

He felt his father take his arm and pull him back. The sound of the returning plane was growing louder now.

David slid down the steep incline and held out his arms to Mike. John watched as Mike pushed his mother's limp body into his father's arms.

Struggling, with Mike pushing from below, David climbed back to the top of the rim of the moat and laid Sarah on the ground.

John gasped at the sight of the arrow in her shoulder. He looked around in bewilderment at the front lawn of the castle —at the bodies—and pieces of bodies—everywhere.

David lifted Sarah back into his arms and began to run in the direction of the woods.

"Run, John! Run!" David shouted as the sounds of the plane grew louder and louder until it seemed the noise of its engines blocked out all other sound.

Mike stumbled after them, tripping once but not falling. The woods were ahead. The entrance of the tunnel was just a few yards from there.

If they could just get to the tunnel in time...

They made it to the woods. John was behind his father and ahead of Mike. Only a few more yards... just a few more feet until...

John heard the sound of the second eight-hundred pound bomb as it sailed home above them.

Susan Kiernan-Lewis

58

It was a direct hit on the castle.

And for that Sarah would always be grateful.

Just a few hundred yards to the east and even the tunnel wouldn't have saved them. It would simply have entombed them.

It was the sound of the bomb as it hit—combined with the agony of coming to consciousness as David dove into the tunnel with her in his arms—that brought Sarah around.

When she opened her eyes, everything was dark. She thought she was dead or blind. Her leg, her face, her arm were in pounding, writhing agony.

But she was alive.

When she heard John's voice in the darkness, she began to cry.

"Mom, you okay? Mom, I'm so sorry. Please don't die. Please I'm so sorry for what I said."

And Sarah sobbed, her hands reaching for her son in the darkness to clutch his shirt and weep into his shoulder. The pain of her physical injuries all but gone with the joy of holding him again.

The sound of a familiar groan made her turn in the dark to the source. She reached out her hand to him.

"Mike," she gasped.

"I'm here, lass," he said, his voice choked with emotion.

"We survived," she said. "We lived through it."

"Aye," he said softly.

The sound of a match striking brought her surroundings into sharp relief. Sarah squinted in the gloom to see they were in a tunnel made of dirt walls bolstered by two by fours.

David pulled out a knapsack and took out a plastic water bottle. He handed it to Sarah but she could only stare at it. Mike took it from him and held it to her lips while she drank.

"Is she going to be okay, Dad?" John asked worriedly.

"The arrow's only in a couple of inches," David said. "Probably hit a bone."

"Will they come back?" Mike asked David.

Sarah had closed her eyes but now they fluttered open.

Of course. David would know about the planes.

David shook his head. "You should be safe now."

"And if we try to rebuild?" Mike asked.

"They won't be back. I promise."

59

Sarah didn't remember how they got from the tunnel and back into the castle. She remembered nothing of her trip up to the clinic either. Fortunately, the clinic was one of the few places in the castle that hadn't been destroyed or so badly damaged that it was beyond use.

Every detail of Mike's den with its mahogany desk and floor to ceiling bookshelves—every first edition and Oriental rug—was now fully visible from the courtyard.

The courtyard was full of rubble from the two castle walls that had caved in on top of it. The back seaward wall was undamaged as were most of the stables—even so the cow had been killed.

The dungeons were completely intact.

And so was every person who had found shelter there.

All of the castle people and all of the villagers survived the bombing.

Before nightfall Mike and his men had gathered up all of Thor's weapons. With three of the four castle walls down they would once more be living exposed and vulnerable to attack but at least they were well armed once more.

When Sarah awoke—two days after the castle was destroyed by the second bomb—she was informed in a very business like manner by Sister Alphonse that she'd suffered a fractured kneecap, a gash across the bridge of her nose where Thor had smashed her with his gun, a ragged but half-hearted canine bite on her shoulder and an arrow hole in the opposite shoulder—thankfully shallow since it hit the clavicle.

Sarah was never so glad to know that most of the castle's morphine supplies had not been destroyed.

That afternoon, the first person she saw was John who sat reading a book by her bedside.

She watched him for several seconds before he noticed she was awake. She just wanted to enjoy the sight of him and feel, deep into her bones, the exquisite pleasure of knowing he was safe and home.

Home.

"Hey, you're awake," John said as he put down his book.

"Hi, there," she said, her eyes misting with emotion. "Have you been here long?"

"Naw. But it's a nice quiet place after all the pandemonium. Da says he'll bring Shivvy in to see you later today."

"Everyone…okay?"

"Everyone survived the bombing," John said.

Sarah shook her head in wonder. "Do we still have a castle?"

He grinned. "Not really. Basically just this clinic. The rest is a pile of rocks."

"Oh, well."

"Doesn't matter. Mike's got plans. We'll put it back together."

"Mike always has plans. And…your father?"

"He's still here. He didn't want to leave until he'd spoken to you."

"And…and you…are you…?"

"I'm not leaving, Mom."

Tears sprang to Sarah's eyes. John shook his head and looked down at his hands.

"I'm really sorry, Mom. I don't know why I overreacted like that."

But Sarah knew. It was because for one horrible moment, John thought his father had killed Cassie and he couldn't face it. So he went after Sarah.

"It doesn't matter, sweetheart," she said, reaching for his hand. "I promise you we'll find out who did it."

"Mike nearly flipped out when I told him. He didn't even know she'd been killed."

"So much happened in just a few hours."

"I know. Both Mr. O'Malleys were killed in the gate tower. They found, like, pieces of them in the courtyard."

"Poor Mary and Liddy," Sarah said. "Anybody else?"

"Well, the old lady that Thor shot. And then the other woman who yelled to you just before all hell broke loose. And of course Mr. Morgan. He was shot after it was all over. One of the bad guys had just enough life in him to pull the trigger."

"I'm so sorry. How are the little boys?"

"Pretty upset. Aunt Fiona is taking care of them for now."

"I guess it could have been much worse."

"I don't know, Mom. The castle's destroyed, you're pretty badly hurt and we lost three people."

But the things that really matter, Sarah couldn't help but think as she gazed at her boy. *I still have those.*

"It wasn't until the bastards shot at us that Dad and I even knew what was happening," John said.

"I don't understand why you didn't just go straight into the woods from the castle passageway. How is it you nearly got caught by Thor's men?" Sarah asked.

John shrugged and looked away. "Dad dropped something out front when he first came to the castle and he wanted to retrieve it."

"What in the world was that?"

John hesitated. "It's not important," he said.

Mike stood in the workshop as Terry worked with his head bent close to his worktable to craft more arrows. Mary came in silently with a cup of tea for both of them. Her shoulders sagged with sorrow.

Mike thanked her for the tea but said nothing more.

She had admitted to destroying the arrows to prove that the girl archers were nothing without their bows and arrows.

Mike had felt forced to impress upon her at the time that she'd very nearly gotten them all killed as a result of it.

"What'll ye do with her, squire?" Terry asked after she left. "Is it enough that she's lost her husband?"

"The archers want blood," Mike said. "They're laying Morgan's death at her feet. Turns out they liked the auld tosser."

"Isn't it enough that she feels responsible for the death of her own husband?"

"Evidently not."

"That's hardly fair."

"Welcome to my world."

The thought of Artemus Morgan pierced Mike with sadness. The bastard would have been a challenge to live with there was no two ways about it. But it would have been better for the castle, without doubt, with him as a part of it.

Regan's words the morning after the attack when they buried Morgan still rang in Mike's head.

"Why do we keeping losing the auld ones?" she'd asked sadly before turning away.

Morgan had fired his gun during the attack and made every bullet count. As it happened, Mike hadn't shot his weapon during the rain of arrows. But he hadn't needed to.

One way or the other, every man holding a hostage had been killed. And except for Sarah, none of the other human shields was hurt.

Because of the way Thor had been holding her, it was deemed nearly impossible to take him down without at least grazing her. His corpse revealed an arrow through one eye.

Regan was now officially the archers' new leader. Aibreann was still in the squad but she had asked to be allowed to work part time in the nursery.

That first evening after the attack while Sarah was in the clinic, David had made the surprisingly helpful suggestion that a separate military tribunal be set up to deal with infractions by the archers.

That way they wouldn't be held to the same laws as the rest of the castle—but in some ways they'd be forced to adhere to much stricter rules. The tribunal would be headed by Sarah and Fiona—the two castle matriarchs. After all, what was a community that was eighty percent women if not a matriarchy? Regan as the archers' leader would also sit on the tribunal, as well as Mike and one rotating member of the castle civilian population—to serve as tiebreaker.

It made sense to Mike that the squad was dealt with separately from the rest of the castle population. He still agreed with their receiving special privileges—their breathtaking skills with the bow in the skirmish against Thor was evidence enough for that—but he saw David's point that that might be better balanced with special responsibilities too.

He was pretty sure Artemus Morgan would have agreed.

As for Morgan's grandsons, Matt and Mac, Mike was gratified to see John had already taken them under his wing. They were grand little lads, both of them. He had made a mental note to talk to Sarah about adopting them.

What was two more?

At the thought of Sarah, Mike shook his head in amazement. Two days ago he'd lost everything—or he was sure he had. To have come so close to losing her—closer than he ever had before—seemed to have altered something fundamentally in him.

Somehow he swore he was never going to feel that terrible impending loss again. He wasn't sure what he could do to ensure it. A part of him had died during that moment when he watched her fall wounded into the moat.

Somehow he was never going to take the chance of that happening again.

"Oy! Governor," Kylie said, entering the workshop. "The newcomers are begging a word."

Mike looked up and frowned to see two figures approach him, backlit through the light of the open, broken, barn door. As they got closer he saw that it was Thor's widow and daughter Rose—*better known*, Mike thought grimly, *as the whole reason for this fecking mess.*

But he knew that wasn't true. Thor was a psychopath. If it hadn't been for the attack on his daughter, it would just have been some other reason.

After the slaughter, the two women had been found huddling in the woods with a few other castle women and two of Thor's men.

The men had been stripped of their weapons and sent on their way.

The women had asked for and were given refuge in what was left of the castle.

Emma and Rose Dennehy now stood before Mike. He had to admit neither of them looked particularly grief-stricken after the recent death of Thor.

"May I help you, Missus?"

"Mr. Donovan," Emma said. "First I want to thank you again for giving us sanctuary, especially after what…after my husband…"

"You're welcome, Mrs. Dennehy," Donovan said abruptly. This was the sort of thing Sarah usually handled. The thought of his wife reminded Mike that he'd been hoping to check in on her before lunch. The last time he saw her, she nearly looked like her old self again.

"I have overheard from some of the others," Emma said, "that you are holding the young man Jordie for the crime against…against…"

"Aye, that's right," Mike said. "Until we can get to the bottom of this. He'll stand trial. Just as I told your husband he would."

"Well, that's just it… my daughter would like to say something about that," Emma said, pressing her lips together in a firm line.

Awww, don't tell me, Mike thought looking at the girl who appeared to be a large thirteen year old but a child in every other way.

"He didn't rape me," Rose said in a small voice.

Mike stared at her. The full realization of what she was saying thundered through him. People had died, good people. And all for what? Because a teenager was having a snit?

"May I ask ye why you said that he did?" Mike asked tightly.

Rose shrugged and looked at her feet. "Sorry," she said.

"Sorry?" Mike said.

"I think… in her defense," Emma said hurriedly, "she had recently discovered she was in the family way and then when she ran into your lad she…she…"

"We didn't do anything!" Rose said. "We just had a laugh and shared a ciggie. But I knew when Da found out I was up the pole, he'd come unglued." Rose looked at Mike. "He would have killed me if I hadn't told him I was forced."

"Marcus had a temper," Emma said. "I didn't know Rose was lying about the rape until yesterday but I can understand why she did it. I'm that sorry, Mr. Donovan and I can also understand if you want us gone from your community."

Kylie snorted from where she stood lining up a stack of finished arrows. Mike turned to her.

"Go find Tommy and have him release Jordie from the dungeon. Then have him send Jordie to me."

Kylie nodded and left the workshop.

"So you're pregnant?" Mike asked Rose, who only looked at her feet.

"She is," Emma said.

"Surely your husband would have known that your daughter's pregnancy couldn't be from a rape committed two days ago?"

Emma looked at him blankly.

Mike felt an exhaustion filter through him. *What the feck did any of it matter now?*

"Thank you for coming forward," he said before abruptly walking down the aisle toward the stable door.

He was seriously afraid he might say something he'd regret.

Susan Kiernan-Lewis

60

David wondered if he would miss this when he was back at base. He didn't disdain the luxuries he enjoyed at MPC—electricity, hot tubs, saunas. But there was something to be said for the purity of the rustic simplicity of this life.

It was perfect in its own way.

But maybe for only short periods of time.

He sat on an overturned wine barrel as the sun began to dip down below the horizon. They'd begun to clear the courtyard although it would never resemble anything ever again by that name.

There were several large, iron cauldrons bubbling with soups and stews over four carefully managed open fires in the green space outside the castle. Several pigs and three cows from the village were tethered nearby until the stables could be repaired.

He watched as John walked out from the broken archway that led down from the second level of the castle. Because the interior wall had been destroyed, the staircase was visible. David watched John as he descended and stepped outdoors.

David raised a hand to get his attention.

"Wow," John said as he joined him. "Dinner smells good. What is it, do you know?"

"Some kind of stew, I'm told," David said. "So how is she?"

John settled down by his father and turned his gaze to the activity around the cook pots as the village and castle women tended to them.

"Sister Alphonse says she'll be up and about in a day or so. And she's not in any pain."

"That's good."

John turned to look at him. "Thank you for going back for her," he said.

"Of course," David said uncomfortably. "I care about your mother. I always will."

A moment of silence extended between them.

If there was any chance, any hope at all that John might leave with him in the morning, David knew that now was the time to make that happen. After they'd rescued Mike and Sarah and returned to the castle, John had given him no indication of how he felt.

But in his heart, David pretty much already knew the answer.

"Is Mom talking to you yet?" John asked.

"She's definitely annoyed with me," David said. "As she should be. Pretty crappy, my running off with you like that. Especially with unfinished business between the two of you. Have you sorted that out by the way?"

John nodded. "I don't know what got into me. I…I loved Cassie and seeing her like that…I just flipped out, I guess."

"I'm sure your mother understood."

"She said she did."

"But I'm still not going to get you to change your mind, am I?"

"I know you want me to help you rebuild the world when the time comes, Dad, but first I need to rebuild my little world right here."

"I understand."

"I hope so."

"I do, son."

"And when you leave? You'll stay in touch?"

"Absolutely. Count on it."

It seemed like every single person in the castle had been waiting for Sarah to open her eyes so they could visit. After the tenth visitor, she was exhausted and Sister Alphonse had shooed the rest of them away.

The outpouring of love and concern felt good. Even Mary and Liddy came to see how she was and for Mary at least that must have taken a lot of courage. Because Jordie had been transferred back to the dungeon as soon as the smoke had cleared, Eliza had been up to beg Sarah to use her influence on Mike for his release.

Fortunately, she'd been the visitor that Sister had decided to begin her *no-more-visitors* campaign on.

If Jordie *had* assaulted the girl, they'd find out in short order—unless it devolved into a situation of *he said she said*, in which case it would probably be dropped for lack of evidence.

The pain medicines helped enormously but Sarah was still fairly uncomfortable and her thirst seemed unquenchable. Plus, she felt guilty because she knew it was a hardship to lug great quantities of drinking water up to the clinic.

The fact was everything was going to be a hardship now. Everything that had merely been inconvenient or uncomfortable before was now going to be problematic or downright impossible. It was hard to believe the castle could be so badly damaged.

Without seeing it with her own eyes—and frankly the clinic looked exactly as it had before the attack—it was difficult to imagine. But visitor after visitor had extolled the extent of the damage.

Fiona and Nuala had brought Siobhan and Ciara in to see Sarah just before dinner and Sarah was gratified to see the child was as ebullient as ever. As far as she and the other children were concerned, they were just camping out and this was only one more experience to add to the adventure that was their lives.

Sarah smiled at the thought of her exuberant daughter, whose face was still smeared with her supper.

Fi had been less welcoming.

"I can't believe you made me think you were going to Mike and all along you were planning on leaving the castle," Fiona had scolded her.

All Sarah could do was point to Ciara and say, "Wait until this one gets old enough to have a mind of her own and then tell me you'd do any different in the same situation."

In the end, they'd hugged—gingerly being mindful of Sarah's various punctures, bites and scrapes—before Nuala and Fiona left to go orchestrate bath time for the children with no way to heat the water or even transport it easily.

Thank God it's still summer, Sarah thought. *How will it be come November?*

She closed her eyes and was listening to Sister Alphonse potter about the clinic, washing utensils and dishes when there was a light tap at the door. Sarah smiled.

She'd recognize her husband's knock anywhere.

"So there's Himself now," Sister said. "Sure I'll put those in water for you."

Mike came through the door, his face grimy from his day's labors, and a bouquet of wildflowers in his hands. Sister took the flowers—a handful of primroses, wood anemones and bluebells—and left the room in search of water.

Sarah smiled as he came to her and kissed her.

"How is it this evening?" he asked as he pulled up a chair next to the bed.

"I'll be able to pull my own weight this time tomorrow," she said with a smile.

"Go on with ye," he said with a raised eyebrow. But his eyes danced with pleasure at her words.

"What's happening in the castle?"

"Haven't your steady stream of visitors filled you in at-tall?"

"They've said it's like we're camping out again. That the dungeons and the clinic are the only rooms left standing."

"So they didn't exaggerate."

"God, Mike. Where is everyone sleeping?"

He shrugged. "There's no rain on the horizon. We'll be fine, so we will, until we can get some rudimentary structures in place."

"God, it seems like all we do is rebuild. I'm so tired of it."

"Aye, lass," he said and took her hand. "It's a hard life now, so it is."

"I'm too old for it to be so hard all the time," Sarah said and then, afraid she sounded like she was whining, she squeezed his hand. "Don't listen to me. I'm due for more drugs soon."

He laughed.

"Eliza is upset about Jordie being in jail," Sarah said, yawning.

"The lad is sprung, so he is," Mike said. "The lass in question came forward to say it was all a yarn."

"You are kidding me."

"Sure I'm not at-tall. And you'll know young Jordie is a bit of hero in the castle at the moment."

"This I have to hear."

"Because of him none of the castle horses were killed in the bombing."

"Well, that's one way to look at it, I suppose. Except they're still missing, right?"

"Aye, they are."

"I think John's decided to stay," Sarah said. "Have you talked with him?"

Mike nodded. "Briefly. Aye, and I'm that glad, too. There's a lot to be done and we're short two men."

"Wow. No wonder he has stepfather issues with you," Sarah said with a grin.

"Sure the lad knows my feelings for him," Mike said. "But that doesn't take away from the fact that we need him now more than ever."

"Well, whatever will get him to stay is fine with me. What about Gavin? Are you thinking of going out looking for him? I guess I don't need to tell you it's been too long."

"Sophia's been doing a good job of telling me that," he said, "as if she needed to. We'll find the horses first and then I'll go."

"I'm sure he's fine, Mike."

"Oh, sure, and why wouldn't he be?" His voice was light but the tension was palpable beneath the surface of his words.

377

"We've been through so much," Sarah said. "Sometimes I can't even believe it all."

"I was so worried, lass," Mike said reaching for her hand and bringing it to his lips. "When I saw ye in the hands of that monster—a gun to yer head…" He shook his head and his eyes filled.

"I know. I'm sorry. I just couldn't help going after John. I just physically couldn't help it. And I made everything worse for everyone. It's a miracle we all ended up in one piece." She nodded at her heavily bandaged shoulder. "Well, mostly one piece."

"Ye know this is a younger man's game, what we're doing."

"You mean surviving in a post-apocalyptic world? What choice do we have?"

"I don't know," he said thoughtfully. "But Regan said something when we buried poor auld Morgan. She said 'why do we always have to lose the auld ones?'"

"And I guess that makes us the auld ones now?" Sarah said with smile and then she sobered. "I'm so sorry about him. I know you really liked him."

"Aye. And he leaves those two lads of his."

"About that," Sarah said, shifting in bed to sit up higher. Mike rearranged her pillow. "Do you think we could take them? I mean, John already loves them and—"

Mike laughed and shook his head.

"Sarah Donovan," he said. "How is it I'm so blessed to have you in my life?"

"I ask the same question, Mike," she said softly, her eyes dewy with emotion. "All the time."

He leaned over and kissed her and then sat on the bed and pulled her gently into his arms. He felt her sigh when she relaxed in his arms. They didn't need to speak any more tonight. They were together. And together the world was grand and the world was just right.

He held her and felt the first peace that he'd experienced since the moment he'd seen her standing with Thor.

When he heard the soft purr of her snores and knew she was deeply asleep, he got up and tucked her blankets around her. He was gazing at her sleeping face when Sister Alphonse came in with the wildflowers in a small glass vase.

She nodded at Sarah and held the door open for Mike.

"Thank you, Sister," he whispered on his way out. He stood in the hall for a moment after she'd closed the door and looked down the hall where the inner wall was now missing and the sounds of the castle preparing for night was suddenly all around him.

A figure stood in the shadows.

Mike approached it. He felt his heart beat begin to race even though he knew he was safe and that there was no danger here.

It was Jordie, his eyes white and fearful in the dark.

Mike walked past him. "Come," he said.

They walked to the next set of stairs. A large section was missing but Mike took it easily in one long step. He didn't look back to see how Jordie was managing it but when he reached the opening to his den—there was no wall or door now—Jordie was behind him.

Mike stepped inside to where his mahogany desk still sat. He hadn't made up his mind whether to keep it or use it for kindling. The entire room had been a joke in the first place.

Plaster, small stones and chunks of masonry littered the Oriental rug and chairs in the room. Mike heaved himself into the large chair behind the desk. A small ceiling fixture sat broken on the surface of the desk and Mike pushed it to the floor with one arm. The sound made Jordie start violently.

"Why are you so jumpy?" Mike asked. "I should think you'd know by now I'm not going to hang you or flay you alive."

"I know," Jordie said, sitting on the edge of one of the leather club chairs.

"And you know the lass recanted her accusation against you?"

Jordie nodded. He continued to look terrified.

"I'm just so sorry," Jordie said. "I'm so sorry for everything."

Mike knew the lad had been through hell when he'd been the juicy prize of a maniac. Plus there was that desperate moment when Mike had held a gun to Jordie's temple and threatened to blow his brains out.

"Look, lad, things happened when that lunatic bastard came to the castle. There's no denying you got the short end of the stick and it's me who's sorry for putting you through that."

"No sir!" Jordie said vehemently. "I deserved it. I deserved everything that happened to me. And more." He looked down at his hands as if forcing himself not to say more.

Mike narrowed his eyes as he watched the man.

Fecking strange behavior for a man just found innocent of a crime.

Perhaps the trauma of that day had really unstrung him?

"Ye deserve nothing of the kind," Mike said firmly. "And there's an end to it. Mr. Donoghue is organizing apprenticeships and you'll be in line to have one. So if there's anything you think you'd like to do, talk to him."

"I will," Jordie said, his head still down.

Mike sighed. "That's all, lad. Go find your dinner if you haven't already."

Jordie got up and went to the doorway from which the rubble-strewn courtyard was visible. And with the eastern castle wall down, so was the coastline for as far as the eye could see.

"I just wanted to say sorry," Jordie said again before slipping away into the moonlit evening.

Mike looked out at the space that Jordie had filled just seconds ago and found himself wondering what exactly the poor plodder was sorry for?

61

The next morning Sister Alphonse helped Sarah walk with the aid of a cane down the hall to Sarah's bedroom.

"There's naught to see," the nun said. "Just rubble and trash. Same as the rest of the castle."

Sarah had prepared herself. After three days living in the clinic she was fairly confident she had a realistic view of the damage that had been done to the castle. The minute she stepped out into the hallway, that delusion was ripped away.

The hall outside the clinic was a freestanding outdoor walkway, open to the sky and the elements. It provided an overview of the devastation below in the courtyard. Most of the castle walls seemed to have ended up there. Sarah found it hard to imagine how anyone could cross the area or reclaim its use.

Sister kept her hand on Sarah's shoulder as Sarah leaned on the cane.

"It looks worse than it is," Sister said.

Sarah nearly laughed. "It looks like a bomb dropped on it," she said.

"Well, then, it looks just as it should, since one did."

How were they ever going to fix this mess? The castle had been reduced to a pile of rocks and landfill.

"How do people get in and out of the stables?" Sarah asked. She knew Terry's workshop—being on the ocean wall —had suffered almost no damage.

"I understand they have a pathway through the debris below although ye can't see it too easily from here."

Sarah shook her head. The job looked too much for any normal, mortal people to put right. With a sigh she reminded herself of the Egyptians and their pyramids and put it from her mind.

They would have to put it back together. What were their options otherwise?

When Sister Alphonse led her to the gaping opening off the walkway that used to be her bedroom—her wonderful, cozy room—for the first time since she'd awakened, Sarah felt like she wanted to cry.

The bed was still there but under most of the collapsed ceiling. All of her books looked like they'd exploded sending a shower of confetti all over the room.

"I'll leave you now, Sarah," Sister said. "Is that all right?"

"Yes, yes. I'll be fine," Sarah said, stepping into the room.

"Mind you don't make your injuries worse! There's a lot to hurt yourself in this room."

Sarah didn't answer but just looked around the room in horror and with a sinking heart as the nun left.

"Whoa! What a mess," said a familiar voice from the walkway.

She turned to see David standing there, shaking his head as he gazed at the wrecked room.

"You're still here," she said before limping over to the bed and knocking some of the bigger pieces of rubble onto the floor.

"We're leaving after lunch," he said as he entered the room, then squatted to pick up an intact book and flip through its pages.

"We?" She turned to look at him but he didn't look up.

"This one's not too badly damaged," he said. "*A Man in Full*. Wow. Didn't you already read this about twenty years ago?"

"You must be thinking of someone else." Sarah sat on the corner of the bed.

He stood up and tossed the book in the direction of an overturned table.

"Yeah, maybe," he said.

"I can't believe you came back for me," she said. "And with a bomber circling overhead."

"Why is it so hard to believe? I was married to you once."

"So you finally accept we're no longer married?"

"I don't know what I accept, Sarah," David said, raking his fingers through his hair. "But I know you're the mother of my only child and someone I care about."

"Even though you were going to let the bomber kill me and everyone else in the castle?"

"It's complicated."

"Wow. You finally got a sense of humor."

"I always had one. You just never understood it."

"And for that I am grateful." She paused. "But seriously. Thank you."

"Look, Sarah. I want you to know that in spite of everything I really do wish you well. I hope you're happy. I wish that for you."

"Thanks, David. I wish that for you, too." She hesitated. "In the spirit of all this uncharacteristic openness, do you mind if I ask you a question?"

"Shoot."

"Did you kill Cassie?"

"For God's sake, Sarah. Do you really think me capable?"

"We're all capable at this point, David. Did you kill her?"

"No. No, for heaven's sakes. I am not a murderer."

"Glad to hear it. Did John ask you if you did it?"

"Of course not."

"Well, he's thinking it. Just so you know."

David dragged a hand across his face and looked in the direction of the door as if he was thinking of jumping up and confronting John. Then he turned back to Sarah.

"I saw your daughter this morning," he said. "Really cute little kid."

"Thanks."

"She looks like you," he said.

"No, she looks like her daddy," she said.

David turned and walked back to the gaping hole where the door used to be.

"Do you need help getting back to the clinic?"

"No, thanks. I want to sit here a little longer."

He nodded and licked his lips as if trying to choose his words.

"I guess what I really wanted to say," he said, "was…I'm sorry." He looked at her and for the first time since he'd entered the room, he looked her in the eyes.

"What for?" she said. "For not coming back all those years ago? For trying to take John?"

He nodded. "For all of it. I'm not sure I'd believe me if I were you but it's true. I am sorry for all of it."

"Thanks, David. I appreciate that."

"Goodbye, Sarah," he said and then turned and left the room.

Sarah sat in the ruined room and listened to the sounds of children playing and the ringing of hammers as the castle worked to right itself. And the sounds of her first husband's footsteps as he walked away.

A few hours later, Mike came to the clinic and carried Sarah down to what used to be the front gate to see David off. The drawbridge still spanned the moat but as Mike carried her across it, Sarah could see that several makeshift bridges of scavenged lumber had been built across the moat.

The tents that they had used when they first set up camp outside Henredon two years earlier were erected once more on the lawn between the car park and the main drive. It had only been four days since the bombing and the debris was considerable even outside the castle.

But the encampment already looked like a small village. Children ran between the tents that encircled a number of cooking fires at the center.

A few of the castle women ran over to greet Sarah when Mike set her down, and one of the castle men put a lawn chair down for her.

David had said he'd leave by way of the IRA tunnels until he came to a designated drop off and pick up site. He'd been very cagey about the specifics of how he was getting back to his "island of secret knowledge" and Sarah didn't press him. She'd already heard more than she wanted to know.

She watched him now as he stood next to John. They were speaking to Terry, Tommy and young Darby. John looked so young but he always did to Sarah when she saw him from afar—or was feeling particularly insecure about his safety.

"You all right, lass?" Mike asked.

Sarah was surprised to discover that she had seriously mixed feelings about watching her first husband walk away—especially with John standing beside him. But she'd already said her goodbyes. There was nothing left to do now but turn to the life she had before her.

And make the best of it.

"I'm fine," she said and laced her fingers through Mike's. The sun was warm but she knew they wouldn't feel it in the tunnel where it was cool no matter what season it was. She swallowed hard as David turned to her and lifted a hand in farewell. She nodded and smiled, but she felt her lips tremble.

Why is goodbye always so hard?

But she knew why.

Because nowadays you never know if it's forever.

Terry and Jill both hugged Tommy, and Sarah watched David throw his arms around John. Father and son stood that way for a long time and then John broke away. He patted his father on the shoulder and walked back to stand beside Sarah.

Tommy joined David and they both waved goodbye to everyone and then walked toward the woods where the tunnel was.

It had been a shock to everyone but John when Tommy had asked to accompany David back to his secret world.

Tommy was an intensely bright boy with a love of electronics, science, and invention and Sarah had no doubt he'd fit in very well there.

John reached for her hand. They watched together until the two figures disappeared in the woods.

"Do you wish you were going?" Sarah asked softly.

John turned and looked at her. "Naw," he said. "Or else I would be going."

Sarah felt an expansion in her chest. She turned and hugged her son tightly before releasing him to wipe away grateful tears.

"Right then," Mike said. "Ready to get back to work?"

62

One week after David's departure, Gavin, Robbie and Frank rode back into camp with all seven castle horses.

Sarah had been sitting in one of the camp loungers, enjoying the sun, when she heard the shrieks of joy that passed from woman to woman until they reached and were heightened by Sophia.

Although they'd gotten quite a bit done in the nearly two weeks since the bombs had destroyed the castle, it was still quite a shocking scene for Gavin and the others.

At noon everyone gathered to eat around one of the campfires. Nuala sat next to Robbie, her two boys on other side of them, her littlest one in Robbie's lap. Gavin held his beautiful Sophia with one arm and little Maggie in the other and together with Frank the three regaled them all with the stories of their adventures.

They'd found the missing castle horses just the morning before, grazing in a nearby pasture, and they'd brought home enough fresh meat from their successful hunting trip to last well into the winter.

The feeling around the camp was jovial. With Gavin returning victorious as he had, everyone felt that there was a new age dawning—in spite of the ruined castle. The village people had brought with them three cows, a flock of sheep and several goats. Although most of their crops had also been destroyed by the ash, they had reserves—thanks to Morgan's careful stewardship—and there was a general feeling of thanksgiving and bounty.

Terry had set up a series of apprenticeships that, surprisingly, many of the archer girls had taken up. Kylie and Mac had both chosen to apprentice with Terry in the workshop to create the arrows and anything else the castle needed made.

Darby Donahue, Terry's own lad, had requested to apprentice as a tailor as the community's constant need for durable clothing had increased with their numbers. Still others had chosen to work with Sister Alphonse to learn medical skills and herbal applications.

Mike had delivered the edict that everyone over the age of ten was required to practice the bow at least an hour a day. Instead of forty archer girls, they would have at least a hundred, both male and female.

And someday they would once again have a high parapet from which to shoot to defend the fortress.

In the two weeks since the attack, Sarah's wounds had almost healed and she was moving easily about the castle although still using a cane. John, who was mourning both Cassie and the loss of his father, played a lot with Mac and Matt and worked closely with Mike on running the castle. It sometimes occurred to Sarah as she watched them together that John was the obvious successor to Mike as leader of the community.

Or maybe that was just her.

As she listened to Gavin's stories and the laughter from his audience—*such a natural storyteller*, she thought with a smile—and as she watched Mike's joy as he basked in the return of his son, Sarah felt her peace begin to erode.

She would need to talk to Mike soon.

Perhaps after lunch when everyone had gone back to their chores.

She scanned the audience to pick out Jordie who was sitting well apart from everyone else. More than one person had commented on the fact that Jordie was a changed man since the attack. Gone were the jokes and silly childishness.

Now he looked at the world as if afraid any moment he was about to be flung from the top of the highest castle rampart.

Or perhaps it was something else he was afraid of?

This morning as Sarah had stood over the washbasin to tackle the stacks of dirty castle laundry, she'd emptied the pockets of a pair of jeans she knew belonged to Jordie.

In one pocket was a couple of polished stones and a cheap rabbit's foot that had been dyed blue.

In the other pocket was a blood-soaked handkerchief. It was trimmed in lace with a name embroidered in a faded cursive.

Cassie.

That evening would be Sarah's first night spent sleeping in the tents instead of the clinic where Mike had insisted she stay there longer than she would have chosen. The clinic was the only place truly sheltered from the rain, and the beds there were real beds—not sleeping bags or blankets stuffed with leaves.

But she was ready to get back to normal. And she was ready to sleep next to her husband again.

Recuperating was hard enough with all the various compromises needed to heal wounds without having to fall asleep alone each night.

At first Mike had slept in the clinic with her on the other bed, but things soon got so busy with the clean up of the rubble around the castle—not to mention the ash which was still everywhere—that he ended up staying more and more in his tent. That's where the people were and where all the problems were.

So that's where Mike needed to be.

Sarah settled herself beside the largest outdoor cookfire. It was a fine summer night. The breeze off the ocean was light and cool and the ground still felt warm from the sun's beat down during the day. She'd started doing more chores—

anything where she could lend a hand—and she felt herself getting stronger every day.

As she looked at all the activity—the children running, the women stirring various pots, and the men laughing and talking over the events of the day—Sarah decided that she didn't even miss the big dining hall. It was grand and dramatic but unless she was mistaken, the hall was also more often than not the scene for too much drama and unhappiness.

She wasn't sure how it could be arranged, but she was going to talk to Mike about rebuilding such that each family had their own dining rooms again—like they had back in Ameriland.

She smiled at the thought of their old compound and her cottage there. It made her think of the elderly Siobhan, and Archie, and Papin, and Regan's parents and so many other dear ones who had not made the trip west with them.

"Mommy sad?" Siobhan said as she ran up to Sarah and slammed on the brakes in front of her.

Sarah smiled. "Not a bit," she said. "Mommy is downright gleeful."

Siobhan gave her an unconvinced look and then shrugged and dashed away again. Fiona's little Ciara was right behind her. As was Fiona.

Her sister-in-law came and sat down next to Sarah.

"God, I'm fagged," Fiona said with a groan.

"You work too hard," Sarah said.

Fiona turned to look at Sarah. "Have you heard the rumor?"

Sarah frowned. "What rumor?"

"Nuala and Robbie are going to announce their engagement tonight."

Sarah's shoulders relaxed. "I'm glad. They're a sweet couple."

"And Mike says you're determined to adopt the twins."

Sarah glanced over the cook fires to see John standing with both boys beside one of the camp dogs.

"Well, John has already adopted them," Sarah said with a smile. "This just makes it official."

"So I understand you'll be joining us tonight down in the ghetto?"

Sarah nodded. "Just like old times. My bed as rock hard as the ground with a pine board for my pillow."

"Sure the villagers are pissed, so they are. Just when we let them in the castle, it gets blown to shite."

Sarah laughed. "It kind of did happen that way."

Fiona snorted and looked away. She waved to someone walking through the tents and then turned back to Sarah.

"Mike told me about Jordie killing Cassie and all," Fiona said.

Mike had made short work of confronting Jordie with the bloody handkerchief. Jordie had broken down in tears and confessed on the spot. It seemed he and Cassidy were horsing around on the same window above the postern where Mac broke his arm and she'd slipped and hit her head.

Fearing this would get him and his mother thrown out of the castle for sure, Jordie panicked and carried Cassie's body to her room where he hid her in the wardrobe.

"It was an accident," Sarah said.

"And Mike really thinks we can use someone that thick?" Fiona asked, shaking her head.

"I'm pretty sure he thinks we can use someone who could really use a second chance," Sarah said to her. "And who never meant any harm. God, if we threw everybody out who screwed up, we'd be down to just...well, just me, I guess."

Fiona guffawed and shoved Sarah on the shoulder, sending electric jolts of pain up and down Sarah arm in the process.

"Good one, ye auld tart," Fiona said, laughing.

After the vibrations of pain began to subside, Sarah managed a smile. If there was anybody who could find the best in any crappy situation, Sarah was pretty sure that was her gift.

Yes, the castle was mostly just a pile of rocks now but they had a bigger community of people—and a much more balanced one because they had more men. Robbie had actually been employed as a bricklayer in his life before the

EMP and had been made responsible for directing the rebuilding of the castle that would better fit their needs as a community.

Sarah had two happy, well-adjusted children—both of them with her and as safe as she could make them. She had her dear friend and sister-in-law, Fiona and the support of a big and loyal community. Her bedrock, her heart and soul Mike, was alive and by her side.

She flexed the hand of her hurt shoulder and felt strong and whole again.

Really, what more was there?

As stupid as it might sound while she was sitting on an old sleeping bag, nursing an arrow wound to her shoulder and staring up at the home that had just been bombed out from under her—somehow the future looked bright to Sarah.

That night after most of the community had settled into their tents and sleeping bags, it took Sarah a little longer than she'd expected to get comfortable.

Mike had dragged one of the beds—complete with mattress, sheets and duvet cover—down into the tent which commanded a site slightly apart and higher up than the rest. In a way, Sarah knew it was because Mike needed to look out over all of them, like a mother hen with her chicks, and be able to see the various campfires burning and know that all was well.

They had sentries, of course. After all there were still the wolves. But they had enough ammunition not to worry too much about it. Plus the constantly burning campfires kept them away—in spite of the lure of roasting meats, the aroma of which permeated the campground most days and evenings.

Mike settled in next to Sarah and eyed her as if not sure she was really ready for this level of roughing it.

"I'm fine, Mike," she said, leaning back onto the bed with a huge pillow behind her head. "And besides Sister Elise needs the bed. Her gout is acting up. But have you thought what we'll do if it rains?"

He glanced up at the ceiling of the tent. It wasn't high enough for him to stand up in, but it was waterproof.

"It'll likely mold," he admitted, indicating the bedding. "But I reckon we'll live."

"That's basically our family motto, isn't it? *I reckon we'll live.*"

He slid his arm around her and waited until he was sure he hadn't hurt her.

"Not a bad one as these things go, I'll wager," he said.

"What did you do to Jordie when he confessed?" Sarah asked.

"You know he'd been sort of confessing all along, right? Just nobody was really listening," Mike said, shaking his head. "I told him he'll clean the bogs out—single-handedly, and mind you I had to stress I wasn't saying *bare-handedly*, the lad's really not the whole shilling—for two months."

"Yikes. That's pretty bad."

"He wept with gratitude, Sarah, so he did."

Sarah shook her head. "Poor Cassie. I feel so bad about her. How did John take the news?"

Mike sighed heavily. "Ah, lass. I hate that our children are having to understand such things. There's no chance of innocence or naivety left at-tall. Not at-tall." He was silent for a moment. "He just said he knew it was an accident because Jordie wouldn't have hurt Cassie. The lad's a wonder, so he is."

Sarah blinked away the tears that gathered in her eyes. She also hated that John had to be so adult so soon. And was eternally grateful that he could be.

And also that it wasn't David who'd killed Cassie after all.

"It's been a long wild ride, Mike," Sarah said, feeling the tension drain away from her shoulders and neck as she nestled into his strong arms.

"Bound to get a little wilder as we go on," he said.

"That's okay. As long as I have you. And John and Siobhan and Gavin and Sophia and Baby Maggie. Oh! And Mac and Matt. That's all I have to have."

Mike leaned on one elbow and kissed her on the mouth.

"Sure that's all I need too, me darlin,'" he said.

The flap to the tent was open so they could catch every whiff and gust of the ocean breeze coming to them now that the castle wall wasn't there to block it. Its reassuring roar lulled Sarah as she let her head rest on her husband's chest.

After all they'd been through, and with the castle now open to the world, it wasn't lost on her the bittersweet irony that at this moment, she never felt more at peace or secure in her life.

The next morning, sunshine awoke Sarah. She was curled up around the pillow on the big bed and reached out to touch Mike only to find him gone as he so often was.

She could smell coffee boiling somewhere outside the tent and she knew the teapots would be steeping about now too.

Yawning, she got up and stood in the doorway of the tent and looked out at the camp slowly coming to life. As she stepped back into the tent, she noticed Mike's gun in his holster was still on his side of the bed.

A needle of alarm pierced her heart at the sight of it.

There was no way Mike would have left the tent without his gun.

Sarah knelt at the foot of the bed to find his trousers where he'd slid out of them the night before.

And his shoes.

She threw on her clothes and raced out of the tent, praying there was some logical explanation.

An hour later, the whole camp was up and reeling.

Mike was nowhere in the camp.

No one had seen him after he and Sarah retired the night before.

No one had seen him this morning.

He had simply disappeared.

ABOUT THE AUTHOR

Susan Kiernan-Lewis lives in North Florida and writes mysteries and dystopian adventure. Like many authors, Susan depends on the reviews and word of mouth referrals of her readers. If you enjoyed *Wit's End*, please leave a review saying so on Amazon.com, Barnesandnoble.com or Goodreads.com.

Check out Susan's blog at susankiernanlewis.com and feel free to contact her at sanmarcopress@me.com.

NOTE FROM THE AUTHOR

I hope you will forgive me for this little cliffhanger at end of *Wit's End* especially when you see where I'm taking you in Book 9, *Dead On*. Trust me, you'll understand there was no other way to get there but this way.

Wit's End

Susan Kiernan-Lewis

Printed in Great Britain
by Amazon